GILBERT MORRIS

✫

Stars in Their Courses

Tyndale House Publishers, Inc.
Wheaton, Illinois

Library of Congress Cataloging-in-Publication Data

Morris, Gilbert.
  Stars in their courses / Gilbert Morris.
    p. cm. — (Appomattox saga ; 8)
  ISBN 0-8423-1674-4 (sc : alk. paper)
    1. United States—History—Civil War, 1861-1865—Secret service—
Fiction. I. Title. II. Series: Morris, Gilbert. Appomattox saga ; 8.
PS3563.08742S73 1995
813'.54—dc20   95-35086

Printed in the United States of America

01 00 99 98 97 96 95
9   8   7   6   5   4   3   2   1

To Alan Morris

A son who has made his father very proud

CONTENTS

Part Four: The Last Act
NOVEMBER–DECEMBER 1863

GENEALOGY OF

THE APPOMATTOX SAGA

THE ROCKLINS

Noah Rocklin (1767–1842) m.1797 **Charlotte Minton (1780–1847)**

- **Stephen (1798–)** m.1816 **Ruth Poynter (1797–)**
  - **Gideon (1819–)** m.1840 **Melanie Benton (1821–)**
    - Tyler (1841–)
    - Robert (1842–)
    - Frank (1843–)
  - **Laura (1818–)** m.1839 **Amos Steele (1816–)**
    - Patrick (1840–)
    - Colin (1841–)
    - Deborah (1842–)
    - Clinton (1843–)

- **Thomas (1800–1863)** m.1819 **Susanna Lee (1801–)**
  - **Clay (1820–)** m.1863 **Melora Yancy (1834–)** m.1840 **Ellen Benton (1820–1862)**
    - Denton (1842–) m.1861 — Thomas (1863–) **Raimey Reed (1843–)**
    - David (1842–)
    - Lowell (1843–) m.1863 **Rooney Smith**
    - Rena (1846–)
  - **Amy (1822–)** m.1839 **Brad Franklin (1810–)** m.1835 **Lila Crawford (1818–1842)**
    - Grant (1840–)
    - Rachel (1842–) m.1862 **Jake Hardin (1836–)**
    - Les (1844–)
    - Vincent (1837–)
  - **Burke (1830–)** m. 1863 **Grace Swenson (1836–)**

- **Mason (1805–)** m.1825 **Jane Dent (1807–1833)**

- **Marianne (1810–)** m.1830 **Claude Bristol (1805–)**
  - **Paul (1831–)** m.1862 **Frankie Aimes (1844–)**
  - **Austin (1832–)**
  - **Marie (1837–)**

- **Mark (1811–1863)**
  - **Allyn Griffeth (1845–)** m.1863 **Jason Larrimore (1835–)**

THE YANCYS

Buford Yancy
(1807–)
m.1829 —————
Mattie Satterfield
(1813–1851)

- Royal
  (1832–)
  m.1854
  Margaret O'Hara
  (1835–)
- Melora
  (1834–)
  m.1863
  Clay Rocklin
  (1820–)
- Zack
  (1836–)
  m.1859
  Elizabeth Stuart
  (1841–)
- Cora
  (1837–)
  m.1855
  Billy Day
  (1835–)
- Lonnie
  (1843–1863)
- Bobby
  (1844–)
- Rose
  (1845–)
- Josh
  (1847–)
- Martha
  (1849–)
- Toby
  (1851–)

Part One
The Actor
MARCH–JUNE 1863

CHAPTER ONE
Early Morning Encounter

"Anybody who would eat goose liver deserves a bellyache!"

As Frank Rocklin strolled down Fourteenth Street he glanced at Willards Hotel and smiled faintly. The structure, outlined in the darkness by the flickering amber of oil-burning streetlamps, brought a quick memory of the very late supper he'd eaten there a few hours ago. The meal had included fried oysters, steak and onions, blancmange, and pâté de foie gras. He rubbed his stomach as he walked along in the predawn darkness.

Rocklin spoke the words aloud, then quickly moved down the deserted streets of Washington. He was on his way home after a long night at the poker table, and his eyes were gritty from lack of sleep. Overhead a sullen moon hid behind skeins of dark clouds, and the silence of the streets lent an eerie tone to the capital. By day the area Rocklin passed through was in essence a Southern town, without the picturesque quality but with all the indolence, disorder, and want of sanitation. When Frank had walked down the same street early the previous morning, lounging Negroes had been a reminder of the war—for many of them were in Washington as contraband. He'd passed through flocks of geese while moving past the Capitol, and hogs of every size and color roamed in the grassy area that surrounded the War Department.

A wagon rumbled by, the driver stopping now and then

to pick up night soil, and the thousands of privies sending forth their rank odors brought a frown to Rocklin's face. "I liked you well enough before the war," he murmured, addressing the city as if it were a troublesome child, "but you're spoiled forever."

He quickened his pace and passed along a row of roughly built structures, anxious to get home. "Should have hired a cab," he muttered. As he spoke, the sound of muffled voices came to him. Glancing up alertly, he strained his eyes trying to pierce the stygian darkness. Slowing his pace, he drew himself up, well aware that the dark streets were the hunting ground for predators—two-legged ones.

As Rocklin advanced along the wooden sidewalk, he realized that the muted voices were coming from a gaping cavity between a hardware store and a gun shop. Placing himself close to the gun shop front, he eased himself along until he stood framed in the opening. The flickering yellow light of the streetlamp threw four figures into relief, two of them bulking large in the murky dimness.

A rough male voice rasped, "All right, let's have that ring, dearie. And I'll have that stickpin from you, fellow!"

A woman's voice answered, quick with fear. "This was my mother's ring. Please, let me keep it, and I'll give you money."

"We'll have the money *and* the ring, dearie." A high-pitched giggle followed, and the shadows melded as one of the roughly dressed men suddenly moved forward. "Don't scream, or I'll have to slit that pretty throat of yours!"

Rocklin moved forward, noting that the woman's companion was backed against the wall of the hardware store, held there by a knife pressed against his chest. The woman was struggling with the smaller of the two hold-up men, pleading with him to leave her ring.

Rocklin stepped closer, then said loudly, "All right, you two—let those folks alone!"

At once both men whirled, both holding knives in fighting position. One of them was very tall, over six feet two or three, and his features were blunt. His smallish eyes searched the opening, and seeing only one man, he grinned, exposing broken teeth. "Well, now, looks like we got us another contributor, Ollie."

The smaller man had a foxlike face, sharp and keen. His lips were thin and now curved into a smile. "Right, mate. Now, suppose you take the gentleman's money."

A glimmer of light traced the blade of the knife, and a hungry grin appeared on the thick lips of the big man. "Let's have it, now—no funny stuff."

Rocklin's hand dipped into his coat pocket, and he came out with a revolver. "Would you say this is funny stuff?" Neither attacker said a word, so Rocklin said casually, "I like this gun. It's a Le Mat—the same kind that Jeb Stuart carries." Lifting it to aim at the head of the smaller man, he observed mildly, "It shoots six .42 caliber slugs, enough to tear a pretty nice hole in fellows like you. But if you survive all that, there's a 20-bore shotgun barrel underneath—see?" He lifted the Le Mat slightly, then added, "Pretty messy thing, getting hit in the belly with shotgun shells."

"Now—just a minute—"

"Drop those knives and get out of here!"

The two men at once threw down their knives and scurried away, disappearing into the darkness like nocturnal animals. Rocklin slipped the revolver into his pocket, then asked, "Are you two all right?"

"I think so," the man said and turned to the woman. "All right, Carmen?"

"Y-yes." The voice was low and trembled only slightly. She came forward and peered upward into the face of Rocklin. "If you hadn't come, it would have been terrible."

"Let's get out of here," her companion spoke up. "They might come back." He moved quickly onto the sidewalk, drew a deep breath, and shook his head. The light falling from the streetlight revealed the lean face of a man in his late twenties, aristocratic and handsome. His voice was a rich baritone as he said with a grateful smile, "And your name, sir?"

"Frank Rocklin."

"Ah, Mr. Rocklin, my name is Roland Middleton—and this is Miss Carmen Montaigne." He hesitated slightly, as though expecting Rocklin to recognize the names, then said, "Come along, we'll have a drink to celebrate our timely rescue."

"Thanks, but it's late—or early, I should say." Frank smiled, adding, "I'd either take to carrying a gun or keep off the streets during these hours."

"Please, Mr. Rocklin, I'd feel much safer if you'd walk with us to our hotel," Miss Montaigne said. She was an attractive woman in her late twenties, Rocklin guessed, possibly older, with black hair and a striking face that had a foreign flavor. Her voice was strong and clear as she urged, "We're staying at Willards." There was a magnetism in her voice, and her eyes were compelling as she turned them fully on him.

"Why, of course," Rocklin answered.

The trio made their way down the street, Middleton speaking of the dangers of the city, the woman saying nothing. She let her arm brush against Rocklin's as though for security, and when they reached Willards she put her hand out. "I'll never forget your help," she said, smiling up at him. "I insist that you give Roland and me a chance to show our gratitude."

"Why, certainly!" Middleton reached into his waistcoat pocket and came out with several small slips of paper. "I don't know if you're a man who likes the theater, but you must come for our performance—tonight, if possible."

Carmen examined Rocklin closely, taking in the tall, strong figure in a glance, then noting the deep-set dark brown eyes under heavy black brows. He had olive skin, a straight nose, and high cheekbones. His mouth was wide, and his slightly waving hair was black as her own. He was a handsome man, somewhere in his early twenties, she estimated. His hands were square and rather thick. He wore a dark brown coat, a pair of tan trousers, low-heeled black boots, and a black hat with a medium brim shoved back on his head in a careless fashion.

Rocklin peered at the tickets, then looked up to ask quickly, "You're with Mr. Booth's company?" He had been aware that John Wilkes Booth, the brother of the most famous actor in America, Edwin Booth, was appearing in a production of *Romeo and Juliet*. He loved the theater and said so. "I'll be glad to come. Which roles do you play?"

"Juliet," Carmen answered. "And Roland here is Mercutio."

Frank nodded. "My favorite in the play, Mr. Middleton."

"Really? Well, I'd rather play Romeo, but John insisted on that role." There was a droll look on Middleton's face, and he grinned suddenly, adding, "But you have good taste."

"I played the role two years ago—a very bad, amateurish production," Rocklin confessed with a half-embarrassed laugh. "I was terrible! But I liked the sword fight."

Carmen Montaigne laughed aloud, amusement in her dark eyes as she cast a mischievous glance at Middleton. "Do you now? Roland *despises* the fencing!"

"Fool sort of thing." Middleton flushed. "Somebody's going to get hurt—and it'll probably be me!" He managed a smile, saying, "Bring a couple of your friends, and we'll have dinner at Willards after the performance."

"Maybe John will join us," the woman suggested.

Middleton turned his nose up in an imperial gesture. "I shall not ask him. He's a pompous bore!" He shook his head, adding, "He's a fire-eating rebel, Mr. Rocklin. I wish he'd go join the Confederate army—then *I* could play Romeo!" He had an engaging wit, and now put his hand out, giving Frank a surprisingly strong grip. "We'll tell the ticket taker to put you in front row seats. And as for your help, I can no other answer make, but thanks and thanks— and ever thanks."

"Hamlet," Frank said with a nod, recognizing the quotation.

"You *do* know your theater!" Middleton stared at him with pleasure. "We'll look forward to the dinner."

"I hope you enjoy the play," Carmen said, putting her hand out. Her hand was smooth and strong, and there was a promise in her dark eyes. When Rocklin turned and left, she waited until he was out of hearing, then murmured, "Most men wouldn't have risked helping us."

"A knight in shining armor, Carmen?" Middleton asked, his gray eyes on her.

Carmen Montaigne knew men well. She had found most of them to be less than they should be—but as she watched the tall figure of Rocklin moving away, she said sharply, "Don't be so cynical, Roland." She turned and moved into the hotel. "There are a *few* good men in this world."

★ ★ ★

Stephen Rocklin looked with satisfaction around the dining room. He had designed and furnished it himself, saying to his wife, Ruth, "We'll be spending plenty of time in here, so I want to feel comfortable." Fortunately, as owner of a prosperous ironworks, he had not been limited, and there was a richness in the room and the furnishings that gave him satisfaction each time he sat down for a meal.

Along one wall rested a large sideboard made by Thomas Sheraton, supporting on its gleaming mahogany top a golden pitcher and sparkling crystal goblets. The serpentine front allowed one to reach easily across and serve with agility. Two large oil paintings directly over the sideboard added color, and the features of Noah and Charlotte Rocklin, Stephen's parents, were finely executed. In the opposite wall was a large fireplace with a walnut mantle that supported patent lamps on gilded tripods. Behind Stephen two ten-foot-high windows were covered with scarlet draperies, a gilt-edged mirror between, and light was regulated by blinds that blocked out a distracting glare. The Wilton carpet was protected by a baize floorcloth, and overhead an adjustable ceiling lamp was suspended to shed a brilliant light over the handsome dining table and chairs.

The room pleased Stephen, but tonight it was the company that gave him the most satisfaction. He ran his eyes around the table, taking in each face, then said to the woman on his left, "I wish Gideon was here, Melanie," thinking of his son, who was on active duty with Hooker.

"So do I, sir." Melanie Rocklin reached over and put her hand on her father-in-law's arm. She was an attractive woman of forty-two, wife of Stephen's only son, Gideon. "But at least we have all three of the boys."

"That's a minor miracle with this war going on," Stephen said. He glanced fondly at the three young men sitting to his left. At the age of twenty, Frank was the youngest—and the most trouble. His brothers had joined the army almost as soon as the war began. Tyler was the oldest at twenty-two, and Bob was only a year younger, and both of the older boys wore blue uniforms. Stephen asked, "Well, Frank, when are you joining the army?"

The question brought a pause in the hum of conversation, and Frank gave his grandfather a rash grin. "I don't have to worry now, Grandfather," he said. "Looks like I'll get conscripted. Lincoln signed the act yesterday."

At once his cousin Deborah Steele, who sat across from him, said sharply, "I don't agree with the president. The North has plenty of young men who'll fight!" She was an attractive young woman with decided opinions. "I read the act, Grandfather. It says that any drafted man can hire another as a substitute for three hundred dollars. This isn't a rich man's war!"

Frank winked slyly at Noel Kojak, Deborah's fiancé, saying, "I didn't know that, Deborah! Only three hundred dollars? Why, that solves my problem. Noel, keep your eye out for a good, strong young man for me, will you?"

Deborah opened her mouth to reply angrily, but Noel squeezed her arm. He was a small young man with light brown hair and gray eyes. He had been wounded at Bull Run and was not fit for active duty, but his writings on the army and the war were becoming more and more popular. President Lincoln had been heard to remark, "Why, that young Kojak can just make a man *see* what's going on—and he's got good sense, too!"

Ruth Rocklin, Stephen's wife, said sharply, "I think it's a good idea. There are plenty of men who have other things to do. You find a decent young man, Frank. I'm sure your father will understand."

"I doubt that, Grandmother," Frank shook his head wryly. "No colonel in the Union army wants his son to sit out this war." He glanced around and saw that only his grandmother favored such a cowardly act as buying a substitute, and he quickly changed the subject. "Ty, what's going to happen next? Will Lee whip us again like he always does?"

Tyler Rocklin wore the uniform of a second lieutenant of artillery. He forced a grin and shook his head almost sadly. "Well, I hope not, Frank. But unless we get a real fighting general at the head of the Army of the Potomac, he just might do it. But the best man would be Grant."

"Old 'Unconditional Surrender'?" Stephen mused. Ulysses S. Grant had scored the most significant Union victories for the North by capturing Fort Donelson and Fort Henry. By a curious coincidence, his initials fit the terms he'd demanded from the Confederates—unconditional surrender—and the name had stuck.

"Grant won't lead the army against Lee," Bob Rocklin said slowly. He was a quiet young man, the deepest thinker of the three boys and the most gentle. He looked more like his mother than the other two, and now he shook his head. "Somebody's got to take Vicksburg. Until we take the whole Mississippi and split the Confederacy, we can't put the rebellion down."

"Bob's right," Tyler agreed. "I expect both of us will be pulling out soon to do that. And it'll be a big job. No port on the river is as well fortified as that place."

The talk went on for thirty minutes, and then Frank snapped his fingers. He fumbled in his waistcoat pocket, pulled out the tickets Middleton had given him, and grinned at his grandparents. "Got a treat for you—I'm taking you to see a play. I've got three tickets down front for *Romeo and Juliet*. And after the play, we'll have supper with a couple of the actors."

Stephen stared at his grandson and snorted. "Me? Go to a thing like that? And eat with *actors?*" He hated drama and despised actors. "I like real people," he said stiffly, "and real life, too. Take my advice, Frank, and throw those things away!"

But Deborah at once said, "Take Noel and me, Frank! I'd love to see the play!"

"All right, unless you fellows want to go," Frank offered, glancing at his brothers. "Or better yet, let's all go. I'll pay for the extra seats."

Tyler said roughly, "That's the play John Booth is in, isn't it? He's a copperhead, Frank! A real Southern sympathizer. I'd pay to send him to the South, but I won't go to see him act."

In the end it was Deborah and Noel who got into the cab. As the cabby spoke to the horses and sent them off at a brisk pace, Deborah said, "I'm not going to listen to John Wilkes Booth make a speech. I want some romance!"

"Well, nothing's more romantic than *Romeo and Juliet*, Deborah," Noel said. He put his arm around her and drew her close. "Maybe I'll get some pointers from this thing. You're always saying I'm not romantic enough." He winked at Frank, who was grinning at him. "Pretty hot stuff, is it, Frank?"

"Never mind all that, Noel!" Deborah sniffed and drew back. "You just stay away from those painted actresses!"

★ ★ ★

The trio enjoyed the play tremendously. Frank jabbed Noel in the ribs when Juliet came onstage, saying, "There she is,

11

Noel. If you like, I'll take Deborah off someplace, and you and Carmen can have a private little supper. That all right with you, Deborah?"

Deborah gave Frank a frosty stare. "She's old enough to be his mother! Juliet's supposed to be fourteen years old!"

"Well, art has its limits, I guess." Frank shrugged. He, too, was of the opinion that Carmen Montaigne was too old for her role, but he had to admit that she *looked* better than any Juliet he'd ever seen. She wore a stunning white gown, and there was a sophistication in her eyes that no fourteen-year-old girl had. She added to the role a most sensuous quality.

Noel said at once, "Well, she's *romantic* enough, Deborah. I'm keeping my eyes on her, that's for sure!" He kept Deborah fuming by his under-the-breath remarks on the "art" of the actress.

Frank was interested in John Wilkes Booth, who played the role of Romeo with too much spirit, he thought. He had little of his older brother Edwin's skill, but moved with overdone gymnastic abandon all through the play. *Why, I could do better than that!* Frank thought. He'd seen Edwin Booth perform *Hamlet* in New York and had been amazed at the ability of the actor.

Roland Middleton was a good actor, but he had obviously been drinking. This surprised Frank a little, for though he was no prude, he believed in giving his best—and liquor never helped a man do that. Middleton did so well under the influence, Frank wondered how good he'd be if he was sober.

Finally the third act began, and Frank leaned forward, for this was Mercutio's death scene. He thought of how the actor had scowled at the thought of fencing, and he wondered at it. He himself was an expert fencer and loved the sport. He watched as the quarrel between Tybalt and Romeo developed, then Mercutio entered. The actor playing Tybalt demanded of Middleton, "What wouldst thou have with me?"

Middleton looked pale, and his hands were not steady as he drew his sword, saying, "Good King of Cats, nothing but one of your nine lives!"

The duel began, and Frank noted how ineffectual Middleton was. The actor playing Tybalt was obviously an expert swordsman, his blade flashing as he circled Middleton. Booth as Romeo played his part well, coming in to thrust up the blades of the two men. In the play, he is attempting to make peace, but the treacherous Tybalt stabs Mercutio under Romeo's arm.

It was a tricky piece of stage work, and Frank remembered how hard he'd practiced with the actors when he'd played in the part. It had to be done carefully or someone could get hurt.

And suddenly he saw it—Tybalt's blade shot under Romeo's arm—but Middleton was too slow to turn aside. The blade took him in the thigh and he dropped his sword, crying aloud. He recovered instantly, so that most of the audience didn't know that an accident had occurred. Turning to one side, Middleton concealed the blood that streamed down his leg as he said his final lines.

He's got plenty of nerve—even if he drinks too much, Frank thought. Middleton's face was pale as he cried, "Go, villain, fetch a surgeon."

A shaken Booth managed to speak his line: "Courage, man, the hurt cannot be much."

And then Middleton turned and happened to look directly into the face of Frank Rocklin. He smiled cynically, saying, "'Tis not so deep as a well nor so wide as a church door, but 'tis enough, 'twill serve." And then he laughed suddenly, giving the most famous pun of Mercutio, "Ask for me tomorrow and you shall find me a grave man!"

The actors helped the dying Mercutio off the stage, and Deborah said, "That looked so *real!*"

"It was real," Frank said grimly. "I'm going backstage."

"We'll go with you," Noel said at once.

The three rose and ignored the glares from the irate

spectators. They made their way out a side door. Frank strolled purposefully down a hall leading to the back of the building and entered the backstage area. At once he saw a crowd of actors huddled around Middleton. He moved closer and bent down to see the wound. He found himself standing next to Carmen Montaigne, who looked at him with distressed eyes.

"Is he badly hurt?" Frank asked.

"I don't know. We've sent for a doctor." She would have said more, but a heavyset man chewing on the stub of a cigar came to say, "All right, get ready, Carmen—the rest of you, break it up. We'll take care of Roland."

Middleton had been sitting on a stool, but now rose. Seeing Frank, he said, "Come along, Rocklin. I may need a little help."

Noel and Deborah went back to their seats, and Frank accompanied the actor to his dressing room, where Middleton collapsed on a chair. "Cut this blasted costume off, will you? Can't see how bad it is with the bloody thing on!"

Frank managed to cut the right leg of the tights off, and he said at once, "Not too bad, Middleton. If the blade had hit an artery we'd see lots of bright red blood."

Middleton looked down, his lips puckered. "Looks like enough blood to me. Are you a doctor?"

"No, but when I was fencing regularly, this sort of thing sometimes happened. You'll be all right."

Soon a doctor came in, a small man with a thin face and intense gray eyes. "I'm Dr. Parnell. Let's have a look."

Frank stood back as Parnell examined his patient. He punched and probed, making Middleton squirm. "By heaven, that's painful!" he gasped. "Is it bad?"

Dr. Parnell stared at him. "You're not going to die—but you're going to have to stay off this leg for a week. A big muscle is torn."

Middleton didn't argue. After the doctor left, he gave Frank a pale-faced look. "Stick around, will you, Frank? Booth is going to hit the ceiling!"

Frank sat down, and the two talked until the play ended. The door opened, and Booth came rushing in. Glaring at Middleton, he cursed vividly, throwing himself around the room. While he was engaged in this, the door opened again and Carmen entered, followed by Noel and Deborah. "Is it bad, Roland?" she asked.

"Bad enough that he can't do his part for a week!" Booth snarled. "What am I supposed to do for a replacement? Blast a drunk anyway!"

Deborah watched the actors as they argued, fascinated by the behind-the-scenes action. She was intrigued by Booth, who was as handsome as he was famous. And she felt sorry for Middleton, who looked pale and sick. She was an impulsive girl and spoke up to interrupt Booth. "Frank, you always wanted to be an actor. Here's your chance."

John Wilkes Booth at once fixed his large, expressive eyes on Frank. "Are you an actor, sir?"

"Why, just in an amateur sort of way—"

"John, he knows the lines, and he's an expert swordsman," Roland Middleton spoke up, anxious to turn Booth's wrath away. "He can be my replacement."

"Do you know the part?" Booth demanded, then said, "What follows this cue: 'And so bound, I cannot bound a pitch above dull woe. Under love's heavy burden do I sink'?"

Frank spoke the next line, lifting his voice, "And to sink in it, should you burden love, too great oppression for a tender thing."

"*Very* good!" Booth said, a surprised look on his face. "A fine voice. Now, what follows this cue: 'In bed asleep, while they do dream on things true'?"

Frank had always loved Mercutio's speech on the fairy, Queen Mab. He spoke it quietly, but his love for the lines shone through his eyes and his voice. "Oh then, I see Queen Mab hath been with you. She is the fairies' midwife, and she comes in shape no bigger than an agate stone on the

15

forefinger of an alderman, drawn with a team of little atomies. . . ."

The room grew still as he recited the long speech, and when it ended, Booth exclaimed, "Why, sir, you *are* an actor, no matter what you say! I've heard no better Queen Mab from any man." He was a handsome man, with black curly hair and magnetic eyes. He had forgotten his anger and said, "Come now, you must help our friend Roland."

"Why, Mr. Booth—!"

"I'd be in your debt—again," Middleton spoke up. He had fine gray eyes, and there was a pleading in them as he spoke.

"Grandfather will disown you, Frank," Deborah said, her eyes gleaming. "But I'd love to see you do it!"

"It would be a favor for all of us, sir," Carmen said, coming to stand by Frank. "Won't you do it?"

Frank Rocklin was a reckless young man. He had done more dangerous things than this, and the idea had a certain appeal. "Why, I'll do my best, but I may smell up your play with my amateur acting."

John Wilkes Booth laughed with delight. He, too, was a daring young man and clapped the newest member of his cast on the shoulder. "Rehearsal tomorrow at ten o'clock. You'll do a fine job!"

Frank Rocklin said wryly to Roland Middleton, "Don't worry about your job, Roland. A week of this, and I'll be glad to hand your job back to you."

But Carmen Montaigne put her hand on his arm in a possessive manner. "Don't be too sure about that, Frank. You may like it better than you think!"

CHAPTER TWO
Dinner at Willards

Frank endured the morning rehearsal and, after satisfying Booth that he could get through the play, left the theater. He'd been more nervous than he'd expected, unable to do more than nibble at the excellent lunch he ordered. The curtain went up at eight, but Booth had warned the cast to be on hand and in costume by seven. Frank paced the streets nervously, dreading the time he'd have to step out on the stage. Finally at six o'clock he made his way to Grover's theater and found it surrounded by a noisy, milling crowd.

"What's the trouble?" he asked a tall, lanky man wearing a stovepipe hat. "Has there been an accident?"

The tall man wheeled and fixed a pair of steely blue eyes on Frank. "Accident? No sir, not an accident—but an outrage!" He lifted his chin and pointed upward to the top of the theater. "Some Rebel has torn down the new flag that Mr. Grover installed on top of the theater—and some of us are ready to tar and feather the traitor!"

Lifting his gaze, Frank saw that two men were raising a mammoth flag. The stiff breeze caught it, and as it rippled freely, he said mildly, "Well, there's another new one."

"And it will stay unfurled, sir! Anyone who dares touch yon banner dies like a dog!"

A grin rose to Rocklin's lips as he thought, *He talks like one of the actors.* He suppressed it, saying only, "I hardly think a Rebel would dare touch the flag in broad daylight."

"There is nothing so low but that the traitors who have rent our Union asunder will stoop to it!"

"I suppose that is so." Frank had no inclination to argue with the man, for Southern sympathizers were legion in Washington and he did not want to be labeled as such. Lincoln's secretary of war, Edwin M. Stanton, had imposed an iron rule on the capital but had not succeeded in obliterating the movement. The city was rife with the rumors of Confederate spies, and Belle Boyd, the colorful Southern spy, had not been troubled with the high cost of living in the capital. She had been given one of the best rooms in Old Capitol prison, which held over two thousand Confederate captives.

A cheer went up as the huge flag fluttered in the breeze, and as Frank made his way through the crowd he wondered if John Wilkes Booth was troubled by the anti-Confederate feeling that brought out such crowds over a single flag. He found the door to the theater locked, but when he knocked, he was admitted at once by Jed Hoskins. "Good evenin', Mr. Rocklin. You's early, sah."

Frank grinned at the tall black man who had been born a slave in Alabama but had fled to the North on the Underground Railroad. "I may leave early, Jed." He shrugged. "I feel as out of place as a frog on the middle of Pennsylvania Avenue."

Hoskins was a serious man, but he smiled with sympathy. "No sah, you is gonna do real fine! Mr. Middleton, he say you a natural-born actor."

"Is he here?"

"Yes sah. He backstage." Hoskins shook his head, a sad expression sweeping over his face. "I wish you could keep Mr. Middleton from likker, sah. He a good man, but dat whiskey is de ruination of him."

"Guess we all have our weaknesses, Jed," Frank murmured. He stood there uncertainly, then shrugged and attempted a smile that didn't quite come off. "If they start throwing rotten tomatoes at me, Jed, I hope you'll stand by with a towel."

Hoskins shook his head vigorously. "No *sah!* I watched you real good in de rehearsal. You do jest fine! And I say a special prayer dat Gawd will be with you. Dat'll answer!"

"Thanks, Jed. I need all the help I can get."

Making his way through the empty theater, Frank found Roland slumped in a chair, a pair of crutches leaning against the wall. He looked up to say, "Hello, Frank. You're early— which is a mistake."

"Coming early is a mistake?"

"Oh yes." Roland pulled a silver flask from his inside pocket, unscrewed it, and offered it to Frank, who shook his head. He lifted it, took two swallows, then shuddered as the liquor bit at his throat. "What awful stuff!" he muttered. "Tastes like varnish remover!"

"Maybe you need to buy better whiskey."

"No, it all tastes the same after a few swallows." Middleton looked tired, and his eyes were red-rimmed. He shifted in the chair, grimaced, and swore. "Leg is killing me!"

"You ought to be in bed, Roland." Frank sat down, gave a nervous glance around, then rose and paced the floor. "Why is it better not to come early?" he asked. He was not really interested in the answer, but was not able to keep still.

"Because you pace the floor like you're doing now and worry about how it will go. But if you come late, other people have to worry." Middleton smiled and lifted his hand to smooth his dark brown hair. "If I were you, I'd leave now. Go to a saloon, have a few drinks, and get back just in time to get dressed."

Frank grinned, his white teeth flashing. "I'd get roaring drunk, and Booth would put that sword right through my middle." Then he realized that his words were an insult to Middleton—who had done just what he had mentioned. "I didn't mean—"

"Oh, you can't insult a drunk, Frank," Roland said with a

trace of bitterness. "There was a time when I'd have called you out for saying that, but I'm past having my pride hurt." He pulled out the flask, unscrewed the top, and then hesitated, lifting his gaze to look at Rocklin. "Want to know why I became a drunk, Frank?"

"Yes."

"Nothing very original, I'm afraid." Middleton stared down at his feet as if he found them particularly interesting. He spoke in a low voice. "I was engaged to a young woman. Very much in love, of course—so much so that I would not beteem the winds of heaven visit her face too roughly." His lips twisted bitterly, adding, "As Lord Hamlet once said of another faithless woman. Well then, I had a friend—or thought I did. Can you guess the rest?"

"Your friend took your fiancée away from you?"

"Yes, so it was, and since that time I have tried to ruin my life by strong drink. You find that despicable, I suppose?"

"I find it tragic, Roland." Frank studied the lean face of Middleton, shook his head, and added, "There are other women—and not all men are like your friend. Take another try." Frank shrugged his shoulders and grinned. "I hate it when people tell me to do the obvious and right thing. When we decide to go to the devil, why, something in us gets some sort of perverse pleasure out of watching ourselves fall apart."

Middleton stared at Rocklin with a startled expression. "Where did you get that from, Frank? You've never been a failure, have you?"

"Some would argue that I'm one right now—my grandfather for one. And maybe even my father—" He broke off as a knock sounded, and without a pause the door opened and Carmen walked in. Frank rose at once, saying, "Hello, Carmen."

"Frank, you're here early." Carmen was wearing a rose-colored dress that set off her figure well. Her cheeks were flushed, and there was a pleased expression in her large eyes. "I'm excited about your premier performance."

Frank laughed self-consciously. "I feel like I'm the guest of honor at an execution. Matter of fact, I'd like to back out of the whole thing."

Carmen came to stand before him. She was not tall and had to lift her head to look up into his face. She was a woman of much experience, but there was a youthful air about her as she said, "No, I won't let you do that. Now, you get into your costume. We'll have time to go over your lines one more time."

"He knows them better than I do," Roland said. He smiled at Frank, saying, "My costume ought to fit you. Step outside, Carmen, and we'll see what he looks like in tights."

Fifteen minutes later Frank was wearing tights for the first time in his life—and feeling like an utter and complete fool. He stared at himself in the mirror on the wall and growled, "Roland—I can't go out in front of people wearing this! Why, it's indecent!"

Roland laughed, but assured him, "You look good, Frank. All of us feel the same way when we first put on garb like that. Don't be nervous—it'll be fine."

Voices were beginning to filter through to the dressing room, and soon Booth breezed into the room, followed by Carmen, and smiled with satisfaction. "I was afraid you might run away, Rocklin. First-night nerves do funny things to a man." Booth was wearing a greatcoat with a flowing cape collared in fur. There was a velvet collar on his braid-bound jacket. He wore a seal ring on his little finger, and a stickpin was thrust in the center of his fine cravat. He was, in short, the picture of nonchalant dandyism. He walked around Frank, examining his costume carefully. "Good! You'll make a fine Mercutio!"

"What if I freeze up or forget my lines?"

"Roland will be sitting in the wings. If you forget a line, he'll prompt you. If you freeze up—" Booth smiled and struck Rocklin lightly on the chest—"I'll stomp on your toe." He laughed, saying, "You'll do fine. The rehearsal was good. See you on stage."

21

As soon as Booth left the room, Carmen said, "Come along, Frank. We'll go over your lines." The two of them went to her dressing room, where Frank stood stiffly, reciting his lines as she gave him the cues. Time dragged by slowly, but finally Jed Hoskins stuck his head inside, saying, "Curtain goin' up! Better git yoahselves in place, please."

"All right, Jed." Carmen had been sitting down, but rose and came to take Frank's arm. "It'll be all right," she said, then turned, and he followed her to the wings. He could hear the muttering voices of the audience, and the actors and actresses were strolling around in a casual way. The older man who played Capulet was reading a copy of *Uncle Tom's Cabin*, deeply engrossed in it. *He's probably been on stage so long it's no more than taking a drink of water,* Frank thought with a tinge of envy.

As the curtain rose Frank's knees were unsteady and his palms were sweaty. He wanted to wipe his face but was afraid he'd smear the makeup that Roland had layered on. Mercutio did not appear in the first three scenes, and the tension grew worse. Finally Booth came to stand by him, his dark eyes excited. "All right, Rocklin?" he asked.

Frank croaked, "All right," his throat dry as dust. When Booth walked out onto the stage accompanied by several other actors, he tried to follow—but seemed to be glued in place. And then Carmen gave him a kick, saying, "Break a leg, Frank!" When he stared at her uncomprehendingly, she smiled and explained, "It's the way we wish each other well in the theater. Now, go do it!"

Frank was half shoved onto the stage by a thrust from Carmen, and the lights blinded him for a moment. The act began with Romeo and Benvolio speaking, and frantically he tried to remember his line but could not have told anyone his name. He stumbled forward, staring at the audience as if he were hypnotized, his mind reeling.

Booth caught a glimpse of Frank and saw at once that he was having a terminal case of stage fright. He'd seen it happen before and now moved close to Frank. He said very loudly the line that introduced Mercutio's first speech: "Give me a torch, I am not for this ambling." He took the torch handed him by one of the actors, then moved so close to Frank that he was touching him. "Being but heavy," he said even more loudly, "I will bear the light." As he said the last of the line, he lifted his foot and brought it down hard on Frank's toes!

Frank grunted involuntarily and spat out his line, running it together so rapidly that most could not understand a word of it: "Nay, gentle Romeo, we must have you dance." As he gasped out the line, he glared at Booth, who laughed at him and whispered, "Now, you're on your own!"

The grins of the actors inspired Frank Rocklin. He saw that they were amused, and for some strange reason this delivered him from the fear that had paralyzed him. He looked over the audience and saw Deborah, Noel, Robert, and Tyler sitting up front. Taking a deep breath, he lifted his voice and spoke his line clearly, "You are a lover. Borrow Cupid's wings, and soar with them above a common bound."

Booth was instantly relieved, and he winked at Frank slyly. He dominated the scene, of course, but Frank was able to throw himself into the play. This had happened to him before, in amateur productions—losing himself. He forgot the audience, or at least was able to concentrate on the action that took place on the stage. And as he did this, he seemed to enter into another realm. The world faded, and all he knew was the tiny cosmos that existed on the small stage.

Why, this is fun! he thought once, and when it came time for him to speak the Queen Mab speech, he was shocked when, at the end, the audience applauded. He blinked with astonishment, and Booth nudged him, whispering, "Blast it all, don't be *too* good, Rocklin! I hate to be upstaged by a bit player!" But he was smiling with approval, and as Frank made his exit, Carmen was waiting, her eyes like stars. She threw her arms around him, whispering, "You were *wonder-*

23

ful, Frank!" And then she was gone, her voice floating to Frank as he stood in the darkness of the wings.

As he stood there, a sense of fulfillment came to Frank Rocklin. He listened to the voices of the actors, and to his total astonishment he found himself *anxious* to get back in front of the footlights. When Jed came by and patted him on the shoulder, whispering, "You done real *fine,* sah! Real fine actin' indeed!" Frank felt a wave of pride and thought, *A man could get used to this!*

Finally the play ended, and Frank was pulled out for a curtain call. He stood there staring down at the audience, noting that his family was beaming at him with pride. Then he was startled, for Booth lifted his hand for silence and, when it came, said forcefully, "I want to give special thanks to Mr. Frank Rocklin, who played the role of Mercutio. He is one of your own, the son of Col. Gideon Rocklin, and his two brothers right in front are, as you see, wearing the uniform of the United States. This was Mr. Rocklin's first professional appearance on the stage, but I know acting, and I insist that if he chooses to make this his profession, why, my family will have to look to its laurels!" He smiled at Frank, and the applause that followed seemed like thunder, sending thrills along that young man's spine such as he'd never felt before.

★ ★ ★

The dining room at Willards would hold fifteen hundred people—or so Mr. Willard boasted—but as the party of John Wilkes Booth was finally seated, it seemed to Frank that the enormous room could not hold one more person.

Booth had charmed the headwaiter into placing them at a good table, and as Frank held Carmen's chair, he said, "Not exactly a private little celebration, is it?"

Carmen turned to face him as he sat down, her lips curved in a smile. "The English hate this place," she said. "They like snug inns with private parties, and one of them told me that all they got here was heat, noise, dust, smoke—and spitting!" She was wearing a pale green dress with a low-cut bodice, and from her ears dangled two jade earrings. Leaning toward him she said, "We'll have a private celebration for your triumph later, Frank, but Booth has to have this sort of thing. He thrives on attention—like all of us in the theater, I suppose."

And she spoke only the truth, for Booth was in his element. He was greeted by many, some wanting his autograph, and more than one stagestruck young woman practically threw herself at the handsome young star. Frank took in the actor, noting the ivory skin, the silky black hair and mustache, the white teeth, and lustrous, heavy-lidded eyes. "He's fine-looking—a little of a dandy."

"Women practically throw themselves at him. But he's not just a dandy, Frank. He's a fencer and an expert pistol shot. Look at his hands—see how strong they are?"

Frank nodded, then turned to Deborah, who was seated on his left, saying, "Get Noel to dance with you."

Deborah smiled but shook her head. "That's not dancing, Frank. That's a can of sardines out there." She motioned to the dance floor, which was indeed packed. The floor was filled with officers wearing white gloves and snowy collars above their wool tunics. The West Point generals were splendid in gold-embroidered shoulder straps and gauntlets, and some of them even kept on their plumed hats. The colors were almost glaring, for the ladies wore dresses of pink and green silk and white tarlatan, and they tossed their curls in the mazes of the dance. Old and young, plump and lean, pretty and plain, the ladies all seemed to find partners. Grave statesmen and stout generals capered as friskily as boyish lieutenants on leave, and the sound of laughter and music and the soft plopping of champagne corks filled the air.

Robert said quietly to Tyler, "You'd never think that our men are dying out there in the field, would you, Ty?"

Tyler shook his head, but didn't answer directly. Instead he looked at Frank with a curious expression. "He was good, wasn't he, Bob?"

25

"I suppose so." He sipped his water carefully, a worried expression on his face. "It's a pretty frothy sort of existence, this acting business. I'll be glad when Frank signs up and we can get away from here. Washington's like some sort of circus these days."

Booth waited until their meal had been ordered, then turned to speak to Noel. "Well, Mr. Kojak, I've read your stories—very fine writing. Honest and clear—a rare thing for a political writer."

"I must say the same for your acting, Mr. Booth," Noel answered quickly, and his reply pleased the actor. Noel added, "I must warn you that I've been asked to write a critical review of your play."

Booth laughed aloud, saying at once, "Well, then, I must flatter you a good deal more than I have, sir! But since one of my company is your good friend, I'll hope you'll spare us the worst."

Carmen said firmly, "I never saw such poise in anyone with so little experience, did you, Mr. Booth?"

"No, indeed I have not." Booth turned to face Frank, his face serious. "Some men cannot be taught to act. Oh, they can memorize the lines and go through the role well enough. But there's a sort of—well, *magic* in drama. Some men and some women can make the audience forget it's in a theater. And those who do are the sort who themselves forget they're in a play. I saw some of that in your performance tonight, Frank. You belong on the stage. I hope you won't neglect the talent God's put in you."

Deborah saw that both of Frank's brothers were uneasy with this statement, and she herself was uncertain that Booth was right. But this was Frank's night of triumph, and so she waited until later to whisper to him, "I hope you don't go on the stage, Frank, as a career." When he looked at her with surprise, she smiled, saying, "You're far too attractive. You'd be besieged by impressionable young women."

"Oh, don't be silly, Deborah!" Frank protested.

"It's true, you know. When you were on the stage, I

forgot that you were just Frank Rocklin, the young man I've known forever. There's some sort of magnetism in some men—Booth is one of them—and I was drawn to you."

"Don't tell Noel. He'd challenge me to a duel."

But Deborah was serious. "Haven't you seen how the women swarm around Booth?"

"Well, I'm no Booth—and not likely to be."

"That's good. Most men couldn't stand such adulation. I'd hate to see you get caught up in that kind of temptation."

CHAPTER THREE
Frank Makes a Choice

As Frank took his final bow at the curtain call along with the rest of the company, he felt a sense of loss. For seven nights he had performed, but now Middleton was fit. Looking out at the audience, he thought, *I'm going to miss all this*. He turned and left the stage, and when he got to the dressing room, he found Roland waiting for him.

"You did well tonight, Frank. Even better than usual."

Frank shrugged and sat down to remove his makeup. "Thanks, Roland," he murmured. He listened as Roland rambled on, speaking of various aspects of the performance, then rose and stripped off the costume. "I'll have these washed for you, Roland," he said.

"Don't bother. I'll take care of it. It'll be good to get back on the boards." He tested his leg, then grinned ruefully. "I hope Booth is more careful with that blasted sword!"

Frank slipped on his trousers, saying, "Roland, don't ever drink before a performance. It's too dangerous trying to handle a sword when you're drunk."

"Amen!" Roland's aristocratic features drew up into a frown. "I've learned that lesson," he said tersely. "I've heard enough about it from Booth." He sat down and grinned faintly. "I'll try to use more discretion in my progress to ruin. I'll only drink before performances that have no dueling scenes."

Frank buttoned his white shirt, then reached for his coat. He slipped it on and turned to study the actor. He had grown fond of Middleton during the past few days, discovering that beneath the cynical facade that the man wore was a sensitive man—and a tortured one. Middleton made a joke of his painful experience with his sweetheart and best friend, but Frank was astute enough to realize that the betrayal of the two had scarred the man emotionally. Now as he sat down and pulled on his soft black boots, he tried one more time to help Middleton.

"You're tired of my preaching, Roland," he said quietly, "but I think we've gotten to be good friends. I hate to see you ruin yourself. You're a fine actor—and if you'd give up drinking, why, you could go to the top." He'd discovered from Carmen that Roland's reputation for drinking kept him from rising in his profession, and now added as he rose to his feet, "You're better than Booth."

"Wouldn't have to be too good to outact him." Roland came to his feet, testing his right leg carefully, then turned to face Frank squarely. "I'm not much at liking other men, Frank, but I like you. But I might as well tell you what you already know—don't waste your time trying to reform me. I'm a hopeless case."

"Don't believe that, Roland," Frank protested. "A man can do what he wants to do." Then he grinned and slapped Roland on the shoulder in a rough gesture of affection. "End of sermon. We'll now have the offering and the benediction."

"What will you do, Frank?"

"Don't know. Go into the army, I expect."

"You feel strongly about the war? You haven't said much."

Frank shrugged his shoulders, saying, "I'm against slavery, but not enough to get myself killed doing something about it. My father and my brothers have all the noble instincts in our family. I'm just a mutt, I guess."

Roland laughed at the expression on Frank's face. "Makes two of us," he said. Putting his hand out impulsively, he gripped Frank's hand with a surprisingly strong pressure. "Let's see each other, Frank. We'll be going to New York next week, but we can have a good time before then."

"Sure. I'll come tomorrow night just to be sure you do a good job." Grinning rashly, Frank added, "Why don't you pink Booth in the arm? Might give him a little humility!"

He turned and left the dressing room, going at once to knock on Carmen's door. When she called out for him to enter, he opened the door and stepped inside. She was sitting at her dressing table but rose at once and came to him. "I guess my brief career on the stage is over," Frank said, grinning ruefully.

"It doesn't have to be." She put her hands out and squeezed his as she looked up at him. "Booth likes you, Frank. He'll find you a place in the company."

"I don't think so," Frank said. They had spoken of this before, but he knew that he had little or no choice. "The only way I could become an actor would be to hire a substitute—and I won't do that."

"No, you wouldn't do that."

Carmen had become very fond of this broad-shouldered young man. Usually it was the men who became infatuated with *her*, but most of them were not men she'd think of seriously. She'd been interested in a few, but they had been married—or had no intention of marrying an actress. For the past week, she and Frank had been together every day, going out after the play to eat. They'd enjoyed each other's company tremendously—something Carmen thought wonderful. Most men would have pressured her into an affair, but though Frank had kissed her more than once, he had not asked anything more of her.

Now that he was leaving the company, Carmen felt a desire to keep him. "You promised to take me riding," she said, holding on to his arm.

"How about tomorrow afternoon?" Frank asked. "I'll pick you up at one. We can have a nice ride in the park." When she nodded, he turned and left the room.

He was on his way toward the exit when Booth stepped out of his dressing room and hailed him. "Frank, hold on there!" The actor came and held an envelope out. "You weren't leaving without saying good-bye—and without your salary?" His handsome face broke into a smile, and he shook his head. "If you're going to be an actor, never forget to take the money."

Feeling extremely awkward, Frank took the envelope, but said, "I didn't do this for money, Mr. Booth."

"I know that—and it's refreshing to see someone who loves the stage for what it is." Booth sobered, his large eyes fixed on Frank thoughtfully. "I've been meaning to talk to you about joining the company."

"Why, you don't need me!" Frank was astonished at the offer. He knew that any young actor would snap up the chance to join the company of John Wilkes Booth. He was not the figure of renown his father was—or his brother, Edwin—still, he was a rising star on the stage.

Booth brushed his dark mustache and said briefly, "Roland's a good actor, but totally unreliable. You know that. He's been released before and will be again. I don't trust him. Why don't you come with me?"

Frank did not even have to think about it. "I appreciate your offer, but I can't accept." He hesitated, not wanting to sound sanctimonious, then faced Booth squarely. "We've not known each other long, but Roland and I are friends."

Booth was very much surprised. He had had no thought but that his offer would be accepted. Now he stared at Frank for a long moment. "Loyalty is a fine thing, sir," he finally said slowly. "I honor you for it. But it might be better placed, I think."

"I've talked to Roland. I think he'll do better in the future."

"Oh, he's always going to do better." Booth shrugged with contempt. "He's promised me a dozen times to lay off the bottle, but he just can't do it. He's hopeless, I'm afraid."

"I don't give up on people," Frank insisted. "But I do

appreciate your offer, Mr. Booth." He found a smile, adding, "My family would probably cast me into the street if I did become an actor. They have little respect for the theater."

"Well, if you change your mind, I'll be glad to recommend you, Rocklin. You've got a real gift, and you're young enough to learn to craft it into something wonderful. I'll be keeping up with you." He smiled at a thought, then added, "Carmen will keep me posted. She's quite taken with you, isn't she?"

Frank shifted uncomfortably, disliking the cynical expression that had come to Booth's face. "I expect we won't be seeing each other much—not if I go into the army."

"You're enlisting?"

"Have to, I guess. It's that or get conscripted."

"You don't think of hiring a substitute?"

"No. I won't do that. I must uphold my family's fine military tradition," Frank said, none too convincing.

Booth stared at him, started to speak—then changed his mind. "Good luck to you," he said cordially, shook hands, and turned back into his dressing room.

He was going to say something to me about the war, Frank thought as he left the theater. He knew that before the war John Wilkes Booth had been very popular in the South. He had, in fact, put on a militia uniform and gone to stand guard when John Brown had been hanged. Middleton had told him, "Booth is a Marylander—one of those who hate the Republican administration and who sentimentalize over the Confederacy. But he'll never join himself to its fortunes."

A light rain glazed the sidewalk as Frank emerged, and he thought of his future. He had no desire to go into the army, and the idea of becoming an actor tantalized him. But as he made his way home, he put those thoughts aside—and thought instead of his riding date with Carmen.

★　★　★

"I'm glad that acting foolishness is out of Frank's system." Stephen Rocklin leaned back in his chair and grunted with satisfaction at Tyler. The two had always been close, and there was a fond light in the older man's eyes as he examined his grandson. Tyler sat loosely in a leather-covered chair, his muscles lax. He was a muscular young man, his chest swelling the fabric of his blue uniform. He had a certain inner strength that matched the power of his sturdy frame, and there was a steadiness in his dark eyes.

"I'm not so sure it's over, Grandfather. You know Frank—when he gets an idea in his head, it takes an earthquake to blast it loose." A sudden grin pulled the corners of his lips upward, and humor glinted in his eyes. "Like you, I suppose."

Stephen glared at his grandson. "I'm *firm*," he snorted. "Frank is *stubborn!*" Then he slapped the desk in front of him and laughed at his own words. "You're right, Ty. I guess it runs in the blood. All Rocklins are pretty stubborn. Well, there are worse things for a man to be."

"Frank is good at things. He just never found anything he liked well enough to stick to. He'll find himself someday."

The two men were sitting in Stephen's office. Tyler had dropped by to spend a little time with his grandfather. It was understood that once the war was over, it would be Tyler who would be a driving force in Rocklin Iron Works. Gideon would never leave the army, and Robert cared little for the business—Frank even less. At the age of sixty-five Stephen Rocklin was strong and vigorous, but now as he looked at his grandson he felt a touch of mortality.

"You'll be sitting behind the desk soon, Ty," he said abruptly. "I wish you weren't in the army. I need you here. The business is too much for an old man. We're three months behind with orders now—and they keep piling up." He waved his thick, square hand at a stack of papers on his desk, adding, "The army can't get enough of anything."

"You know how I love to work with you, Grandfather," Ty said gently, "but I have to wear the uniform." He changed the subject at once, saying, "Frank needs to get into the company with Bob and me. That way we could watch out for him."

"Will he do it, Ty?"

"I talked to him yesterday, and he said he'd let me know."

"He told Bob he'd sign up for ninety days—but no more."

Ty frowned, saying, "Ninety-day wonders, we call those fellows. They're almost worthless. Not enough time to be trained, and as soon as they are, they're looking forward to getting out of the army. If a man's due to get out in a few weeks, he'll hold back when it's time to charge the enemy. We don't need that kind!"

The two men sat there speaking quietly, and finally Stephen asked, "What about this woman Frank's been seeing? What's her name?"

"Carmen Montaigne."

Stephen snorted and gave his grandson a cynical look. "I'll bet she was born Mary Smith!"

Ty laughed and rose to his feet. "I wouldn't be surprised, sir. If Frank went on the stage as a professional, he might change his name to Launcelot Fourtenier!" He picked up his hat, but said before he turned to go, "That's another good reason for getting Frank away from here. She's a pretty sultry package. Enough to turn any man's head."

"Well, get him out of here, Ty," Stephen said, coming to put his hand on the thick shoulder of the younger man. "And watch out for him and Bob as best you can." His gray eyes grew troubled, and he said quietly, "I couldn't bear to lose any of you!"

★ ★ ★

The presidential residence was dismissed by most travelers from overseas as an ordinary country house without taste or splendor. As Frank and Carmen rode past the structure, Frank nodded toward it, saying, "Looks pretty much like a Southern plantation home. Sort of out of place here in Washington."

Carmen was hanging on to the reins of her mare tightly. She disliked horses and had agreed to ride with Frank only to spend time with him away from the city. Now she looked at the iron fence with large gateways that enclosed the grounds, and she shook her head. "It's not very pretty."

Frank laughed, turning to face her. "Smells bad, too."

"What *is* that awful smell, Frank?"

"All this area used to be a marsh. It was used as an outlet for sewage. And right over there is the old city canal. It used to be an inland waterway between the Potomac and the Eastern Branch, but now it's mostly a sewage canal. Come along. We can get away from all this."

Thirty minutes later they were walking their horses slowly down a lane shaded by huge oaks. "This is where most of the officers come for their rides," Frank said. "Pretty nice, isn't it? Wonder how long it will take the engineers to find it and mess it up."

They reached an opening where green grass carpeted the ground, and Carmen exclaimed, "Oh, look at the flowers!"

Frank glanced at the carpet of wildflowers and nodded. "Want to gather a bouquet?"

"Yes!" Carmen allowed him to help her to the ground and made a face. "I'm going to be sore tomorrow!" She laughed up at him, adding, "I'm no rider, as you've found out."

Frank tied the horses to a sapling, then walked with her across the open ground. Carmen was delighted with the flowers that grew profusely and, as she picked them, asked, "I wonder what these are? They're so pretty."

"That's bloodroot," Frank answered, looking at the blossom, which was white with a golden center. "Be careful you don't get any of that juice on your dress." He pointed at a drop of red bloodlike liquid that oozed from the wounded stem. "The Indians use this to decorate their faces and their weapons."

Carmen stared at him with amazement. "How in the world do you know that?"

"My mother likes wildflowers. She used to take all three

of us to the woods and fields." He stooped to pick a delicate flower with a purplish tint and held it out to her. "This is a wood anemone," he said. "William Cullen Bryant wrote a poem about it." Frank quoted a few words, touching the blossom with a forefinger:

> *"Within the woods,*
> *Whose young and half transparent leaves scarce cast*
> *A shade, gay circles of anemones*
> *Danced on their stalks."*

Carmen took the flower and held it gently, saying, "I've never known a man who knew wildflowers."

"No money in it," he said with a shrug. He was embarrassed and laughed ruefully. "None in poetry either. What I need to do is get into selling life insurance or something profitable."

"You'd never like business," Carmen answered. The two wandered along the fringe of trees that outlined the open field and came finally to a large tree that had fallen. "I suppose you know what sort of tree this is?" she asked, sitting down on it.

"Elm," he remarked, then sat down beside her. The air was still, and he could smell the scent of violets in her hair. She was wearing a hunter green riding outfit, and a small gray hat with a yellow plume sat on her head. As with all her clothing, the garment clung to the rich curves of her body. "This is nice, Carmen," he said quietly.

"Yes, it is." Carmen held a pink blossom to her cheek as she studied him, then asked, "What are you going to do, Frank?"

"I signed up for a ninety-day enlistment this morning."

Disappointment came to her face, but she was too experienced to protest. "I'll miss you," she said. "We've had fun, haven't we?"

"We'll have more when I get out. Three months isn't long."

37

Carmen dropped the flower, which fell to the grass. Turning to face him, she whispered, "Yes, it is—a very long time."

Reaching out, Frank put his arms around Carmen and drew her close. She came to him willingly, taking his kiss fully, even eagerly. When he released her, she said, "You've had experience with women."

"Not too much," he protested.

"You're the sort of man who has his way with women."

Frank was stung by her remark and said almost roughly, "And you're the sort of woman who can make a man do anything."

"No, that's not right." Carmen placed her hand on his cheek, a smile coming to her lips. "If I were that, I'd have kept you with me. I tried hard enough."

He was a little shocked at her blunt response. "I've got to go, Carmen. There's no way out of it."

"I see that now." She was afraid that her aggressiveness had shocked him. Drawing back, she put her hand up and smoothed her hair. "What will you do when you get out, Frank?"

He stood up and gazed around at the field, noting that a flight of blackbirds was rising out of the lank grass across the field. She stood with him, and he shook his head. "I don't know, Carmen. Maybe go to work for my grandfather at the factory."

"I suppose that would be good for most men. It's a good business, isn't it?"

"Yes, very good." The thought of going to work behind a desk depressed him, and he said abruptly, "No sense thinking about that now. I've got three months to think about it." He was restless and said, "Let's ride over and see the Potomac. Maybe we'll see one of the new gunboats."

They spent the rest of the afternoon making their way in a leisurely fashion along the banks of the Potomac, and when Frank left her, she offered her hand. "Come back safely, Frank."

★ ★ ★

The next morning Frank accompanied Bob to the camp, where he was issued a uniform and the tools of his new trade. When he'd put his uniform on, Bob said with satisfaction, "Well, you *look* like a soldier, Frank. Now let's see if we can make you into a first-class fighting man."

The training period for the new recruits was almost over, and a week later Frank climbed aboard a railway car stuffed with yelling soldiers. He and Bob squeezed their way into a seat, and when they cleared the station and the men quieted down, they listened to the reckless talk of the recruits. One of them, a lanky young man with flaming red hair, said, "Why, we'll take Vicksburg in a week!"

A yell of agreement rose from the young soldier's friends, but Bob said quietly, "I think it'll take a little more time than that."

As the train crawled around the curves outside of Washington, squeezing between the banks of stone, protesting as the grade grew steep, a strange thing happened to Frank. He was looking around at the fresh, youthful faces of the members of his company—and the thought leaped into his mind, *Some of us who are so alive this morning will be dead before Vicksburg is taken.*

He tried to ignore the thought, but it came back, as persistent as a tune that goes on inside one's head. Finally he began to consider his own death. *What if I get killed?* It was an unsettling feeling, and as the train whistle uttered a shrill protest, it seemed to him that many things he'd always put a high premium on were not as important as he'd assumed. Finally he joined a noisy poker game and managed to shake off the feeling.

The train turned southward, bearing the men who were to be thrown into the struggle for control of the mighty Mississippi. All day long it clattered over the joints of the rails, and as night fell and the men slept, there was a doleful sound as the engineer tugged at the cord over his head, sending what seemed to be a hoarse warning to the countryside. Into the ebony darkness the iron wheels propelled the men of Company H, and Frank Rocklin was not the only one aboard who could not shake the thoughts of battles that loomed ahead.

CHAPTER FOUR
Advance to Vicksburg

"He looks like a man who's lowered his head and seems determined to ram it through a two-inch-thick oak door!"

Thus one of the aides of Gen. Ulysses S. Grant described his commanding officer. And it would take a man like this—stubborn as any officer who wore the Union uniform—to accomplish what *had* to be done before the Confederacy could be severed. Lincoln had said as early as 1861, not long after Manassas: "The war can never be brought to a close until Vicksburg is in our pocket. We may take all the northern ports of the Confederacy and they can still defy us from that stronghold!"

For nine months the Union struggled to take Vicksburg, but experienced nothing but humiliating defeat in five separate attempts. Why were the powerful Union army and equally powerful navy unable to storm this bastion of Southern power?

Gen. William T. Sherman, who was as scrappy a soldier as a man can be, lost heart in the struggle. "No place on earth," he stated flatly, "is favored by nature with natural defenses as Vicksburg, and I do believe the whole thing will fail." He pointed out that the city stood on a series of frowning bluffs above the Mississippi River. Fortifications along these precipices reached as high as three hundred feet, so that any gunboats had to face the fire of heavy land-based guns while unable to return the fire. As for attacking the city from the landward side, this was even more difficult. To come from the north meant that an army with heavy guns and wagons would bog down in the soft, low ground turned into a mire by the Yazoo River. To approach from the other side meant a terrible journey through bayous—with no supply lines. In this territory, the Union soldiers were hindered by chilly, rainy weather in low, swampy country. Everything—clothing, tents, bedding—was wet and stayed wet. Malarial fever and smallpox broke out, and under these terrible conditions any man except Ulysses S. Grant would have given up.

Finally the winter passed, and Grant was ready to attack. But he was like a prizefighter who had been floored too many times. The gunboats of the navy would not take the city, nor could the engineers find a way to get at the stubborn Confederates. Something else would have to be tried, and the soldiers of both armies waited to see what Grant would do.

★ ★ ★

Ty Rocklin sat down on a log beside Frank, saying, "Well, Private, you've been yelling for action ever since we left Washington. Now it looks like you're going to get your wish."

Frank glanced up quickly, noting the excitement on his brother's face. "We're going into action?" he demanded. "When?"

"Well, Gen. Grant hasn't given me all the details of his plan," Ty said, a gleam of humor in his eyes. "But I think the waiting is over." He reached and took a piece of hardtack from the skillet, juggling it to keep from getting burned. A few drops of the grease Frank had been frying it in fell on his boot, but he ignored it, since the caked mud hid the leather completely. "You know, this hardtack isn't too bad," he commented, nibbling at it cautiously.

"Not if you like shoe leather soaked in wallpaper paste," Frank answered. He glanced up as Bob came out of the tent, and said, "The general here says we're going to whip the Rebs, Bob. Here, you'd better eat some of this. It'll make you fight better."

"What's the plan, Lieutenant?" Bob asked, squatting down in front of the small fire. The April breeze blew the gray coals into a swirling funnel, and he turned away to avoid the smoke. He was thinner than he had been, for sickness had laid him low for the past week.

"Don't know much, except that Gen. McPherson just called a staff meeting."

"I didn't know a lowly second lieutenant gets in on those things," Frank jibed. He picked up the blackened coffeepot, filled his tin cup with the tarlike substance, then asked, "What'd you and the general decide?"

Ignoring Frank's remarks, Ty looked down at the muddy waters of the Mississippi, where it purled around a stand of cypress trees. He studied it thoughtfully, then shook his head. "We'll never take that place from the river. That hairpin curve just below it forces the gunboats to slow down to a crawl. Makes them sitting ducks for those big guns up there." He was a slow-talking man, like his father, and he now paused and nibbled at the hardtack. "We're going to head south along the west bank of the river. When we get out of range of the guns, we'll cross over."

"And what will that get us?" Frank inquired. He sipped cautiously at the scalding coffee, grimaced, and blew into the cup. "They'll be ready for us when we get around them, won't they?"

"I suppose so—but at least they can't turn those big guns up on that bluff at us." He sat on the log, a big man seeming entirely indolent. He spoke for a time of the tactics of the campaign, then rose and grinned. "Be sure you take some dry socks on this march. I've got a feeling we're all going to get our feet wet on this one."

"Word is that Grant is sending a big cavalry force out to draw the Rebs away," Bob said.

"That's right, he is. Col. Grierson's taking his troops out

to stir up trouble. If he can draw Pemberton's force after him, it'll give us a chance to cross the river without the Rebs finding out about it. And Grant's leaving Sherman here to demonstrate against Vicksburg."

"But the boats are all north of Vicksburg," Bob argued. "We'll need them to get across the river."

"Adm. Porter will take them downriver," Ty said. "While the enemy is busy with him—and with Sherman and Grierson—we'll sneak down the river, cross over—and then we'll have them!"

Later in the day marching orders came, and Frank was exultant. "I'm sick of sitting on this old riverbank like a bullfrog in a mud hole," he said as he lined up beside Bob in marching order. "Anything would be better than more of this!"

But as with most battle plans, the execution of Grant's scheme proved to be more difficult than it seemed on paper. Some of his officers doubted that the plan would work, and truthfully it was hazardous. All communications and supply lines would be cut off once the army crossed the river. If they were defeated, all would be lost. But Grant was stubbornly determined to hit the Confederates, and he gave the orders for the operation to begin.

On the night of April 16, 1863, Adm. Porter led the Union fleet past the Vicksburg batteries. "I want absolute silence," Porter ordered. "Leave your pets behind—-and the chickens, too!"

Gen. Pemberton and his senior officers were enjoying a ball that night, but when Confederate pickets spotted the spectral shadows of the approaching ships, the ball ended abruptly. The batteries opened up, and several buildings were set ablaze. Barrels of pitch on the east bank were ignited, and suddenly, as Fred Grant, Gen. Grant's twelve-year-old son, would recall later, "The river was lit up as if by sunlight."

The passage of the fleet was agonizingly slow. For five hours the bombardment lasted, but only one transport was sunk. Thus the first part of Grant's plan was successful. The second part was launched at once, as Grant sent Col. Grierson on a raid that drew off many of Gen. Pemberton's men. Grierson's cavalry made a great deal of mischief, as ordered.

All of this was academic to Frank Rocklin, for he was one of those who spent most of April struggling through the muddy bayous and swamps of Louisiana. They fought the heat, mosquitoes, snakes, sickness, and when they finally arrived at their destination, Frank exclaimed in disgust to Bob, "If fighting is any worse than this, I don't think I can take it, Bob!"

Bob Rocklin, struggling with the beginnings of a malarial fever, was pale, and his face was covered with a sheen of sweat. He glanced across the river silently, then said abruptly, "Frank, this has been bad—but if we get into a fight tomorrow, I'd feel a lot easier knowing that you were all right."

"Why, I'll be fine, Bob," Frank answered at once. He understood instantly that his brother was not speaking of the physical danger. "I guess you're worried because I've never joined the church."

"It's more than that, Frank," Bob said. "None of us know when we'll die. A man can get thrown by a horse on his way to a party. But in battle, the odds are shorter." He wiped his face with a damp handkerchief, then turned to say, "Why haven't you ever given your heart to God, Frank? It's been a grief to all of us—especially to Father and Mother."

"Can't say why, Bob." Frank was a man who could always find something to say—but now he discovered that he had no answer for his brother's quiet question. "I know God exists. I believe the Bible, too. But somehow it's just not come to me as it did to you and Ty. Guess some folks are just naturally drawn to such things—and I'm one of those who just isn't."

"That's wrong, Frank," Bob said instantly. He pulled out his worn New Testament, opened it, and read, " 'For the grace of God hath appeared to all men.' " Looking up, he asked quietly, "Do you believe that Jesus is the Son of God?"

"Why, of course! I've always believed that."

Bob began to read the Scripture. He was a quiet young man, not flamboyant or outgoing. But there was a steadiness in him that Frank had always admired, perhaps because he himself lacked the quality. It had been Bob he'd gone to all his life when he needed help or advice. Their father had been gone on duty for long periods, but Bob had always been there. More than once it had been this brother who'd steered Frank out of trouble or who'd been there to help when he'd gone wrong.

Finally, when Bob fell silent, having done his best to present his beliefs, Frank said, "Bob, I guess men don't have words to say some things—not like women do. But just in case something does happen—" Frank paused and looked down at his muddy shoes, then lifted his face, his eyes fixed on the other. "Just in case, I want you to know that I—well, I love you, Brother. You've been the best friend I've ever had." Embarrassed by the voicing of his deepest feelings, he looked off across the river, studying the Federal gunboats as they steamed back and forth like huge beasts.

"Why, I appreciate that, Frank," Bob said. He was weak, and his hands were not steady, but he smiled, adding, "I believe that God will get all three of us through this thing, but we ought to say such things to each other." He hesitated, then nodded slowly. "I'm not going to pester you with sermons, Frank. I know that won't do. You've heard the gospel just like Ty and I have. But I want you to know that I'm praying for you all the time."

Frank took a deep breath, then expelled it slowly. "Thanks, Bob. I reckon I knew that." He clapped his brother on the shoulder, noting that it seemed thin and frail. "Well, let me do one thing. That fever's got you down. You still won't go to the surgeon?"

"No. I didn't come to be sick."

"Then I'll carry your pack on the march. No arguments.

You had to carry *me* once, remember? That time we were coon hunting and I fell into a hole and twisted my ankle?"

Robert smiled, his face lighting up. "That was a good time, wasn't it? What were we, about thirteen?"

"You were, and I was mad because *I* wanted to be in my teens." His face changed, and the thought of that dim past had its way with him. His eyelids fell and his lips seemed to soften as he answered, "Funny how we're never satisfied to be what we are." Leaning back and clasping his leg he continued, "When we're little, we want to be in our teens. But when that comes, we want to be grown men. I guess we're always looking for something better. . . ."

Bob listened quietly as Frank spoke. The scent of cooking meat was in the air, along with the lush, rank smell of the bayou. Overhead the sky was blue and looked hard enough to strike a match on. The air was filled with the sound of an army preparing to move—the clatter of equipment, men cursing mules who struggled to pull heavy guns through the soupy mud, a babble of voices, most with hard Northern accents. Excitement filled the air, and Bob thought, *Some of these men who are laughing right now will be dead or shot to pieces before this thing is over. Why can't they see what's coming?*

"Well, you stretch out and take it easy, Bob," Frank said. "I'll scout around and see what I can scrounge. Lots of grub here, but when we cross that river there, we won't be able to run to the store and buy a few groceries." He stood up on his feet, looked across the chocolate brown river that looked as strong as time itself, then shook his head. "I expect we'll do some fighting when we get on that other side."

He left Bob and spent a few hours scrounging food. He had the instincts of an old soldier and, by the time Ty found him, had collected quite a store. "You look like the quartermaster, Pvt. Rocklin," Ty joked as he looked over the stock. "Going on a picnic?"

"No, sir, Lieutenant. Just tired of hardtack. Made a little dicker with a farmer and his wife." He waved at the stock of food with pride. "They were just about to start eating dinner, and I bought it from them. Look, got some ham, pork chops, baked potatoes, two loaves of fresh-baked bread—and the biggest part of a chocolate cake. Here, have a taste."

Tyler took a slice of the cake, ate it with pleasure, then wiped his hands on his handkerchief. "You're just a chocolate soldier, Private," he teased. Then he looked over toward where Bob was lying flat on the ground and sobered. "He ought to go to the hospital. He's in no shape to go into action."

"Won't hear of it." Frank shook his head. "Never saw him act so stubborn, Ty."

"Well, if he gets worse, I'll order him to go. Meanwhile, you look out for him."

"I don't think he can make a march. He's weak as a kitten, Ty."

Tyler thought for a moment. "I'll assign him to one of the supply wagons as a helper. That way he can ride. When we go into action, we'll have to see."

"That'll be better."

"Frank—"

Something in his older brother's voice caught at Frank. He glanced up quickly and saw that Ty's eyes were filled with concern. At once he said, "You're worried about us, aren't you?"

"Yes. It's going to be pretty hard, Frank. Some of us aren't going to make it."

"Bob's talked to me." Although Frank had not been as close to Tyler as he had been to Bob, he respected and admired him. Now he wanted to say so, but found it difficult. "I know all of you are disappointed that I've not been a church member," he said slowly, searching for the right words. "Maybe it will come to me, but a man can't force a thing like that. I'll just have to wait, Ty. I can't become a Christian just to please other people."

"No, but I'm hoping you'll find Christ for your own happiness, Frank." Tyler Rocklin was basically a private person and found it hard to speak of his faith. "I'm no

preacher, Frank, but without Jesus, I'd be the most miserable man in the world!" He shook his shoulders together and
his lips grew firm. "End of sermon."

"I told Bob how much I admire and respect him," Frank
said awkwardly. Again he was embarrassed, and his face grew
slightly red. "Well, you've been a fine older brother to me,
Ty—and I want you to know I—I count myself lucky." He
grinned suddenly, adding, "I can spout poetry by the yard!
Why can't I say what I feel about my own family? Blast it all,
Ty, I love you—and you'll just have to put up with my
blathering! Must be the ham in me!"

But his words had pleased Ty, and he put his heavy hand
on Frank's shoulder. He said only, "I feel the same about
you, Frank." Then he was gone, and as he disappeared,
Frank felt good. *Should have said those things a long time ago.
It's a shame it takes a war before people can say what they feel!*

★ ★ ★

On April 30, the Union army crossed from the west bank of
the Mississippi river to Bruinsburg on the east shore, a
village thirty-five miles below Vicksburg. Grant wrote about
his arrival in Bruinsburg, "I felt a degree of relief scarcely
ever equaled since. . . . I was on dry ground on the same side
of the river with the enemy. All the campaigns, labors,
hardships and exposures that had been made and endured
were for the accomplishment of this one object."

Gen. Pemberton, Grant's opponent, telegraphed President
Jefferson Davis for help, but Pemberton moved too slowly.
Instead of striking at once for Vicksburg, Grant moved to-
ward Jackson. He knew that once Jackson was taken, the
Confederate supply line to Vicksburg would be cut.

Few Union military campaigns were as successful as that
of Grant in the days that followed. He defeated a Confederate force at Port Royal on May 1, then was joined by
Sherman to begin what would be called almost eighty years
later a "blitz." The Union army defeated the Confederates
at Raymond on May 12 in drenching rain, and it was in this

battle that the Rocklins were fiercely engaged. Company H was part of the First Brigade, the Third Division of the Seventeenth Army Corps. They were led by Maj. Gen. James B. McPherson, a handsome young man from Baltimore.

As the army moved forward, Lt. Tyler Rocklin was disturbed about the condition of his men. He wrote in a letter to his mother, "The men need time to rest, but there is no time. The marches have been severe, and nearly one-third of our men have no shoes, having worn them out on the marches. Supplies are short, and the men are so tired, I've seen the whole company asleep as they trudge along the muddy roads. I'm especially concerned for Bob. He's weak after his bout with malaria. Pray for him, Mother, and for Frank, that he will find God. Much hard fighting ahead, but we must trust in the mercies of the Lord."

Jackson fell to Grant's army on May 14, and the army then turned to Vicksburg. Grant whipped Pemberton at Champion Hill, then again at Big Black River Bridge. Pemberton sensed defeat and ordered his troops to retreat to Vicksburg.

It was a great victory for Grant. In 18 days his army had marched 200 miles, fought 5 victorious battles, and captured more than 6,000 prisoners and 67 pieces of artillery. The relatively low Union cost was 4,500 casualties. Lincoln's faith in the squat and tough Ulysses Grant was amply justified!

★ ★ ★

"Now I guess we can get a little rest." Frank spoke as he looked down at his shoe, the sole of which was held in place by a piece of rawhide string. He was tired to the bone, and looking around at the squad, he knew that they were all played out. Bob was slumped in his blankets, and Kyle Morton—at the age of seventeen, the youngest man in the squad—had gone to sleep holding his bowl of stew. "Wake up, Kyle," Frank called out. "Eat that stew, then go to bed."

Kyle gave a start, looked around wildly, then grinned

wearily at Frank. "Who made you a general, Pvt. Rocklin?" he demanded. He lifted the spoon, ate the rest of the food, then looked around with bleary eyes. "I been a hero long enough. I want my medals now, Frank." He was an engaging young man, thin as a rail, but strong and active.

Frank had gotten close to the boy, feeling protective of the youngster, and now teased him, "If Martha Ann could see you now, she'd find another sweetheart."

"No, I'm too good-looking," Kyle said with a wink. He had only faint wisps of beard on his smooth cheeks, despite all his desire to grow a fierce beard. "She's too much in love with me to look at any other feller."

At that moment, a voice called out, "Form up! Form up!" The members of the squad groaned, and Kyle said, "Aw, Lieutenant, give us a break."

Lt. Rocklin's face was lined with fatigue. "We're moving in—we'll be skirmishers. Load your muskets and follow me!" He turned to Bob, who was acting sergeant. "Get them moving, Sergeant," he said, then whirled and left to go down the line.

"Bob, we're in no shape to attack!" Frank whispered, pulling his belt on. "We're in poor condition."

"We'll make it, Frank. Watch out for yourself!"

But the attack was a failure. Grant, overconfident after his success, was determined to take Vicksburg by storm. The Confederates had been able to fortify the approach, and the Union troops had great difficulty getting through the felled trees and steep ravines.

Frank's squad was in the thick of the fight. They advanced through the thickets, bullets screaming overhead. "Keep down!" Bob called out. "Crawl on the ground!"

Frank was beside Kyle as Bob called out. He turned to relay the order to the young man, but a bullet caught Morton in the stomach at that instant, driving him backward.

"Kyle!" Frank cried out. Dropping his musket, he leaped to kneel beside the wounded man. Kyle stared up at him, his face filled with astonishment and pain.

"Why—they shot me, Frank!"

"Take it easy, Kyle. You'll be all right."

But young Morton looked down to see his stomach drenched with crimson. He knew as well as any that the chances of a man recovering from a stomach wound were almost nonexistent. He lay there quietly, and finally said, "It don't hardly hurt at all, Frank." But the blood was pouring from the wound, and he looked up to stare at his friend. "I'm going to die, Frank. Write my people for me."

"I'll get you to the hospital."

"Won't make no difference. Promise me you'll write to my ma. Tell her I died trusting in Jesus. And write to Martha, too."

The air was filled with the explosion of shells, and the musketfire was like thousands of sticks breaking. The cries of the wounded grated on Frank's nerves, but he nodded. "I'll . . . do it, Kyle."

Morton reached out, and Frank took the bloodstained hand. Kyle's face was pale, and he looked no more than fourteen years old as he lay dying. "Glad you stopped," he whispered, squeezing Frank's hand. "Wouldn't like . . . to die . . . alone."

Frank's throat was thick, and his eyes blurred. He sat there holding the young man in his arms and finally heard him whisper, "Martha." Then he seemed to relax, his hand going limp.

Frank Rocklin sat on the battlefield holding his dead friend. Soon the squad returned, beaten back by the Confederates. He looked up to see Bob standing over him. "He's gone, Bob," Frank said tonelessly. Getting to his feet, he gave one angry look at Vicksburg. "He died taking that place. I don't think Martha will think it's worth it."

Bob said only, "He was a Christian, Frank. He's with his Lord now."

But Frank shook his head, a bitterness in his expression. "I'm going to bury him, Bob. It's the last thing I can do for him." Lifting his eyes to stare at the city, he said nothing more.

Bob knew him well. *He's going to be bitter over this,* he thought. Then he said gently, "I'll get some shovels, Frank. We'll have a little service. It'll be something to tell his people." He saw that his words meant little to Frank, but there was nothing else he could say.

CHAPTER FIVE
Special Mission

A pale white sun poured heat over the ditch where the six sweat-soaked soldiers crouched. From time to time one of the Federal cannon would fire, and the men would blink and look upward. Sometimes it was possible to actually *see* the missile, or at least a faint black line, as it scored the summer sky. When it struck with a muffled *whump,* they would all relax.

That was when one of their own cannon fired; but when a shell rose from one of the Confederate batteries, that was a different story! They had all learned to identify the muffled cough of the Rebel artillery, and when it came, every man would draw his head in like a snapping turtle. Frank knew it was silly, for if a shell hit in his section of the trench, such a thing would not save him—but it was an involuntary action.

Now as he crouched in the dust with his legs drawn up, Frank heard the familiar sound and hunched himself into a fetal position. As the enemy shell rose, it screamed like a banshee, and for one moment Frank thought of the shell as a living thing—a sharklike demon with white teeth gleaming as it sought to find its prey of living flesh. Then the explosion came, some fifty feet behind him and to his right. He turned his head to watch the geyser of dust rise and then muttered, "Rotten shot, Reb!" He rolled over and pulled his canteen from underneath his side with a grunt, uncapped it, and took three small sips of the rank, tepid water. It tasted of metal, but he would have willingly drained it all. But water was short, and all along the twelve-mile length of the Union line, men were as thirsty as he.

Flies swarmed around his head, and he ignored them for the most part. But when one of them crawled over his lips, he couldn't stand that and shook his head, blowing out with a mild curse. He was tired to the bone and from time to time would doze off, only to be awakened by a howling shell and the shattering explosion that followed. Sleep came at night, and he longed for the searing heat of day to pass into the relative coolness. Mississippi was a hot place, and only during the darkness did he get any respite from the humid air that kept him bathed in sweat.

The siege had begun on May 18, and now it was growing toward the middle of June. Not a long time, relatively speaking, but digging holes in the ground under the sultry, burning southern sun all day while dodging shells and the fire of lynx-eyed sharpshooters made it seem like an eternity. As he lay there, Frank heard the sound of singing and was forced to smile despite his misery. Both sides sang at night, but this was a new one—obviously composed by some witty Confederate. They'd sung it every night for a week and now had decided to serenade themselves under the sun. It was sung to the tune of "A Life on the Ocean Wave," and Frank hummed along with his Rebel foes:

> *A life on the Vicksburg bluff,*
> *A home in the trenches deep,*
> *Where we dodge "Yank" shells enough,*
> *And our old "peabread" won't keep.*
> *On "old Logan's" beef I pine,*
> *For there's fat on his bones no more;*
> *Oh! give me some pork and brine,*
> *And truck from a sutler's store.*

"Sounds like the Rebs are getting hungry, don't it, Frank?"

Frank lifted his head cautiously to meet the eyes of Lafe Sutter, a lanky young man from Maine. He was something of a musician himself and cocked his head critically. "That ain't their regular tenor," he remarked. "Hope they ain't nothing happened to him. That there feller taking his place is pretty bad."

Frank grinned at the young man, saying, "They'd be sorry to hear their performance doesn't please you, Lafe. Maybe we ought to let them know that we've got a particular judge of music over here on our side." As the song started again, he thought of how strange it was that Lafe was concerned about the well-being of a man who was trying his best to kill him. But then much of war was ridiculous, he had learned, and he listened to the rest of the song.

> *Old Grant is starving us out,*
> *Our grub is fast wasting away,*
> *Pemb' don't know what he is about,*
> *And he hasn't for many a day,*
> *So we'll bury "old Logan" tonight,*
> *From tough beef we'll be set free;*
> *We'll put him far out of sight,*
> *No more of his meat for me!*
>
> *Texas steers are no longer in view,*
> *Mule steaks are now "done up brown,"*
> *While peabread, mule roast and mule stew,*
> *Are our fare here in Vicksburg town;*
> *And the song of our hearts shall be,*
> *When the Yanks and their gunboats rave;*
> *A life in a bomb-proof for me,*
> *And a tear on "old Logan's" grave.*

As the ragged chorus of voices faded, Frank squirmed around to ask, "Bob, you ever stop to think that one of those fellows in those trenches might be named Rocklin?"

"Sure, I have." Bob was sitting with his back braced against the trench. His face was sunburned, and he was still weak from the fever that had plagued him from the beginning of the campaign. He traced a complicated geometric figure in the dust as he thought back, then glanced at Frank. "I think a lot of those cousins of ours," he murmured. "Can't forget that summer we spent there, all three of us—you and me and Ty. It was the best vacation we ever had."

"Sure was," Frank agreed, thinking of the summer of '57. He'd been fourteen and had run wild in the hills of Virginia. The three of them had stayed at Gracefield, where they'd learned to know their Southern cousins for the first time. He thought of the long, slow nights with the scent of magnolias and how he'd fallen madly in love with one of his cousins. "Remember how I fell for Rachel Franklin, Bob?" he asked. "Never did understand just how close kin we were, but I was sure crazy about her."

"She's married now," Bob said, then smiled. "You were pretty gone on her." He paused, then said more slowly, "I got real close to Dent. He was pretty wild, but I liked him." He glanced involuntarily toward the Rebel line of fortifications, saying softly, "Sure would hate to meet up with Dent. Don't see how I could pull a trigger on him."

"You think any of our kin might be in those lines?"

"Most of them are with Lee." He fell into a silence, then shook his head. "This isn't like fighting some army from Spain or Germany. That would be easy. But to fight your own kin—it's hard!"

Frank said nothing, for he had thought of this. It was a brothers' war, with many families split right in two. *There's no way to sort this mess out,* he thought wearily. He hated the war, and he hated the trench warfare worse than battle. As he sat under the blazing sun, he thought, *When my ninety days are up, I'll get out of this!* He knew Bob and Ty were expecting him to reenlist, but he could not endure more of this sort of misery!

The day wore on, and finally he grew more angry. Yanking

off his cap, he put it on the end of a stick and lifted it above the trench. Almost instantly, he heard a sharp *crack,* and the cap jerked as a minié ball struck it, then continued to plow a track in the dirt behind the trench.

"Rocklin, stop that blamed foolishness!" First Sgt. Jake Mulhullen, a square box of a man from Vermont, had been crawling down the line and had seen Frank's action. His face was the color of a ripe tomato, and he barked angrily, "If you want to play games, come along with me. I've got one you'll love!"

"Aw, Sarge, I was just seeing if the Rebs were awake!" Frank protested.

Mulhullen only glared at him. "Diggin' latrines—that's a good game, Rocklin. Just about your speed!"

Frank gave a despairing glance at Lafe, who shrugged, saying, "Have a good time, Frank."

For the rest of the long afternoon Frank joined the miserable crew who had displeased their superiors as they dug long, shallow trenches. One of his fellow sufferers paused long enough to say, "Well, at least we won't get picked off by one of them sharpshooters!" His sentiments might have been astute, but Frank was furious. For a while he took his anger out by making the dirt fly, but the short private to his right hissed, "Cut it out will you? You're making the rest of us look bad. What you tryin' to do, set us a good example?"

Frank simmered down and settled into a slow, methodical motion that he refused to increase even when prodded by the sergeant in charge of the detail. Finally the sun began to set, and the air cooled. Sgt. Mulhullen came to say, "All right, Rocklin, if you had enough fun, you can get chow. But if I catch you playin' around again, you'll dig a trench ten miles long!"

Frank stomped to where his squad had been pulled back far enough to have their evening meal. Several of the men laughed as he came to get his plate of beans and pork. "Gonna' win the war by digging them ditches?" one of them jibed, and when Frank glared at him, he threw up his hands

59

in mock fear. "Hold him, you fellers! It's that trench-diggin' terror, Frank Rocklin!"

Frank started for the soldier, but Bob was there to hold him back. "Here, better get some of this grub before these gluttons eat it up," he joked. He pulled Frank aside, saying, "Got a letter from Mother. It's to all of us, I guess. Ty's already read it." Bob watched as Frank read the letter, then folded it and handed it back. "She's worried about us, of course, and about Pa, too."

Frank was still angry and, when Ty came by, said, "I didn't join the army to dig sanitary trenches!"

"They've got to be dug. We've lost more men to sickness and disease than we have to Reb bullets." Tyler considered the stubborn expression on the face of his younger brother and then glanced at Bob. Something passed between the two men, and Tyler said, "Got some chores of my own. Got to detail a private to the job of taking care of the staff's horses. Be a change for you, Frank."

Frank gave the lieutenant a grateful look, but said, "I don't want any special treatment."

"You won't get any," Tyler said with a smile. "Far as I see, Private, there's no such thing as a soft job in this kind of fight. Report to me first thing in the morning."

Afterward, Bob had a chance to speak with Tyler alone. "He's pretty touchy. Good for you to have him where you can keep an eye on him."

Tyler nodded thoughtfully. "He's not like us, Bob. We're pretty steady fellows—like Father, I suppose." Taking off his hat, he wiped his brow, then replaced the hat, settling it firmly on his head. "Frank's more impulsive. He's the kind you can count on when things are hot and the action is heavy, but he's not built to take boredom too well. I'll be glad when this thing is over," he concluded. Staring through the darkness, he shook his head. "Wonder what the Rebs are thinking? No way for them to get out. Gunboats on the river, and seventy thousand of us to stop a breakthrough. They must be worse off than we are!"

★ ★ ★

Tyler Rocklin had been entirely correct in his analysis of the character of his youngest brother. That Frank was impulsive with a highly volatile streak all the family well understood. But two days after Frank had been assigned to take care of the chores for the staff of the corps commander, Gen. McPherson, Lt. Tyler Rocklin got the shock of his military career.

"Lieutenant, Gen. McPherson wants to speak with you. Report to his headquarters at once." The order came in the form of terse, clipped speech from a slight, young major named Benning. He snapped caustically, "The general doesn't like to be kept waiting, Lt. Rocklin."

"Of course, Major!" Tyler fell into step beside the officer, asking, "Do you have any idea what the general wants with me?"

"Gen. McPherson will do his own talking, Lieutenant."

Tyler's mind raced as he accompanied Benning along the line of tents toward the headquarters of the commander. *I must have done something pretty bad,* he thought, but though he searched his memory frantically, nothing came to him. He was a tough-minded young man and knew that he'd done his duty, so when he arrived outside the tent of the commander, he was curious, but not at all rattled.

Maj. Benning leaned to put his head inside the tent. "Sir, Lt. Rocklin is here."

"Come in—and you remain as well, Major."

Tyler stepped inside and found the general seated at his portable desk. He rose at once and returned Rocklin's salute. He was a trim young man in his thirties, with a pair of intense gray eyes and a firm mouth. "Good to see you again, Lieutenant. I hear good things of your company from Col. Wesley."

"Why, thank you, General!"

"I served with your father once—fine officer! I know you're proud of him."

"I am indeed, sir!"

Gen. McPherson studied the tall young officer for an

61

extended moment, then said, "You have two brothers serving with your company? Tell me about your youngest brother—Pvt. Frank Rocklin, isn't it?"

Tyler's heart grew cold, for he was now certain that Frank had committed some frightful blunder! But he lifted his head and said firmly, "My brother Robert is enlisted for three years, General, and will rise in the ranks. Frank is— well, different from Robert and me. He's very impulsive, sir, and he's had hardly any training. No time for it before we left Washington." Tyler spoke slowly, giving an honest judgment, and finally asked, "Is Pvt. Rocklin in some sort of trouble, General?"

At once McPherson shook his head. "Why, no, Lieutenant, not at all." He smiled then, adding, "I can see how you might think so—getting called up before the corps commander to explain your brother. But it's not what he's done. It's what he *wants* to do."

"Sir?"

"Gen. Grant is going to have to make an attempt to take the city. We all know that, don't we? The country's eyes are on this place. It's become a symbol for the whole war. If Vicksburg falls, the end of the war is in sight. It's important that we have this victory."

As McPherson went over what every officer in the army knew, Tyler was wondering what under the sun all of this had to do with Frank. Finally the general said, "Well, your brother's been listening to the camp gossip. Everyone wants to know if the enemy is ripe for an attack. How strong are they?" A smile touched McPherson's lips, and he shook his head with a sort of wonder. "These ninety-day men don't have the awe of generals that regulars do, Lieutenant. So this brother of yours came to my aide with a request to see me. Maj. Benning here was quite shocked, but when he heard the plan, he thought I should hear it."

"I still think it won't work, sir," Benning snapped. "He'll never pull it off."

"Pull *what* off, sir?" Tyler burst out. "What in the world does Frank want to do?"

"Why, he says he can get through the Confederate lines, scout out the situation, and get the information back to us."

Tyler stared at the two officers in dismay, but asked cautiously, "And how does he propose to do all this, sir?"

"Says he's an actor," Benning snorted. "He's going to put on a disguise of some sort and just walk right into the city! Nonsense!"

"But if it worked, Major," Gen. McPherson urged quickly, "it would be an invaluable piece of information." He put his steady gaze on Tyler and asked, "Is he capable of doing this, in your judgment?"

Tyler thought rapidly, then nodded firmly. "It's the kind of thing *he* would do, sir. I couldn't do it, but I think Frank might be able to accomplish a mission like that."

McPherson laughed loudly. "He says it'll be better than digging latrines! I like his spirit. Now, Lieutenant, I want you to see to it that he gets what he needs. Anything! But it must be fast!" He hesitated, then added, "You must see that he understands that he'll be shot at once if he's caught. He'll be out of uniform—a spy. We'd do the same if we caught one of theirs."

"I think he knows that, sir. He's no coward."

"Well, he'll be doing us more good in this way than taking care of my horse. Have him come and see me before he leaves. I'll have a few instructions for him, and you tell him what sort of military items he needs to look for—guns emplacements and so on."

"Yes, General." Tyler saluted, and as he left he thought, *Only Frank would think up a scheme like this!*

★ ★ ★

"Contraband Negro to see you, General."

Gen. McPherson turned to find Maj. Benning, who had approached the rise that was covered with tall oaks. He'd come here to study the twisting line of battle—and to think.

63

It was a quiet spot, and one of the few places where he could find some solitude. He frowned as he said shortly, "You can take care of these things, Major."

Benning was a stubborn young man, and he held his head high. "Sir, he says he's been in Vicksburg, that he knows something that might help us. He won't speak with anyone but you, sir."

"Very well!" McPherson stood still as the black man advanced. *He might know something—but he looks almost senile.* "Yes, Uncle, what is it?"

The man was very old. His kinky hair was white as snow, as was the beard that adorned his dark cheeks. His eyes were dark brown but almost hidden under droopy lids, and there was a slowness in his thick speech that made him almost impossible to understand. He walked painfully, leaning on a cane made from a sapling, and his snuff-colored hands trembled violently. "Is Marse Linkum heah?" he quavered in a rusty voice.

"President Lincoln? Why, no, he's not here. What do you have, Uncle? Tell me about Vicksburg!"

"Yassuh, I done seed it." The features of the old man twisted, and his hand fluttered as he fumbled with the cane. He licked his thick lips, then seemed to forget that he was in the presence of a general. He mumbled about someone named Carter, then cackled in a high-pitched laugh, saying, "No suh, us ain't been kotched—them pattyrollers ain't get us!"

McPherson gave the major a disgusted look. "See he gets something to eat, Maj. Benning—he's no help." He turned but then stopped when a strong voice said, "Pvt. Rocklin reporting, General." Wheeling to face the man, McPherson stared with incredulous eyes as the bent figure straightened up and the eyes opened wide—and a broad smile split the darkened face. "Ready for duty, sir!" he said, a light of humor in his dark eyes.

McPherson burst into laughter. "Well, Pvt. Rocklin," he

said, "if you can fool the Rebs as well as you fooled us, you'll be all right. Did you know him, Major?"

"No, sir." Benning was as taken by surprise as the general and gave one of his rare smiles. "Maybe there is *some* use for actors in the world, Pvt. Rocklin. You'll have a chance to prove it to me and the general."

The three men spoke for over thirty minutes as darkness fell over the land. Frank saluted, then faded away without a backward glance.

"Do you think he can do it, sir?"

"I think he's got brass enough for it, Major." McPherson added, "I think we might take time to wish that young man luck—and a prayer if you've got one!"

★ ★ ★

Frank had found that a single man getting into Vicksburg after dark was not the problem he had feared. The lines were thin in spots, and he had moved stealthily through the darkness, grateful that there was only a sliver of a moon. Keeping to the line of trees that flanked some sort of rough cattle trail, he passed out of the Union lines. Once he heard a sentinel call out on his left, "Hey, Charlie, you got a chaw of terbaccy?" He froze at once, but when the guard left to get his chaw, he at once moved forward.

"Well, I'm in Vicksburg," he murmured as he made his way up the incline. He had no map nor any sort of paper to identify himself, but Maj. Benning had shown him on the regimental map where the city lay behind the lines. Soon he encountered a series of houses that he recognized as the outer limits of the city. The silence was broken occasionally by one of the Union batteries firing on the town. Frank made his way carefully toward the bulk of buildings and then decided to wait until morning to proceed.

He took shelter in a clump of trees, but dared not light a fire. He had no canteen, but he had brought a piece of beef he'd scrounged from the general's mess, which he gnawed as he lay on the dew-soaked ground. It was tough and stringy, but better than hardtack, and it was something to do. The beef was salty and he grew thirsty, but he decided not to try to find water until daybreak.

It was a long night to him, and he could not sleep. As the shells exploded, making red dots in the blackness of the night, Rocklin thought with a gust of amusement of what he was doing. "Of all the fool stunts I've ever pulled, this takes the prize," he murmured, shifting to avoid a sharp stone that dug into his back. There was a strange mixture of humor and fatalism in him; he knew that if he were caught, there would be no long drawn-out trial. The thought that he might be lying dead in a shallow grave in a few hours came to him, and he discovered that he was somewhat frightened by the concept. It wasn't death that troubled him, but the notion that life would be cut short. *Lots of things I want to do. If I get caught, it's all over.* He tried to think of what it would be like to be dead, but all he could make of it was that he would be out of the only place he knew. *When you're dead, it's the end of the world. Your family will still be living, and the war will be going on—but not for you.* He thought of the sermons he'd heard about hell and judgment, and he grew sober. He was no doubter and was convinced that he would face God one day. It had always seemed like something that was far away, a distant threat like thunder heard far off—only a low rumble. Now it was very close, and as the hours crawled by, he was silent, thinking about God and what it would be like to stand before him.

When the first few gleams of gray appeared in the east, he was up and moving. Finding a small creek, he drank thirstily, then ate the rest of the beef. When he emerged from the trees, he put himself on the road, careful to assume his role. Hobbling painfully, he leaned on his stick and kept his head down. The first person he saw was a woman who came out of her house and stared at him for a moment. She didn't speak, and Frank pretended not to see her. The brief encounter sharpened his thoughts, for he realized that just one false step with just one person would be a disaster.

As the sun rose, he encountered more people. He passed a gaggle of small children playing some sort of game that involved a ball, but none of them paid him the slightest attention. A man driving a scrawny cow appeared out of a side trail. He was a short, muscular man wearing a pair of faded overalls. "Better watch yourself," he called out as he passed close to Frank. "One of them shells wouldn't do you any good."

"No sah," Frank mumbled. "Is it dem Yankees?"

"Shore. They won't git in heah, you can bet. Gen'ral Joe Johnston, he's on his way with 'bout a million of our boys." The stocky man nodded emphatically, adding, "He'll run them Bluebellies all the way back to ol' Abe!" The cow had stopped to pull a few mouthfuls of grass, and Frank stood there, listening and saying a word now and then. He risked looking the man fully in the face, and to his relief, got no reaction. When the farmer asked him if he was looking to be free, he shook his head and mumbled, "I belong ter Mistah Edward Sullins. Ain't studyin' no freedom, no sah!"

The man grinned, then said, "Watch fer them shells, Uncle. You'll get to glory quicker than you think if one of them derned things lands on you." He tapped the cow with the long slender sapling he held and moved away.

Frank expelled his breath, feeling a little drained. He'd conceived this role of an older slave, but hadn't been certain he could pull it off. He'd been around blacks when visiting in Virginia, but that had been several years earlier. Fortunately he had a good ear for dialect, and the thick speech of Box, an elderly slave who was the blacksmith at Gracefield, had stayed with him.

People emerged from their houses as he passed through the residential areas. All of them scurried quickly along, ducking their heads when a cannon shell exploded. There was a determined look on most of their faces, but there was fear as well. Once when a shell exploded beside a small white frame house not fifty feet from where he walked, Frank almost darted away. The shell blew the side of the house apart, sending splintered fragments sailing into the air. A woman who was working in a garden in the back threw the hoe down and screamed, "Betsy! Betsy!" Frank watched as she ran in the back door, then felt a gust of relief as she emerged carrying a small, naked child. Neighbors came running to the pair, and as the dust settled, Frank heard the woman say, "Take Betsy with you, Helen. I'll go see to the house."

All morning Frank roamed the town, moving slowly toward the river. He noted the artillery mounted in parapets made of timber and earth. He was studying the batteries and had decided that they were rifled thirty-two pounders, but he wrote nothing down. As he passed along the front, he stopped to watch as one gun crew carefully took aim and fired at a Federal gunboat that was edging along the far side of the river. When the missile bounced off the armored side of the vessel, the gun captain swore roundly, then shook his head. "We only got twelve charges left. We can't waste no more on them iron gunboats."

He grew hungry after midafternoon and bought three potatoes, ten pears, and a loaf of fresh-baked bread from an old man selling vegetables. He ate one of the pears as he sat watching the soldiers who guarded the inner lines. Once he gained some information that he knew would be worth the risk he was taking. He'd hobbled toward the Confederate lines that faced the Union invaders and had been greeted by a sergeant. "Come to jine up with the army, have you?"

"No sah!" Frank said. "Jes bin to see could I fin' some fresh vegetables for Mist' Sullins. My ol' legs, dey 'bout give out."

The sergeant nodded at an empty box, saying cheerfully, "Set fer a while." He turned away, but later came to stand beside Frank, who offered him one of the pears. He took it, bit into it, then chewed it slowly, savoring the juicy fruit.

A lieutenant soon joined him, and Frank was more alert. He kept his head down and listened as the two spoke.

"Hope the Yanks try another bust in here, Lieutenant,"

the sergeant said. "They nailed us last time. Them Mississippi rifles warn't no good. Half of 'em blowed up—and a sharpshooter couldn't hit a bull elephant ten feet away."

The lieutenant nodded grimly, but then grinned. "It'll be different next time they try it. These new Enfields will stop them!" The English-made Enfield rifle fired an elongated ball and was highly accurate. "We were lucky to get these rifles," the lieutenant grunted. "They were almost taken, but got here still in the crates."

"I got the men all set with muskets loaded like shotguns, too, sir," the sergeant replied. "We'll let the Bluebellies get close, then rise up and give 'em what they come fer!"

Frank sat on the crate for some time, soaking up information, then rose and hobbled off. The sun was going down, and he made his way to a hill on the northeastern part of Vicksburg, intending to spend the night in the woods.

As he moved down a worn path, he heard a voice say, "Stop!" and a sudden warning ran along his nerves. But when he turned he saw only a young girl and an old man dressed in a suit. "Yas suh?" Frank said, bobbing his head. "Kin I hep you, sah?"

"What's the word from town?" The man was in his late sixties, but his eyes were sharp and his voice strong. "Any word come about Gen. Johnson?"

"He comin', dey says," Frank spoke slowly, thickening his accent. "But dey doan know when."

The elderly man nodded, then said, "I don't know you. Who do you belong to?"

"Mist' Sullins, sah. His place ovah close to Simmsville. He sent me heah to find out 'bout his girl, Ellen. She live in Vicksburg. He say fo' me to take care of her."

At that moment a shell exploded not far away, and the man said, "Come on—they've got our range!" He grabbed the girl's hand and pulled her around. Frank saw no house, but when the man shouted, "Come on—get out of this, Uncle!" he followed him.

Frank saw an opening in the steep bank and realized that

it was a cave. When he stepped inside, he saw that it was furnished like a house. A woman was cooking on a wood stove that was set back, and to the left a carpet covered the raw earth. A couch, several chairs, and a table were illuminated by two lamps, and the elderly man waved his hand, saying, "We've moved here until the siege is over. Too dangerous in our house. Sit down, Uncle."

Frank eased himself into a chair and for the next two hours learned about what war was like for helpless civilians. The family was named Taylor and were fine people, he decided. He said little, but the girl chattered to him like a parrot. She was a pretty thing with bright red hair and sparkling blue eyes. She was a singer of songs and a teller of stories, Frank discovered, and Mrs. Taylor warned him, "Patty will talk the hands off the clock!"

Finally when the meal was ready, Mrs. Taylor handed Frank a plate of beans with a morsel of salt pork. His portion, Frank noted, was the same size as theirs. Mr. Taylor asked a simple blessing, and then they ate their supper. After they were finished, Frank pulled out his sack, saying, "I thanks you, and I is got something sweet." He passed out the remainder of his pears, and the family ate them at once. Afterward, Frank left, and as he hobbled away he thought, *Why does war have to be so hard on old people and children?*

He stayed in the city for three days and then made his way back through the lines under cover of darkness. He was cautious, for the Union pickets were trigger-happy at times. The next morning he appeared at the tent of Gen. McPherson, who was delighted to see him. "Well, what have you got for us, Private?" he asked at once. He listened carefully, along with Maj. Benning. Frank ended with the words, "They're tough people, General. It's not going to be easy."

"I think you're right, Private," the general said. "You don't see any signs of their weakening?"

Frank pulled a piece of paper out of his pocket. "They've taken a lot, but they've still got a sense of humor, General. I took this from the wall of a hotel."

BILL OF FARE
SOUP
Mule Tail

BOILED
Mule Bacon with Poke Greens
Mule Ham Canvassed

ROASTS
Mule Sirloin
Mule Rump Stuffed with Rice

ENTRÉES
Mule Head Stuffed à la Mode
Mule Beef Jerked à la Mexicana
Mule Hide Stewed New Style Laid On
Mule Spare Ribs Plain
Mule Liver Hashed

SIDE DISHES
Mule Salad
Mule Hoof Soused
Mule Kidney Stuffed with Peas

JELLIES
Mule Foot

PASTRIES
Cotton Seed Pies
China Berry Tarts

LIQUORS
Mississippi Water Vintage 1492 Superior $3.00
Spring Water Vicksburg Brand $1.50

Meals at all hours. Any inattention on the part of servants will be promptly reported at the office.

Jeff Davis & Co.
Proprietors

Gen. McPherson lowered the fragment of paper, his face grim. "No, they're not whipped," he murmured. "You've done a fine job, Private. I'll see that your father hears of it."

71

Frank saluted, then left the tent. He found himself greeted warmly by his squad, and when he had time to talk with Ty and Bob privately, he said, "Those people won't give up."

"We've got to take it, Frank," Bob insisted.

Frank stared at the two. He was thinking of the bright eyes of Patty, the small red-haired girl in the cave. For him she had become the symbol of the futility of war. He had made a decision on his way back to the camp, and now he said flatly, "I'm out of it. When my ninety days are up, I'm going home." When his brothers started to argue, he cut them off shortly. "You do what you have to do. But I'm through with this war—and that's that!"

CHAPTER SIX
A New Start

As Frank stepped off the crowded train, he found himself strangely despondent. Grabbing his gear, he fought his way through a noisy crowd, found a cab, and quickly tossed his knapsack into it. The driver, a lantern-jawed individual, stared at his private's uniform with a jaundiced eye. When Frank gave his parents' address, he muttered, "Cost you two dollars, Solger."

"I think I can rake it up." Throwing himself into the cab, Frank tried to ignore the depression that had begun when he'd said good-bye to his brothers. They had not rebuked him for leaving the army—at least not with words. Both of them had wished him well, but there had been an uncomfortable feeling about the parting. Now as he rode through the crowded streets of Washington, he felt sullen and discontented. *What's the matter with me? I wanted out of the army—so I've got what I asked for.*

Moving his feet restlessly, he stared out the window and saw a huge crowd gathered in one of the park areas. He heard raucous shouts that sounded like threats; over to one side of the park a line of infantry stood with muskets at half rest. "What's going on?" Frank demanded of the driver.

"Why, it's them nigger solgers," the hulking driver said. Turning to give his fare a hard glance, he shrugged, adding, "Been tryin' to get a nigger regiment ever since we got chopped up so bad at Chancellorsville. Ain't goin' to work though!" He sent a stream of amber tobacco juice onto the street, disgust in every move.

"Why not?"

"Because they ain't enough of 'em, fer one thing. All the free niggers got good jobs as teamsters or laborers. And them that *do* sign up fer the army is likely to get shot at from *both* sides." Noting Frank's confusion, the driver added caustically, "Lots of whites in the North are from the South. They hate niggers being raised up and would just as lief take a shot at one of them for spite. And if the Rebels capture a nigger in a blue uniform, why, he's gonna' put a ball in his head, don't you reckon? And one of the police right here said he'd shoot down a nigger wearing a uniform jest like he would a yeller dog!"

Frank stared at the thin line of black soldiers who were wearing army uniforms, wondering what would come of this. He said mildly, "Some of them are good fighters. I've just come from Grant's army in Mississippi. The Negro troops fought at Fort Hudson and Miliken's Bend as well as any men could." He got a cold stare from the driver and made no further attempts to speak of the matter.

Getting out at his parents' home, he paid his fare—to the penny, then walked toward the house, ignoring the furious stare of the driver. "You'll see about them niggers!" he called out spitefully. "They ain't got no souls like us white people."

Frank dismissed the driver with a thought of disgust and opened the front door. He found his mother alone, and she greeted him joyfully. "Why, Frank, come in! Are you hungry?"

Frank grinned as he held her tightly. "You'd offer a meal if the world was coming to an end, Mother." However, he allowed her to fix him a plate of gravy and biscuits, which he devoured with relish. As he ate, he gave her the news of Ty and Bob, then asked about his father.

"Why, he's with Gen. Meade, going to stop Lee."

"Meade? I thought Hooker was in charge."

"He was, but President Lincoln replaced him. I guess he was unhappy with the way he failed at Chancellorsville." Melanie's face suddenly turned heavy, and she gave Frank a troubled look. "I'm afraid for your father. He'll be right in the thick of the battle—like he always is."

Frank felt the same sense of discomfort he'd felt with his brothers and said abruptly, "I've left the army, Mother."

"I know, Son." Melanie put her hand over his and shook her head. "It's a thing no person can decide for another."

"Do you think Pa will despise me?"

"Of course not! You know your father better than that, Frank!"

"Well, he's army to the heart, and I thought—"

Melanie shook her head, noting the uneasy expression on the tanned face. This son had always been more trouble to her and her husband than the other two. She studied his brooding expression, noting how much he resembled his father. *He looks like Gid, but Ty and Bob are the ones who act like him.* She smoothed his raven-dark hair back from his forehead, wondering what lay ahead for this youngest of her sons, but said only, "Well, what will you do with yourself?"

Frank looked up, his eyes suddenly bright. His broad lips turned upward in a grin, and he said, "Going to disgrace the family, Ma—I always knew I would."

"Why, Frank!"

Frank rose and took her in his arms, squeezing her. "You're still the best-looking woman in Washington," he said, grinning down at her. Then he held her at arm's length and shrugged. "I'm going to try my luck on the stage, Mother. I know you and Father will hate it, but I feel I've got to do it." When he saw the alarmed look on her face, he laughed, adding, "Don't worry—I'll probably be terrible. It'll be the shortest career in the history of the theater!"

"You'll do well at whatever you set your mind to, Frank Rocklin!" Melanie insisted. "Let me go—some letters came for you." He followed her into the drawing room, where she took several letters off the mantel. Handing them to Frank, she could not help observing, "They're from a woman. I can tell by the handwriting."

"Yes, from Miss Montaigne," Frank said. "I told her to write me at this address." He looked up from the first envelope and, seeing the curious look on his mother's face, asked innocently, "Do you want me to read them aloud, Ma?" He laughed when she flushed and left the room in a huff.

"You didn't get any of your insolence taken out of you in the army!" she observed acidly. "I don't care a pin about your old letters!"

Frank sat down and read all three of the letters at once. The first two were witty and full of descriptions of New York, where Carmen had been with Booth's troop. The play had been a success, and in the second letter, she spoke of how it was likely that Booth would bring the company back to Washington for a play—she wasn't certain what it would be.

The third letter caught at Frank instantly. It was dated only a week earlier, June 21, and was very brief. She wrote,

> We are back in Washington to do *Hamlet*. I will be Ophelia, of course. Booth will play Hamlet, and Roland will play Laertes. I fully expect Booth to kill Roland! The sword fights are so intense! Mr. Ford is building a new theater. The old one he had, the Athenaeum, was actually a *church*! Remodeled, of course— but still I expect several deacons and pastors must have rolled over in their graves at some of the lines that were spoken in that place! We will rehearse at the old theater, but the play will open in Mr. Ford's new theater sometime around the first of July.
>
> I have no idea when you will return, but long to see you! Write if you get this! I still remember our times together with pleasure!
>
> Carmen Montaigne

Frank did some mental calculation, rose, and called, "Mother, I'm going downtown. Don't wait supper for me!" He went to his room, washed, and shaved carefully. Placing the uniform in a drawer—and feeling some sort of regret he couldn't understand—he put on his best clothing. The outfit consisted of a pair of white trousers tapered at the ankle, a white silk shirt, a square-cut waistcoat, and a double-breasted maroon frock coat. He stared at his reflection in the mirror, smiled wryly, and muttered, "Well, Mr. Rocklin, if looking like a fop will get you into the theater, you're well qualified!" Then he picked up a gleaming black top hat, stuck it on his head at a rakish angle, and left the house.

★ ★ ★

The rehearsal had not gone well, and John Wilkes Booth was in a rage. He had laid aside his fine clothes and wore a pair of gray trousers and a white cotton shirt—both now drenched with perspiration. His handsome face was drawn into a scowl, and as he glared at the actors across the stage, fury burned in his dark eyes. "Have any of you *read* the play?" he shouted. Slapping his hands together in a rash gesture, he moved like a cat around the stage, his voice ripping them like a rapier. "Before heaven, I've never seen such an insipid, mewing bunch of amateurs in all my experience!" A table barred his way, and he kicked it viciously, sending it flying over the edge of the stage to crash into the seats below. The gesture, Carmen realized, was typical of Booth. She paid little heed to his ranting, for long ago she had discovered that under the fine looks of the actor lurked a rashness, an anger that would flare out at times. The rehearsal had not been good, but Booth himself had performed poorly. However, none of the cast dared to say so. Therefore they stood there enduring the harsh words with as much patience as they could muster.

Finally Booth seemed to exhaust the fit of anger and slumped down on a couch, moaning, "We'll *never* be ready for opening night."

77

Roland Middleton, looking tired and leaner than usual, said, "Well, Mr. Booth, we've done harder things. I'm sure we'll be all right."

But his words brought no comfort to Booth. He muttered, "If you'd learn to handle a blade, Middleton, that would help a great deal." He got to his feet, looked at them, then shook his head. "Well, let's do it again—and this time, let your voices fill this place. You're all mewing like sick kittens!"

Frank Rocklin had entered the theater just a few moments before Booth had exploded into rage. He stood back under the balcony in the darkness, dismayed at what he had witnessed. The theater was dark, only the stage lit by footlights, so he could not be seen. Now as he watched the company struggle on through the act, he thought, *This is not the best time to ask for a part*. He watched Carmen for the most part, admiring her as she played her role very well. She was wearing a simple light green dress and her hair was done up in a new fashion—but he admired her beauty. He'd forgotten how attractive she was, and now the thoughts of their times together floated back into his memory.

Finally Booth said wearily, "That's all for tonight. Be here at ten in the morning."

Frank moved forward, and as he came into the range of the lights Booth turned abruptly, catching the movement. He blinked and put up a hand to shade his eyes—then called out, "Bless us! Is this Rocklin that I see before me?" He ran to the edge of the stage and jumped over it, which caused the older woman playing the role of Gertrude to cry out a warning. But Booth was half acrobat, and he landed on the floor of the theater with perfect balance. He smiled and came with his hand out. "I thought you were in the army," he said, then took in Frank's fine clothing and added, "but I don't recognize that as a uniform of the Union."

Booth's hand was hard and firm, and Frank was astonished that the actor showed such pleasure. "I'm an ex-soldier now, Mr. Booth. I did my ninety days and am now ready to bore you all with lying tales of how I saved my regiment from death and destruction."

Booth opened his eyes widely and smiled, exposing perfect teeth. "Let me get dressed," he said in an animated tone. "We're going out to dinner. I want to hear what you've been doing." As he wheeled and practically ran across to the side door, Roland came down the short flight of stairs, his usually glum face alive with pleasure. "Welcome home, the conquering hero!" he exclaimed, grasping Frank's hand. "When did you get home?"

"He can tell us all about it at dinner." Carmen had come to stand before Frank, and putting out her hands, she smiled warmly. "I'm glad to see you," she said huskily. "I'll go change. Don't go away."

As she left, Middleton said eagerly, "Are you home for good, Frank?"

"Yes. I've done my soldiering, Roland." He smiled, saying, "You looked good up there."

"I was as bad as everyone else. The play's sour before it even starts."

"Why is that?"

Roland shrugged. "No one can say why it happens, Frank. Sometimes everything is wrong, but the actors catch fire. Sometimes everything looks good, but nothing happens." He hesitated then said, "I think Booth's upset over the way the war's going. He's pretty pro-Southern, you know. He doesn't talk about it much—that wouldn't be smart. But his emotions go up and down according to the way the Confederacy prospers. When the South wins, he's high as the moon—but when they suffer a setback, he's impossible, like you saw him tonight."

"He'll be more upset, then—because Vicksburg is going to fall."

"Really? Well, that's good news for the country. But watch Booth when it happens."

Middleton left, and an hour later Frank was sitting at a table at Willards with Booth and Carmen. The other members of the cast had not come, and Booth at one point confided, "The cast is not doing well, Frank."

"It'll get better, I hope."

Booth shrugged, then asked eagerly, "Tell me about Vicksburg. How does it look?"

Frank hesitated, then said honestly, "It's hopeless for Pemberton, Mr. Booth." He saw the disappointment wash across Booth's face as he went on to describe the situation. He ended by saying, "The only hope the South had was to unite the armies of Pemberton and Johnston. Once Grant cut in between them and penned Pemberton up in the city, there was no real hope."

"Perhaps Johnston will come to relieve the city."

"Perhaps. But if he doesn't, it's just a matter of time. The people of Vicksburg are living in caves, and the food can't last."

Booth pondered this, and as Frank talked with Carmen, he noticed that the actor was in some sort of deep thought. Finally Booth shook off his mood and asked, "What's for you now, Rocklin?"

Frank laughed shortly, his face flushed. "I want to learn the art of the theater," he said. "I might be no good, but I'd like to try."

Booth brightened up instantly. "Why, I think you'd do well, Frank!"

"Why don't you let him play Laertes?" Carmen suggested. "Roland hates the role, and after seeing Frank play Mercutio, I think he'd be a fine Laertes."

"Why, that's true! Both of those fellows were hotheads, too quick with their swords!"

"I won't take the role," Frank said instantly. "Roland's a friend."

"Don't let that hinder you," Booth said. "Middleton loathes the role, especially the swordplay. You've seen how inept he is, and the duels in this play are more demanding. You could handle that part of it perfectly. Middleton can take the role of Rosencrantz. Do you know the play?"

"I've seen it three times and read it quite often," Frank said, then admitted, "but I'd have to memorize the lines and the actions."

Booth sat staring across the table at Rocklin, and it was one of those times for Frank when he felt that he'd come to a crossroads in his life. If Booth turned him down, he had no other contacts. But then Booth nodded and slapped the table hard. "All right—you're on! If you can't do it, I'll have to let you go, of course." He turned to Carmen and smiled with slight mockery. "I don't suppose you'd have time to teach Frank the part, Carmen?"

But Carmen gave him a steady smile and reached across the table to put her hand over Frank's. "I'm always glad to help a fellow performer, Mr. Booth."

After the meal, Booth left them alone, and it was Frank who said, "I don't know if I can do this, Carmen. It's one thing to play a role for a week that you know pretty well, but it's something else to make it your life."

Carmen leaned toward him, the lights bringing out the coral of her skin. There was a strain of imagination in her and a wild depth of feeling that leaped out from time to time. Despite the hard life that all actresses led, she had retained a warmth and even a gentleness that she revealed to only a few. Now as she sat before him, her lips were in repose and there was a longing in her brown eyes that she didn't try to hide.

"You'll be successful, Frank," she whispered. "You have a great talent. And I'll help you."

There was a promise in her words, and Frank felt again the reckless spirit that he'd seen in her, but now was conscious of a deep, mysterious glow that he had not seen before. Slowly he reached out and, when he held her hand, said slowly, "You know how to draw a man, Carmen." He saw that his words pleased her, and he laughed aloud, the memories of the bloody violence at Vicksburg gone from his mind.

PART TWO
The Actress
JANUARY–AUGUST 1863

CHAPTER SEVEN
Lorna

Lorna Grey started violently as a heavy hand slid around her waist and a sly voice whispered, "Now that's wot I calls a fine piece of work!"

Without hesitation Lorna lifted the hot pressing iron in her right hand and slapped it against the meaty hand of her employer, Mr. Norval Bates. The results were spectacular, for the hand was jerked away abruptly and Mr. Bates yelped with pain as he hopped around trying to jam the wounded member into his mouth.

"Ow! You burned me!" Bates stopped long enough to glare balefully at the young woman who had turned to watch him—holding the iron up in a defensive position. "I'll teach you—"

"What's happening here?" Mrs. Phoebe Bates materialized as if by magic, her agate hazel eyes fixed on the pair. She was a thin, sallow-faced woman, who for some unfathomable reason felt that every woman in London was a danger to her marriage. Her insane jealousy was beyond the comprehension of Lorna, who abhorred the man. He had put his hands on her at the first opportunity after she began working in the shop, and since that day she had found that boredom and weariness were the least of her problems. She had searched for another job, but work was scarce, and now she lowered the iron, saying quietly, "I'm afraid I burned Mr. Bates with the iron. I was too careless."

Mrs. Bates glared at her but, having no direct evidence of wrongdoing, turned to her husband. "Come along, dear. I'll put some ointment on that burn." She made comforting sounds as she led the hulking man out, but turned to say harshly, "I've warned you before, but now you'll have to decide. You can't do two jobs. Either you give your notice to that music hall, or I can't use you."

Lorna yearned to throw the iron at the woman, but the thought of hunting for employment came to her. "Yes, Mrs. Bates," she said wearily. "I'll give my notice tonight."

Her answer dissatisfied the woman, but she only grunted and left the room. As Lorna turned and began mechanically ironing a delicate white blouse, a young woman with a pale face and a sour mouth grinned from where she stood ironing a similar garment. "I wisht you'd stuck that iron in 'is ear! Why, 'e ain't nothin' but a beast! Can't never keep 'is blasted 'ands to 'imself." Whipping the blouse off the board, she placed it on a stack of finished ones, then said, "Yer ain't gonna quit your actin', are you, Lorna?"

"I'll have to, Annie. It doesn't pay much, and I've got to live."

"Wot a shame—and you so good at it, too!"

Lorna put in the rest of the day, and as she was leaving, Mrs. Bates stopped her, saying, "Remember, you give your notice to those people. No self-respecting young woman would allow herself to be seen with them! And be here early in the morning!"

"Yes, Mrs. Bates."

Lorna left the building, noting that the bricks were so stained with smoke from thousands of London fireplaces that the original color was completely obscured. Her legs were trembling with weariness, for the day had been long—and Mrs. Bates did not believe in breaks. Twelve hours of standing over a hot iron was enough to drain the energy from anyone—and now as she moved across the dirty snow that covered the walk, she felt the weight of depression. Her room was located in a rough part of town, and several times men spoke to her, but she had learned to ignore them. Finally she arrived at her room, where she looked longingly at her iron bed. The mattress was lumpy, and the covers long since had lost any grace or beauty—still she longed to fall into it and lose herself in sleep.

"Tomorrow I can come home and sleep," she said aloud, then forced herself to clean up as well as she could. There was no bath, of course, and the room was icy cold. But she endured the cold water, washing herself even as her teeth chattered. Moving slowly, she put on her only clean dress and then sat down and fixed her hair. She had beautiful hair, long and the color of honey. Her eyes were gray, and there was a delicate beauty in her oval-shaped face. She studied herself dispassionately, then applied a little rice powder to her cheeks. Finally she rose and pulled on her thin black coat and settled a rust-colored hat over her head.

Leaving the room, she made her way along the streets, moving toward the theater. The smell of roasting meat came to her, and she considered treating herself to a kidney pie, but settled for tea and crumpets in the cause of economy. She was still hungry, but had learned to live with that.

The Gem Theatre was not the place for royalty, and as she reached the rather grimy two-story brick building almost hidden on a side street of Soho, she felt a quick pang of despair. Memories of the green countryside of her home came to her, and she stopped dead still in front of the side entrance used by the cast. The dancing heads of sprightly flowers and the carpet of emerald green grass on the rolling hills were strong in her mind. Regret sliced through her, but then she tightened her lips and scolded herself silently. *You hated your life there—buried like a potato in the mud! Couldn't wait to get away from the boring existence and get to the glittering world of London! Well, you're in London—and on the stage, so stop moping and do your job!*

She forced the memories of Yorkshire from her mind,

entered the theater, and moved quickly to the shabby dressing room she shared with six other girls. The odor of strong, cheap perfume and sweat struck her at once, but that was part of the world of the Gem. Quickly she removed her street clothes and slipped into her costume, a gauzy pink dress exactly like the ones the other six girls wore. As she sat and arranged her hair, a voice from the past seemed to speak: *You'll lose your virtue if you go on the stage—it happens to all them actresses!* Lorna had heard her mother say that often enough and now wondered if there had not been wisdom in the warning.

Glancing around at the five young women who chattered like squirrels, she knew that all of them were free with their favors. They went out with the rather seedy men who came seeking female companionship, and they were contemptuous of Lorna for keeping herself aloof from men. She had made no friends among them, and now as she put on her makeup, the thought came to her, *How long will it be before I become as cheap and tawdry as they are?* The depression that had troubled her for days grew heavier, and as she rose when the stage manager bellowed "All right—get with it, girls!" she thought with some relief, *Well, this is my last night— good-bye to the stage for me.*

The production was something called *Springtime in Dover.* It was a rather dreadful and unsuccessful attempt to join a light drama with some sort of musical score. But the producer had not wasted money on talented musicians or on singers. Most of the girls who made up the chorus had flat voices and either sang in a strident off-key manner or made no more music than a cricket. The story was so banal that Lorna was sick of it the second time she was exposed and could not explain why anyone would come to such a pitiful excuse for entertainment.

The Gem was, of course, a music hall, and it made no pretense of grandeur. The seats were filled with working-class people, desperate for any break in their monotonous lives. And as Lorna joined in the chorus, she felt a sense of defeat, for her dreams of being an actress had come to this. And now even this pitiful excuse for a stage career had come to an end.

When the time came for her one solo number, Lorna put herself into it. She had a fine contralto, untrained but clear and sweet and strong. As always the audience grew still as she sang, and it was the one moment of time in her bleak life that was vivid and alive. The song was not deep or profound—merely a ballad about a girl whose sweetheart has gone to war—but she always managed to get across the poignant grief of a girl who had lost her love. Her clear voice rose and fell, swelling with power, then falling to almost a whisper as she finished.

And, as always, when the song ended the audience broke into loud applause, and there were calls of "That's the way to sing it, girlie!" Lorna blinked back the tears, knowing that it was the last time she would feel such—such *magic*—for such it was to her. She craved the stage as a drunk craves liquor, and she had to turn aside to dash the tears from her eyes. *Well, that's that!* she thought grimly, and as the performance ground to an end, she paid little heed, thinking of the grubby room she would go back to—and fighting off Mr. Bates the next day.

In the dressing room she mechanically removed her makeup and was about to put on her dress when the manager stuck his head in the door and said in an excited fashion, "Hey, Lorna, get yourself dressed! There's a real swell askin' for you!"

"Tell him I can't go with him, Barney."

Barney gave her an outraged stare. "Hey, this ain't no joke! I know this guy, Lorna." He paused and said impressively, "This is *Michael Dennis!*"

Every one of the five young women swiveled their heads to stare at the manager. "Aw, you're puttin' us on, Barney!" a sharp-faced girl named Sally jibed. Then she shot a calculating stare at Lorna, adding, "If you don't want 'im, Lorna, I'll take 'im off your hands!"

Lorna had seen Dennis once, spending too much to see him perform. He was the most popular leading man in England, and curiosity rose in her. "Tell him I'll be right out, Barney." Conscious of the envious stares of the other girls, she quickly changed and left the dressing room. Barney was standing close to the door, nodding his head toward a tall man who was lounging farther toward the exit.

As Lorna approached, she felt a quickening interest. "Mr. Dennis?" she said, coming to stand before him. He turned to face her, a smile coming to his lips. He was six feet tall, very erect and athletic. His hair was a dark chestnut with a slight wave, and he wore a small mustache of the same texture. His light brown eyes, large and direct, were his best feature, and he fixed them on her, saying, "Miss Grey, I apologize for coming unannounced."

"Frankly, Mr. Dennis, I'm surprised that you're in a place like this at all."

Instantly Dennis grinned broadly, two creases springing up at the edges of his lips. Casting a look around the dilapidated interior of the Gem, he shook his head. "Frankly, I don't come to places like this often. But a friend of mine told me about you."

"About *me*? Why, I can't imagine why, Mr. Dennis." Lorna was perplexed, and then a thought came to her. "If you're looking for—female companionship," she said firmly, her eyes meeting his glance, "I can introduce you to several of the actresses who'd be charmed to join you."

Michael Dennis was accustomed to adulation. It was part of his life as an actor. Perhaps he was sated with female companionship, for he found himself intrigued by the firm rejection of what many young women would fight to obtain. He cocked his handsome head to one side, studied her, then said, "I appreciate the warning, Miss Grey. Actually I want to speak with you about another matter. Would you join me for a late supper where we can discuss a professional matter?"

Lorna was mystified, but humor came along with a stab

of curiosity. "I'll be glad to join you, but I must warn you: I'm starved. It will be an expensive meal."

Dennis's white teeth gleamed as he smiled and offered her his arm. "I've never heard a woman admit that," he remarked as they left the Gem. He handed her into a cab, told the driver the name of a restaurant, then got in beside her. He was cheerful as they drove along the dark streets, commenting on the weather but saying nothing of his purpose. When they reached the restaurant, Lorna felt badly out of place with her inexpensive dress, but she kept her head up as they were seated.

The next hour went quickly and very pleasantly. Dennis tactfully helped her to order, then while they waited, asked her a few questions. He listened as she spoke, and when she finished, he told her amusing stories of the theater. The meal arrived, and Lorna ate hungrily. Afterward, when the waiter brought fresh tea, Dennis announced, "I want you to read for a part in my new play."

Lorna stared at him. If he'd told her she was going to the wilds of Africa she would not have been more shocked. Her eyes grew large, and finally she asked, "Is it your custom to recruit for your company in third-rate music halls like the Gem, Mr. Dennis?"

Dennis had expected the young woman to leap at his offer and was taken somewhat aback when she questioned him so. He lit a cigar, taking his time; then when the purple smoke was rising languidly, he leaned back and observed, "You don't trust people too much, do you, Miss Grey—or may I call you Lorna?"

"If you like—and I suppose I do have some caution." She smiled slightly, her full lips curving in a most attractive manner. Her long blonde hair caught the gleams of the chandeliers, and there was a piquant expression in her gray eyes. "I've not had many famous men beating a path to my door asking me to go on the stage." She sipped the tea and studied Dennis carefully. "Why me, Mr. Dennis?"

"You'll work cheap!" Dennis laughed aloud, then leaned

91

forward. "You're an honest young woman," he said abruptly. "Let me be equally honest. I'm getting a cast together to do a new play. I'm tired of paying managers and investors. This one will be all mine. Let me tell you about the play. . . ."

Lorna listened as Dennis spoke with excitement about his project. In essence, he was putting up all the money, so he needed a cast who would work for modest salaries. He ended by saying, "You would be perfect for the character of Jenny in the play."

"You've never seen me act."

"No, but I've seen your face and I've heard you sing. This character, Jenny, isn't a major character, but she's vital to the play. She's a sweet girl with a beautiful voice, and she dies in the second act. Her death is the center of the action, and I can teach you what you don't know about acting." Dennis leaned forward and said quietly, "A friend of mine saw your performance and asked me to come to see you. Now that I have, I think there's a good chance you could do very well. As I've told you, I can't hire well-known talent. As a matter of fact, only the leading lady and I are established. I'm picking up the rest of the cast as best I can. Would you like to read for the part?"

Lorna agreed. "I love the stage, Mr. Dennis. If you think there's a chance for me, I'll work very hard."

Dennis was watching the girl's face carefully. *She's got whatever it is that makes people watch her. Never saw a good actress who didn't have it.* He smiled. "I think we're going to be working together. Let's have a toast." He lifted his cup of tea and, holding it toward her, said, "To a long and successful career for Miss Lorna Grey!"

Lorna felt a sudden rising of hope. She had given up, but now out of nowhere this man had come to offer her what she wanted most in the world. Gratitude filled her voice, and her lips trembled slightly as she lifted her cup, whispering, "Thank you, Mr. Dennis!"

She could say no more, and he saw that her eyes were

brimming with tears. He reached over and took her hand, squeezed it gently, then said, "I'm glad I found you, Lorna Grey!"

★ ★ ★

Lorna felt Michael squeeze her hand hard, and she turned to smile at him. The footlights caught his face, and he whispered over the cheers of the audience, "You have them, Lorna! They love you!" He bowed again and led her off the stage, then turned at once and kissed her full on the lips, saying warmly, "You were wonderful, darling!"

Lorna had grown accustomed to Michael's caresses, and now she flushed with pleasure, ignoring the grins of the stagehands. "Let me get dressed, then we'll go out for dinner."

"All right, but it'll be a special dinner tonight." He released her, and she moved quickly to her dressing room. As she entered and began undressing, she thought of how opulent this room had been four months earlier. It had been the dressing room of Alice Fortiner, the actress starring with Dennis. But after the success of that play, she had been given the starring role in his second venture and had inherited the star's dressing room. The play was a costume drama, and she carefully removed the ornate silk dress, then the farthingale and the numerous petticoats. Quickly she hung the costume in a wardrobe, then put on her new dress. It had the fashionable pyramid shape, with bell-shaped sleeves and a tight-fitting bodice that closed around the neck in a V shape. Carefully she arranged her small straw hat so that it tilted over her brow, plucked up a matching silk parasol, and left the dressing room.

Michael met her, dressed as usual in the latest fashion. He looked dashing in a royal blue double-breasted frock coat, and around the gleaming of his white shirt blossomed a cravat with fringed ends. He hurried her outside, spoke to the driver, then got in. He was in a fine humor and soon had

her laughing over some of the amusing things that had
occurred during the performance.

Lorna sat close beside him, enjoying his witty conversation. He had been careful not to press her into private
meetings for the first month of the play's successful run. He
had spent long hours going over her part, rehearsing her
until she was perfect—but it had been purely professional.
After the first play closed, he had been excited about a new
play—one that would allow her a starring role. Not as fat as
his, of course, but second place to the brilliant Michael
Dennis had been thrilling enough for Lorna.

The carriage stopped, and when Lorna stepped down, she
looked up to say with surprise, "Why, this is your hotel,
Michael. I thought we were going to the fanciest restaurant
in London."

Dennis smiled and squeezed her arm. "Something better
than that, Lorna. Come along now and don't ask questions.
I've spent a lot of time planning this evening."

Lorna allowed herself to be led into the hotel, noting that
Michael was greeted with deference by all the help. The
manager came to say, "All is ready, Mr. Dennis. I think even
you will be pleased with what I've managed to come up
with."

"Thank you, Louis. I'm looking forward to it."

Lorna had been to Dennis's hotel suite twice, both times
accompanied by other members of the cast. But now as she
entered and looked around, she saw only two waiters, who
were standing beside a tabled covered with a snowy white
cloth. One of them said, "Whenever you're ready, Mr.
Dennis."

"We're ready now, Andrew." He waited while one of the
servants took their coats, then led Lorna to a chair at one
end of the table. When she was seated, he nodded at the
waiter, saying, "Let's have some wine—and some music,
Andrew."

Lorna turned as a door opened and three men came in, all
carrying stringed instruments. She turned to Dennis, her

eyes shining. "You *have* planned all this, haven't you, Michael? How lovely!"

It was an evening such as Lorna had never imagined. The string trio played all her favorite tunes, and the meal was the best she'd ever eaten. Michael was charming, and his words of approval over her performance in the play excited and pleased her.

Finally the table was cleared, the musicians played one final medley, then left after receiving warm approval from both Dennis and Lorna.

But the night that had been so wonderful for Lorna soon turned unpleasant. While talking on the couch, they had moved rather close to one another. Michael gently kissed her, but soon his kisses had become forceful. As his hands began to roam, she struggled against him and fought clear of his embrace. "I think it's time for me to go home, Michael," she said, disappointed in his behavior.

Dennis rose and came to stand before her. He caught her hands and asked, "Lorna, don't you care for me at all?" When she said rather awkwardly that she *did* care, at once he began telling her how much he loved her. Lorna was drawn to Michael as she had not been attracted to any other man. For many weeks she had felt herself in love with him, yet what he was suggesting was impossible for her.

"Michael, I—I don't know how to say this," she said quietly. "I know actresses are—well—lax in their relationships with men. But I can't be like that. When I marry, I want to be able to come to my husband as a pure woman."

A silence fell on the room, so that the loudest sound was the ticking of a large rosewood pendulum clock. It seemed to Lorna that the slow beat of the instrument was an echo to the beating of her own heart. She stood quietly before Dennis, offering no arguments, but there was a steely pride in her erect posture that he admired. Despite her rigid posture, there was something soft and gentle and appealing in her, and he said quietly, "I do love you, Lorna. I've never known a woman who was beautiful—and firm." He came

95

closer to her, put out his hands, and when she surrendered hers, held them gently. "I can't think of a woman I'd rather marry. Most actresses have egos as big as this hotel. You're not like that."

Lorna listened to him speak, and she was relieved to hear him finally say, "I'll take you home now." All the way back to her hotel, he was quiet, and when they stood outside the door of her room, he made no attempt to kiss her. He did stand before her quietly, his eyes taking in her face as though seeking for the answer to some mystery. Finally he said, "We'll talk about us later, Lorna. Good night."

Lorna entered her room and slowly began preparing for bed. She was shaken by the experience and knew that there was little safety for her in repeating such things. When she had put on her nightgown, she sat down at the small desk beside her bed, took out a small book, and opened it. She had begun a journal six months earlier, when she'd first joined Michael's cast. Now as she read the pages, she saw clearly that she'd been falling in love with him. Finally she picked up her pen, opened the small bottle of ink, and began to write. She recorded the scene as clearly as if she were an objective reporter. Then she paused and lifted her eyes, remembering how his caresses had brought an excitement to her. Then she wrote in her neat script, "I am in love with Michael. That is very dangerous, for even if he loves me, he has loved many women." She hesitated, wrote slowly for a moment, then paused to look at the words she'd put on paper. "I am not certain if I am strong enough to keep myself from him. God help me to do so!"

Then she closed the diary, replaced it in the drawer, and blew out the light. Getting into bed, she thought of what it would be like to have a husband—and the memory of Michael's hands as he'd caressed her was disturbing. *What kind of a wife would I be? Can I please a man?* She had no answers and finally let herself drop off into a disturbed sleep.

CHAPTER EIGHT
End of a Dream

"Ah, this is a most beautiful gown—the finest I have ever seen." The diminutive woman with the slight French accent who had shown the best of her goods to Lorna stroked the pale blue silk nightgown with a sensuous gesture. Madame Dubois was curious about the beautiful young woman who seemed rather nervous when shown the finest of undergarments. *She must be getting married. But she's behaving strangely about her underclothes—and about this nightgown.* She was good at her job and suggested with a smile, "Are you getting married, mademoiselle?"

Lorna had developed into a fine actress, but the question brought a rich flush to her smooth cheeks. Aware that the woman was smiling at her in a knowing fashion, she grew flustered, saying hurriedly, "Why—I will be—that is, I'm going on a short vacation—" She broke off, aware that she was only arousing the sharp-eyed woman's curiosity. "I'll take it—and that will be all."

"Certainement! I will have them wrapped carefully myself, mademoiselle." She took the garments into a back room and, as she wrapped them, gave a wicked smile to an older woman who sat at a table sewing a blouse. "That one, she is up to mischief, *ma Tante."*

"Why do you say that? She looks respectable enough."

"So I thought." Wrapping the garments expertly, the

97

small woman shook her head with a definite motion. "Only two kinds of women buy the sort of lingerie this one has chosen: the one who is going to be a bride—" she paused long enough to give the string a final knot, then looked at the older woman with a gleam in her dark eyes—"and the woman who wants to please a man who is *not* her husband." Holding the package, she hesitated, her eyes moody. "I thought I knew both kinds, *ma tante,* but this one deceived me. She has the innocence of a bride—but she is not. *Voilà,* she is a woman out to snare a man!"

When Madame Dubois handed the packages to the young woman, then took the cash for them, she smiled slightly, saying, "I hope you enjoy your vacation."

Lorna caught the emphasis on the word *vacation* and could not meet the woman's eyes. She turned and left the shop quickly, conscious that the sharp-eyed woman had seen something in her that she thought she had concealed.

The sky was a leaden color as she walked along the busy street, the brilliant blues of spring fading. Soon summer would come, then fall, then the dreary winter. London was not a pleasant place during the winter, at least not to Lorna. She loved the summer and spring, but the dreary months when the city was shrouded with fog, smoke, and dirty snow depressed her.

Turning into her hotel, Lorna was greeted by a stubby man in a rather flamboyant suit. She recognized him, saying, "Mr. Cooper, how are you?"

Thomas Cooper ducked his head, smiling at her hopefully. He had a reddish face, a shock of orange-red hair, and an abundant crop of freckles. "I'd be better if you'd consider my offer in a more agreeable light, Miss Grey." He added eagerly, "Now that your run is over, you'd be free to take another engagement. Now I'm willing to offer you the best terms I can, and it would be an *international* tour! All the way to America!"

Cooper had been insistent with his offers, and Dennis had laughed at them. "He's a poor show for a manager," he'd told Lorna. "Never had much success in this country, so now he's going to try it overseas. Don't give it a second thought, Lorna!"

Being kindhearted, Lorna had tried to let the man down as easily as possible and now said, "I'm very sorry, Mr. Cooper, but I have no desire to leave England. I wish you well, but you really must accept this as my final answer."

Cooper was not at all dismayed; he grinned cheerfully, saying, "Well, I don't want to be a pest, Miss Grey—but if you change your mind before the sixteenth, let me know. I'll always make a place for *you!*"

Cooper left, and as Lorna moved across the lobby, she returned the greeting of the desk clerk absently, then turned to say, "Harold, I'll be gone for the next week. Will you hold any mail that comes for me?"

"Certainly, Miss Grey." The clerk was a fervent admirer of the young actress and said, "I was at the final performance of your play last night. You were *wonderful!*" He beamed at her, then asked, "Will you be doing another play with Mr. Dennis?"

"I'm not sure, Harold."

"Oh, I *do* hope so! You two seem so—well, you act together so very well." Like most other fans of Dennis and Lorna, Harold Grimsely had spent much time wondering if the love scene that the pair acted on the stage was a reflection of what went on offstage. Harold had been besieged by endless questioning concerning the pair and was disappointed that he could not give a report to his questioners. He compensated with innuendos and self-righteous proclamations: "Why, it would be unethical for me to say anything about Michael and Lorna!"

As Lorna turned away, the clerk could not conceal his avid curiosity. "Are you going on a trip with—" He halted abruptly as Lorna whirled, her eyes filled with anger. "I mean, will you be coming back soon? I believe I can hold your room for you, Miss Grey."

Lorna bit back the scalding words that leaped to her lips, saying only, "I can't say now, Harold."

When she was safely inside her room, she tossed the packages on her bed, then took two or three turns around the room, grasping her hands tightly. Her face was stiff and her lips drawn into a tight line. Restlessness stirred her, and she moved to the window and stared out at the pale sun that seemed reluctant to touch the dusky streets with light. Finally she turned slowly and moved to the mahogany chest and, opening the bottom drawer, pulled her diary from underneath the underclothes.

I'm ashamed to have anyone read what I've written in here for the last few weeks! she thought, an unusual bitterness rising in her. She flipped through the pages of the thin volume, noting that her relationship with Michael had grown more physical. She had managed to keep herself from making the final surrender, but the flesh had been stronger since he'd begun telling her he loved her. She was a young woman who longed for love, and his caresses drew her toward a consummation that he insisted would prove that they were truly *one.*

Sitting down, she read the last entry, her brow drawn together in a worried expression. Her writing, she noted, was erratic and scarcely readable—quite unlike her usual neat script.

I don't know what to do! Michael has said that he loves me—and that we will be married! When he said that tonight, I wanted to give myself to him. But somehow I *could* not! He urged me to show my love and said that we would never be complete until we knew the limits of love. But when I asked him *when* we would be married, he said that we had our careers to think of. He said that the public wants a romance *off* the stage as well as on. When I told him I didn't understand this, he laughed and kissed me, saying, "Why, sweetheart, the people see that we're in love. And they'll come to see us play on the stage what they know is true in real life. We'll give them another play—a highly romantic one—and we'll announce our engagement. Then we'll be married and give them a dozen romantic dramas!"

The sounds of traffic floated in, and Lorna paused for a moment. She looked at the wallpaper as if it might have some sort of message, then shook her head and began writing again:

> I've agreed to go away with him for a week. He was delirious with happiness, telling me that we'll be truly one, that I'll know what love really is. But I'm afraid. It isn't right, and I know it. He says what matters is that we love each other and that one day soon we'll be married. He says that the marriage is only a formality.
>
> Perhaps he's right. I'll go with him, for we can't go on like this. I love him so much—and the thought of losing him is more than I can stand. God help me—but I must have him!

Slowly she blotted the ink, then stood and moved to the packages on the bed. Unwrapping them, she held up the silk nightgown. As she gazed at her reflection in the mirror, she found something in the sight that disturbed her. Slowly she began to pack and, when she came to her diary, had an impulse to throw it away. She held it over the basket for a long moment, then put it into her suitcase and closed the lid.

★ ★ ★

Brighton was like nothing that Lorna had ever seen before. When she walked along the boardwalk for the first time, her eyes grew large with wonder and she gasped, "Michael! It's like a fairyland!"

"The prince of Wales created it to look like that," Dennis said. "Nothing like it in all England."

The centerpiece of the city was something like an Indian mogul's palace with a great onion-shaped dome. Radiating out from this magnificent structure rose domes and minarets and cupolas. And the interiors of the buildings equaled the outer appearance. Within the Royal Pavilion, huge gilded rooms were filled with treasures, ornate and oriental. Lorna gasped as Michael took her into the famous banqueting room, stunned by a table set with priceless silver. She marveled as she saw, hanging from the ceiling, a giant palm tree out of which hissed a dragon!

Finally as the afternoon drew on, Michael said, "It's been a long trip, sweetheart. Let's go to the hotel and have dinner." He took her to the dining room, where he ate with obvious enjoyment. The meal included a delicate turtle soup, lamb cutlets with asparagus, roast saddle of venison, plover's eggs in aspic jelly, and finally ices and pineapple cream along with chocolate cream.

Lorna ate a little of each, but had little appetite. She was dreading the moment when they would be alone together, but she did not allow her fears to show. Finally when Michael finished the last of the tea and rose, saying, "Well, shall we go, my dear?" she followed him out of the dining room.

Their room was on the second floor, and a servant brought them hot water in covered vessels, then left. Lorna sat down as Michael spoke with animation about the new play that he was planning, but she was not able to keep her mind on what he was saying. Finally Michael gave her an odd look, then said, "Why don't you get ready for bed, sweetheart? I'll just take care of a little book work."

"Of course." Lorna rose at once and left the sitting room. The bed was turned back, her trunk open at the foot. Slowly she took the silk gown from where it lay on the top, held it for a moment, then changed. She felt uncomfortable in the thin garment, and she turned abruptly and slipped into the bed. Pulling up the cover, she tried to relax but discovered that her muscles refused to obey her will.

For what seemed like a long time, she lay there, forcing

herself to unclench her fists. Her mind was filled with fears and confusing thoughts, and she wished that she had chosen another way.

Finally she heard the sound of voices from the sitting room and grew curious. At first she thought it was Michael talking to a bellboy, but there was a strident sound to at least one of the voices. She sat up in bed, for she recognized that one of the voices—the loudest one—belonged to a woman. She listened hard, then, as the voices grew louder, crawled out of bed. Slipping into a blue silken robe that matched her gown, she moved to the door and placed her ear against it. She listened for a time, and what she heard made her cheeks turn pale. Opening the door quickly, she stepped inside and saw a woman with an angry expression standing opposite Michael.

"Who is this woman, Michael?" Lorna demanded, turning to face him. His face, she saw, was pale, and he dropped his eyes, as though unable to face her. When he said nothing, she turned to the woman, demanding, "What are you doing here?"

The woman was in her thirties and was rather attractive in a hard sort of fashion. She was tall and well formed, with a round face and pretty features. She was dressed in expensive clothing, and there was an aggressiveness in her voice as she said, "What are *you* doing here would be a more fitting question." She had a pair of smallish blue eyes that studied Lorna with obvious disgust. Turning to Michael, she demanded, "Is this your latest trollop, Michael? I must say, she's prettier than some of the others."

"Michael! Who is this woman?"

"I'm his wife, that's who I am!" Anger and triumph flashed from the woman's eyes, and she cried out, "Well, tell her! I suppose you didn't bother to tell her you had a wife, did you?"

The room seemed to swim before Lorna for just one moment. *It can't be true!* was the thought that screamed through her mind—but when she steeled herself and looked at the face of Michael, she knew that it *was* true. Dennis's expression was filled with guilt. He stroked his mustache in a nervous gesture, saying, "Now, don't be upset, Lorna. I can explain—"

"Can you explain that I'm your legal wife and you're here with another woman?"

Dennis stepped forward, making an angry gesture toward the woman. "Get out of here, Lillian! We've said all we have to say to one another!"

The woman saw something in Michael's expression that caused her to shut her lips into a thin line. She blinked at him, then muttered, "All right—but I want the money, Michael. If I don't get it, you know what will happen!" She turned and left the room, slamming the door.

Dennis stood still for a moment, his chest heaving, then gave a look of black despair to Lorna. "Well, there it is," he said heavily. "I wanted to tell you, but I was afraid I'd lose you."

"She's really your wife?"

"Yes, unfortunately." Dennis turned to her, saying, "Sit down, Lorna. It's a long story."

Lorna sat down numbly and listened as Dennis spoke bitterly of his past. In essence, he told her how he'd made a rash marriage when he was seventeen. He'd separated from his wife after a short time and had lost contact with her. After he'd become a star, she'd come demanding to take her place as his wife. He ended by saying, "I don't love her—I *never* loved her! I pay her to stay away from me, and she keeps promising to give me a divorce. That's what she came for tonight—to up the price."

"You should have told me, Michael."

"You'd have left me, wouldn't you?"

Lorna nodded and got stiffly to her feet. "I have to leave here."

Dennis protested, but saw that it was useless. He said finally, "I'm sorry, Lorna. Stay here tonight. I'll get another room, and I'll see you back to London tomorrow." He hesitated, then said, "I hope we can work together—even after this."

"No, Michael," Lorna said quietly. "I never want to see you again."

★ ★ ★

Thomas Cooper opened the door of his hotel room and was shocked to see Lorna Grey standing there. "Why, Miss Grey!" he exclaimed, "I didn't expect to see *you!* Come in!"

"I'm afraid that would not be appropriate, Mr. Cooper."

"No, of course not. Let me get my coat. We'll go down to the restaurant."

A few minutes later the two were seated at a table, and when Cooper had poured two cups of tea, Lorna asked without preamble, "Would you still like for me to join your company?"

The question was so unexpected that Cooper almost dropped his cup! He recovered it, then stared at the young woman. "Why, of course! It would be exactly what I need."

"Very well, give me your terms."

Cooper began to talk rapidly, and after he had set forth his terms and the time he planned to be in America, Lorna nodded. "I'll accept. When will we leave, Mr. Cooper?"

"Why, now, I'd say we're ready for the day after tomorrow. Would that be too soon for you, Miss Grey?"

"No, not at all. I'll be at the Sterling Hotel. Let me know when the ship leaves." She rose and left with the briefest of good-byes, and Thomas Cooper sat down and sipped the last of his tea thoughtfully. When he rose and paid for the tea, he went back to his room, thinking, *I'd like to know what changed her mind*.

For the next two days Cooper drove himself frantically, but finally late one afternoon he stood braced against the rail of the *Priscilla* watching the shores of England fade into the dusk. Noting the latest addition to his company standing alone, he moved to take his place beside her. "Well, now, we won't be seeing England again for a time, eh?"

105

Lorna turned to him, and he was shocked at the emptiness in her eyes as she said, "I don't care if I ever see it again." She turned and walked away from Cooper, the wind blowing her hair. Her back was stiff as she moved to the bow and stood watching the white froth as it flew by. She lifted her gaze and seemed to be trying to look over the thousands of miles of open sea to where America lay waiting for her. But there was a cynical twist on her lips as she whispered, "I hope it's better in America than here, but I think it's all the same no matter where you go!"

The gulls circled, their voices raucous. Their white breasts formed a glaring contrast to the iron-gray sky and the sea beneath, and Lorna watched them until they rose, circled, then turned back toward the shores of England.

CHAPTER NINE
The Winds of War

The war hovered over the North like a huge dark shadow during the early summer of 1863. The winter had passed with a sullen discontent, but by mid-June new defenders poured into Washington. But there was no relief in the city for, louder and more perilous than the distant roar of guns at Vicksburg, an ominous rumble had sounded beyond the Blue Ridge. Daily hundreds of rumors flew along the streets of the capital. Frank Rocklin listened to these avidly, anxious for his father. The details were varied and contradictory, but one thing was clear: Gen. Lee and the Army of Northern Virginia were marching north.

Frank Rocklin, caught up in trying to master a new profession, was troubled by all of this. He spent as much time with his mother as possible, and the two of them waited impatiently for word from Tyler and Bob. Vicksburg was invested and the siege was on, and though Frank said nothing to his mother, he felt that the worst was yet to come for his brothers.

On June 16 the report of Rebels crossing into Maryland spread. A week and a half later, as Frank made his way from his home to Ford's Theater for the evening performance, he was aware that crowds were gathering in front of the newspaper offices. When he stopped to listen, he heard one of the editors repeating to the nervous listeners how Rebel troops were in Chambersburg in Pennsylvania. A sense of panic seized the city, and that night the audience was scant.

Booth was excited, the cast saw, and after the performance, he disappeared without a word. Frank knew the actor was sympathetic to the Confederate cause, and this troubled him.

On June 27, Washington listened to heavy artillery fire from the direction of the Bull Run Mountains. Gen. Hooker was abruptly relieved of command of the army and replaced by Gen. George G. Meade the next day. Meade was a little-known commander with a bleak scholar's face, and he at once moved to meet Lee's army.

The two armies groped blindly and finally found each other at Gettysburg. For three days Washington held its breath. All during the evening of July 3 and for most of the night, the burning of firecrackers, squibs, and rockets ushered in the celebration of Independence Day.

Late in the afternoon of the fourth, Frank was with his mother at home. He looked up startled when a neighbor came running down the street, waving a paper. "Lee's been beaten!" he yelled, and Frank and his mother went out on the front porch at once. Harold Dement's face glowed as he yelled, "We whupped the Rebels! The Army of the Potomac's whupped Lee!"

"Thank God!" Melanie whispered, leaning against Frank. "Now if we can just hear that your father's safe!"

Frank hugged her, saying, "He'll be fine, Mother! I know he will! And Tyler and Bob—we'll have them all home again soon." He held her tightly, speaking cheerfully, but he knew the odds of battle too well. *Three of them—and that's three chances for us to lose at least one of them!* He tried to brush the thought away, but as the two of them moved back into the house, he had a strange feeling that the men of the Rocklin tribe would not escape the fires of this battle unscathed.

The next day the news came that Vicksburg had fallen to the forces of Gen. Grant. The double victory sent the nation into a heady celebration. Across the North boomed the salutes of guns. Bells rang and buildings were adorned with garish banners. People cheered the names of Grant and Sherman, the heroes of the hour.

But Meade did not destroy Lee's army. He could have done so, for the Confederates were broken, but he did not move. The Army of Northern Virginia crept back to Virginia bleeding but not destroyed.

"Meade let them get away!" Frank exclaimed with disgust. "He had Lee in his hand but didn't have the nerve to push at him!"

Lincoln felt the same way, and he wrote a scathing letter to Meade—then refused to mail it. "I wasn't there," he said sadly. "I can't judge Gen. Meade from the safety of Washington."

And so the Union was not saved, and a longer war loomed ahead despite victories at Gettysburg and Vicksburg. The golden opportunity slipped away from the North, and grimly both North and South prepared for the bloodbath that all knew would come.

★ ★ ★

The city of Washington was not at all what Lorna Grey had expected. She had come to believe that the capital of the country would be somewhat grand, and when she got her first glimpse of the city, she was shocked at its crude appearance.

As Thomas Cooper took the company from the station to their hotel, she noted that there was a random sort of feeling connected with Washington. Outside the area where the population was concentrated were lonely tracts of woodlands and commons, broken at intervals by large estates, planted and bowered in trees. But adjoined to the rather attractive sections she saw shantytowns, their dusty streets lined with dingy buildings. Rain had turned the roadbeds into channels of mud, and the open sewer of the canal sent a malignant stink over the area.

Cooper kept up a running conversation as the carriage

took the company down the city's main thoroughfare, Pennsylvania Avenue. "Now then, ain't this fine!" he exclaimed, apparently excited by the view of the restaurants and shops that were all located on the north side of the avenue. Lorna thought the hotels, which were a recent development, ugly to a fault, but said nothing.

Unfortunately the company arrived in the capital when Congress was in session. At such times the hotels and all their halls, dining rooms, and bars were packed. The din as they entered their hotel, a smallish one called the Morgan House, was frightful. Cooper's face dropped when he negotiated the price for the room, for rates were high and the clerks haughty and short-tempered.

Finally Lorna found herself in a very small room with a bed, a table, one chair, and a washstand. Eileen Fenton, her roommate, took one look at the lumpy mattress and complained, "I think I'll try the *floor*. It looks *far* more comfortable than that *bed!*" Eileen was a short, rather overweight actress who, at the age of twenty-nine, had passed the point of playing youthful heroines. She had been rather successful in such roles when she was eighteen and still persisted in trying to recapture her early triumphs. Cooper, desperate for actors and actresses to join him in the rash venture, had agreed to give her better roles than she'd been able to find in England. She was a nervous, high-strung woman who complained constantly, and now as Lorna unpacked her trunk, Eileen moved about the room finding fault with every element from the wallpaper to the water pitcher, which had a minuscule crack on the handle.

"We'll just have to make the best of it, I suppose," Lorna offered mildly. She was actually sick to death of Eileen's constant complaining and longed for nothing more than peace and quietness.

"I'm going to *demand* that Thomas get me a *private* room!" Eileen could not speak without emphasizing far too many of the words she uttered—which in effect meant that people soon stopped paying any heed at all to what she said.

Now she turned and left the room, her shrill voice raised as she said, "How does he *expect* an actress to *perform* when she has no *privacy!*"

Lorna sighed with relief as the door slammed. She was exhausted, for the voyage had been stormy and the accommodations poor. For weeks the ship, a converted merchant ship with the unlikely name of *Pride of Albion,* had wallowed in the troughs of the roaring waves for what seemed like months. Eileen had been seasick and so frightened that she'd kept Lorna by her side constantly.

"I should have stayed in England," Lorna murmured, then shook her head in a firm manner, knowing that she could not look back. She had little money, and her only hope was to make the best of the situation. Removing her dress, she stared down at her petticoat, which was a new style, the forerunner of a hooped crinoline. It had been fresh and stiff once, but life at sea had offered no opportunity for keeping clothing in that condition. Stripping it off, she examined the parallel rows of stitching around the bottom that stiffened it, noting that the threads were pulling loose. She took advantage of the moment of privacy to strip off the Greek-style *zora,* which consisted of a silk garment wrapped around her upper body, then the lace-trimmed pantalettes. She had not had a thorough bath for days, and now she used all the fresh water, luxuriating in the smell of soap and the sensation of cleanliness. Quickly she dried herself with the rather skimpy towel and put on a cotton nightgown. Fatigue struck her, and she stripped the covers back, fell into the bed, and was asleep instantly.

She awoke to the sound of Eileen's voice, complaining as usual. "And I told *him* that if I didn't get my *own* room— why, he could get *another* artist!" Eileen looked over and saw that Lorna was awake, and said, "We're all going to the *theater,* Lorna. I *told* Thomas it wasn't likely we'd see any *acting,* but he says we *must* scout out the competition."

Lorna, refreshed by her bath and rest, rose and dressed. She had brought a small trunk filled with clothing and now slipped into ankle-length pantalettes, a plain petticoat, and a crinoline "pouf" with the hoops and ribbon ties to hold the front closure in place. Her dress was striped satin, blue and white, and after checking herself one last time, Lorna said, "I'm ready, Eileen."

The two found the rest of the company waiting, and after a rather poorly cooked meal they left the hotel and, with some difficulty, packed themselves into a carriage. Since there were eight members of the company Lorna found herself squeezed between Jonathan Bratton, the leading man, and Lyle Defore, who played either villains or heroes as was needed. Both of them had made advances to Lorna, which she had fended off so adamantly that each had made a truce with her. Across from Lorna three rather seedy actors shared the seat with Eileen. They all were tired and uncertain and therefore said little. Eileen's complaints, however, made up for that.

Lorna was relieved when they arrived, and when they were seated in Ford's Theater, she was pleased to find herself seated between Cooper and David Talbot, a young man of seventeen who was very shy—for an actor.

"What's the play, Mr. Cooper?" Talbot asked.

"Why, it's Mr. Booth's *Hamlet.*" Cooper turned to add, "It's John Wilkes Booth—not his famous brother."

"Have you seen him act?"

"No, but if he's anything like his father or brother, he's excellent."

As it developed, Lorna was not at all impressed by the star of the play. He was, she thought, more of a gymnast than an actor. She watched as Booth cavorted about the stage, sawing the air with his hands constantly. Finally she whispered to Cooper, "I don't care for him. He's like some sort of puppet that one winds up—and he goes until he runs down."

"I must say he's a bit *much,*" Cooper agreed. "Some of the rest of the cast aren't bad. That young fellow playing Laertes is rather good. What's his name?"

Lorna peered at the program she held, then whispered, "Frank Rocklin." She watched as the sword fight was enacted, then commented, "I must say, Booth is better with a sword than he is with a line." When the play was over, they went backstage and met the star and his cast. Booth welcomed them and wished them well in their new venture. He frowned, adding, "There's need in our country for English excellency on the boards. I'll expect to hear great things from your company, Mr. Cooper."

Lorna shook hands with Booth, then turned to find the young actor who'd played Laertes standing beside her. She hesitated, then said, "I enjoyed your performance, Mr. Rocklin."

"Why—thank you, Miss . . . ?"

"Lorna Grey."

"Miss Grey, I'm so new to this profession that I gather up any crumbs of appreciation that fall in my path." Rocklin was impressed with the poise of the young woman, as well as with her serene beauty. "Have you been acting long?" He listened as Lorna gave him a brief answer, then smiled at her. "Welcome to America. I wish you a prosperous tour." He was very handsome, his raven dark hair and dark eyes set off by olive skin and even features. "I'll come to see you if I can. Where will you be playing?"

"We open in a week," Lorna answered. "At the Belleview Theater." She saw something in Rocklin's face change as she named the theater, and she asked, "Is something wrong, sir?"

"Well, not really." Frank Rocklin hesitated, then said honestly, "The Belleview isn't quite as ornate as—well, as Ford's. But it's the performance that counts, not the place," he added quickly. He bowed and moved to speak to others who were waiting, but his reaction stayed with Lorna.

On their way back to the hotel, she thought, *The Belleview must be a pretty dreary place. I could see Mr. Rocklin was a little shocked that we'd be playing there.* She thought of this, then shrugged, for there was nothing to be done. She did remember more of Rocklin than she did of Booth in the days to come. There was an intensity in him that impressed her. *He's going to do well,* she thought. *He has talent, looks, and he knows what he wants.*

★ ★ ★

"You're going to do *what?*"

Frank stared at his mother blankly, certain that he had misunderstood her. Since the news had arrived that Gideon had been captured at Gettysburg and taken to Richmond as a prisoner of war, Melanie had been quiet. Frank had been bitter, for he had heard of the terrible conditions of the camps and prisons where captured men suffered. He'd come down for breakfast and had been shocked as his mother faced him and spoke of her intentions to go to Richmond.

"I'm going to Richmond to take care of your father, Frank." There was an iron quality in Melanie's voice, and Frank knew that when his mother had that certain glint in her eyes, argument was useless. He listened as she told him that Clay had sent her a letter telling her of Gideon's location and condition. "You can read the letter," Melanie said, holding it out to him.

Frank scanned the short letter, then frowned. "I was hoping he was doing better. But going to Richmond can be dangerous," he protested.

Melanie answered emphatically, "I don't care. Your father is sick, and he needs me."

"But you don't know that you can get to him!"

"God will be with me."

Frank protested the rest of the evening and thought he had convinced his mother to wait for official channels to help his father. But the next morning Frank found a note from his mother saying that she had left for Richmond and not to worry. "God will take care of me" was the last line of the note.

Upset that his mother left on such a dangerous journey, Frank couldn't sit around the house. He dressed and went out for a long walk. His square shoulders were slumped and his mouth was a bitter line as he wandered D.C. He went to the newspaper office and read the list of dead, wounded, and captured that was posted on the outside, his eyes bleak.

He straightened when he found no mention of his brothers, and a gust of relief passed his lips. "Well, there's hope," he muttered. Still, he knew that after a battle, many soldiers killed in the action were buried in mass graves and it was as if they had disappeared.

That would be the worst, he thought, turning to make his way to the theater. *Not to know—just to think about their bodies thrown into an unmarked grave!* He shook his shoulders, forced the thought out of his mind, and walked rapidly away. *They'll be all right—God won't let them die!*

★   ★   ★

A faint but persistent banging noise brought Frank out of a sound sleep. He had been dreaming of some ridiculous escapade in which he was vaguely aware that it *was* a dream. It involved a party in which he was involved with several animals that were making strange noises. Somehow the cries of the animals were transformed into a persistent knocking sound, and he came out of sleep abruptly, sitting up in bed with a start. Staring around wildly, he realized that someone was knocking at the door.

Scrambling out of bed, he grabbed his pants, struggled into them, then when he dashed across the room, kicked a low stool he'd forgotten was there.

"Blast!" he groaned, grabbing his shin and hopping on his other foot. The steady rapping continued, and he hobbled out of his bedroom. He groped his way to a table in the hall, found a jar of matches, and managed to light a lamp. Replacing the chimney, he made his way to the front door. Slipping the bolt, he pulled the door half-open and peered at the dark, shadowy figure of a man outlined in the opening.

"What the blazes do you want?" he rasped, holding the light up so that the amber light fell on the face of the visitor.

"Hello, Frank."

Frank blinked with astonishment as he recognized the drawn features of his oldest brother. "Tyler!" he exclaimed, and at once reached out and pulled him inside and closed the door.

"I thought nobody was home," Tyler said, taking off his coat.

"Did you get our letter about Dad getting captured at Gettysburg?" Frank asked.

"Yes."

Tyler looked exhausted, and he had a guarded expression on his face. At once alarm shot through Frank, and he grabbed Tyler's arm, his voice going tense. "Where's Bob?"

"Well—"

"He's dead, isn't he?"

"No! Nothing like that!" Tyler shot back. "He was wounded, but I got him out of Vicksburg."

Frank saw that Tyler was groggy with fatigue and worn thin with the rigors of battle. "Come on," he said, "I'll fix you something to eat while you tell me about it." He led the way to the kitchen, and shoving Tyler into a chair, he fired up the stove.

By the time the eggs and bacon were cooked, Frank had told Tyler all that he knew about their father's capture. Tyler began to eat hungrily, washing the food down with greedy gulps of strong black coffee. When he was finished, he shoved the plate back and began to speak of the last days of Vicksburg. He sketched the battle quickly, then said with a bitter note in his voice, "Bob got hit just four days before the surrender."

"How bad is he, Ty?"

"A shell went off just over the trench we were in. Killed two men. Bob got some of the blast from the powder in the face. One piece of shrapnel got him in the chest. I got him to the surgeon, and he patched him up. He got a fever after the operation, and I thought he'd die." Tyler leaned his head down on his hands in a gesture of utter fatigue. He

116

remained there for a few moments, then lifted his head to stare at his brother. His voice was hoarse as he said, "He's blind, Frank."

Frank bit his lips, and he lowered his head to stare at the table. "Any chance he'll ever see again?"

"The doctors gave us no hope."

"That's bad," Frank said quietly. "What about the wound in his chest?"

"Making a good recovery. I left him in the hospital—used to be the old Union Hotel, but they've made a hospital of it."

"I'll go right down," Frank said, rising to his feet. "You go to bed, Ty."

"Think I will." Tyler rose, his eyes bleary with want of sleep, then pulled his shoulders back as he looked at Frank. "I'm grateful all three of us are alive," he said quietly. "But it's hard to take, Bob losing his eyes."

Frank could not speak of that, but said bitterly, "He didn't have that kind of thing coming to him, Ty—not Bob!"

"A lot of good men got a rough deal, Frank, and some of them wore Confederate gray." He turned and made his way out of the kitchen, his back bent with fatigue. At once Frank cleaned up the kitchen and went to dress. There was a dullness in him as he saddled a horse and mounted. As he made his way along the darkened streets, headed for the hospital, bitterness rose in him.

"Why'd it have to be Bob?" he spoke aloud, then clamped his lips together. He'd never been good with people who'd suffered tragedy. Going to a home where death had come had been a terrible thing for him. He could never think of a single thing to say that made any sense at all. Now he had to go to his brother who'd lost the great gift of sight.

What can I say to him? If it were me, I'd kill myself, I reckon. He went over the situation in his mind and found guilt rising in him. *Maybe if I'd stayed with him, it wouldn't have happened,* he thought, and though the rational part of him told him there was no certainty of this, he could not shake it off.

When he dismounted and tied his horse in front of the Union Hospital, he had tried himself and returned a guilty verdict. As he mounted the steps and passed inside, bitterness had seared his spirit like a hot iron.

Pausing before a large woman who sat at a table, he said, "I'm looking for Robert Rocklin."

The woman was rolling bandages, and there was a light of pity in her face as she looked up. "I'm Miss Alcott," she answered. "Your brother Tyler said you'd be coming."

"Can I see him?"

"I expect he's asleep. You can sit beside him if you like."

"I want to."

Miss Alcott rose and led Frank down a hall, then into a long room filled with cots. Lamps burned faintly at each end, giving nurses enough light to see by. She stopped by a cot and whispered, "Are you awake, Robert?"

"Yes."

"Your brother Frank is here." She busied herself getting a chair and placing it beside the bed, then whispered to Frank, "You have a fine family, Mr. Rocklin."

When the nurse left, Frank sat down and cleared his throat. "How do you feel, Bob?"

"Not bad. My chest hurts a little sometimes, but Miss Alcott gives me something for it. I'm pretty fuzzy right now."

Frank hesitated, then said, "I came as soon as Tyler got home." He struggled to find words, and anger ran through him at seeing his brother stretched out blind and helpless. He fought it down, then slowly reached over and took Bob's hand. At once he felt the pressure and returned it.

"I'm glad you're back safe, Bob," he whispered finally. The pressure on his hand grew, and the two sat there in the darkened room holding to each other. After a time, Frank whispered, "I'm sorry about—" He could not finish what he'd planned to say, and then he saw that Bob was asleep. He clung to the still hand, and slowly the tears ran down his cheeks unheeded.

CHAPTER TEN
"God Let It Happen!"

The staff of Union Hospital had grown accustomed to the visitor, for he came often. Louisa May Alcott had asked one of the male nurses about the stout, gray-haired man and had been told, "Why, his name's Whitman—Walt, I think his first name is. Some kind of a writer."

It took Miss Alcott some time to discover that Walt Whitman had written a slender book of poems entitled *Leaves of Grass.* It was reputed to be vulgar, so she didn't read it, of course. She herself had begun to be known as a writer of tales and poems and made it her business to get to know Whitman.

"My brother was wounded at Fredericksburg," Whitman told her when she engaged him in a brief conversation. "I came to see him and got caught up in our brave wounded fellows." The poet was slow-moving and had opaque, heavy-lidded eyes and wore no tie. His spotless white shirt was Byronic, and there was an unusual daintiness about the big man. He was only forty-four years old, but seemed older.

"The men are grateful for your faithful visits, Mr. Whitman," Miss Alcott said. "It's good of you to come so regularly. Do you have your own business?"

"Oh no, Miss Alcott! I do a little clerking, a little hacking for newspapers." Whitman shrugged. "I do some copying in the paymaster general's office for two hours or so each day."

His bluff, reddish face grew sad, and he added, "I see some of our wounded men climbing to the top floor, and sometimes they find a hitch in their papers and can't get paid. It's a sad thing to watch."

"How terrible! But you always bring little presents—and the men are so grateful."

"I wish I could do more. I've asked some friends and my family to help, and they do." He lifted the haversack in his hand, his soulful eyes grown warm. "Look, I brought pens and pencils, writing paper and envelopes. And I brought some pickles and horehound candy—and some jelly, you see?" He smiled as she exclaimed over his small store, then added, "I give them plugs of tobacco, and sometimes I can spare a little cash to buy the fresh milk that's for sale in the wards."

"Are you a minister, Mr. Whitman?"

The woman's question seemed to amuse Whitman. "I believe we're all ministers, Miss Louisa," he said quietly. He left her then and passed into the ward. For three hours he moved from bed to bed, writing letters, reading to some, sometimes playing Twenty Questions. Walt Whitman believed in the curative properties of affection, and he often stroked the hands or feverish brows of the sick men, whispering encouragement.

"Well, now, how are you today, Robert?" he asked, coming to sit down beside the soldier whose eyes were bound with a linen bandage.

"Fine, Mr. Whitman." Bob Rocklin turned his head to face the man who sat down beside him and smiled. "Did you bring your poems today as you promised?"

"Oh yes. But I brought something sweeter." Rummaging in his knapsack, he came up with a small orange and placed it in Bob's hands. "Nothing sweeter than a good orange!"

"Why, I've always been partial to oranges, sir. I'll eat it later."

"I've got the latest edition of the newspaper. Let me read the gist of it. . . ."

Whitman read in a clear tenor voice, stopping to comment from time to time on the news. Finally he noted a young man in rather dandified dress approach, and he stopped reading. "You have a visitor, Robert," Whitman said. He got up, but the young man shook his head. "I'll get this stool, sir," he said and moved a three-legged stool to the opposite side of the bed. "How are you, Bob?"

"Fine, fine. This is my brother Frank—and this is Mr. Walt Whitman."

Frank leaned over and shook the man's hand, saying, "Nice of you to visit with our men, sir. Miss Alcott tells me you rarely fail."

Whitman shook off the praise and said quickly, "I'll leave you two to visit—"

"Not before you read some of our poetry, Mr. Whitman," Bob broke in. "Frank's the real authority on poetry in our family. He'll probably have to explain to me what it means after you leave."

Whitman smiled gently, then took a small book out of his knapsack. Opening it, he found a page and began to read:

> *"A child said* What is the grass? *fetching it to me with full hands;*
> *How could I answer the child? I do not know what it is any more than he.*

> *"I guess it must be the flag of my disposition, out of hopeful green stuff woven.*

> *"Or I guess it is the handkerchief of the Lord,*
> *A scented gift and remembrancer designedly dropt,*
> *Bearing the owner's name someway in the corners, that we may see and remark, and say* Whose?"

"Why, even I can understand that!" Bob exclaimed. Turning to Frank he demanded, "Why didn't you tell me poetry could be so easy?"

Frank was puzzled by the poem and shook his head. "Your poetry's not like any I've read, sir. I'd like to read more of it."

Whitman reached into his knapsack, pulled out another volume, and handed it to Frank. A humorous grin touched his full lips. "I have a library of two thousand books, sir, and I wrote every one of them."

Frank laughed, liking the man. He opened the book and began reading aloud where Whitman had left off:

> *"Or I guess the grass is itself a child, the produced babe of the*
>   *vegetation.*
>
> *"Or I guess it is a uniform hieroglyphic,*
> *And it means, Sprouting alike in broad zones and narrow*
>   *zones,*
> *Growing among black folks as among white,*
> *Kanuck, Tuckahoe, Congressman, Cuff, I give them the*
>   *same, I receive them the same.*
>
> *"And now it seems to me the beautiful uncut hair of graves.*
>
> *"Tenderly will I use you curling grass,*
> *It may be you transpire from the breasts of young men,*
> *It may be if I had known them I would have loved them,*
> *It may be you are from old people, or from offspring taken*
>   *soon out of their mothers' laps,*
> *And here you are the mothers' laps."*

Frank's voice was deep and rich, and when he paused, Whitman said, "You read very well, Mr. Rocklin."

"I've never seen poetry like this," Frank repeated. "Which poets did you model your work on?"

Whitman shook his head. "We must speak with our own voice. It may be the world will not hear a new voice, being content with old ones, but every man is different. In that book I say, 'I celebrate myself.' Some have said that is egotistical, but we are all specially made, all of us different."

"That's so, Mr. Whitman," Bob said, his voice quiet and certain. "And all made by God to serve him."

"Do you believe in God, sir?" Frank inquired.

Whitman was not offended. He looked at the book in Frank's hands, saying, "Read on ahead, sir."

Frank scanned the page, then read slowly:

> *"I wish I could translate the hints about the dead young men and women,*
> *And the hints about old men and mothers, and the offspring taken soon out of their laps.*
> *What do you think has become of the young and old men?*
> *And what do you think has become of the women and children?*
>
> *They are alive and well somewhere,*
> *The smallest sprout shows there is really no death."*

Frank looked up quickly, a frown on his brow. "It's hard for those who've buried their dead to believe this, Mr. Whitman."

"Death is not the end, Frank." It was Bob who spoke up, and there was a firm smile on his lips as he turned to face his brother. "Jesus came out of the tomb—and all of those who believe and trust in him will do the same."

The eyes of the poet and the actor met across the body of the stricken man, and it was Whitman who said gently, "I honor your faith, Robert." He rose, saying, "I trust you will find something in my verses to your liking, Mr. Rocklin."

Frank watched the sturdy figure move away, then shook his head. "What do you make of him, Bob?"

"He loves people. You can feel it, can't you?"

"I guess so. But he's sure a different kind of poet from any I've read." He sat beside Bob, giving him the details of his day. Finally he said, "You look better. More color in your cheeks."

"I feel better. The doctor says I'm keeping a real sick man

from a bed." Bob shifted and said, "I'd like to come home, Frank."

"I'll talk to the doctor." He remained for another hour, mostly reading from Whitman's book of poetry, then rose, saying, "I'll see you tomorrow. Ty will be in as soon as he gets back with the company—probably next week."

Frank left the ward and stopped by the table where Miss Alcott was working on her bandages. "Do you have a minute to spare?" he asked.

"Why, certainly, Mr. Rocklin." Miss Alcott rose and nodded to her left. "Come along, and I'll see if we can't have some tea."

Ten minutes later the two were sitting at a table in the mess hall, and as she talked, Frank studied her. Louisa May Alcott was thirty-one years old, he had discovered, and was plain and quite strong. She was a large, bashful woman with dark eyes and long hair bundled up in braids at the back of her head. Frank had watched her in action, and like other inexperienced nurses, she shed tears often, smoothed brows, and sometimes sang lullabies and placed nosegays on pillows. She joked and gossiped, played games with the patients, and armed herself with a bottle of lavender water to drown out the bad smells.

"How did you happen to get into nursing?" Frank asked. He liked this woman a great deal and knew that she had done much for his brother.

"Oh, I've always been a romantic," Miss Alcott confessed shyly. "I suppose I want to be like Clara Barton—rush to the battlefield as she's done—but I'll never do that!" She leaned forward, placed her chin on her hands, and smiled at herself. "I remember when I came here my first time. Forty wagons filled with wounded men were lined up right out there, Frank. They were brought in, and I nearly fainted! A more pitiful-looking sight you never saw! Ragged, gaunt, and pale, muddy and with bloody bandages untouched since they'd been put on."

"And what did you do?"

"A nurse put a block of brown soap in my hands and told me to start cleaning the men up. I was flabbergasted—but there was no way out of it. There I was, a spinster lady, and I was to wash those men!" Laughter ran over the nurse's face, and she giggled. "My first man was old and Irish, and I scrubbed him down and stuffed him with soup. After that, it was all right."

Frank enjoyed listening to Miss Alcott, but finally got to the subject of Robert. "How is my brother, Miss Alcott?"

"The wound in his chest is healing well. Dr. Anderson said he didn't anticipate any difficulty there."

"But his eyes?"

"Poor boy! Dr. Anderson said he'd never see again! So sad!"

"He wants to go home. Do you think he could?"

Miss Alcott thought hard, then nodded slowly. "You'd have to check with one of the doctors. But with good nursing, he could go, I think. But unless you've got somebody to stay with him, he might be better off here until his wound is completely healed."

"My mother would do it, but she's out of town." Frank got to his feet, saying, "Thanks for the tea—and for all you've done for Bob."

"He's a dear fellow!" Tears welled in the dark eyes, and Miss Alcott shook her head. "He'll need love to get over the loss of his sight. I wish his mother were home. There's nobody like a mother in a case like this."

"Perhaps she'll be home soon. I'll ask Dr. Anderson if he'll release him."

Dr. Anderson said much the same as Nurse Alcott. "He'll need some care, but he'll be fine with that."

Frank then faced the doctor squarely. "Is there *no* chance he'll ever see, Doctor?"

Anderson was a burly man of sixty, with much experience in battlefield wounds. He was accustomed to giving bad news, but he never had learned to like it. Now he said bluntly, "I hate to raise false hopes, Mr. Rocklin. Better to face the facts, I think." He thought for a moment, then said evenly, "The eyes are intact, but there's a great deal of damage apparently to the optic nerve. We don't know too much about that part of the body—and practically nothing about how to treat such injuries."

When Anderson paused, Frank stared at him hard. "So there *is* a chance, even if it's small? Is that what you're saying?"

"Don't allow yourself to hope—and don't offer any to your brother. Miracles happen—at least things that we can't explain," Dr. Anderson shot back. "In Robert's case, that's what it would take. It's almost—" He sought for a way to put the concept into words, then shrugged his thick shoulders. "It's almost the same as saying that a man who's lost an arm would have to grow another arm. I never heard of such a thing. It would be unwise for Robert to spend his life counting on it."

Frank nodded slowly, then said, "I'll find someone to take care of him, Doctor. And as for the rest—"

"He'll have to fill his life with other things, Mr. Rocklin. It's not the end of the world. He has all his other senses; he can walk and learn to do some kinds of work. I'm sorry I don't have better news for you."

Frank thanked the physician, then left the hospital. He moved through the performance that night, his mind on the problem of finding someone to stay with Bob. After the play he was surprised to see his aunt Laura Steele enter the backstage area. She was accompanied by her husband, Amos, a minister. Laura came to him with a bright smile, saying, "You were wonderful, Frank!"

Frank took her kiss on his cheek, then turned with a smile to her husband. "I'm surprised to see you here, Uncle. I thought you were opposed to the theater."

Amos Steele was a tall man with piercing hazel eyes. He was not a man of great humor, but he smiled now, saying, "Your aunt is educating me, Frank. I suppose I'll be going to bet on horse races before she's through with me." He put his hand out, saying, "I'm impressed with your play. Always loved *Hamlet.*"

"Come now, we've come to kidnap you," Laura teased. "We're going to feed you, and you're going to tell us all about the wicked ways of the theater!"

Frank truly enjoyed the meal with Amos and Laura. He'd always been fond of them and was aware that they had come to the play to show their loyalty to his choice. He listened as they talked about their children, especially about the coming marriage of Deborah and Noel. Clinton, their youngest son, was in college, while Colin and Pat were both in the army.

Finally it was Laura who asked about Robert. The pair listened as Frank told them of the tragedy. His voice was unsteady, and he said bitterly, "God let it happen! It didn't have to be like this!"

Amos Steele resisted the impulse to launch into a theological debate, but with the aid of one warning look from his wife he said merely, "I'm sorry, Frank. We're very fond of Robert."

"When can he come home?" Laura asked.

"Oh, he can leave the hospital now," Frank said. "But I'm gone every night, and with Mother in Richmond there's nobody to take care of him."

A swift glance passed between Amos and his wife. "He'll come with us," Laura said firmly. When Frank started with surprise, she added tartly, "Don't look so shocked. We're family, I suppose you know? And you're coming to live with us, too. You'll be company for him."

When Frank tried to protest, Amos said sharply, "Don't argue, Nephew. Laura and I rattle around in that big house with all the children gone. It'll be nice having young people there again. Besides," he added, "you know how well Robert and I always got on. He was planning to study with me. Well, we'll do it now!"

Frank felt a lump in his throat at the kindness, and nodded. With some difficulty, he said, "I'll bring him tomorrow."

"It'll be a blessing having both of you," Amos said.

"Uncle Amos—I didn't mean to speak so—about God."

"I know, Frank," Steele said gently. "But he's probably used to our foolish speeches. Come now, let's look to him in all things!"

★ ★ ★

The next day Frank came to stand beside Bob, who was sitting up on his bed. Something about the helpless attitude of his brother struck a sad chord in Frank, and he covered it by saying brusquely, "Well, you've soldiered on me long enough. Come on, time to move on."

"Move on?" Bob's lips tightened slightly. "I can stay here, you know."

"No, you can't." Frank had brought fresh clothing, including a flannel gown and robe. "Here, get into this. We're going to live with Aunt Laura and Uncle Amos—at least until Mother gets home."

Bob made no protest and slipped into the garments. Frank had paid two of the attendants to carry Bob on a stretcher, and they made the trip with no trouble. When they arrived, his uncle and aunt came down the steps. "We've made up Patrick's room for you, Bob—and you can have Colin's room, Frank. You'll be close together that way."

Amos came over to stand beside the still form of Bob lying on the stretcher. "Well, now, Robert," he said loudly, "now we'll be able to get this matter of sanctification straight, won't we?" Leaning down he took the young man's hand and squeezed it warmly. "I trust that I'll be able to—ah, *enlighten* you on that doctrine." Then he straightened up and dismissed the attendants with a nod.

As Amos got Bob settled, Frank spoke with his aunt. "It's wonderful for you to take us in, Aunt Laura," he said. "I was about out of ideas."

Laura smiled, then kissed him on the cheek. "We're going to see God do great things, Frank. Now, you go up and stay with Bob. I'll make one of those peach pies you both love so well." She went to the kitchen and stood there for one moment silently. Then, looking up, she lifted her hands and pleaded, "Lord, do a mighty work in Bob, and in Frank, and in all of us!"

★ ★ ★

Thomas Cooper had gathered the company into the stage area early in the afternoon. Most of the cast assumed that they were going to be asked to rehearse and were sullen. But something about the pale cast of Cooper's face caught Lorna's attention. *He's afraid of something,* she thought, and she listened closely as the stubby manager called for their attention.

"Well, now, I wish I had good news for you," Cooper said in a strangely flat voice. He took out a limp handkerchief and mopped his brow.

"Well, what *is* it, Thomas?" Eileen demanded. "What's wrong *this* time?"

Others of the company began complaining, and Cooper suddenly lifted his head. "Might as well give it to you straight." He hesitated one moment, shrugged, and said, "The tour is off."

Every member of the cast stared at him, and it was Lorna who spoke. "What's happened, Mr. Cooper?"

"It's a bust, that's all. You've seen how the house has been off. And two of the theaters I thought were booked have canceled." He gave them a defensive look, adding, "I'm sorry, but that's the way it is. I've got tickets to get us back home—and that's what we've got to do."

What followed was a tide of angry recriminations and threats of lawsuits. Most of the actors, however, were hardened to the facts of touring and made the best of it. When Cooper said that the ship would sail on the next day, there was a bustle to get to the hotel and pack.

Lorna stopped Cooper as he turned to leave. "Mr. Cooper, could I have my ticket, please?" she asked.

"Why, it might be better if I kept all of the tickets, Miss Lorna."

"I'm going to cash it in." Seeing the surprise on Cooper's homely face, Lorna said quickly, "I'm not going back to England—not yet, at least."

"But what will you do?" Worry etched itself on the plain features, for he felt responsible for the young woman.

"Don't worry about me, Mr. Cooper. I'll be all right." It took some persuasion on her part, but finally the manager saw that she was adamant. He gave her the ticket reluctantly; then she gave him her hand. "You'll be very busy, so let me say good-bye—and thank you. You've been very kind."

"Aw, now, I wish it hadn't come to this," Cooper muttered. "You take care of yourself, now! You've got talent, and looks, too. When you get back to England, you look me up. We'll do better another time!"

The next day Lorna waved good-bye as the ship bearing the company sailed down the river; then she turned and made her way back to the hotel. She had no idea what she would do, and fear came to her as she sat down in her room. She had very little money, no friends, and no marketable skills. Closing her eyes she prayed for the first time since she was a small child.

"Oh God, I'm frightened! Take care of me, please, will you? Don't let me go wrong!" She sat there quietly and was somewhat surprised when, after her rather desperate prayer, a sense of peace came to her. It wasn't much, but as the fear left, her courage rose, and she stood to her feet and left to face the world that lay before her.

CHAPTER ELEVEN
Mr. Pinkerton
Makes a Call

"Nothing smells better than a mimosa blossom, does it, Aunt Laura?"

Bob Rocklin stood shaded from the blistering August sun, holding a delicate bloom to his nose. The fine hairlike tendrils tickled his nose, and he smiled broadly. "I wonder why young women haven't come up with a way to make perfume out of this? I'd fall in love with anyone who smelled this good!"

Laura Steele had come to sit in the backyard, hopeful of catching some faint breeze. She looked up from the purple-hulled peas she was shelling and smiled at her nephew. "We called those silk flowers when I was growing up," she remarked. "The trees are always small enough for a child to climb, and I made many a bouquet of silk-tree blossoms."

Bob walked from under the tree, holding out his hands as he approached the house. He wore a pair of dark smoked glasses instead of the bandages he'd worn when he first came. Carefully he reached out until he touched the side of the house, then turned and leaned against it. He wore a pair of faded blue cotton trousers and a thin white shirt of the same material. His face had some color, and he showed little trace of the wound he'd taken.

"Did you change your bandage this morning, Bob?"

Laura asked. She had been his nurse for a week after his arrival, but he soon rebelled, insisting that he could take care of his own needs.

"Don't really need one, Aunt Laura." Touching his chest, he nodded, saying, "The scar is all formed; no need to keep a bandage. I think the air is good for it."

"That's good. You need to gain a little weight, though."

"If you keep on stuffing me, I'll be as big as Mrs. Skeffington." He referred to a brood sow that he had raised as a young boy. He smiled at the memory, adding, "Just like an ornery boy, wasn't it, to name a sow after the pastor's wife."

"Well, Sister Mae *was* overweight," Laura admitted, then smiled. "I wonder if she ever heard about that sow?"

"I hope not. Boys are pretty heartless." Squatting down on his heels, Bob ran the palm of his hand across the stiff tongues of grass, then dug his fingers into the ground, loosening the soil and letting it run through his fingers. Laura caught this and thought suddenly, *He has to be touching something all the time—to make up for his lack of sight, I think.* "I brought the newspaper out." She put the pan of peas down and picking up the paper began to read.

After the crisis of July, August had been fairly quiet. Robert E. Lee had led the Army of Northern Virginia home to rebuild, and there had been little major military action. On July 13, New York City had been rocked by a draft riot. The draft headquarters had been stormed, residences raided, and businesses looted. Only the troops returning from Gettysburg had stemmed the riot, but it had broken out again in other parts of the city for the next two days.

"It says here that Gen. Lee has offered to resign from the army," Laura commented.

"Davis will never let him do that," Bob spoke up. "Lee's the one indispensable man in the South. They could do without Jefferson Davis, but it's the South's veneration for Lee that keeps them going."

"The navy is attacking Fort Sumter." Laura read the

account of the attempts to retake Charleston Harbor, then lowered the paper. Her eyes were thoughtful as she said quietly, "It seems like a lifetime ago that the war started—right there at Fort Sumter."

Bob was listening carefully to his aunt and caught the sadness in her tone. He had always been good at reading people, and since the loss of his sight, his hearing seemed to be more acute. "You're worried about Pat and Colin, aren't you, Aunt Laura?"

"I grieve over all of our men. It's like a fog over the land." Her face grew sad, and there was a faint trembling of her lips as she added, "No matter where you go it's the same. Everybody's got someone in the army or the navy—and they're all in harm's way. We live under the shadow of death. And in the South, I know it's the same."

"One day it'll be over. Until then, we have to trust God, don't we?"

Laura found his faith encouraging. He'd never once complained about his injury, but had manifested a cheerful spirit. "I wish Frank wasn't so bitter," she remarked. "He's turning into a sour man, and that's going to destroy him."

"I've tried to talk to him, but he's full of hatred. I think he takes my blindness worse than I do."

"He's worried about Gideon, too."

"Yes, he is. So am I, Aunt Laura, but the Scripture says that with God all things are possible. God can keep Dad alive and get him home safely." Bob stood up and lifted his face upward as though seeking some sort of answer to the problems that faced them all. Then he turned his face toward her. "It's good for him to be here—with you and Uncle Amos. It would be good for anyone."

Laura rose and came to take his hand. "You have a sweet spirit, Bob. But don't you ever get depressed? Most people would."

"Sometimes I do," Bob admitted. "But then I know that God has something for me to do. If he didn't have, I'd have been taken home in the battle. I don't know what it is yet, but God will tell me when I'm ready for it. But one thing I can do now—while I'm waiting to find out God's will."

"What's that, Bob?"

"I can go to the hospital. I can visit with the men, take them little gifts, like Mr. Whitman does." This was something that had come to Bob as his strength had returned. He had planned it out, and now his face glowed with excitement as he spoke of his plans. "If you'll bake some cookies or a cake, I could take it to the hospital. And even though I can't read to the men, I can talk to them." He laughed and seemed almost boyish. "And I can practice preaching to them. If God calls me into the ministry, I'll have some experience."

Laura smiled at that and at once joined in helping with a plan. "I'll do the baking, and you do the preaching! When do you think you'll feel up to going?"

Bob was so enthused he was ready to begin that day, but Laura and Amos saw to it that he waited for a week. Frank listened as Bob spoke with enthusiasm of his venture, and he said at once, "I'll go with you as often as I can, Bob." He was glad that Bob had come up with something to throw himself into, and on the first visit to Union Hospital, he'd been glad to see the reception that Bob got.

Miss Alcott's eyes had grown large, and she'd come at once to hug Bob, exclaiming, "Why, Robert Rocklin—look at you! You're brown as a berry!" She had taken him at once to the ward, where Bob was greeted by calls from his friends.

Frank stood to one side, leaning against the wall, watching with a faint smile as Bob moved from bed to bed. He wished that he could join in, but a strange mood had come upon him—one he couldn't shake off and couldn't explain. Ever since he'd learned of the maiming of his brother, he'd been oppressed by some sort of dull-spirited moodiness. He was able to conceal this from people and had carried on with his work, but it was always there. He was worried about his father, and at times he thought that was his trouble.

At night he would toss on his bed, assailed by a bitterness

at the tragedy of his brother. It did him no good to realize that Bob himself had accepted his blindness. Somehow he still had the nagging doubt that if he had stayed at Vicksburg, this might not have happened. He was aware that most of the men in his family wore the uniform—and this troubled him as well.

They're fighting and risking their lives for the Union—and I'm playacting! Even now as he watched Bob speak to a young man with two stubs for legs, Frank felt self-disgust rise inside him. He'd been a man of strong self-esteem, but now that seemed to have been replaced by loathing for what he was. He was in this sort of mood when a voice beside him said, "Good afternoon, Mr. Rocklin."

Frank snapped out of his gloomy reverie and turned to find Walt Whitman had come to stand beside him. "Oh, hello, Mr. Whitman."

"Your brother is doing well," Whitman said. "I'm glad to see it."

"He's still blind."

Whitman's eyes narrowed at the flat tone of Frank Rocklin's voice. He was a perceptive man and at once understood the bitterness that marked the voice and eyes of the young man next to him. "It's a cruel war—but then, there's no such thing as a 'kind war,' is there?"

"He's taking it better than I am," Frank said in a spare tone. "I'd like to line up the men who got us into this war and shoot them all! The South started all this!"

Whitman listened as Frank Rocklin spoke with fervent bitterness of the war and what it was doing to the country. He made no attempt to speak, for he realized that the young man was using him as some sort of confessor. He was a good listener, this gray poet. He'd heard many voices speak to him what they were ashamed to speak to family or friends.

Finally Frank halted abruptly and shook his head, a half-shamed and bitter smile on his lips. "Didn't mean to dump all my hard feelings on you, sir. Don't usually do things like that."

"I think we all need to speak what's in our heart, Mr. Rocklin. We think we're alone, that nobody else is as bad off as we are. But we're all alike, really. The whole land is filled with men and women who've suffered loss. Don't think you're alone, my boy!"

"I feel alone, sir!"

Whitman's eyes were large and luminous as he put his hand on Frank's shoulder. "You must not feel so. We are all tied by blood—all of us!"

Frank listened as Whitman spoke, and when the poet left, he thought, *He's a strange one! Wish I could feel like he does—but I can't!* He watched as Bob spoke to the wounded men and could not fathom how a man who'd been stripped of his sight could be so happy. Finally they left the hospital, and on the way home, Bob said, "Poor fellows! I wish I could do more for them!"

Somehow this love Bob had for the men in the ward came as a rebuke to Frank. He had to force himself to be cheerful, and when he left the house to go to the theater, he muttered almost angrily, "I can't go on like this! I'm getting to be like a mean dog. Next thing I know I'll be snapping at people or biting myself!"

★ ★ ★

August was hot and sultry, but as it came to an end, the cooling breezes touched Washington with a soothing hand. The discontent that had shaken the city during the summer was less rampant, but everyone knew that the war was simply smoldering. In the West, Rosecrans and his Federal Army of the Cumberland were edging toward Chattanooga—where Bragg and his Army of Tennessee waited. The Army of Northern Virginia was being reformed, and any force that moved toward Richmond would have to contend with it.

As for Frank Rocklin, he struggled with moodiness, performing at night at Ford's, but less and less content with his life. He spent much time with Bob, but Amos Steele had taken his nephew in hand, and the two of them spent long hours in the study of the Scriptures. Frank roamed the city aimlessly for hours, trying to find some sort of escape from the discontent that had destroyed his peace of mind.

One night after the performance, he was greeted by Tyler, who had regained his lost weight and looked tanned and fit. "Come along, little brother," Ty said after they'd greeted one another. "I'm starved. You can buy me a steak." The two went out to dinner, and as they ate, Ty recounted his activities. "No fighting—just marching around from one place to another." He drank from his coffee cup, then said, "The play's still going well?"

"This is the last week. Booth told us last night we'd be closing."

Ty gave his brother a curious glance. "What happens then? Will you go into another play?"

"Don't know, Ty." Frank stirred restlessly in his chair. "Bob needed me for a while, but he's busy with Uncle Amos."

"I expect he'll make a preacher," Ty commented. "He was always bent that way."

"Can a blind man be a preacher?"

Ty caught the bitterness in Frank's voice. "What's the matter with you, Frank? You're down in the mouth. It's not like you."

Frank hesitated, then began to speak of his moodiness. Finally he ended by saying, "I can't get it out of my mind that if I'd stayed with you two, Bob might not have gotten blinded."

"Or he might have gotten killed—or *you* might have been maimed." Shaking his head, Ty said strongly, "No sense in thinking like that, Frank. You can't go back. And even if you could, you might make things worse." He spoke for a time, then leaned forward with a speculative look in his eyes. "You've got something on your mind, haven't you?"

"Well, I guess I have." Frank moved his legs restlessly, then blurted out, "I'm thinking of going back into the army, Ty. Never should have left it in the first place. What good have I done? Nothing but prance around on a stage spouting poetry!"

Ty stared at Frank, saying nothing for a time. He knew this younger brother of his fairly well, and finally he said, "It's more than that. I think you'll make a great actor."

"Can't win the war playing Hamlet!"

The two finished their meal, and when they parted, Ty said, "Don't be too quick to jump into a uniform, Frank. Think it over."

"I've got another week of the play. When that's over, I'm going to reenlist."

For the next two days, Frank grew more and more certain that he would enlist in the Washington Blues as soon as he was free. He said nothing to his family, not really wanting to hear their advice. But then he was met again by Tyler after the performance on Wednesday. "Got to talk to you, Frank," he said abruptly.

"All right." They left the theater and Frank asked, "Want to get something to eat at Willards?"

"No. There's a little place over on Elm Street. We'll go there." He led Frank to a small, dingy restaurant wedged between a hardware shop and a laundry. As they entered, he said to the waiter, "We'll eat with that gentleman back there."

Frank followed Ty to the table, where a man wearing a plain brown suit looked up at them. "Sit down," he said quietly. He was a smallish man with a clipped brown beard and a pair of small, steady eyes. "I take it this is your brother, Lieutenant?"

"Yes. Frank Rocklin."

"I've seen you in the play, Mr. Rocklin. Fine performance."

Frank said, "I didn't get your name, sir." He was aware that Ty had not given the man's name and was certain that the omission was deliberate.

"My name is Pinkerton, Allan Pinkerton."

Frank stared at Pinkerton, for he was aware that this was

the famous head of the Secret Service. "Glad to know you," he murmured. He glanced at Ty, who shrugged but said nothing.

"Will you order now?" The waiter had appeared, and after he had taken their order, Pinkerton said, "I suppose you're wondering what this is all about."

"I don't meet with Secret Service men often."

Pinkerton found this amusing. "I suppose not." He had a tight mouth, opening it to speak, it seemed, with some reluctance. "Tyler, perhaps you'd better explain why I'm here."

"Yes, of course." He turned to face Frank, asking, "You remember how I was wounded at Bull Run?"

"Yes. You were laid up for quite a while."

"Do you remember the young woman who nursed me? Frankie Aimes?"

"Why, certainly. She married our Uncle Paul, didn't she?"

"Yes, but what you don't know is that she was an agent for Mr. Pinkerton—and so was I."

Frank stared at Ty with surprise, saying, "I didn't know that!"

"Neither does anyone else, and I'd appreciate it if you'd keep it to yourself," Ty said at once. He hesitated, then said, "Ever since you told me you were going to reenlist, I've been thinking about something. Finally I went to Mr. Pinkerton and laid it out. He was very interested, and I think you should hear what he's got to say."

Frank turned to look at Pinkerton, who said at once, "It's commendable of you to want to reenlist, Mr. Rocklin, but I think I've got a better plan." He smiled briefly, asking, "Perhaps you can guess what it is?"

But Frank was mystified. "What kind of a plan, sir?"

"I want you to join my force," Pinkerton said, smiling slightly at the shock that came to the face of the young man. Turning to Tyler he said, "He's as surprised as you were when I asked you to join us."

"Me? Become a spy?"

"An *agent,* Mr. Rocklin!"

"I don't see that calling it something different makes it better." Frank shook his head. "I'd be no good at that sort of thing—decoding messages and so on. I can shoot, and that's what I'm going to do."

Pinkerton grew stern, his voice firm. "You're determined to serve your country, but don't you owe it to your country to serve in the best way you can?"

"Yes, but—"

"We have one hundred thousand men to fire muskets, Mr. Rocklin, but almost no one can do the job I need *you* for." When Frank stared at him with an unbelieving expression, Pinkerton spoke rapidly. "We've lost battles because our generals had almost no reliable information. This war is going to be bloody to the end, so we must do all we can to end it quickly! And one way to do that is to provide accurate information to those who have to go in and do the fighting."

Frank listened as Pinkerton spoke with a simple eloquence about the job of the Secret Service. Finally he shook his head, saying, "I don't disagree with what you say, Mr. Pinkerton. But I'm not fitted to do such work."

"Most of our men started as amateurs. There's no West Point to train agents. Your brother performed well, and I'm convinced that you can do a fine job."

"But why *me?*"

"Ah, you're in a position to move at once into place—because of your profession."

"You mean acting?"

"Exactly! What I propose has never been done—and that's why it will work!"

"Just what is it you have in mind, Mr. Pinkerton?"

"I want you to assemble a company of actors and take it to the South, to New Orleans and especially to Richmond." Pinkerton's smallish eyes gleamed as he spoke rapidly, outlining his plan. "Actors move often, and they meet everyone. You'd be invited to social events where people speak freely."

"But I'm not a star! It's not like I was Edwin or John Booth! I'd never be accepted."

"But Booth doesn't have a family named Rocklin—some of the men in the Confederate army," Pinkerton shot back. "All you have to do is indicate that you're sympathetic to the Southern cause and say that's why you've chosen to bring your company to the South."

Frank was stunned by the idea, but even as he thought of it, he saw the adventure and the difficulties. "But it would take money—"

"That's no problem. The government will foot the bills," Pinkerton said quickly. He was a quick-witted man, and for the next twenty minutes he spoke rapidly, covering most of the difficulties. Finally he demanded, "Will you do this job, Mr. Rocklin?"

Frank was an impulsive young man. Despite his guilt over Bob, he had dreaded the idea of going into the regular army, but this was different. The romantic side of his nature drew him to such a venture, and he said at once, "I'll do it, sir!"

Relief washed across the face of Pinkerton. "Fine! Now, your play is over this week. Can you begin as soon as you're free?"

"Yes, sir, I can do that."

"Good! Now, you'll have trouble getting a company. No successful actor or actress will leave here to go into enemy territory. Get whomever you can—but secrecy is vital!"

"Yes, sir. But how do I get information back to you?"

"You'll be given very specific instructions, and you'll be contacted by a very good agent." Pinkerton rose, saying, "Be in front of the Capitol tomorrow morning at ten. You'll be contacted, and we'll give you what training we can. I'm grateful you'll be with us, Frank."

When Pinkerton was gone, Frank stared at the table, wordless for once. Tyler clapped a hand on his shoulder. "Well, it beats digging trenches, little brother. But if you get caught, you'll be executed—so be careful!"

Frank looked up and smiled. "It's a little more in my line,

isn't it? I was never a good soldier—like you and Bob, and Dad, of course."

"It's like Pinkerton says, Frank. You might be able to help shorten the war."

Later as Frank made his way to the Steeles' home, he was surprised to discover that the gloomy despair that had oppressed him for days had lifted. He smiled briefly, then murmured, "Well, it looks like I'm going to have to be a pretty good actor. I can't afford to put on a bad performance for the Rebels, or they'll stretch my neck!" He laughed aloud and with a zestful air found himself looking for the adventure that lay ahead of him.

CHAPTER TWELVE
A New Sort of Company

Frank felt constrained to mention his plan to form a repertory company to John Wilkes Booth. The actor stared at him with a gleam of interest, then demanded, "Why to the South? Do your sympathies lie in that direction?"

"Well, Mr. Booth, I have family there, you know, so I am not exactly anti-Southern," Frank said. "But the truth is, I'm not able to compete with you and the other established stars here in the North."

"But can you make a go of it financially? Things are pretty bad there, I understand."

"I'll have to pay short wages, but it'll be good experience. I think I can get some young people who haven't caught on here and maybe a few who are, well, past their best days."

Booth smiled and offered his hand. "I wish you luck. By the way, I have some friends in the profession there. I'll write you a letter of introduction. It'll open a few doors."

"Why, that's generous of you, sir!" Frank shook Booth's hand and went at once to rent a room at Willards Hotel. He placed an advertisement in the paper, then made his way to the Steeles. Finding Bob in the parlor with his uncle, he said, "Well, I'll be out of your way by the end of the week."

"Are you *sure* you want to do this, Frank?" Bob asked. He'd been surprised when Frank had spoken of his new venture, but then so had the Steeles. "Seems to be a pretty risky sort of thing."

Amos nodded, anxiety on his plain face. "I agree with Bob. As I understand it, acting is a pretty precarious sort of life at best, but to go to the South—!"

"Now we've been through all that," Frank said with a polite smile. He'd been reluctant to leave Bob, but he'd seen that Amos and Laura were what he needed. With that settled, he was happy in a way that none of his family could understand—except for his grandfather, Stephen. The old man had grunted, "He's not got all the foolishness knocked out of him yet. Got to let some of that life in him get spent. He'll probably go broke, but he'll have good memories to keep."

Frank said as he studied Bob carefully, "I'll try to get to see Dad. Mother could probably use some help taking care of him."

"Well, that's true," Bob agreed. "I'm hoping he'll be exchanged soon. When do you leave?"

"As soon as I get a company hired." Frank grinned as he added, "I don't have a lot of experience to get in the way. Talk about shoving off to sea in a sieve!" He laughed at his own foolishness, then said, "I'll be staying at Willards until I'm ready to leave. But I'll be by to say good-bye before we shove off."

After Frank left, Amos said in a puzzled tone, "He's changed, Bob. He was pretty low for a while."

Bob said only, "Frank's not like Ty and me. He's got a reckless streak. But I'm glad he's got something to challenge him." He shook his head, adding, "He's never gotten to know God, Uncle Amos. I think he's put that out of his mind."

"Well, God knows all about Frank, as he knows about every man. When he wills it, Frank will get his call."

★ ★ ★

The job of recruiting a company proved to be less difficult than Frank had anticipated. He was somewhat shocked when applicants came thick and fast on the first day. Most of them lost interest when they discovered that the tour would take place in the South, but by the end of the second day, he had five solid volunteers.

One of these was Carmen Montaigne, which both pleased and disturbed him. She had smiled at his protests that the whole thing would probably fold up, saying, "It'll be fun, Frank. We'll smell the magnolias together." He'd warned her about low pay and poor conditions, but she'd leaned against him and put her hand on his cheek. "I'm tired of what I've got here," she murmured. There was a light in her black eyes as she whispered, "We'll go dancing in New Orleans. It's a romantic place, I hear."

The very first volunteer was a young man of seventeen named Albert Deckerman. He had apparently slept outside Frank's room, for when Frank opened the door to go to breakfast, he'd practically stumbled over the boy. Albert had only amateur experience, but he had enough theatrical ambitions for *ten* actors. Albert was thin and had long blond hair, of which he was inordinately proud. He also had a booming voice and was willing to serve as a props man and all-around handyman.

The prize of the company, Frank felt, was the Hardcastles—J. Harold and Elizabeth. They were both in their late fifties, but strong and hale, and they had a wealth of experience. J. Harold was a short, overweight man with thinning gray hair and bright blue eyes. He had a bombastic manner of acting, a fashion out-of-date for thirty years, but he could play any role in the older age category.

Elizabeth Hardcastle was a dignified woman of some fifty-five years. She was thin and alert and had great presence. She had been an actress all her life and said in a regal tone, "We in the theater have a special calling, Mr. Rocklin. We must lift our audience *up*."

Frank was not exactly certain of what that meant, but he was grateful for the Hardcastles.

It was a word from Carmen that gave him another member of the company. "Roland's in jail," she had said grimly. "He publicly insulted the secretary of war. Go pay his fine, Frank. He'll be glad to come with us."

At once Frank had gone to Pinkerton, explained the situation, and on that same day Roland had been released with the condition that he get out of Washington.

Frank had offered him a job, warning him, "It's not going to be easy, Roland. We may be tarred and feathered by those Rebels in Richmond."

But Roland was happy to be out of jail—and glad to have work of any kind. He promised to remain reasonably sober and, as he looked over the script with Frank, beamed as he exclaimed, "We'll have a triumph in the land of cotton, my dear fellow!"

★ ★ ★

Lorna had risen early, determined to find some sort of work. She had her breakfast at the Northern Pride Restaurant, which included one egg, a small portion of fried ham, and biscuits.

Ora Jenkins, the owner, cook, and manager of the Northern Pride, passed by, paused to study the tired expression on the features of the young woman, and said, "I been asking around about some work for you, Miss Lorna. You could get on at the iron factory, but that's too rough for you."

"I'll have to take it, Ora."

Jenkins smiled ruefully, saying, "Well, I'll keep looking around. Something will turn up. Like the fellow in the Bible says, 'I've never seen the righteous forsaken, nor his seed begging bread.'" The thin owner had a Scripture for all occasions. He left Lorna's table, but was back in five minutes holding a paper in his hand. "I'll bet you didn't see this, Miss Lorna," he beamed, handing it to her. "Read that right there!"

Lorna took the paper and read the small advertisement under Jenkins' bony forefinger: "Wanted—actors and actresses willing to travel. Company being formed to leave immediately. Contact Mr. Frank Rocklin, Room 222, Willards Hotel."

"Now, if that ain't the good Lord providing for you, I never seen it!" Jenkins was smiling broadly and added, "Was I you, Miss Lorna, I'd hie myself over without no preliminaries."

"I will, Ora. Thank you!"

Lorna's spirits rose as she walked the five blocks to Willards. *I wonder if Mr. Rocklin will remember me* was the thought that came to her. *I doubt it—he's met a great many actresses.* As she entered the hotel, she was conscious of both hope and nervousness. *I've just got to get on with this company! It's that or go back to England.*

She knocked on the door firmly, and when it opened, she smiled, saying, "Am I too early, Mr. Rocklin?"

"Why, no, of course not!" Frank stepped back, and when she had stepped inside, he asked, "I suppose you've come about the new company?"

"Yes. I'm very much in need of work."

Frank liked her straightforward admission, and he admired her appearance. She was wearing a stylish dress, light blue with white cuffs and collar. She had, he saw at once, the mobile features that were so necessary for anyone in the theater. He started to speak, then hesitated. "Have we met before? You look familiar."

"You have a good memory for faces," Lorna commented. "I came backstage after one of your performances. I was with Mr. Cooper's company."

"Why, yes, of course. You were with the troupe from England as I recall."

"Yes. My name is Lorna Grey."

"Sit down, Miss Grey." Frank waited until she was seated in one of the two chairs in the room, then sat down across from her. He spoke briefly, setting his intentions to take a troupe south, and ended by saying, "It's really a rather risky venture, I'm afraid."

"Because of the war?"

"Well, there's always some danger of being caught in some of that, but I was referring to the professional risks."

"Aren't all plays risky? Most of the companies I've been with haven't made anyone rich. I think it's the nature of the theater."

Frank nodded, pleased by her sharp analysis. "That's true, Miss Grey. And you must understand that I've had almost no experience in this sort of thing. But I think this will be excellent experience." He smiled, his teeth white against his tan, and added with a wry tone, "I think I'm afraid of the competition here in the North. Where we'll be going, the critical response won't be so severe."

"I admire your ingenuity, Mr. Rocklin." Lorna was impressed by Rocklin's dark good looks and wondered how long it would be before he used them on her—if she got the part. "As I said, I must have work. Could I read for you?"

Rocklin knew that he would offer the young woman a place with the company, but decided to make the thing look professional. He rose and picked up a book from the desk, found a page, and handed it to her. "You know this speech from *Romeo and Juliet?*"

Lorna glanced at the page and smiled. Putting the book down, she rose and walked to the window, looking down at the street for a moment. Then she turned and began the familiar speech:

> *"O Romeo, Romeo, wherefore art thou, Romeo?*
> *Deny thy father and refuse thy name,*
> *Or if thou wilt not, be but sworn my love*
> *And I'll no longer be Capulet."*

Frank was highly impressed by the young woman. Her beauty was set off by the pale yellow sunshine that filtered through the window; the bars of light caressed her long honey-blonde hair, giving off faint reddish gleams, and her large gray eyes were lustrous. Her lips were full and well shaped, and there was a regal quality in her bearing that he had rarely seen in a woman.

She ended her speech, saying, "Romeo, doff thy name, and for thy name, which is no part of thee, take all of myself."

Frank at once came to her, smiling and giving Romeo's response. "I take thee at thy word. Call me but love, and I'll be new baptized."

Lorna answered, and the two played out the scene. They made a fine team, which both of them realized, and finally when they reached the end of the scene, Frank cried out, "By heaven, we'll have to do this play together."

Lorna was excited by how well she had done. "Am I accepted then?"

"Accepted?" Frank's eyes glowed with admiration, and he took her hands and held them tightly, "Why, my dear Lorna, you will be a brilliant light in our little company." He was aware of her firm hands in his and released them at once. Smiling ruefully, he said, "I wish the salary were commensurate with your talent, but I'm afraid I can't pay much."

They talked for a time of the terms of her employment; then Frank slapped his hands together, saying with pleasure, "Now, that's settled. I can't tell you how pleased I am to have you with us."

Lorna was feeling lightheaded with relief. Her future had been dim and murky, but now she had a place and something to do. "I'm the one to be grateful, Mr. Rocklin—"

"Frank, if you will."

"Yes, Frank, then." Lorna smiled at him, confessing, "I was in a pretty grim situation. Getting a place with your company is like a gift from heaven." She smiled and her eyes glinted with humor. "You're not an angel in disguise by any chance?"

"After you see me in a few rehearsals, you won't accuse me of anything so nice as that! Many would say I'm rather spoiled." He looked very virile and masculine as he lolled in the chair across from her. "I hope *you're* not spoiled. Two prima donnas is one too many!" The two sat there, each of them feeling very good over finding the other.

"What play will we do first?" Lorna asked finally.

"When we get to New Orleans, we'll do *Romeo and Juliet*," Frank said. "Some of the company were in Mr. Booth's version, and we can cut back—do an abbreviated version. Plenty of Union troops there with Union cash. We can use that!" He rose and picked up a sheaf of papers, then handed it to her. "Here's what we'll do when we're in Confederate territory. It's called *The Return of the Prodigal.*"

"What's it about?"

"It's about the evil Yankees who've come to destroy the South. I play a noble young man who goes wrong, but is brought back to the ways of righteousness—and to a place in the Confederate army—by a beautiful Southern girl—and that's you. There's a villainous Yankee officer, some fond parents, and so on."

"I don't think I know the play."

Frank grinned ruefully. "Not too surprising since I'm writing it myself!"

Lorna looked up, startled. "You're a playwright?"

"No, I'm a desperate amateur manager of a company who needs a surefire success in his first venture." There was a light of humor in Rocklin's eyes, and he suddenly laughed aloud. "I'll probably have us all come out waving Confederate flags and singing 'Dixie'! Anything you can think of to pander to the folks of the Confederacy, don't hold it back, Lorna." He shook his head, saying, "I'm afraid it's not very artistic."

"It'll be fun," Lorna maintained stoutly. She rose, saying, "I'll leave you now." Putting out her hand, she gave him a firm grip, saying seriously, "I'm not a very religious person, but the owner of the Northern Pride Restaurant told me that God worked in getting me this job. I'm very grateful to God and to you, Mr. Rocklin."

"We'll be good for each other, and hopefully it'll be some

fun, as you say." He reluctantly released her hand, saying, "Can you leave on short notice?"

"I can go *today.*"

"Well, not *that* short! But possibly tomorrow." A thought came to him, and he asked, "Are you married—or anything?"

Lorna's lips curled upward in an amused smile. "I don't know what *anything* means to you, but I'm not married."

When Lorna left the room, Frank moved to the window and watched until she emerged from the hotel. He followed her with his eyes until she moved out of his sight, then clapped his hands together with a sharp gesture, exclaiming, "Well, now, *that's* a stroke of luck." He was excited by the addition of a capable actress and walked around the floor making plans. "We can do *Romeo and Juliet,*" he muttered under his breath. "She's a lovely woman, and she's not married—or *anything!*"

He thought of what she'd said about God being in her coming to him, and grew sober. *If she knew what this thing was all about, she wouldn't be so quick to bring God into it!*

The thought depressed him, and he sat down and wrote for some time, making the arrangements for the tour. Finally he stopped and looked at the wall blankly. He was a little astonished to find that much of the bitterness that had driven him into this venture had left him. *I'm still going through with it, but I don't feel all the anger that I did for a while after Bob got hurt. I wonder why that is.*

He had no answers, and finally went back to his papers. A thought came to him even as he wrote: *She's a beautiful Juliet! I'd like to do that play with her.*

PART THREE
The Company
AUGUST–OCTOBER 1863

CHAPTER THIRTEEN
Under Southern Skies

Dark, rolling clouds obscured the skies as the *Saratoga* plowed through the choppy waters. Lorna drew her coat more closely about her and peered to her right seeking for a sight of land, but found none. The iron-gray August heavens were bleak and cheerless. Far off in the distance, she knew, lay the sunny climes of Florida and the Gulf of Mexico. But now the sharp tang of the Atlantic breeze bit at her face, causing her to shiver slightly. Shoving her hands in her pockets, she thought almost longingly of England, but quickly drove those thoughts out of her mind.

"I've made up my mind," she murmured, a look of defiance in her eyes. "There's no turning back. I should have found that out by this time." She was interrupted when someone called her name, and she turned quickly to find Frank Rocklin approaching her. He was wearing a pair of light-gray trousers and a loosely cut blue frock coat. The wind ruffled his dark hair, and as he approached he tried to smooth it with his hand. "Cold out here. Hard to believe it's still summer. It'll be warmer if the sun comes out, though." Leaning on the rail, he peered out into the foggy outlines of the sea, then shook his head. "I don't like ships much. It's too far to swim home." He turned to face her, and his broad lips broke into a smile. "If a horse goes lame or the wagon wheel rolls off, you can always walk home. Not out here, though."

"How far are we from New Orleans?"

Rocklin considered her question, then shook his head. "I don't really know," he admitted. "It's somewhere around five days to a week, the captain says." He shook his shoulders together and said, "We've been invited to eat at Capt. Woods's table. Are you hungry?"

"Yes, I am." Lorna turned from the rail and matched her steps to his as they walked down the deck. "Does Elizabeth feel any better?"

"I don't think so. Seasickness is a pretty bad thing."

Elizabeth Hardcastle had gotten sick almost the moment the company had come onboard the *Saratoga*. Even when the ship was as steady as a house, the aging actress had begun to turn pale. And when the ship had drawn anchor then plunged out into the stream with a sharp dipping motion, she had gone abruptly to her cabin. Thinking about her, Rocklin shook his head. "I had a friend once that made the crossing to England. He was sick all the way over and all the way back. Said it was the worst thing that ever happened to him." A thought struck him as the ship bucked slightly, catching a broadside wave. He took her arm and held her until it settled down, then released it. "He said for a while he was afraid he was going to die." His eyelids came together with a hint of humor as he added, "And then he said after a while he was afraid he *wasn't* going to die."

Lorna smiled faintly. "I had just a touch of it on my way over from London," she said. "It didn't last long, but it's very bad." She stepped through the door, and the two of them walked down the corridor to the dining room.

The *Saratoga* was a combination cargo ship and passenger vessel, a little less of the latter. Some of the space had been carved up into cabins, and the dining room was fairly large for the twenty-five or so passengers that had gathered there. She might have been a fancy ship at one time, but age and smoke and hard wear had worn off whatever elegance she had once possessed. "The captain's waiting for us," Rocklin said, and the two of them approached the table. Frank pulled out Lorna's chair, and after she was seated he sat down between her and Roland Middleton. Albert Deckerman was flanked by Middleton and Carmen. There was a certain sickish look about Middleton's face, and Lorna suspected it was because he had been drinking.

"Well, it's good to have acting folks on board," Capt. Leonard Woods said. He was a tall, broad man of fifty-five with pearly white hair that was always exceptionally clean. His blue eyes were almost hidden by the wrinkles after a lifetime of staring into the sun reflecting off the ocean. He looked around the table and smiled. "I don't suppose any of you ever crossed the equator?" When no one responded, he shook his head. "That's a pity. Now there's a voyage for you. No piddling around on these little creeks or rivers or in the blasted Gulf Stream!" He waved his fork around with violent gestures as the steward began to serve them. "Pitch in," he commanded brusquely. "We don't have fancy cabins, but we do have good grub."

Frank had been somewhat surprised to find out that the food on board the *Saratoga* was good. He had discovered that Capt. Woods demanded the best on his table and had imported his own Chinese cook, whose wages he supplemented out of his own pocket for a special fare.

"How is your wife doing, Mr. Hardcastle?" Lorna inquired.

Hardcastle shook his head mournfully. "Not at all well, I'm afraid. She's no sailor." He plunged into his food, eating heartily. He was a man with a big appetite, Lorna had already discovered. As he put the food away, she was aware that he was one of those men who can never say no to any kind of food.

The talk ran around the table for some time, and finally Carmen asked, "Do you think we'll have a good run in New Orleans, Frank?"

"Not sure." Frank shrugged. He looked at the captain

and asked, "What's it like in New Orleans, now that the Union army's taken over?"

"Lots of tension," Capt. Woods said. He turned to the first mate, Charles Hardin, a tall, dark man of twenty-eight. "What was that that you found out about Butler last time we hit port there?"

Hardin had been lifting a glass to his lips. He put it down and said with a grin, "Well, the ladies of New Orleans have been rather arrogant, I'm afraid. They treated some of the Union officers with disrespect." He glanced over at Carmen and smiled. "Some of them even spit on him, so I understand. Not very ladylike, but feeling is strong in New Orleans. Anyway, it got Gen. Butler a new nickname." He picked up the water again, sipped it and, when he put it down, added, "They call him 'Beast' Butler now. He gave an order that any woman who insulted a Union officer would be arrested and jailed as a prostitute."

Frank stared at him. "That's pretty strong medicine!" he exclaimed. "I wouldn't think he could get by with that."

"Butler can get by with about anything, sir," Capt. Woods said. "He's a pretty sorry general from a military standpoint, but he knows how to bring the votes in. Lincoln knows he's going to have to run for reelection, so I guess the Union army will have Butler on its hands as long as this war lasts."

The talk ran around the table, and Lorna found herself enjoying the conversation. Both Woods and Hardin had traveled widely, and the two entertained them with stories of their voyages over the past several years. When the meal was over, Lorna excused herself and went to her room. The ship began pitching slightly as the weather grew worse, but after a while it seemed to go calm again. For a time she sat down and studied the script of the play that they were to do in Richmond, *The Return of the Prodigal,* and agreed that it would appeal to the emotions of the Southern people. It was a thriller about a young man who had joined the Confederate army, a romantic sort of play that was not to her liking. Then she turned to the abbreviated version of *Romeo and*

Juliet that they would perform in New Orleans. Lorna was cast as Juliet, and Carmen was assigned the part of the nurse. Soon she put it aside and lay down. Ordinarily the rocking of the ship would have put her to sleep, but sleep eluded her. She heard bells ring from time to time and slept a little, but finally was glad when she awoke and saw the beginning of a gray dawn out of the window. Quickly she rolled out of bed, washed her face and hands, dressed, then sat down and did her hair. When she left the cabin and made her way along the rail, she saw a solitary figure and identified Roland Middleton. Stopping beside him, she said, "Good morning! You're up early."

Middleton turned at once to face her. He was wearing a rather disreputable brown jacket and a soft felt hat pulled down low over his brow. "Couldn't sleep," he muttered. "Never did like ships."

"Shall we go down and get some breakfast?"

"After a while, I suppose." He turned to her and studied her carefully. He was somewhat of a connoisseur of women, and he admired the well-made structure of her oval-shaped face. There was a liveliness in her gray eyes, although now they seemed a little clouded with some sort of troubled thought. "How do you like it here in the States?" he asked finally.

Lorna shrugged slightly. "All places are about alike, aren't they?"

Middleton was caught by her answer. He traced the iron rail with one long forefinger, thought about what she had said, and finally stated, "That's for an old cynic like me to say, not a good-looking young woman like you."

Lorna's lips curled up into a smile at his distinction between them. "Men and women are about alike, aren't they, in some ways?"

At once Roland shook his head. "Now that's where you're wrong. All places may be alike, at least to some of us, but men and women are no more alike than . . ." He hesitated, searching for a simile. "They're no more alike than birds are

159

like turtles." He laughed at his own inept phrasing. "Not very well said, but you know what I mean."

He stood there awhile, and the two of them spoke of the trip. Middleton had found that she was a sensible young woman, but sensed that there was something unpleasant in her past. It had brought the serious look that so often came to her face and was reflected in her wide-spaced eyes. Finally he murmured, "It's odd what you said about one place being like another." He looked out over the iron-gray ocean that seemed to crawl under the dim light of the feeble sun, moving in an undulant fashion as far as the eye could follow it. "A little bit like this ocean—no trees, no mountains, no rivers." He waved his arms, saying, "It's all just alike, isn't it? If we stopped right here, it'd be just like stopping where we'll be two hours from now. And that's the way life is. Doesn't matter whether I'm in Washington, Chicago, or New Orleans. Scenes change a little, but they're all pretty much alike."

Lorna was interested in Middleton. Despite his dissipation and the thin strain of cynicism that lurked beneath his manners, she had found him to be a sensitive man and able to laugh at his own weaknesses. "I'm not sure it's really that way," she finally admitted. "I think we carry our own places about inside of us." She glanced up at the sky, where the last flickering stars were still barely visible through the broken cloud cover over to her left, before saying, "They say those stars are a million miles apart." For a moment she hesitated, then reached up and tucked a strand of her hair under the hat that she had pinned on. "It scares some people to think about all that empty space, but it doesn't frighten me. I think we have it in ourselves—empty places, I mean—far more frightening than anything up there."

Once again, Middleton was intrigued. "You're not old enough to think thoughts like that," he protested. "Have you had an unhappy life?" he inquired.

"No worse than some." The answer was clipped short, and Roland almost felt she had hung a Do Not Disturb sign over her past. He said nothing for a while, then finally she asked him about his own life. Roland began to speak slowly. They were alone, and he was lonely. He began to speak of places he had been and things he had done. He spoke about his childhood briefly, which had not been unhappy. Finally he shrugged. "I'm afraid I have no excuse for being the miserable company that I am. My family was good. I can't blame them for what I've become—a drunk."

Lorna was shocked at the depth of self-loathing that had suddenly leaped into Middleton's tone. Looking at him quickly, she saw it was reflected in his face. His lips were drawn into a bitter line, and there was a dim hopelessness etched over his features. Without thinking she put her hand on his arm, saying, "I'm sorry. I didn't mean to pry."

"You didn't. I don't often talk like this, though," he said. "Might as well tell it all." He turned once again to stare out bleakly over the sea and let the moment run on. Finally he said, "I had great hopes once. I have some talent. Not very easy to see it since I'm drunk most of the time. But I could've been more than I am on the stage."

"Why didn't you?" Lorna asked quietly.

"I knew a woman once. I thought the sun rose in her. I had heard before of those loves when someone became more than food or drink or even air. Didn't think it existed, though, until I met her."

When he said no more, Lorna asked quietly, "You lost her, did you, Roland?"

"Someone took her away—I lost her—in any case she's gone now." He turned and said, "Now, Lorna, *please* don't tell me there are other women in the world! I've said all that to myself a million times. I'm just a weak character."

The waves made a chafing sound as they slapped against the side of the iron hull of the *Saratoga*. The breaking whitecaps made startling flashes ahead as the prow of the ship dipped into the ocean, breaking the gray waters into flashing bits of froth. Lorna said slowly, "I know something about that." Her voice was quiet, but there was a tone in it that drew his gaze. "I've been disappointed, too, in love."

When she said no more, Middleton felt a sense of kinship with her. He did not ask any questions as the two of them stood there alone. Tentatively he put his hand on her shoulder and squeezed it. "We're two of a kind, Lorna. But you're young. You'll find somebody."

His words brought her eyes up, and she shook her head suddenly. "I guess I'm like you, Roland. I'm just not looking for anybody. Not anymore."

★ ★ ★

"This sun feels so good, doesn't it, Frank?"

Carmen and Rocklin had been walking around the deck after the noon meal. The days had grown steadily warmer and the bad weather had blown itself out. As they rounded the Florida peninsula the sun shone brightly. The blue-green waters of the gulf seemed to flicker with millions of tiny lights. The *Saratoga* had picked up speed and was now headed across the gulf in the direction of New Orleans.

"It beats what we've had, doesn't it?" Frank observed. He took a deep breath and enjoyed the salty tang of the air. Though the breeze was sharp, it was not like the northern breeze they had left. "Let's go back to the stern. Some of the sailors have put out lines. Maybe they'll catch something."

"All right." Carmen was happy as they walked along. She had shed her heavy clothes for a lightweight cotton dress that was an odd shade of bluish green. The wind flattened it against her figure, and her black hair was disturbed by the stiff wind. When they arrived at the fantail, they sat down and watched as one of the sailors, an older hand who smoked a pipe, watched over several lines tossed over the rail. He gave them a curious glance, but said nothing. Finally one of the lines made a *thunking* sound, and he leaped to his feet.

"What is it?" Carmen asked with excitement.

"Don't know, miss." The sailor shook his head. He picked

up the line and gave it a tentative pull. The muscles in his arm kinked, and the line hardly gave at all. "It's a big 'un," he said with satisfaction. "Maybe a marlin. Most likely a shark, though."

Frank and Carmen watched with excitement as the sailor worked the fish in. The *Saratoga* was making at least twelve or fourteen knots, and whatever the sailor had hooked had that much going for him. Hand over hand, the sailor would haul for a while, then lean down, bracing the rope against the rail to rest his arms.

"Can I give you a hand?" Frank asked with excitement.

"Why, it's hard work, sir."

"Always liked to fish. Never caught anything that big, whatever it is," Frank said. Moving over, he reached out and grasped the line with both hands and hauled back. A look of surprise spread across his features. He considered himself a fairly strong man, but discovered that he could not do with both hands what the sailor could do with one!

Carmen caught his expression and laughed. "Come on, Frank! Let's see you haul him in. You've seen how it's done."

A look of chagrin crossed his features. Frank gritted his teeth and began to pull at the line. He did succeed in making some progress, but the sailor said, "Here, sir. You ain't got the hard hands for this. You'd better let me do it."

Frank surrendered the line and looked down at his palms, which indeed were rubbed raw. He stood there glaring at them, then forced a smile. "Every man to his trade, I suppose."

The two watched and finally they could see a long, slim body trailing twenty feet behind the ship. "What is it?" Frank demanded.

"Shark," the sailor said quickly. He lifted his voice and cried with a stentorian voice, "Hey, Charlie! Come—get a couple of hands. Let's haul this fellow onboard."

Twenty minutes later, after a tremendous struggle, Frank and Carmen stood looking at the monstrous beast that was flopping on the deck. One of the sailors took an ax and hit him on top of the head, but it made no difference. "That's a tiger shark," the older sailor observed. He looked at the great length, torpedo-shaped, and then at the row of enormous white teeth spread into a grin. "Could take your leg right off, that fellow could."

"Is he dead?" Carmen asked.

"Dead! Well, bless you. No, miss. Why, you could cut his head off, and twenty-four hours later I would vow he could still bite you."

"Just like a snapping turtle," Frank said. "What will you do with him?"

"Nothing much. Not fit to eat. They get hunted for their livers, though."

Carmen and Frank watched as the sailors got the enormous hook out of the jaws of the shark and flipped him overboard. "Will he live?" Carmen asked.

"Them fellows are mighty tough," the sailor said. He baited the hook, threw it back over, and shook his head. "Ain't good for nothing, them things aren't. Now if it was a big king mackerel, marlin, or a sailfish, then we'd have something to eat. Don't know why God made things like that."

As Frank walked away, he observed, "I've wondered the same thing about mosquitoes and bugs like that. Why does God make them?"

Carmen looked at him curiously. She said nothing about that, but looked around and said, "This is fun, isn't it, Frank? I wish we didn't ever have to get to New Orleans."

He laughed at her. "It'd be a long trip. I think we'd get bored with it. No, I like to get places."

Frank kept a sharp eye on the troupe now that they were approaching New Orleans. They had had plenty of time for rehearsal, and that night he persuaded Capt. Woods to let them have the dining room to run through it. They all worked hard moving the tables and chairs out of the way, then running through the play, stopping to work on the more difficult scenes. Albert Deckerman, as usual, over-played his part. He could not speak, it seemed, without waving his arms around, and once Frank said in disgust, "Albert, you don't talk with your arms. You talk with your mouth."

"Why, I've seen Mr. Booth. He waved his arms around something fierce," he protested.

Frank would not criticize another actor, but he said, "Never mind Mr. Booth. I'm going to fix you, Albert."

"What are you going to do?" Albert asked, his eyes growing large. He quickly found out, for Frank procured a length of line from a sailor and tied Albert's hands to his sides. The effect was ludicrous. As they ran through the play Albert would open his mouth, but nothing would come out. This was hilarious to all the members of the company, and finally Lorna begged, "Don't be mean, Frank. Let him move his arms around if he wants to."

"Well, all right. I guess one of these days he'll just fly off, but looks like that's the way it'll have to be."

After the rehearsal they all had a cup of tea while they talked about what was to come. Elizabeth Hardcastle was much better, although still pale from her ordeal with seasickness. "I'll be glad when we get off this boat," she said. "I'll never get on another one."

"Now, my dear, don't say that," her husband said. J. Harold leaned over and patted her fondly on the shoulder. There was a loving relationship between the two that everyone noted. Neither of them had ever achieved any fame, but you would never know it to listen to them talk.

Later, when everyone had broken up to go to their cabins, Carmen and Frank stayed to clean up. "That's sweet, the way the Hardcastles love each other," Carmen said.

"Yes, it is. Something you don't see too often."

They worked together, speaking from time to time, then he said, "I'll take you to your cabin."

When they were outside, Carmen walked slowly with him till they reached her door. But instead of going in, she turned and went to the rail. He joined her, and the two stared out at the waters. The engines of the *Saratoga* were throbbing, and the boat moved swiftly through the waters. The moon was up and made a long, inverted V-shape. "The Vikings called that path of light the Whales' Way," Frank observed.

Carmen turned to him. "How'd you know that?" she asked in surprise.

"Part of my useless education," Frank laughed. He thought about it for a moment and said, "I had a friend who loved to read about the old Vikings. He told me, I think."

"Tell me about the Vikings."

For a while Frank stood there speaking quietly, feeling the ship quiver beneath his feet. She seemed interested and Frank finally said, "They had a pretty hard life, those Vikings, as I recall. Very short lives, most of them. Either killed in battle or by disease."

"I guess all of us have short lives compared to those up there." Carmen waved her hand at the stars. "I wonder how long they've been there?" She seemed preoccupied and said, "Tell me some more about the Vikings."

"One thing I always will remember about them, it's kind of sad," Frank said. He stroked his jaw thoughtfully, letting the memory come back. "My friend said their idea of what this life is like is strange. He said one of their poets said that life is like a bird coming out of a raging storm, beat and about dead. This bird flies into a nice warm building where there's heat, light, and peace. He gets his feathers all dry, and no sooner is he all over the storm, he flies out into the storm again." Frank leaned on the rail, stared down, and said thoughtfully, "He said that's what the Vikings thought life was—coming out of nothingness into a warm place where there's a little joy, a little fun, and a little light, and then flying out again into cold nothingness."

"Is that what you believe?" Carmen asked soberly.

Frank turned to her, his face serious. There was a steadiness in him that she admired, a rocklike quality that she had not found in many men. "No, I don't believe that," he said.

"What do you believe?"

"I believe the Bible," he said, then added quickly, "Believe it, but don't do it. At least not much."

"I don't know much about God," Carmen said, a sad note in her voice.

Frank looked at her. In the light of the moon, her face seemed to glow. He was curious about her and asked abruptly, "Were you ever married?"

"No."

"Ever engaged?"

She turned to him and lifted her face. "I never found a good man." She was studying him carefully, then her hands went up. They came to rest on his chest and she repeated, "I never found a good man, Frank."

He reached out and pulled her toward him. Her arms went around his neck, and when he lowered his head and kissed her, she met him fully. There was an urgency in her that shocked him. He realized that this was a lonely woman, despite the fact that she had known men. He knew from her statement that she had been disappointed. Her lips were soft under his and returned his pressure. As her body leaned against him there was both a tenseness and a surrender. She was a woman who had led an adventurous life but had never found what she was looking for. All of this came through to him as they clung to one another. Then she pulled her head back and put her hands on his chest. Her lips trembled and she whispered, "Good night, Frank. Don't think bad of me."

"No, I won't," he murmured. But she had turned and stepped inside her cabin. When she was inside, she shut the door and leaned back against it. She bowed her head and for some inexplicable reason tears came to her eyes. She had tasted life and its pleasures and found it to be bitter. Now there was a hope in her. It was like a light that someone sees far, far down a dark, dangerous road. Only a faint light, but it was more than she had had in a long time. Slowly she moved across the tiny cabin, got undressed, and finally lay down on her bunk. She thought of the kiss and knew that it would not leave her mind. Then she whispered, "He's different from most men." The thought seemed to comfort her, and she let her mind run over the times they'd had together, until finally she dropped off to sleep.

★ ★ ★

New Orleans was a beehive of activity. As Frank made his way down the gangplank, his ears were assailed by the polyglot of sound. There were cries of the sailors who were engaged in docking ships, captains screaming at mates, and mates shouting harshly at the hands.

When all the members were on solid ground, they heard the soft sound of French coming like a layer over them. Most of the deckhands seemed to be dark-skinned men with very white teeth. Not black slaves, but Cajuns, as they found out later. Frank and Middleton worked together to get the luggage separated and finally, along with Albert's help, they managed to get it into two carriages.

"You know a good, cheap hotel?" Frank asked the carriage driver.

"Sure, I know a good one, me." The driver was a swarthy man with a patch over one eye. He looked suspiciously like a pirate, but he turned out to be fairly reliable. He located a reasonable hotel not far from the French Quarter. When he had gotten all their bags inside, he said, "You going to like it here, I'm telling you. This hotel, my uncle, he owns half of it. I get you a special rate."

Frank tipped him liberally, and then the members of the cast went to their rooms, tired from their voyage. By the time the day had ended, Frank had found a local building that had been used as a theater but now was vacant. When he got back he said, "Well, we're ready for tomorrow. I've had posters put up all over town, so we'll see what kind of actors we are."

The next night they did *Romeo and Juliet* and, surprisingly, received a standing ovation. The audience was a mixture of Union soldiers and native-born citizens of New Orleans, with a dash of foreign sailors from other ports.

After the theater was cleared, Frank said, "Well, they're easy to please." There was a roguish grin on his face and he shook his head. "I thought we pretty much made a hash out of it."

J. Harold Hardcastle cried out, "Not at all, sir! Not at all! First nights always seem like that." He fondly put his hand on his wife's shoulder and said, "Your performance was beyond anything I've ever seen, my dear."

"Thank you, Harold. As for you, the crowned heads of Europe would be privileged to see such a performance as you gave tonight."

Carmen was standing close to Lorna. "You did very well, Lorna," she said. "I wish I had an English accent."

Lorna smiled. "I just hope I can remember to change to a Southern accent when we go to Richmond."

Albert Deckerman had played the role of Mercutio and was highly satisfied with himself. "Did you hear the applause when I gave my best speech?" he asked. His thin, lank, blond hair fell from beneath his cap. He had a wonderful voice, and Frank thought that it was a shame the young man's acting wasn't as good. "Wait till tomorrow. We'll show them what acting is!"

"Well, we've got a couple weeks here, then we'll be moving to Richmond," Frank said. He looked around the circle. "I don't see much point in rehearsing. I think they'd applaud if we had stood on our heads."

"The best kind of audience imaginable," Roland said. He had played the role of Tybalt and done the sword duel with a minimum of complaint. "But I'll be happy to survive these blasted sword fights. Don't you think we might use pistols instead, Frank? A bit out of time, but more comfortable!"

They played New Orleans for two weeks, leaving the Crescent City on the tenth of September. As they boarded the train for Richmond, Middleton had a worried look. "Somehow I feel a little bit strange, a Yankee like me roaming the South. Does it bother you, Frank?"

Frank thought of his real purpose in going to Richmond. He thought, *If you only knew why we're really going, you would be upset!* But he only said briefly, "Nobody takes actors seriously. They don't think we have any politics."

As the train rattled over the rails headed north, Frank couldn't help thinking, *One false slip and I could be hanged. I wouldn't mind being shot in a battle, but I can't think of anything worse than dying like that!*

CHAPTER FOURTEEN
An Officer, But No Gentleman

The travel from New Orleans to Richmond was difficult. It meant moving from Union-held territory into the heart of the Confederacy. The acting troupe, however, had less trouble than most. Several times they were eyed sharply by what appeared to be those in charge of the train, sometimes military officers and sometimes the crewmen, but no one questioned them. They were forced to change trains several times. The North had a fine system of railroads—a network that covered practically the entire area. The South, however, had only bits and pieces of small roads. Some of them didn't even use the same gauge of tracks. In addition to this, the Union army nibbled away at the rail system so that in one month the Confederacy might have a particular line but, after being forced back, would have to reroute all traffic on a completely different system.

"I really don't see how these people keep up the battle," Frank murmured. He was sitting by Middleton, and the two men were staring out the window. They passed through part of the war-torn countryside where the battles had raged in previous months. The train clanked and rattled and had already stopped four times for what seemed to be major repairs.

Middleton looked out at the beautiful countryside. The

hardwoods were beginning to turn scarlet, brown, and gold. "Reminds me of home," he said.

"Where's that, originally?" Frank inquired.

"New Hampshire."

"Ever get back there?"

"No, there's nothing to go back to. Family's pretty well given up on me," Middleton observed. He seemingly cared little for discussion of his past. As the train clicked over the joints of the rails, he began to speak of the company. "Do you really think this run will be successful, Frank?" he asked.

"I don't know. I wanted to try it though."

"Why the South?" Middleton inquired. He raised one eyebrow and shrugged his shoulders. "From what I hear, the country's broke—Confederate money's not worth the paper it's printed on even now. If I wanted to take a troupe somewhere, it wouldn't be here."

It was the kind of question that Rocklin tried to avoid. "I don't know, Roland," he said uncomfortably. "My roots are here, in a way. My great-grandfather built a plantation in the middle of Virginia. Some of our people are still there. There're some Rocklins fighting right now against the Union." He stared out the window and thought about the situation, then shrugged, saying, "There's no use thinking about this. Anyway, I just thought this would be a good time to break in a company. If the South is as broke as everybody says and they're as sick of war, any play will be a hit. Time to sharpen up our skills; then we can go back to the North and put it on the road."

The train finally limped into Richmond after what seemed to be an interminable journey. When the passengers disembarked, once again there was a scuffle for baggage. Middleton found a man with a wagon who agreed to take their luggage to the Spotswood Hotel. "They say it's the best," he advised Frank. "It might be expensive, but Union money will buy anything, I suppose."

Middleton proved to be correct. The clerk's eyes widened when Frank paid for the rooms for a week with gold coins.

He picked one of the coins up almost reverently, weighed it in his hand, and then shook his head. "Don't see too many of these, Mr. Rocklin. We're glad to have you staying with us."

"Glad to be here. I have some people in this part of the world. I don't suppose you know any of them? Clay Rocklin, perhaps?"

The clerk's eyes opened wide. "Why, certainly, sir. Mr. Clay stays in this hotel often when he's in town. Of course, I think he's out with his command now."

The accommodations were rather crowded. Richmond was a seething mass of people, as they soon discovered. It was the center of the Confederacy in more ways than one. For one thing, it housed many factories, most of them small, but the Tredegar Iron Works employed a host of people. It was practically the only foundry in the whole Confederacy capable of producing cannons and rifles.

The streets themselves were filled with soldiers, tradesmen, and workers on their way to the various factories. Frank, on his first foray into the city, found some difficulty in obtaining a place to stage the play, despite the contacts he'd gotten from Booth. He tried first to find an empty building and, seeing none that would answer, in desperation asked for the office of the mayor.

"Mayor Johnson, that'll be," answered a tall man with a stovepipe hat. "Right over there, sir. You'll find him on the second floor."

The building housed the mayor's office over the courtroom. Frank, as he passed through, noticed that the courtroom was filled to overflowing. "What's the trial?" he asked one of the clerks who was hurrying along.

"Big murder case. Clifford Haynes shot his wife's lover. He won't be convicted, though," he said confidently. "It'd be hard to convict a million dollars, and that's about what he's got, I guess."

Rocklin managed a grin at this bit of worldly sophistication, then inquired about the mayor's office. Following the clerk's instructions, he climbed a steep stairway, but he found Mayor Johnson a hard man to see. The office was full of applicants, but Frank managed to cut through them by leaning over and whispering confidentially to the clerk, "I have a proposition that might be financially enticing to the mayor."

The clerk peered up at him from under bushy eyebrows. "Financially enticing, is it? Well, I'll see what I can do."

Five minutes later, Frank was in the mayor's office, having found that in Richmond money talked, as it did elsewhere. "I'm looking for a place to put on an extended theatrical production," he said. He had worn his most expensive suit, a fawn-colored pair of trousers, a brown frock coat with a white ruffled shirt, and a pair of shiny black boots. "My company and I have just returned from a triumphant tour in Europe," he lied blatantly. "We decided that the South deserves the best in art, Mr. Johnson. But I'm a stranger here, so could you perhaps advise me about a theater?"

Cletus Johnson could indeed. "As it so happens," he said, "I'm part owner of a building that could easily be converted to a theater. I would be happy to work out any details with you—Mr. Rocklin, is it? Any relation to the Rocklins at Gracefield?"

"Yes, indeed. Clay Rocklin is my uncle," he said at once. He understood instantly that identifying himself with the Rocklins at Gracefield or any of the relatives in Richmond removed all suspicion and most questions about why he was in the South. "I understand that Uncle Clay is on duty right now, but I hope to see him during our stay."

Johnson called his clerk, gave him some rapid instructions, and then shook hands firmly with Frank. "We'll work out an arrangement, I'm sure, and you can expect to see me on opening night. What play will you be doing?"

"*The Return of the Prodigal* is the name of it," Frank said. "It's about a young Southern boy who flees his responsibility to the Confederacy and later comes to his senses and becomes a hero to the cause."

"Fine! Fine!" Johnson said. "I'm certain you'll have a good audience."

Frank spent the rest of the afternoon with business matters. He discovered that having posters printed was somewhat difficult. Paper was becoming more and more scarce in the Confederacy all the time. The printer finally said, "I have some wallpaper here. I could use the backside of it. Will that do?"

"Excellent! Just so the print's big enough and it gets posted. When can I come back for them, sir?" He made the arrangements with the printer and spent the rest of the afternoon scraping together enough chairs for the theater, which was in effect a barn that had been converted into more or less of a meetinghouse. He found it necessary to hire a carpenter to put up a stage. By the time he had rounded up enough material for a curtain and engaged a seamstress to put it together, darkness was beginning to fall.

When he got back to the hotel, he found the others waiting. "Let's go have dinner," he said, "and I'll tell you what I've done."

Dinner in the Spotswood restaurant was a pleasant enough experience. The room was crowded, mostly with officers and their ladies, and also with black-coated businessmen. The main dish was chicken—as well as the secondary dish. "This war's hard on chickens," Middleton remarked, holding up a crusty fried leg. "I must say, they do know how to fry chicken here in the South."

"That's right," Albert Deckerman replied in his booming voice. "I always said you can't fry chicken north of St. Louis. Something happens to it. It's in the air, I reckon."

Lorna laughed and bit into the chicken carefully. "We don't have anything like this in England," she said. "We always bake it or broil it there."

Carmen studied the fare and said, "I should tell you about some of the meals I've had and some of the out-of-the-way places I've been. This is heaven compared to that."

As they were eating, Frank described what he had done

and finally shook his head. "We're set to go on day after tomorrow night. I think the stage, the seats, and the curtain will all be finished." He shook his head dolefully. "It's not Ford's Theater," he said. "It's frontier style."

"I've played in a few of those," Roland said. "A small place, I suppose?"

"Yes, not too large."

"I thought so," Roland said. "The thing about that is the audience is right up in your face. If they don't like you, you don't have to wonder about it." He grimaced, his face twisting into a wry smile. "I hope they don't bring rotten tomatoes. They know we're Yankees."

"Not possible, sir!" J. Harold Hardcastle pounded on the table. "Audiences understand that the actor is not to be confused with the role he plays. I'm not a supporter of the Confederacy, but an artist must subdue his natural tendencies." He began to speak rapidly, saying, "After all, when an actor plays Hamlet he doesn't have to be a prince, he just has to pretend to be a prince. When he plays Macbeth, he doesn't have to be a murderer filled up with ambition. That would be most retrograde!"

"You don't think it would help to be a murderer to play a murderer?" Lorna asked, amused at the older man's insistence.

"Why, indeed not! That is the essence of our art, to seem to be that which we are not."

"Then I reckon that most of the world could be actors and actresses," Middleton said, "because most people pretend to be what they're not. What's the difference between us then, Mr. Hardcastle?"

"We get paid for it," Albert Deckerman boomed out and laughed at his own joke.

Frank was amused by Hardcastle's definitions, yet grew serious. "I've wondered a lot about acting," he said. "Why is it that people like to see plays? It's not real."

Middleton said at once, "Neither is a painting real. You know it's on a flat surface—that those mountains don't have any curves or bumps—but we like to see a painting, especially of places we've been to, that we know. We're just made so that we enjoy that sort of thing."

"I think drama does that when it's good," Lorna observed. "Was it Dr. Johnson that said, 'Shakespeare holds the mirror up to life'? When we see someone in a play, if they do it well, we're reminded of what we are. That's what drama is, I think. To show us what life is really like."

Carmen was listening to all this very carefully. "I never thought of it like that," she said. "I just thought it was for amusement."

"Well, it has to be that," Frank said. "Nobody's going to come see a play unless they're amused. But I think Lorna's right. There's something about a play that catches us. Why, there's something in the Bible about drama."

Middleton was interested, as well as the others. "What do you mean by that, Frank?" he asked. "I wasn't aware that there was drama in the Bible."

"Well, not drama actually. But do you remember in the Old Testament when David committed his great sin? Somehow he didn't seem to know it. He fell in love with Bathsheba, and after she was with child, he had her husband killed so he could marry her." Frank was caught up in his explanation, his dark eyes intent as they swept the table. "Then the prophet Nathan came to him. Do you remember what he did?"

"What was it?" Middleton inquired when no one spoke up.

"Why, he told a story, which is a form of drama," Frank explained. "He told about a man that had one little lamb that was like a member of his family. He'd carry it around because it was very special to him, and he'd feed him from his own table. Then there was a rich man who had thousands of lambs. He saw that one little lamb that the poor man had and took it from him."

"How awful!" Carmen said, her eyes flashing.

"That's what David said," Frank continued. "He said,

'Who has done this deed will die for it.' I can't quote it exactly," he said. "But he intended on having that fellow's hide, and that's when the prophet looked right at him and said, 'Thou art the man!' It hit David like a ton of bricks," Frank observed. "As soon as he heard those words, he saw himself for what he was. So, the prophet used drama, in effect, to show David what he'd actually done. That little story—a drama if you like—made his crime come alive for him."

"Well, I didn't know I was quite as noble as all that," Carmen laughed. "I'll be asking for a raise now that I know what my profession really is."

Frank laughed at her. "I'm not interested in nobility right now, Carmen. If we can just keep these Rebs amused and entertained and make a little money, that's enough for me."

Frank rose early the next morning and set out to find his mother. When he walked into her hotel room, she was as surprised as he'd ever seen her. "Why, Frank! What are you doing here?" she demanded.

"Right now, I've come to take you to breakfast," he said with a grin, squeezing her tightly. "After that, I want to go visit Dad. Come along." He took her to a restaurant, and she listened intently as he told her of his new profession. She was surprised, of course, but said only, "I hope you succeed, Frank." After breakfast, they went to Libby prison, where Frank was finally admitted after some difficulty. When they entered the huge open room, his mother led him to the section beside a high window. Gideon stood up at once, shock in his eyes. "Why, Frank!" he exclaimed.

Frank embraced his father, shocked at how pale and wan he seemed. The wound he'd taken at Gettysburg had sapped his strength, and there was little of the vigor of the man he'd last seen. After a quick explanation of why Frank was in the South, Gideon said, "Tell me about Bob."

It was a difficult time for Frank, but he concealed his bitterness and gave them the best report possible. Finally he said, "He's handling it better than I would. Uncle Amos and

Aunt Laura have helped a lot. It wouldn't surprise me if Bob became a preacher."

"Any chance at all of his getting his sight back?" Gideon asked quietly.

"The doctor says it would take a miracle."

Gideon considered that, then a smile touched his lips. "I guess there are precedents, aren't there?"

The three of them talked for an hour, and as the visitors were leaving, Gideon hugged Frank again. "I'm glad to see you, Son. I've missed you!"

Frank only nodded and muttered something. When they got outside, he said, "I wish I could get him out of that place. That'll take a miracle, too, won't it?"

Melanie hugged him at the door. "Miracles can happen, Frank. Don't forget that."

★ ★ ★

Two nights later, the play opened. Frank had hired a man to sell tickets on the mayor's recommendation that he was tolerably honest. In their jammed-up dressing rooms, which had once been several feed stalls, they heard the crowd filing in.

"Noisy bunch, aren't they?" Middleton said with a grin as he came out, dressed in his uniform. He loosened the sword, sighed, and said, "I hope I don't have to use this to protect myself."

Lorna came out, along with Carmen, wearing their costumes. Carmen looked very calm, but Lorna was somewhat pale. Listening to the crowd's noise, she asked, "Is that sort of thing usual? It sounds more like a circus than a drama."

"Oh, they'll be all right, Miss Lorna," Albert spoke up. "They're just folks like anybody else. They'll appreciate good drama when they see it."

"All right, everybody get ready!" Frank commanded. He felt a fine sheen of perspiration on his forehead, and he tried to avoid any appearance of nervousness by speaking loudly. "We'll knock 'em dead. Let's go!"

When the curtain opened, the crowd burst into loud applause even though they had seen none of the acting. As the drama proceeded, Frank realized at once that this was a different kind of audience from anything he had ever seen. Primarily, he saw that the uniforms of the Confederate army made up most of the audience. Here and there were a few ladies, but it was a rough bunch of soldiers who had come to see the opening night performance. As the drama proceeded, the group made several blunders. But the audience readily went along with it. "You're all right there, boy!" one of them yelled when Albert forgot his lines. "Just sing a song if you forget what you're supposed to say."

Lorna was well received by the soldiers. Several of them called out endearments to her, such as, "I'll meet you after the play, sweetheart. You're a real Confederate flower!"

Unaccustomed to this, Lorna faltered. But the crowd was good-natured and soon settled down to enter into the production.

The play itself was not much. The story was simple enough: a young man, played by Frank, who ran away from home, went bad in his youth and became a prodigal, breaking the hearts of his parents, played by the Hardcastles. Later on, he redeemed himself by joining the Confederate army, where he became a hero.

Middleton, who played the villain, was constantly hissed and booed by the audience. Once when they were behind the stage waiting for their entrances, Middleton grinned at Lorna. "I like being the villain," he said. "You don't have to please anyone. The worse you are, the better they like it. I just hope they don't try to charge. Some of those soldiers look pretty raunchy."

Finally, the play came to an end. The curtain was drawn, and Frank said quickly, "Let's take a curtain call, if they know what that is."

The audience did indeed know what it was. They whistled and applauded, all standing, and before they were satisfied, the cast had made five curtain calls, and finally Frank said, "That's enough. They'll have us going out all night."

They soon discovered that Southern theater, at least this one, was a little different. Part of the audience felt no compunction about simply strolling back behind the curtain, and the actors were soon besieged by admirers. Frank was amused by all of this, but he soon got a shock when a young Confederate lieutenant walked up with an attractive young woman by his side. "Mr. Rocklin?" the lieutenant asked with a grin on his face.

"Yes, Lieutenant. I hope you enjoyed the play."

The lieutenant put his hand out and when Frank took it he said, "Well, I guess I had to like it, seeing as we're kinfolk. My name's Lowell Rocklin."

"Clay's son, of course!" Frank remembered his genealogy. "Well, I'm glad to have you here, Lieutenant. It's always good to have kin in the audience."

"This is my fiancée, Rooney. Rooney, you've heard me speak of my uncle Gideon. Well, Mr. Frank Rocklin here is his youngest son."

"I'm pleased to know you, sir." Rooney said. She was an attractive, vivacious girl, nicely dressed in what seemed to be a new sky blue outfit.

"When will be the big day?" Frank asked.

"About a month away—October twenty-fourth to be exact." Then she changed the subject by saying, "I thought the play was so good." She hesitated, then said, "Of course, I haven't seen many plays."

"Why, Rooney, that's no way to talk to an actor," Lowell said. Then he turned to Frank. "I've seen quite a few plays and I tell you, this was one of the finest ones. Father will be glad to see you when he gets back. How's your family in the North?" He spoke of the Northern Rocklins quite easily as the three of them stood there talking. Finally, Frank introduced them to the rest of the cast. Then he turned to the young couple. "I think I'm going to offer my relatives an early bridal supper."

"A bridal supper?" Lorna asked at once, coming to stand beside Rooney. "You will have a beautiful bride, Lieutenant," she said to Lowell.

Frank took the pair out for a meal, and on the way over, he noticed Lowell favoring one foot. Lowell was very quick, and he said, "I do limp a little. I lost a leg fighting you Yanks, but I'm with the cavalry now. Man in a saddle doesn't need two good legs like an infantryman."

"You're much to be commended, Lowell," Frank said earnestly. He was fascinated by Lowell. He had always been interested in his Southern relatives, and his first introduction to them was most pleasing. Finally the supper was over, and Lowell said, "Mr. Rocklin—"

"Oh, call me Frank."

"Well, Frank, then. I'd like to invite you to a tea tomorrow afternoon at Mrs. Chesnut's home."

"Mrs. Chesnut?"

"Yes!" Rooney said eagerly. "Mrs. Mary Chesnut. Her husband is a colonel, one of the advisors to President Davis. Everybody comes to their house, don't they, Lowell?"

"They surely do. I've seen Gen. Lee, Gen. Jackson, Gen. Stuart, all three there—and I don't know who else—in the same room. I'd be pleased to have you as my guest. Let the flower of Richmond's society see that we Northern Rocklins have *one* artist, at least, in our family."

Frank's mind was working quickly. He was thinking about being able to pick up some information, and it sounded like an excellent place to do it. "I'd be happy to come," he said.

"Oh, and bring as many of your cast as you would like. There's always plenty of room at the Chesnuts'," Rooney said.

"Rooney! You can't invite a host of people to the Chesnuts' house," Lowell protested.

"Oh, it's all right," Rooney said. "I'll go by and mention it beforehand. She's so interested in books and art and things like that. She'll be glad to meet a real company of actors."

Lowell was not so sure, but he had learned that Rooney had a way of taking things into her own hands. "All right, then. But you'll have to make it right." He nodded and said, "Good night, Frank. I'll tell the rest of the family to be sure and come to the play."

"Will your father be back soon?" Frank asked.

"I think so. He's been out with the company on a scouting mission looking for the Union troops to make a drive from the northeast. That's where we've got all our forces scattered." Lowell spoke assuredly, and Frank filed that fact in his head. *It might be something Pinkerton needs to know,* he thought. But he smiled and said, "Fine. What time tomorrow?"

"Two o'clock. Ask anyone—everyone knows where the Chesnuts live."

★   ★   ★

"Miss Grey, I believe?"

Lorna looked up to find a tall Confederate officer wearing the uniform of a major. He had come to stand slightly behind her, and when she turned, he said, "I haven't had the pleasure of seeing you perform, but I propose to take care of that immediately." He was in his late twenties, she judged, with light blond hair and very light blue eyes. His face was thin in an aristocratic fashion, and his hair was cut fashionably long. He looked rather like a dandy to Lorna, but his eyes were intelligent and his manners were better than average.

"My name is Maj. Miles Taliferro. May I take you for some refreshments?"

"That would be very nice, Major." Lorna had arrived with the rest of the group at the home of the Chesnuts. She had been impressed by the graciousness of the house, with its heart pine floors, the stately windows, and the polished, gleaming furniture. The house, as Lowell Rocklin had warned her, was very crowded. There were no privates in this room, however. As a matter of fact, few lowly lieutenants. It was the cream of Richmond's society. Lorna had been very impressed by Mary Chesnut, who had charmed her at once by identifying her accent. "From England, I see. We're glad to welcome you to the South, Miss Grey. You must tell me more about how you got here."

Lorna allowed Taliferro to take her to the table. He placed a slice of cake on a fine china saucer, handed it to her, then proceeded to procure some for himself. Armed with this and a cup of delicious punch, the two sat down. "You're from England, I understand," Taliferro said. "How is it that you find yourself in this country?"

Lorna explained her coming very simply and was aware that Taliferro was very attentive. There was something about him that warned her that he knew women—perhaps better than a man should. Some men, she had long ago discovered, were primarily hunters. They perceived any attractive woman as their quarry, just as a hunter in the woods looks at a deer as his legitimate property. They felt that every woman was to be pursued. Not that he was rude or in any way forward in his manners. On the contrary, he was very smooth. The two sat talking, and finally Frank came over and introduced himself to the major. Taliferro greeted him and asked, "I take it you've been traveling quite a bit. Has your troupe been in the South long?"

At once an alarm went off in Frank's head. There was something about the question that seemed so innocent, yet perhaps was not. There was a sharpness in the major's light-blue eyes, and instantly Frank decided to tell as much of the truth as possible. "Why, no. As a matter of fact, we came from New Orleans, where we played for a couple of weeks. Before that we were in the North. In Washington, to be exact."

"Ah." Interest lighted Taliferro's eyes, and he said, "Have you ever played before the president?"

"As a matter of fact, he did come to a play. I was a minor actor, of course. I've never met him. He does like the theater, although he likes comedy rather than serious drama."

"So I understand," Taliferro agreed. He sipped his punch and said, "I'm surprised you decided to bring your troupe to the Confederacy." A smile turned up the corners of his lips. "At the moment, we're engaged in business quite different from drama."

"I suppose it's natural that you would wonder," Frank said at once. He frowned slightly and looked down at his own refreshments. "As a matter of fact, Major, I probably made a mistake coming here."

"Oh, and how is that?"

"Well, it's obvious enough that the South is hungry for drama. I suppose any nation wants its entertainment, but—" he shrugged his shoulders eloquently—"it's not easy to make it a paying proposition."

"I suppose not, but then you knew that before you came."

"Yes, I did." Frank decided to be a little daring. He was certain that the major knew of the Northern branch of Rocklins, so there would be no danger in admitting it. "My father is in the Union army, and so is my uncle Mason. But our families have been very close—that is, with those here in Virginia. The war, of course, has come and broken most of our communications. Frank looked up directly into the major's eyes and said as simply as he could, "I've only visited briefly in the South. I don't understand it. I think a lot of us from the North have that difficulty, so I thought I would come and see for myself."

Taliferro seemed interested in the explanation. "Well, I'm glad you've come, Mr. Rocklin. You have a fine family here, and I'm sure your own family back in the North are the same. It is a tragedy that we couldn't settle our differences without a war, and hopefully the day will come when we can sit down in peace once again."

It was a straightforward speech, and Lorna listened to it carefully, feeling gratitude for the major's temperance. He turned to her suddenly and said, "We are depending, of course, here in the Confederacy on *your* country for support, Miss Grey. When you were last in England, did you hear any talk about England recognizing the Confederacy?"

Lorna hesitated. "There's always talk, and there are people who feel strongly on both sides of the question." She stopped, then said, "I'm not much of a politician, I'm afraid. But I love your country, what little I've seen of it."

Taliferro said, "I'm sure. I'll be glad to show you more." He smiled engagingly. "After all, you only perform at night. That leaves all your days free."

"But not yours, surely, Major." Lorna gave him back his smile. "Soldiers have plenty to do, don't they?"

"Well, there are different kinds of soldiers." Taliferro hesitated, then said, "The combat soldiers, of course, are on the front lines. But there is much to be done before they reach that stage. An army and a nation, especially a new army and a newly born nation such as ours, require a great deal of attention. I'm one of those who attempts to make it possible for my country to survive."

Soon Frank wandered off and encountered Mrs. Chesnut. She was a charming woman, no longer in her youth, nor was she beautiful. But there was some quality in her that drew men. Frank had seen it before in women who were almost plain. He spoke with her for some time, then nodded to where Taliferro was speaking with Lorna. "The major seems quite taken with our leading lady," he said.

"Oh yes. Maj. Taliferro is not averse to pretty young ladies."

"Does he lead a battalion or some other unit in the Army of Northern Virginia?" Frank asked carelessly.

"Oh no. He is on the staff of the secretary of war." She hesitated, then said, "It's fairly well known that he's one of the leaders of what you might call the secret service. I suppose every company has that sort of thing."

Frank's heart lurched, but he kept a straight, even face. "Yes, of course, they're necessary, I suppose." He continued speaking to Mrs. Chesnut until it was time to go. And finally, as they were on their way back to the hotel, Lorna asked him, "What did you think of them, Frank? Southerners, that is?"

"They're very gracious. But then, I knew that." He looked at her, paused, and then said, "The major was quite taken with you."

"Oh yes. He was very attentive, very gallant." She seemed almost uninterested, and when Frank prodded her, she shrugged her shoulders lightly. "Men are interested in actresses. They see them as easy game, I think."

Frank was a little shocked at her way of putting it. "Well, that's speaking right out. How long have you felt like that?"

"Why, I've always known that. I don't know as much of the history of theater as I should—not as much as you do—but I think in the early days actresses were almost always women of low morals." She hesitated, then bit her lip. "Many of them, I suppose, still are."

"Not all though," Frank said quickly. "I've met some fine ladies in my short experience. And then there's you."

She looked up to see him smiling at her and returned it. "You do pay a nice compliment once in a while. But as for the major, I don't suppose I'll be seeing much of him. He'll be gone off to fight, I'd imagine."

Frank shook his head. "No, he's not that kind of a soldier."

"Not a fighting soldier? Don't tell me he's some sort of a clerk?"

"A little bit more than that," Frank admitted. "Did you enjoy yourself tonight?"

"Very much. They're not like I thought they would be—Southerners, I mean. Back in England, we hear the awful stories of slavery, and I'm sure it's as bad as they say. But you'd never know that these people are cruel taskmasters."

"Not all slave owners are cruel," Frank said at once. "I know that much. My uncle's family owns slaves, and I've heard my father talk about how much care he takes with them."

"I'm sure you're right," she said.

When they got back to the hotel, Middleton spoke for a moment to Carmen. "Well, we were in fancy society tonight. The cream of the Confederacy. I fully expected Gen. Lee to walk in."

"That major was taken with Lorna, wasn't he? I hope she's careful with him. I've seen his kind before."

Middleton gave her a quick glance. "Yes, I saw that. Well, I'm sure Lorna's able to take care of herself."

"I don't know that she is."

Middleton, surprised, gave her a direct look. "What does that mean?"

"Oh, I think you know, Roland. Lorna's not like most actresses. She has a—I don't know—she's vulnerable. A man could hurt her easily."

"But not you, eh, Carmen?"

Carmen dropped her eyes for a moment, then lifted them and smiled. "I thought I was past being hurt, but maybe I'm not. Good night, Roland."

Roland went slowly along the hall to his room. When he got there, he sat down on the bed thinking about the evening. Slowly he pulled out the whiskey bottle that he kept in his suitcase. He uncapped it and lifted it to his lips, then suddenly shook his head and put the cap back on. Putting it away, he undressed and went to bed. Before he went to sleep, he muttered, "Lorna's vulnerable all right, but then so am I—so are all of us!"

CHAPTER FIFTEEN
Rose Attends a Play

Josh Yancy counted the worn bills carefully, laying down each one on the table. When he had finished, he gathered them and shoved them into his pocket. Slowly he got up and walked around the room, staring aimlessly at the furnishings. The Yancys' house was a typical southern cabin with few luxuries. It was comfortable enough, most of the furniture having been made by Buford Yancy and his sons. The walls were covered with pictures clipped out of magazines and newspapers by the girls, except for a few drawings of Stonewall Jackson and Robert E. Lee, which had been collected by Josh.

Josh sniffed at the smell of meat roasting, then walked over to the fireplace, pulled his bowie knife from his belt, and pushed it into the carcass of the turkey that was slowly turning on a spit over glowing coals. The juice dripped to the coals, sending a heady aroma into the room. "You're going to be durned good," he muttered with satisfaction. "You'll do us a lot more good for supper than you did running around out there l-loose." The slight stutter irritated him, but he shrugged, thinking of how the habit was practically gone. He had shot the turkey only the day before and now had lingered around the house most of the morning watching it slowly broil.

The door to a bedroom opened, and his sister Rose

189

emerged. She walked over to the turkey, stared down at it, then commented, "Looks good. Be sure you don't let it burn, Josh." Rose was a tall, willowy young woman of eighteen. She had the same black hair and light green eyes as her sister Melora and the same almost unearthly beauty one sees in a mountain girl from time to time.

"You watch it awhile," Josh said. He looked up and asked, "Where've you been, Rose? I didn't hear you go out this morning."

"Oh, I went over to see Sarah Green." Rose came and poked at the turkey with a kitchen knife, then tossed it to the table and sat down. There was a restless dissatisfaction in her face.

"What's the matter with you?" Josh demanded. "You've been moping around like a sick possum for weeks now."

"Nothing's the matter with me."

"Well, I hope I don't have to look at that sour face you got on for the rest of your life," Josh snapped. He shoved his knife back in his belt and started out the door. "You watch that turkey. Pa ought to be back by dark, and I promised him we'd have it for supper tonight."

"Where're you going?"

"I'm going out to check the pigs."

"I'll go with you." Rose called for Martha to come and watch the cooking bird. When the younger girl arrived, Rose grabbed a man's coat from a peg in the wall and slipped her arms into it. The two left the house, and Josh looked carefully at the sky, searching for the flight of wild ducks. He was a woodsman and a hunter, as were all the Yancys, and his pale green eyes missed nothing as the couple made their way down a path that led through the woods. He knew every inch of this ground—every hill, every valley, and where the bees hummed around their trees. He had shot deer, wild pigs, rabbits, coons, possum—all the wildlife that made up the diet of a typical backwoods Southerner.

"I reckon you must be pretty bored if you want to go look

at the pigs," Josh said finally. "What's wrong, Rose? You can tell me."

Rose kicked at a root that rose out of the ground and seemingly tried to snatch her foot. She was wearing a pair of heavy shoes and a rather ugly brown dress. "Oh, I don't know, Josh. Nothing really," she said. The quick gestures of her hands and the twitching of her shoulders told Josh differently. She gave him a quick glance and summoned up a smile. "You and I don't talk as much as you and Melora used to. I wonder why that is?"

"No telling about those things," Josh said. "But it's not too late to start, Sis. Something bothering you?" he asked for the third time.

Rose tried to match the long steps of the boy. At sixteen, he was slightly taller than she was, with the same lean build. She wore no ornaments, and the worn, rough coat concealed the curves of her young body. "I sometimes think I'll go crazy on this place, Josh!" she exclaimed finally. Biting her lip, she shook her head. The motion sent the black hair cascading across her shoulders. She was a lively girl who liked fun and hated to see the parties and dances that took place from time to time end. "I guess you're right. Any girl that'll go watch pigs is pretty bored."

Josh said nothing for a while. He seemed to be slow thinking, but actually he was very thorough in his mind. "I guess so. You don't hunt and you don't like to read like Melora does. It must get boring for you out here." The two walked on for a while before he said, "I'm taking Rena to the play in town."

"A play?" Rose's eyes brightened at once. "Tell me about it! What kind of play is it? Who's in it?" she asked rapidly.

She listened avidly as Josh described the play and ended by saying, "The actor in it, why, he's kinfolk of the Rocklins. Mr. Frank Rocklin's his name. I think he's a nephew of Mr. Clay. Anyway, I've been saving up money from the hides that I sold, and I'm going to take Rena to see the thing."

Instantly Rose grabbed his arm and turned him around with surprising strength. "Oh, take me, Josh! Please?"

Josh was surprised at the intensity of her gaze. He really cared deeply for this older sister of his, as he did for Melora, but the two women were very different. He had known for a long time that Rose didn't like the farm, but he thought that was just part of growing up. Now when he saw her lips trembling with anxiety, he said quickly, "Why sure, Rose. We'll all three go. We'll have a good time, too. I've got enough for us to have supper, I think."

"Oh, Josh!" Rose threw her arms around him and squeezed him so hard he grunted. When she stepped back, her eyes were dancing and she said, "I'll wear my green dress, and maybe Melora will let me wear her locket. What time will we leave?"

Josh grinned at her, pulled off his hat, and scratched his head. "Well, I guess about ten o'clock in the morning. Think you can be ready?"

"Yes!" Rose exclaimed. As she smiled, the dimple that adorned her right cheek suddenly popped into view. "You two need a chaperone. You're too old to be going out with a young woman without someone to watch you." She was merry the rest of the time, even at such a mundane chore as feeding the pigs. That night when she told her father that Josh was taking her to the play, the younger children set up a howl to go.

"No, you let Rose and Josh go this time," Buford Yancy said. He was one of those tall, lean mountain men who never seem to grow older until they simply stop living one day. He said to the younger members of his family, "There's going to be a circus in two weeks. If you'll stop your yowling, we'll all go. I hear they got a critter there that you won't even believe when you see it. That be all right?" He smiled as the younger ones agreed and said to Josh, "You and Rose go on and have a good time. If there's anything in that play a young man orten to hear—" he winked at Rose—"you just reach out and clap your hands over his ears."

★ ★ ★

Rose Yancy had never had such a good time! She said so more than once as the three young people were sitting in the theater. Josh was wearing a new black suit that he had bought from his earnings when he worked for the Rocklins at Gracefield. Rena looked prettier than ever in a charcoal-colored dress with a saucy new hat pinned into her hair. "That was the best supper I ever had, Josh!" Rose exclaimed. "I wish we could eat out every meal."

"Aw, Rose, you'd get tired of that fancy café cooking pretty soon, I think. Why, they didn't even have any fritters and no grits a'tall!" He winked at Rena, who smiled back at him. "An ol' country girl like you, why you'd go crazy if you didn't get some pig's feet every now and then."

"Oh, you hush!" Rose said. Her cheeks were glowing, and many of the younger soldiers were casting admiring glances at her.

Rena said, "You'd better be careful, Rose. These soldiers haven't seen anything as pretty as you in a long time." Rena was fond of Rose, but had spent little time with her. She had always been very close to Melora, but this younger sister she knew hardly at all. "I've got to spend more time with Rose," she whispered to Josh. "I never knew she was so much fun to be around." Then she halted when Josh said, "Look! The curtain's going up."

Rose had never seen a professional drama before. She had been to entertainment of various kinds and one circus. But as she sat there watching the drama unfold, she was caught up in the action. She had nothing to compare it to; for her the acting was real. And when the hero was thought to be dying, tears rose to her eyes. When he revived, she found herself clapping her hands, saying, "Good! Good!" The dresses of the women seemed very beautiful, as did the women themselves. Once she leaned over and said to Josh, "Isn't it wonderful, Josh? I'd give anything if I could see a play every night!"

193

Josh nudged her with his elbow, saying, "No, it would get old every night, but it's a treat once in a while."

When the play ended, the audience rose to give a standing ovation, none applauding more than Rose. Finally Josh said, "Come on."

"Why? Where're we going?" Rose asked in bewilderment.

"Going back to meet the actors. After all, they're Rena's kinfolk. Lowell and Rooney went back to meet them. I guess we can, too."

Josh led the way and Rose followed timidly. Josh immediately spotted Frank Rocklin and said, "Come on, that's your kinfolk, Rena."

Walking purposefully, he stopped in front of Frank and said, "Mr. Rocklin?"

"Yes?"

"This here's your kinfolk. This is Miss Rena Rocklin, Mr. Clay's girl. And I'm Josh Yancy, and this here's my sister Rose."

Frank looked instantly at Rena and smiled. When she put out her hand, he took it and bent over and kissed it in an eloquent fashion. "I didn't know I had such lovely relatives in Dixie. I'm glad to meet you."

Then he turned, and Rose blushed to the roots of her hair. Frank smiled, reached out and took her hand, and kissed it also. "I'm glad to meet you, Miss Yancy. Did you enjoy the play?"

"Oh yes. It was—it was wonderful!"

Frank laughed, his white teeth flashing as he said, "I wish the critics thought so."

"Why, it's a great play, Mr. Rocklin," Josh protested. "Makes them Yankees look like low-down dogs and makes us Confederates look pretty good."

"Well, that's what we wanted to do," Frank said. He liked the fresh appearance of the trio and added, "Let me introduce you to the rest of the cast."

Then followed the most memorable evening of Rose Yancy's life. She found herself caught up in a movement to go out and eat, as was the custom of the cast. And when they were in the restaurant, she was seated between the beautiful young woman, Lorna Grey, and the actor who had played the villain. She was a little standoffish with him, and Middleton at once understood the reason. He turned to her, saying, "You don't see many plays, do you, Miss Yancy?"

"No, this is my first one."

Winking at Carmen across the table, Roland assumed a ferocious look, "Well, how'd you think I played my part? Was I nasty enough to suit you?"

Rose blushed and dropped her head. Then she raised her eyes to his and said, "You're real mean. Once I almost got out of my seat and came up to—to—"

Everyone laughed, and J. Harold Hardcastle, who was listening, said, "Now *that's* the mark of a fine actor—one who can inspire that kind of emotion!"

Carmen leaned across and said, "You mustn't confuse the role with the man. Roland here is as harmless as any man could be. He wouldn't hurt a fly. He's not a Yankee officer."

"Oh, I'm so sorry!" Rose gasped. She turned to face Middleton, and he was captivated by the sight of her lips, which seemed very red and very vulnerable, and by her wide-spaced, enormous green eyes. He said to himself, *She is a rose out here in this desert of ignorance. Never saw a prettier one.* But he reached out, patted her shoulder, and said, "Don't apologize, Miss Yancy. I understand."

As the meal progressed, Rose began to gain courage. She listened avidly to all the talk that went on about acting. Eventually, she began to speak with more freedom to Roland Middleton. He answered her questions easily. And finally she said, "It must be heavenly to be an actor or an actress."

Middleton caught Carmen's eyes and the cynical twist of her lips. Shaking his head, he said, "Well, it's a job. Not a very good one at times. A very few rise to the top and make a lot of money or get a lot of admiration from the public. Most of us are just poor drudges doing our job."

"But you get to move around and go from place to place.

And you get to do new plays, don't you? You don't always do this one."

"Well, that's true, of course."

"Tell me about the plays you've done," Rose demanded.

Even after the meal was over, she was still listening, and Middleton felt flattered by her interest. Afterward they sat around drinking tea, and several officers came up to speak to Middleton, glancing at Rose, but he fended them off successfully. He sat looking at the young woman and said, "You remind me a great deal of my sister."

Rose lifted her eyes to his with surprise on her features. "Do I look like her?" she asked.

"A little, but she's excited easily, and her whole face lights up when she's pleased—just like yours. When I left home, she was about your age and about as crazy about the theater as you are."

"Did she go on the stage?"

"No, she married a barber, and they have four children now."

Rose wrinkled up her nose. "That sounds almost as dull as taking care of the pigs like I do."

Middleton was amused. "Some things about acting are about as bad as taking care of pigs," he said.

"I don't believe it!" Rose insisted. She made a fetching picture as she sat there, the dark green of her dress setting off the light green of her almond-shaped eyes. Her hair was as black as hair can be and hung down her back in a thick cascade. She had a heart-shaped face, and her features were delicate and at the same time strangely sensuous in an innocent way.

"Maybe you ought to leave the pigs and become an actress," Middleton teased her.

Rose stopped smiling at once. Her eyes grew smaller as she looked at him, and she whispered, "I'd do anything if I could do what you do, Mr. Middleton. Anything!"

Middleton was aware that she was totally serious and shook his head. "It's not as glamorous as it seems, Miss Yancy." He had no time to say more, for Josh and Rena had come to stand beside them, Josh saying, "It's time to go, Rose."

Middleton stood at once and smiled down at Rose. He looked rather handsome in his ash gray suit and said, "I hope you'll come back to see another performance. It's refreshing to have someone youthful like you admiring what we do."

Rose shook her head and said bitterly, "No, I'm afraid I can't come back, Mr. Middleton. So this is good-bye."

As the three left, Carmen came over and said, "Pretty little thing, isn't she, Roland? I suppose she's stagestruck."

Roland said nothing for a moment. He was watching the trio as they left, his eyes fastened on the form of the tall young woman. "Yes, she is. She's bored out of her head at that farm she lives on."

Carmen shook her head. "She's probably better off there—she'll marry a farmer and have a dozen kids." She turned to leave, but Roland stood for a long time thinking about the aching desire in the eyes of Rose Yancy.

Josh and Rena talked excitedly about the play on the long ride back to Gracefield. When they let Rena out, she gave Rose a swift look, then reached up and pulled Josh's head down and gave him a resounding kiss on the check. "That's a thank-you for a wonderful evening, Josh," she said. Then she turned and ran into the house.

Josh climbed back into the wagon, spoke to the team and slapped them with the line, "Giddyap!" The team started out with a sprightly pace and Josh said, "It's gonna be late by the time we get home. Do you want to lie down in the back and go to sleep, Rose?"

"No, I couldn't sleep."

Josh turned to look at her. A full moon was high in the sky, and the silver light bathed her face. "You really liked it, didn't you?" he asked.

"Better than anything."

Josh hesitated and then said, "You talked a long time to that actor fellow, didn't you?"

"Yes. He was so interesting. He told me all about the stage."

"Well, you have to be careful with fellows like that," Josh observed. "Not that you're likely to see him again. But if you were, I'd have to tell you actors aren't all that nice in their behavior to women."

Rose sniffed. "How would you know? You don't know any actors."

"Everybody knows about actors."

Rose glared at him and pulled her coat more firmly around her shoulders. "You don't know anything, Josh, except that farm, just like me. We're not much better than those pigs out there rooting around!"

Josh stared at her. "That ain't so," he said. "What's the matter with you, anyhow? Here I bring you all the way to Richmond and take you to the theater, and you gripe all the way home."

Rose said nothing, but settled back, her arms crossed over her chest. The wagon rattled over the road, and the harness tinkled from time to time. The horses snorted, the sound of their hoofbeats making a cadence that made Josh sleepy. When they finally got to the house it was long past three o'clock. Josh hopped down, saying, "Not much sense in going to bed." When Rose didn't answer, he came over to her and put his arm around her. "I didn't mean to be sharp with you," he said. "But I hope you'll learn to like it on the farm."

Rose looked up at him, and he saw that there were tears in her eyes. "I'll always hate it here," she whispered. She turned and disappeared into the house, leaving Josh looking after her. Finally he turned slowly and led the team to the barn, where he unharnessed them and turned them loose in the corral after feeding them. Then he stood for a moment, leaning against the fence, thinking of Rose. "Women sure do know how to complicate things," he said aloud. Then he struck the top rail of the fence so that it gave a humming sound, turned, and walked into the house.

★ ★ ★

After the performance, Frank had excused himself and wandered down the streets of Richmond. He stopped idly in front of Planter's Bank, standing under the light of an oil lamp. Soon a man appeared out of the darkness to say, "Do you have a light?"

Frank reached into his pocket, obtained a match, and struck it. As the man leaned forward to hold his cigar to the burning match, he said, "The Union . . . now and forever."

Frank looked around nervously, then replied, "Liberty at all costs."

The man nodded, saying, "Come along. This place is too public."

Frank followed the man, a short, barrel-shaped individual wearing a rather worn suit and a cap pulled down over his eyes. When they found a place in the shadows in a vacant lot across from a blacksmith shop, Frank said, "What's your name?"

"Right now, it's Dave Perkins. Folks around here think I'm a jobber, a yard goods salesman. I even carry a few samples around. Nobody has any money to buy, of course, and I can't stay long. What've you got?"

Frank rattled off the things he had discovered in his short stay and watched as the dark eyes of Perkins seemed to register it all. He had a catfish mouth that was pierced in the middle by the cigar. Finally when Frank had finished, he pulled it out and sent a puff skyward. "Not bad. You'll get more as time goes on. What did you find out at the Chesnuts'?"

"There was a man there named Taliferro. He's secret service, I hear."

"Sure. Pretty sharp, too. Watch out for him." He continued to feed Frank information and finally said, "That's all for now. Meet me here again Tuesday night. I'll have some orders by then. Maybe you'll know something about military movements. Watch out for Taliferro." Without a good-bye he faded away into the darkness. Frank turned and walked back toward his hotel slowly. The wind was blowing, making a keening sound that sent a chill over him, and he turned his coat collar up and trudged heavily toward his hotel.

CHAPTER SIXTEEN
An Addition to the Company

The skies were clear, but a stiff October breeze ruffled the blond hair of Miles Taliferro as he approached the long, low red brick building that housed the Signal Corps of the Confederate army. A smile tugged at his lips as he thought with a stab of amusement, *If Pinkerton knew that the Secret Service Bureau was in here, he'd love it.*

He entered the building, turned to his right, then walked across a large room where at least twenty men labored at battered desks. The Secret Service had come to include ten captains, twenty lieutenants, thirty sergeants, and scores of enlisted men from the ranks of army regiments. Many of those were out of the office the majority of the time, however, leaving only enough men to keep up with the book work. "Is Maj. Norris busy?" he asked a dapper-looking sergeant working on a cipher.

"He said for you to come right in, Major."

Taliferro nodded and stepped inside the office of the chief of the Confederate Secret Service Bureau. Maj. William Norris, a tidy, bearded man, looked up from a paper that he was signing. "Come in, Major," he said. Shoving the paper aside, he waved at a chair, saying, "Sit down." When Taliferro was seated, Norris questioned him for some twenty minutes about his activities on the mission he had just completed, and finally he nodded with approval. "You did a fine job," he said.

"Thank you, sir. I hope it will be of some help."

Norris rose to his feet, moved over to the window and stared out of it moodily. "It would help if some of our leaders had more confidence in the work that we do."

"You mean Gen. Lee?"

"He's one of them." Norris's tone was clipped, resentment obvious in his features. Robert E. Lee was a general who believed in the old, honorable ways of warfare. He wanted to be free and clear of spies, or scouts as he called them.

"He's a great general," Norris said, "but he's behind the times." Turning from the window, he marched up and down the floor in a jerky fashion, stroking his beard. "Of course, some of our agents are excellent," he argued. A frown crossed his face as he reached over and picked up a newspaper with *Southern Illustrated News* across the top. It was the most important newspaper of the Confederacy. Maj. Norris said, "Look at that, Miles."

Miles took the paper and saw rather crude woodcuts of a woman on the front page. He grimaced and read aloud, "Miss Belle Boyd, the Rebel Spy." Shaking his head angrily, he said, "How does Belle expect to be a spy if she's got her picture on the front of every newspaper, North and South?"

"She's practically worthless," Norris answered. "It's not her lack of brains, but the woman loves publicity. That story there is fabricated out of half-truths and rumors. She ought to start writing novels!" he grunted.

"They're calling her the 'Siren of the Shenandoah,'" Taliferro said. "Or sometimes the 'Secesh Cleopatra.'"

The two men stared moodily at the paper that Taliferro had tossed on the table, then Norris said, "I've got something for you to look into. I hear from one of our agents in Washington that Pinkerton's stepping up his activities. Word we got was that he's going to be flooding us with new agents." Walking over to his chair, he sat down heavily and shook his head. "Sometimes I think we have more of their agents in Richmond than we do of our own."

"Any information about what they look like—names, descriptions?"

"Some information is on the way. I think we're going to have to take on more men. But I want you to go to all of our agents now and privately tip them off to be looking for new suspects."

"Yes, sir. And as soon as you hear anything from our man in Washington, you'll pass it along?"

"Of course." Maj. Norris waved his hand and said, "We've got plenty of rope. As soon as we catch them there won't be any long, drawn-out trials, Maj. Taliferro!" With only a careless nod he went back to the papers he was signing, and his visitor left the room, closing the door quietly.

★ ★ ★

"You are a very persistent officer, Major." Lorna smiled slightly at Taliferro as the two of them walked along the promenade outside the hotel. Lorna was wearing an oyster-white dress, over which she had put a lightweight woolen jacket made of a beautiful sky blue material. The hat that perched on her head was the latest fashion, and she looked fetching as they moved along.

Miles Taliferro was a man who appreciated beauty in a woman, and he found it in Lorna Grey in abundance. He had learned, however, that she was wary of overt compliments, having heard too many of them, he suspected. "I'm considered to be rather firm," he admitted as they stepped aside to allow a woman pushing a large baby carriage to pass. When they resumed their walk, he said, "That's supposed to be an admirable trait in an officer. I hope you're not offended by my persistence, as you call it."

"Not at all." Lorna had rejected three invitations by the major, and each time he'd merely smiled and asked her in another form at a later date. "I suppose officers get accustomed to giving orders."

"I hope you don't think I've tried to do that with you," he said quickly. "I've desired your company—as have half the men in Richmond it seems. But I'm sure you understand that we officers get lonely at times."

"So do women, Major."

Taliferro half missed a step and turned his head to look at her. "That's the most revealing thing you've ever said. Why should you be lonely, Lorna? You could have as many men as you want."

"How many men does a woman need?" she countered. Her lips turned up in a slight smile, and she added, "I think one's enough—if it's the right one."

"A wise reply. And you're right. One man, one woman. Is that it?"

"I think that's the biblical formula. Although it doesn't always work out in our society, does it, Major?"

"Would you please call me Miles? I keep expecting you to salute," he said with some asperity. "Yes, you're right."

"I think you look on women as a challenge to your ability," Lorna said.

Her words caught Miles off guard, and he flushed slightly. "Women have played games with me and I've responded. I think some of them expect such things." Quickly he added, "Not you, of course."

Lorna's gray eyes studied him for a moment, then she shrugged. "It's the only game women have, Miles. Men can have a career, but for most women their only option is to find a husband."

"Unless they're actresses, or perhaps schoolteachers."

"Never the twain shall meet!" Lorna exclaimed.

They had come to a side street, and he took her arm as she stepped down. "It will do me no good to tell you this," he said abruptly, "but you're very close to being the most beautiful woman I've ever seen."

"Thank you," she said easily. "I never know what to say when someone pays me a compliment." She laughed suddenly. "What would you think if I said, 'Yes, I am beautiful, aren't I?'"

Her wit amused Taliferro. "Well, we'd be agreed in that case." The two walked on down the street and afterward stopped in a shop, where he bought her a cup of sassafras tea. As they sat there, she said, "I've never tasted this before. What's it made of?"

"Some sort of root, I believe." He sipped the liquid, frowned, and shook his head. "Like everything else in the Confederacy, we're having to use substitutes. One day it'll be different."

"Will you be leaving Richmond for your duties, or are you stationed here all the time?"

"I sometimes get called to other parts of the Confederacy," he said guardedly. He studied her for a moment, and as he moved the glass around, leaving a trail of water on the table, he asked, "What's it like in the North now? Does everyone there hate us?"

"Not everyone. There's a strong Peace party that would like to end the war, and many there, best I could tell, have strong Southern sympathies. But since I'm a foreigner, you'll have to ask others." She gave him a covert look, then said, "I understand that you're in some sort of antispy organization."

Miles shook his head sadly. "It's supposed to be the *Secret* Service, but of course, it isn't. Everyone knows what's going on." He laughed suddenly, saying, "Would you like to know where we get most of our information about the movement of Federal troops?"

"Yes."

"From the Northern newspapers." Taliferro laughed aloud and leaned back in his chair, his thin aristocratic face showing amusement. "Fortunately there are many more newspapers in the North than we have in the South."

Lorna was fascinated. "Are there many spies in Richmond?"

"I'm afraid so." He leaned forward suddenly and put his

hand over hers. "Perhaps you're one of them. After all, it would be a natural thing. You're English, and that wouldn't put you under suspicion. Actors travel everywhere, pick up all kinds of information. No one worries about their being spies. Are you a spy?" he asked with a smile.

Lorna was conscious of his hand over her own. She let it remain there, pressing hers lightly, and smiled at him. "I will see if you're a good-enough Secret Service man to find out. If I am, I will certainly report to Mr. Pinkerton that one Southern officer is very alert."

The two of them had a pleasant walk together. When they finally returned to her room, the corridor was vacant. She turned to say good-night, but Taliferro pulled her forward, holding her tightly and kissing her. It was something he did very well, and Lorna did not struggle. When he released her, she smiled and said, "There. I surrendered that kiss to you. Now you'll tell me more of your secrets when we go for a walk. Good afternoon, Maj. Taliferro."

Taliferro was amused and tantalized. *She's a beautiful one,* he thought, when she had closed her door. *I've never met anyone like her.* As he left the hotel, he was already planning new ways to entice her into spending more time with him.

★ ★ ★

As soon as Josh entered the house, he took one look at his father and asked abruptly, "What's wrong, Pa?"

Buford Yancy gave his son a troubled glance. "It's Rose," he said. "We had a fight."

Josh tossed the package he'd brought onto the table and turned to ask, "What was it about?"

"The same thing it always is," Buford said. "She's tired of the farm. She wants to go live in Richmond."

"Why, she can't do that!"

Buford Yancy reached up and rubbed the back of his neck. His pale green eyes were as sharp as when he'd been a younger man. He had only a few lines around his eyes, and it was the sinking in of his cheeks that showed his true age.

"Well," he grunted giving his head a disconcerted shake. "She may have done more than talk this time."

"Where is she, Pa?"

"Gone to visit that friend of hers—Millie—the one that lives just outside Richmond."

"You shouldn't have let her go there."

"She's eighteen years old. What am I going to do? Tie her up to the hitching post?" Buford was disturbed. With the help of Melora, he had raised a large family without a wife. Most of the children had been easy to raise, but there had been a rebellious streak in Rose almost from the time she could walk. He remembered when the girl was first learning to walk. He had tried to get her to hold his hand, but she'd pulled back, arguing, "No, I do it." No matter how many times she fell, she never asked for help. Buford walked over and sat down heavily in the chair. He had not shaved in several days, and the bristles of his beard formed a white shadow on his cheeks. "I dunno whut to do with that girl, Josh," he said finally. "If I hadn't let her go, she'd have run off."

"I'm afraid for Rose." Josh suddenly slapped the wall of the cabin with his hand, then turned to his father. "I'll go bring her back, Pa."

"No, I said she could stay for a week."

"What good does that do? This place isn't gonna change. She'll hate it just as bad."

A harried look came to Yancy's eyes. "I'm gonna talk to Melora. She's the nearest thing to a ma that Rose ever had."

Josh shook his head. "She loves Melora, but she won't listen to her. She won't listen to anybody." Josh was not accustomed to this sort of problem, and he said in a way that made Yancy look up, "What are we going to do, Pa? We gotta do something!"

Josh had not asked questions in such a plaintive way in a long time. He was a sturdy boy, able to take care of himself—almost a man. But something about the look in his eye reminded Buford Yancy of when he'd been a small boy. He wished he had an answer, but he had none. Deep in his heart, he was afraid there was none. Sighing deeply, he shook his head. "Young'uns grow up, Josh. They leave their home and make their own way. Some go right, some go wrong. Me, you, and Melora will just have to pray that Rose turns out to be one who went right."

★ ★ ★

"Come in." Roland Middleton half turned, his hands raised to put on his makeup. He was surprised to see Rose Yancy enter the small dressing room. "Why, Miss Yancy!" he exclaimed, getting to his feet at once. He had not seen her except for the one time, but was now once again impressed by her fresh beauty. Now, however, he saw that her eyes were wide and her lips were drawn tight. "Is there something wrong?" he asked immediately.

"Mr. Middleton, you've got to help me!" Rose was wearing a simple brown dress and over it a worn wool coat. Her hair had been blown by the stiff breezes, and she put her hand up, smoothing it down unconsciously. She seemed to be out of breath, which indeed she was, for she had come at almost a run to arrive at the theater before the performance.

"I—I don't know how to tell you this," she said breathlessly. There was a poignancy in the girl's green eyes, and she had a charm that was not polished, but natural and free. "Can I talk to you for a minute, Mr. Middleton?"

"Well, we have about—oh, ten minutes before the curtain goes up. Can it wait till afterward?"

Rose hesitated, then nodded. "Yes, sir, I can wait that long."

"Fine! Why don't you sit there and let me get this blasted makeup on, then after that we'll talk." As he applied the makeup, he spoke quietly to the young woman, wondering what had brought her to his dressing room in such a state. When someone called, "Places! Places everybody!" he said, "Why don't you watch the play from backstage? It'll give you a different view of the theater."

"Oh, could I do that?"

"Certainly. Come on. I'll find you a place where you won't get run over by the thundering herd."

Rose spent the next two hours standing at one side of the stage. She was not visible to the audience, but all of the cast members were aware of her and spoke to her as they made their entrances and exits.

For Rose it was a fascinating two hours. She was disturbed over her argument with her father but soon lost herself in the action of the play. Surprisingly enough it was the intricacy of the thing that interested her. When she had seen the play from the side of the audience, she'd lost herself in it. Now, however, her interest sharpened as she saw how the play really worked. Several of the players acted multiple roles, so they were constantly charging to a dressing room and whisking out in a new costume, talking to themselves as they made the adjustment. She was especially amused at Albert Deckerman, who played not only the role of a young man, but the role of a much older man. He stopped once beside her, muttering to himself, then turned and said, "Are my whiskers on straight?"

Rose saw that he had glued a set of false whiskers on with some sort of substance. They were crooked, and she reached out and straightened them. "Now they look fine. You're doing so well, Mr. Deckerman. I don't see how you remember all those lines."

Albert Deckerman was not accustomed to being complimented by beautiful young women. He was highly pleased, for he got few compliments on his acting ability. "Not hard once you get the hang of it," he said airily. "Well, there's my cue." He shot off onto the stage, his booming voice dominating the theater as it always did.

"He's loud, isn't he?"

Rose turned to find Carmen Montaigne standing beside her. The actress was dressed in a beautiful gown of some wine-colored material. Her hair was wound around her head in a fashion that Rose had never seen before, and her eyes were curious. "Oh yes," Rose said. "He sure is. You look so pretty," she burst out.

Sophisticated as she was, Carmen appreciated the obviously earnest compliment. "Thank you—Miss Yancy, isn't it?" She hesitated, then said, "You came to see the play?"

Rose hesitated and dropped her head, showing confusion. When she lifted her eyes, she saw that the older woman was looking at her with compassion. "Yes, well, I did want to see the play—" But at that moment, Carmen's cue came and she moved out on the stage.

Rose was almost sorry when the play was over, but it had given her time to think. Middleton came by and said, "Let me get out of this costume, and we'll go someplace where we can talk. Maybe have a cup of tea or coffee." He left at once and was soon back. He led her out of the theater to a café two doors down. It was only half full, and he chose a table near the rear of the room. As soon as the waiter had taken their order, he said, "Now, I can see you have some sort of problem. You want to tell me about it?"

Rose began to speak nervously. She twisted her hands together, and her youthful face was almost painful to watch. The actor, accustomed as he was to hard times and his own troubles, found himself feeling an unexpected burst of pity for the girl. It was an old story to him, of course: a young girl wanting to go on the stage. He was rehearsing his speech, one that he'd given several times. It always began with "I know you want to be on the stage, but there's more to it than you see. . . ."

Finally Rose said, "So you see, I *can't* go back to that old farm, Mr. Middleton. I hate it there."

Roland shook his head and traced a pattern on the top of the table with his forefinger. "There're worse places than a farm, Miss Yancy. I've been in some of them myself."

"Oh, I know that, but I've just *got* to do something else. I can't go on taking care of pigs the rest of my life."

"A pretty young thing like you wouldn't have to worry about that."

Rose flushed at the compliment. She made a charming picture in Middleton's eyes as she sat there. Her skin was almost translucent, as beautiful as anything he'd seen. Her long eyelashes curled upward, and her widely spaced eyes looked at him with an innocence and yet a pain that he found hard to meet. "I could get married," she said simply. "But it would be just moving to another farm. I don't want to spend my life doing that. I want to do something with a little color in it. Something different!"

"Well, the theater's different, all right. May I call you Rose?" he asked suddenly. "I've gone through this with many young people, young ladies and men. The theater seems glamorous enough when you're sitting out there— bright lights, fancy costumes, moving from place to place." He leaned back, his eyes moody, and he shook his head. "It isn't like that really. It's just another job after you've done it awhile. And not a very good job at that—except for a few." He sat there and waited for her objections, which came as he'd expected. He listened for a long time and wished that he had the wisdom to counsel this girl. He knew, however, that it was not wisdom that she needed. Her mind was made up to leave, and there was no mistaking that.

Rose dropped her head finally and bit her lip. "I—I shouldn't have told you all this, I suppose." She looked up, and her lips were soft and warm and vulnerable as she added, "But I had to talk to somebody. And you were so nice to me before, just like you are now."

Roland Middleton had known many women, but never had he known one with the charm, innocence, and un- spoiled beauty of Rose Yancy. A thought came to him: *Someone's going to sell her a bill of goods. She's fair game for some adventurer who doesn't have any compunction about things like that. She'll wake up one day and find herself totally lost.*

His mind worked quickly and he said finally, "Well, Rose, it's not my company. Mr. Rocklin would have to say. I'm not hopeful, but at least we could ask him." At the use of the word *we,* Rose smiled tremulously. "Would you go with me to talk to him?" she asked quickly. "I'd feel so much better if you would."

"Yes, I'll do that. But you mustn't get your hopes up."

Twenty minutes later they were standing in Frank Rocklin's hotel room, where Rose was making her plea.

Frank listened carefully, and once his glance met that of Roland Middleton, as if to say *Why did you bring this to me?* Finally when Rose was finished, he shook his head. "I'm sorry, Rose. This is a small company. We just don't need another actress."

"But I'll do anything," she said. "You need someone to keep up with the costumes and the guns and the things you use in the play. . . ." Rose's voice almost fell over itself. Her eyes were pleading as she stood before the two men. "Just let me go with you. You wouldn't have to pay me. Just a place to sleep and something to eat, that's all I want."

Frank was troubled by the girl. "Does your father know you're here, Rose?"

"He—he knows I'm in Richmond," Rose said. "He thinks I'm at a girlfriend's house. But he wouldn't mind. Not if you asked him, Mr. Rocklin."

"I couldn't be responsible for you," Frank said. Disappointment leaped into the young girl's eyes. "You can see how it is: a young woman going all over the country with a bunch of actors and actresses. I don't think your father would agree to it for a moment."

"I'm eighteen years old, Mr. Rocklin," Rose said, straightening up. She had removed the coat, and she made an attractive picture. She lifted her chin and said, "I'm not afraid to work. You won't have any trouble with me. I just want to leave the farm."

Middleton had been thinking and said suddenly, "Frank, we could use some help with the costumes. Especially when we go on tour. Nobody's really responsible, and we've got some walk-on parts with just short dialogue. It'd save Lorna and Carmen from having to make all those changes."

Frank gave Roland a disgusted look. He'd hoped that the actor would realize the difficulties. "Are you volunteering to be responsible for Miss Yancy, Mr. Middleton?" he asked sarcastically.

A sense of surprise ran through Middleton. He was not accustomed to putting himself out for anyone else. For so long a time his only concern had been drowning himself in drink and satisfying his own needs. Now he found himself saying, "She'll be all right. I'll do all I can—so will you. Lorna and Carmen will be her chaperons. It's respectable enough. After all, we're respectable people, aren't we?"

He caught a caustic look in Frank Rocklin's expression and was forced to grin. "Well, *you* are respectable, and it might do me good to have some responsibility." He hesitated, then said, "Give her a try, Frank. At least while we're here in Richmond. See how it goes."

Frank Rocklin felt he was making a mistake. He argued for five minutes, then threw up his hands. "All right, you can stay. I can't pay very much, and I'll have to talk to your father. He'll have to agree. You understand that, Rose?"

"I'll talk to him," she said breathlessly. There was a joy in her face that was obvious to both men. Her lips trembled as she turned and said, "Thank you, Mr. Middleton. I won't give you any trouble, I promise."

"I'm sure you won't, Rose," Middleton said. He was somewhat shaken now that he realized what he had promised. And when Frank told him to see about getting the girl a place to stay, they left, and Middleton turned to her and said, "Well, I guess I'm elected to take care of you." He grinned uncertainly. "I never had a daughter before, so I don't know how to start."

Instantly Rose looked at him. "You're not near old enough to be my father!" she said in a sprightly fashion. "An older brother, maybe."

Of course the whole plan had to be worked out. The next day, Rose sent word to her father. Yancy came, accompanied by Josh, and the pair talked with Frank Rocklin and Roland

213

Middleton for a long time. Finally they called Rose in and Buford Yancy said, "Rose, these two gentlemen have promised me to do their best to see you do right. They can't *make* you do right anymore than I can. They'll be here for two more weeks. I've said you can stay that long, then we'll talk again."

"Oh, Pa!" Rose ran to her father and threw her arms around him, squeezing him hard. When she looked up, there were diamonds in her eyes, and she whispered, "I'll be good, Pa. Don't you worry."

Later on, Frank said dryly to Roland, *"Don't you worry,* that's what she told her father. And I'm not going to. She's *your* responsibility. You take care of her."

Then a hard expression formed around Frank Rocklin's lips. "Roland, I like you, but you're not much good. I'm telling you this—I don't want that girl abused! You understand me?"

Roland Middleton was not offended. "Don't worry, Frank. I haven't done many good things with my life. Maybe if I can help Rose find herself, it'll be one mark in my favor." He turned and walked away, his head already filled with thoughts of what to do with this young girl, so alive, so vulnerable, so ready for life—so unaware of how life *really* was!

CHAPTER SEVENTEEN
A Matter of Loyalty

For the first few days of Rose Yancy's apprenticeship with the Rocklin Theatrical Company, things went well. Rose herself was ecstatic over the excitement and color of her new life, and finding work for her was no problem. She threw herself into keeping the costumes clean and in perfect condition and was always available for any errand or piece of work. Albert Deckerman had previously strewn his various costumes recklessly, so that from time to time he appeared on the stage wearing the wrong costume. His booming voice was often heard saying, "Rose, I don't know how we got along without you backstage."

The other aspect of Rose's new job included prompting the actors, although this was scarcely ever needed. On her fourth night, however, she was permitted to make a brief appearance on the stage. The play had called for a neighbor of the heroine to appear, say a half dozen lines, and then disappear. Either Carmen or Lorna had been forced to change costumes, make a quick appearance, and then rush backstage and change again. It had been Middleton who had said, "Rose, I think you ought to do a little acting." His eyes had sparkled with fun. And when she had taken a deep breath and nodded vigorously, he had gone to Frank and suggested that the girl be given a chance. Frank Rocklin had been happy enough, and both Carmen and Lorna had been really helpful. Neither of them relished the quick change, and together they had helped Rose find a dress that would do and coached her on the scene.

Just before Rose was to go out, Middleton had been standing beside her, soothing her nerves. "You'll do fine, Rose," he said. "Just forget about the audience and look right at Frank as you say your lines. Did you ever play any make-believe games when you were little?"

Rose was nervous, but his remark caught at her. "Yes, I always did. We playacted all the time. I made my brothers and sisters be in plays whether they wanted to or not."

"Well, it's just like that now. We're all playing a big game up here. Sometimes when I was first beginning, I'd pretend there was a big brick wall at the footlights, that no audience was actually sitting out there. It worked pretty well for me. I got to the point where I could just ignore the audience." His face grew a little glum and he said, "I still do that sometimes, when I do a bad job."

"You never do a bad job, Mr. Middleton!" Rose argued quickly. Her eyes were shining, and she added, "I sure appreciate what you've done for me. I know Mr. Rocklin would never have let me come to work unless you had agreed to look out for me."

Roland Middleton shrugged off the compliment, but actually it pleased him. "I'm glad I could help, Rose. But you mustn't get too caught up with this kind of life. It's a very fragile way to live. Look, there's your cue. Out you go now!" He reached and patted her on the shoulder as she moved onto the stage.

Rose saw that Frank Rocklin was standing in the middle of the stage waiting for her. She did not do as Middleton suggested, however. She took a quick glance at the audience and saw the faces packed in the long rows, all looking at her. But for some strange reason, it did not frighten her. She turned calmly to Frank and spoke her lines clearly. Frank smiled at her and winked, his back being to the audience, as he returned his own lines. And when she went offstage, J.

Harold Hardcastle and his wife, Elizabeth, were waiting for her. They both hugged her and said, "You did fine, child, just fine."

"It was such fun!" Rose beamed. She turned to Middleton, saying, "Oh, Roland, you didn't tell me it was such *fun!*"

Middleton noticed that it was the first time she had used his first name, and he was pleased. "I'm glad you enjoyed it. Maybe I'll write in a few more touching scenes or add a new motif to the play."

"What's a *motif*?" Rose demanded instantly. But he had no time to answer, for he heard his cue.

After the curtain had fallen and they had taken their curtain call, Roland stopped long enough to say, "Still excited over your opening night, Rose?" He smiled at her, the smile making his face look much younger.

Rose started to answer, "Oh yes, Roland, I've—"

"Hey there, pretty gal! I've come to take you out on the town."

Middleton and Rose both turned to see a burly, red-faced soldier wearing a sergeant's uniform. He had come backstage uninvited, as was the custom, but they both saw at once that he had been drinking. His face was red, and his speech was slurred. He suddenly took Rose by the arm. "Hey! I've been looking for a purty little thing like you. Come on now, let's you and me go out and celebrate."

Middleton at once scowled, "You're welcome to congratulate the lady, Sergeant, but that's all."

The burly soldier stopped smiling. He was one of those, Middleton saw at once, who turned ugly when he drank. And now his small, piggish eyes were squeezed almost shut as he said loudly, "Well, you're almost as pretty as she is." He laughed vacantly and added, "But I ain't taking *you* out. On your way, purty boy!"

Middleton stepped forward at once and struck the forearm of the soldier so that he dropped Rose's arm. "Let's not have any trouble about this. Life's too short for things like that," Middleton said. He turned half away and only caught a flash of the hamlike fist of the soldier as it came. He managed to pull himself partly out of the way, but the fist struck him on the shoulder and drove him backward. He almost lost his balance, but caught himself and then turned. The sergeant laughed raucously, saying, "I guess you need a lesson in manners, purty boy. Get outta here 'fore I give it to you." He turned to make another grab at Rose, and as he did Roland stepped forward and hit him squarely in the nose. It drove the soldier backward, and instantly his nose started bleeding. He looked down in bewilderment at the crimson stain spreading across his shirt. The blow had sobered him up, and when he realized what had happened, he uttered a wild roar and threw himself at Middleton.

Roland Middleton was not an expert in the art of brawling. He had had a few fights as a youth, practically none since he had become fully grown. The sergeant, on the other hand, obviously was a brawler of some experience. He came in, catching Roland high on the temple with a tremendous left hand. Roland tried to block the blow, but the sergeant was simply too strong for him. Flashing lights seemed to dance before his eyes as he was knocked backward. Before he could recover, another blow caught him square in the mouth. He fell at once to the floor.

The sergeant laughed and drew back his foot, yelling, "You won't be a purty boy when I git through with you!" But before he could deliver the kick, someone grabbed his foot and wrenched it high in the air. "Hey, what the—!" The soldier fell face down, trying to break his fall, but his forehead banged against the floor. Before he could move, a steely arm went around his throat and he was jerked to his feet. He struggled wildly, but the arm tightened mercilessly, and all he could do was gag. His arms thrashed and he tried to pull away, but as the oxygen grew thin, he became frantic. His voice gurgled in his throat, and he felt himself helpless against his unseen assailant.

Lorna had been shocked at the scene. As little as she knew

about fights, she realized that if the kick had been delivered it would have broken Middleton's ribs. She had not seen Frank Rocklin, but he had come from nowhere, yanking the soldier's foot upward. And when he hit the floor, Rocklin had grabbed him around the throat and hauled him to his feet. Lorna grew frightened as she saw the sergeant's face grow a brilliant red as he tried to suck air into his lungs. Frank's face was tense with anger, and for one moment she was afraid that he would kill the soldier.

But Rocklin loosened his grip and instantly applied a hammerlock to the sergeant and pulled him across the room. As everyone stared, he walked to the door, opened it with his free hand, and said, "Sergeant, I'm going to allow you to leave this time. If you come back, it'll be unhealthy for you." With that he shoved him through the door. The sergeant hurtled out, and as Frank shut the door, they heard the sergeant gasping as he fell. Frank turned and walked over to Middleton, "You all right, Roland?"

Middleton's mouth was bleeding, and there was a raw scrape over his right temple. He tried to struggle to his feet, and Frank leaned down and pulled him up. "That was one of the roughs," he said. "Come along. We'll get you patched up. That's a bad cut on your lip there."

"Oh, I can do that," Rose said quickly. The fight had taken place so quickly that she had had little time to think, but now she led Middleton away to his dressing room. She shut the door and said, "You sit down right there."

Middleton's head was swimming, his head and mouth giving him considerable pain. Rose disappeared and came back soon with a pan of water and clean cloths, and he sat quietly while she dabbed at his wounds. "I don't think I'm going to go into boxing as an occupation," he muttered.

"He was *mean!*" Rose said with indignation. She was standing very close to him—so close he could smell a faint scent of lavender. Even though he was hurting badly, he was aware of the smoothness of Rose's skin and the clearness of

219

her large green eyes. "I wish Mr. Rocklin had broken his dumb old neck!"

Middleton grinned, which hurt him, then inquired, "Have you had a lot of experience nursing beat-up actors?"

Rose was carefully dabbing at his mouth. She lowered the cloth and touched it with her hands, her touch gentle as possible. "That's going to hurt. I wish I had my medicine from the farm," she said. "It'd take some of the pain away."

"I'll be all right," Middleton said. He stood up and ran his tongue along the cut.

She watched him and whispered, "I sure thank you, Roland. You—you didn't have to do that."

"Why, sure I did. I'm your big brother, aren't I?"

Rose stared at him, an unspoken thought in her eyes. Finally, she said, "No, you're not my big brother. You're my friend, though. The best friend I have in the world."

★ ★ ★

Early the next morning, Lorna sat beside Middleton at the breakfast table. "How do you feel?" she asked quietly.

"Why, pretty well," he said. "My mouth's going to be a little sore, but it could've been worse." Roland shook his head. "Wonder where Frank learned to roughhouse like that? If he hadn't pulled that brute off me, I wouldn't have a whole rib in my body."

"He must have learned it in the army. He's very quick—and strong, too."

"Good thing for me he is." He looked down the table where Rose was sitting, talking to Elizabeth Hardcastle in an animated fashion. "I wonder what it would feel like to be fresh, unspoiled, and excited about life like Rose."

Lorna's gaze switched to the young woman, and she said, "I wonder that myself."

It was not the first time that Lorna had aroused Roland's curiosity. He had made such a tragic affair out of his own life. He hated to see anyone as young and beautiful as this English girl headed down that same road. "I hate to see you so low, Lorna," he said finally. "You've got everything. Oh, you've had a bad bump, but don't feel sorry for yourself. That's worse than getting kicked in the ribs by a drunken sergeant," he said bitterly. "The ribs heal up easier than the heart, I think." He laughed aloud rather harshly, saying, "I sound like a real bad romance novel, don't I? *Ribs heal easier than the heart!*"

Lorna gave him a quick glance. "Why, I think you're right, Roland. Any doctor can tie ribs up. Getting at the heart—that which is inside of us—who knows how to do that?"

"The preachers say it can be done," Roland observed.

"Do you believe that?" Lorna asked instantly. "I hadn't thought of you as a religious man."

Middleton hesitated, then said, "I can't forget my mother. Every time I hear people talk about how Christians are hypocrites who don't mean what they say and there's nothing to religion, I think about her. My father and I didn't get along. He was hard. Still is, I guess. But my mother never gave up on me." He leaned back in the chair, toyed with his coffee cup, finally lifted it and drank. He flinched as the hot liquid hit the cut in his mouth, and then he said, "Every time I think of her, I know there's something to it. God was in her. No question about it."

"I've known two or three people like that," Lorna admitted. Then she looked over and smiled bitterly. "But not us. We're too smart for that, aren't we, Roland?" He didn't answer, and finally she shook her head. "I'm sorry. I don't mean to be so caustic. I don't know what's the matter with me." She tried to smile, then reached over and put her hand on his arm. "We'll be all right, eventually. We just haven't found our way."

Frank had been watching the two talk together and wondered what they were talking about. As always, he was impressed by the fresh attractiveness of Lorna, and the thought came to him, *What if those two fell in love? It wouldn't be good for her. I think a lot of Roland, but he can't*

221

even take care of himself. Finally he spoke up, saying, "I've got an announcement to make. We have an invitation."

"An invitation to what?" Albert Deckerman questioned loudly.

"An invitation to a fancy ball." Frank pulled a note out of his pocket and held it up. "My relatives, Uncle Brad and Aunt Amy Franklin, have invited the whole company out to Lindwood, their plantation. We're all invited to come. Would you all like to go?" At once, the voices of the company assured him that they would. He stuck the paper back into his pocket with a grin and said, "All right. You'll have to behave yourselves, though. I don't want my Southern relatives to find out what a disreputable company I've really got!"

Rose came to Frank afterward, a little distressed. "You didn't mean me, did you, Mr. Rocklin?"

"About what, Rose?"

"About the party at Lindwood."

"Well, of course you're going. The note's from my aunt. She especially asked me to bring you."

Rose's face colored as she smiled and said, "Well, I just wasn't sure about it. We Yancys aren't great folks, you know. Not like the Rocklins or the Franklins."

Frank smiled, for he found this touching. "Well, *I* think you're great folks," he said. "It'll be an honor for them to have you. I'm sure your sister and all of them will feel that way, so put your best bonnet on because we're going to a ball."

★ ★ ★

The sun was setting as Clay and Melora rode into view of Lindwood. The cool October air brought a flush to Melora's cheeks as they rode in the open carriage. They both looked impeccable, dressed for the autumn ball given every year by Clay's sister, Amy, and her husband, Brad Franklin. Clay sat ramrod straight in his ash-gray uniform complete with a crimson sash around his lean middle. He had come home only two days before, and the two of them had been as loving as if they had just gotten married. Clay looked at Melora and nodded at the dress, a plum-colored fare of silk that he'd paid far too much for in Richmond. "You look beautiful," he said simply.

"Why, thank you, sir," she answered demurely. "And you'll be the handsomest man at that ball."

"Don't tell Rooney that. She thinks Lowell is."

"He is fine looking. So are Dent and David. All you Rocklin men are handsome devils." Then she asked suddenly, "What do you think about Rose? Going to be on the stage, I mean?"

Clay shook his head. "Took me off guard. What do you think?"

"I don't know," Melora said, shrugging her shoulders. "She never was like the rest of us. Always unhappy on the farm—you know that, Clay."

"Maybe she needs a good spanking. But I guess at eighteen, it's too late for that. I'll have a good talk with my Yankee nephew. I hope he's got some of Gid's good sense. Never thought of having an actor in the family. Almost as bad as having a jockey or a lawyer, isn't it?"

"Now you hush," she said quickly.

Clay grew serious and shook his head. "She's a sweet girl, but not like you at all. She always craves excitement, and the farm just doesn't give it to her."

They had reached the front steps of Lindwood, and Clay pulled the horses to a stop. Bruno, one of the Franklins' stable hands, took hold of the horses, and Clay stepped down from the carriage and walked around to Melora's side. "Come along now."

He helped her down, and the couple made their way inside and met Brad and Amy, who were greeting guests as they arrived. Then they turned and entered the ballroom. "There's Rose," Melora whispered. "I know who that is with her. He's got the Rocklin look."

The two approached, and as soon as they were there, Melora gave Rose a hug. "How pretty you look!" she said.

Rose had worn one of Lorna's dresses and said at once, "This is Mr. Frank Rocklin."

"You don't have to introduce us," Clay said. "I remember you well, Frank—you, Ty, and Bob."

"That was a long time ago, sir," Frank said. "We had a good time, even though it didn't last long enough for us. I hope that soon we will all be able to gather here again." He turned and said, "I'm happy to meet you, Mrs. Rocklin." He took Melora's hand and bent to kiss it. "My grandmother's letters did not do your beauty justice." Frank gestured toward a small group and said, "Here's the rest of my troupe. Let me introduce them to you."

Frank introduced his company, and when he was finished, Clay said, "I'm halfway tempted to ask you to put on your play tonight since the whole group's here. But I'll let you off this time. Come and sit down with me. I want to hear what's happening with your brothers—and your whole family, for that matter."

Frank followed Clay Rocklin to an alcove, where they sat down. For the next thirty minutes, they chatted, with Frank doing most of the talking, about his family. Finally, Clay said, "I'm glad to hear the family's doing well. I wish your father were out of Libby. I'm trying hard to get him exchanged." The two spoke of Gideon for a time, then Clay hesitated and said, "Frank, I've got to talk with you seriously. I hope you won't take it wrong."

"Why, of course not. What is it, Uncle Clay?"

"It's about Rose. Melora's worried about her. She's not sure—about the life of an actress."

Frank at once said, "I understand your concern." He went on to explain how Rose had come to him and how he had offered her a place for as long as the company was in Richmond. "Her father came by," he said. "I explained it to him. Did he tell you?"

"I haven't seen Buford. But if he told you it was all right, then of course it is."

Frank said, "I can't guarantee anything. All I can say is Mr.

Middleton and I will do our best to watch out for the girl. But you know she's a handful. Actually I hesitated to take her, but she begged so hard that I just couldn't say no."

Clay grinned rashly, his white teeth gleaming against his golden brown skin. "Those Yancy girls have a way of doing that," he said. "Well, you watch out for her the best you can, Frank. That's all I ask."

The two returned to the party, and the evening was a pleasant one for all of them. Frank danced with his relatives and spent a most enjoyable thirty minutes with Susanna Rocklin, his great-aunt. She was a beautiful woman at the age of sixty-two, with a sharp wit. Finally he found himself dancing with Carmen, who had been besieged by some of the young officers gathered for the ball.

"You're a hit," he said as they went around the polished floor.

"Any woman who wasn't actually hideous would be a hit here," she said. "Officers are all the same, North or South, aren't they?"

"If you mean that they appreciate a beautiful woman, you're right," he said. Then he asked, "What do you think of this place?"

Carmen looked around the floor at the colorful dresses of the women, the gray uniforms of the men, the flashing of brass buttons reflecting the chandeliers, and shook her head. "It's beautiful," she said. "But it isn't really the South, is it?"

"No, not really. There are few plantations and lots of poor folks, but the North has far more poor than rich, as well," he countered.

"Do you think they will let Rose stay with the company?"

"It looks that way. We'll have to be very careful about her, though. These Southerners are very protective of their young women."

"Roland seems to be doing a good job at that," she announced and nodded toward the two who sailed by, gliding in a waltz in and out among the dancers. "Have you noticed that Roland's doing better? He's not drinking. Do you suppose Rose has a good influence on him?"

"I think so. He doesn't like to look bad in front of her, which could be a good thing—or a bad thing."

"What could be bad about it?"

"If he fell in love with her. That would be bad."

"Why? Roland's a good man."

"Sure, but you know Roland. He can't even take care of himself, much less a wife and a family."

Dissatisfaction and something almost like pain swept across Carmen's face. "He can change, can't he, Frank? Anyone can change, given the chance."

Surprised at the intensity in Carmen's voice, Frank looked carefully at her. She was beautiful in her crimson dress, a daring one that not many women could wear. "Of course they can, but they have to want to. I'm not sure Roland wants to."

Carmen wanted to talk more with Frank, but the dance stopped. She was at once claimed by a tall colonel, who swept her off for the next dance.

Frank wandered around the floor awhile and finally saw Lorna slip out one of the side doors. Quickly he followed her. The sound of the music faded as he stepped outside and closed the door. Lorna turned to face him, and he said, "It's cool out here. Should I get your wrap?"

"No, I'm not staying long, Frank." She studied him then said, "I like your family very much."

"My father thinks the world of Clay," he said. He came to stand by her and smelled the jasmine that was in the scent she wore. Overhead the stars twinkled brightly against the velvet sky, and he said, "The story is that my father and Clay Rocklin were both in love with my mother—and Clay lost."

"It must've been a hard choice for her. Your father must be quite a man to have beat Mr. Clay Rocklin out. He's so fine looking! Such a fine man, too, from what I understand."

"Yes, he is. But he wasn't always that way." He hesitated, then said, "He had a bad experience in marriage, and it's taken him a long time to come back. The family talks about it sometimes. His first wife was not amiable, but Clay was always faithful to her, even though he loved Melora for years."

"I think that's very sweet. Melora's very beautiful." She let the silence run on, then said, "It's not very often the story turns out like that, is it, Frank?"

"You mean happily? Well, I suppose some of the time it does, some of the time it doesn't."

"But mostly it doesn't," she said.

Frank was interested in this. "Why do you say that, Lorna? I've wondered about you." He turned her around and stood facing her. "You're a puzzle to me."

"I think I'm a very simple woman," Lorna said quietly. She looked up, facing him, and said, "I think men put complexities in women that aren't really there."

"And sometimes," Frank countered with a slight smile, "women have complexities that they try to cover over with simplicities." He reached out, took her hand, and held it for a moment. "I didn't mean to sound like a half-baked philosopher. But I've been waiting for a chance to tell you how much I appreciate your coming with the group. You've been a great help."

Lorna was very conscious of his warm hand holding hers. She was troubled by it at the same time—or troubled by something that went on inside her. "I was glad to get away from England," she said quietly. Then the memories from the past rose in her and her face grew sad. "I wouldn't want to go back again."

Frank Rocklin was suddenly conscious of the vulnerability of this young woman whose hand he held. Her flesh was soft, warm, and vibrant, but there was a fragility in her that he could not identify. He wanted somehow to see her put it aside and manifest the joy that a beautiful woman should let the world see. "What's to be so sad for?" he whispered. "I hate to see that in you."

They were very close, and Lorna looked up intending to

227

speak, but she found she could not. The sadness that lay not too far beneath the surface suddenly caught up with her, and Frank Rocklin saw it. "Don't be sad," he said. "Life is good." He reached out and drew her close. She lowered her cheek against his chest, and he held her there quietly. There was a strength in him that she yearned for. His arms closed warm and strong around her and that moment she felt safe and secure. There was a sudden desire in her for whatever it is that a man brings to a woman. She had missed it, and in missing it she had feared she would never have anything like love again. And now for this one moment as he held her tightly, she felt something of what a woman ought to feel when a man protects her.

Frank was moved by her surrender. She was, he knew, a strong woman, not one to give herself easily. There was nothing in her but an intense femininity—that mystery that is woman, female—that the male must have. And now as she leaned against him, almost like a tiny bird nestling in a set of strong hands, he felt protective of her. Reaching up, he touched the back of her hair, caressing it, and when she looked at him, he said, "Don't be sad. You have so much, Lorna." He wanted to kiss her, but felt that would be wrong. Instead he touched her cheek with one hand and said quietly, "I want you to have what every woman should have. And you'll have it one day, I promise you."

Lorna was moved by his words. She had expected him to try to kiss her and when he did not, paradoxically she was both disappointed and relieved. Taking a deep breath, she nodded and stepped back. "I'm sorry, I don't often let these moods throw me," she said. "I suppose we'd better go back in."

"Are you all right?" he asked quietly.

She smiled, her face becoming quite serene. The moment had done something for her, and she knew she would think of it often. "Yes, Frank. I'm all right now. Let's go inside."

CHAPTER EIGHTEEN
The Secret Discovered

Maj. Miles Taliferro was dissatisfied. His profession lent itself to disappointment, for being a spy in both the North and the South was of necessity a matter of amateurism. There had been no professional spies, as such, when the war began. But now, both sides realized the need for information about the movements of the enemy.

Since his superior had warned him that an influx of agents from the North was to be expected, Taliferro had worked hard at instilling in his subordinates the necessity of rooting them out. This, of course, was most difficult. Some of the agents they had apprehended had *seemed* more Southern than those born in the South. Some of them had, indeed, been born in the South but had given their loyalty to the North. Now as Taliferro looked over the paperwork scattered on his desk, he grew irritable. Finally he shuffled the papers around and shoved them into a folder. Moving across the room, he leaned down and twirled the dial of a huge safe. It had been in a bank once, but Taliferro had managed to obtain it for storing his own files. The doors swung open. He put the folder carefully on top of a stack, shut the safe, and spun the dial again.

Moving swiftly, he left the office, saying, "I'll be gone for the rest of the day, Sergeant."

"Can I reach you at any particular place, Major?"

"I'll be moving around quite a bit. If you have to find me, I'll eventually be at that makeshift theater where Rocklin's company is playing."

The sergeant grinned. "I saw that play myself. It ain't bad, is it, sir?"

"It's all right, I suppose."

For the rest of the afternoon, Taliferro moved from point to point. He had a phenomenal memory for names and faces, and when he saw someone who looked slightly out of place, a stranger he didn't recognize, he managed to discover something about the party. Sometimes he did this by striking up a conversation directly, and other times he would move around, following the suspect and asking others for information. By five o'clock he gave up and moved to the Spotswood Hotel, where he entered the dining room. It was only half-filled this early, and he was able to obtain a good table. He was in the process of ordering when he looked up and saw Lorna Grey enter. At once he said to the waiter, "Hold on. I hope to have company." Moving across the floor, he came to stand in front of Lorna, saying, "Have pity on a poor, lonesome soldier—have dinner with me."

"I'll be glad to, Major." Lorna allowed him to escort her to the table. He seated her, then negotiated the meal, warning the waiter he'd have the place closed if the food wasn't prepared just right.

As the waiter left, Lorna smiled at him, amused by his threats. "Would you really have the restaurant closed?" she asked idly.

"I'd be shot if I did." Taliferro grinned. "This is the best place to eat in Richmond." He studied her for a moment, then asked, "How's the play going?"

"Very well, I suppose. At least all the seats are filled every night."

"I suppose that's due to many factors."

At once, Lorna understood his meaning. "Not very complimentary, Major. But true enough. Any kind of entertainment would play to a full house around here. It's not a very good play, I'm afraid."

"Not a good one for you, at least. You should be doing something quite different. Tell me about your career."

But Lorna, after touching on the subject, chose to lead him away from it. She spoke of the company, and when she mentioned Rose, Taliferro glanced sharply. "Rose Yancy? Who is she?"

"A girl from the country. Her sister's married to Clay Rocklin."

"That's unusual. I didn't know the Rocklins went in for the theater."

"The girl comes from a very poor family, I think. I understand she's not going to be with the company for long. When we leave Richmond, I'm not sure her father will let her accompany us."

"Mr. Rocklin—has he said when you'll be leaving?"

"No, he hasn't mentioned it. But he did say when we left Washington that we'd be touring the South, so I presume we'll be performing in some other cities down here."

They talked idly until the food came, and then as they ate, Taliferro picked up the threads of the conversation again. "As I told Mr. Rocklin, it seems a strange thing to bring a theatrical company here." A sour look came to his face and he said, "I'm sure you've discovered that Confederate money is worth very little." He took a bite of the steak before him, chewed it thoughtfully, and said, "Mr. Rocklin said he wanted to see the South again, but it doesn't seem to be a wise or professional move."

"I suppose that's so. But I know nothing about Mr. Rocklin's plans."

"He visits his father every day, I'm told."

"Yes, he does. I think he's very concerned about his condition."

For some time, they sat there talking. And finally Lorna became aware that there was some sort of pattern to the conversation. Taliferro would speak idly of certain things, but his questions always came back to the company, especially to Frank Rocklin. She said nothing to him about this, but filed it in her mind. Later on, after they had parted, she asked herself, *I wonder why he's so interested in Frank?* The thought would not leave her, and from that moment on she began to pay more attention to Frank's movements.

★ ★ ★

The skies had grown completely dark, and as they left the theater after the performance and moved back to their hotel, the company had little to say. Middleton was walking with Rose, and once he looked up and said, "We'll have rain before morning."

Rose followed his glance and agreed, "Yes, it smells like that, doesn't it?"

They arrived at the hotel, and the company said goodnight and went to bed. But Lorna suddenly remembered that she had left her purse at the theater. It contained all the money that she had, and she was not certain that it would be safe. She went to Frank's room to get the key, but to her surprise he was not inside. Puzzled, she thought, *But he just came here. Where could he be?*

Albert Deckerman took care of the props, and she knew that he had a spare key. She went to Albert's room, borrowed his key, and told him she'd return it the next morning.

"You'd better let me go with you if you're going back to the theater," he proposed.

"No, I'll be all right. I'll take a cab. You go to sleep, Albert."

"All right, but I'd be glad to go."

Lorna did not take a cab, for the theater was only a few blocks away. She walked along the sidewalks, the oil lamps casting enough light for her to see clearly. When she arrived at the theater, she went inside and found her purse in the dressing room. Then she left the theater, locking the simple hasp back in place. Turning to go, she saw a man across the street and was surprised to identify him as Frank Rocklin. He was walking with his head down, for a few drops of rain had started to fall. Lorna remembered her conversation with Taliferro, and on impulse crossed the street. She kept far enough behind Rocklin so that she could not be identified. Frank walked for two blocks, then stopped suddenly as a man came out of an alley. The two spoke to each other, then moved back into the darkness of the alley.

Alarm ran along Lorna's nerves, and she moved closer to the building and waited. *What could he be doing here? And why's he so secretive about it?* she asked herself. She knew little of Frank Rocklin's business. There could be any number of reasons or explanations of why he was meeting someone at this time of night, but she couldn't think of one. Finally, Rocklin came out and turned back toward her, and she saw the other man emerge and turn in the other direction. Rocklin was headed straight for her and, fearful of being seen, Lorna turned and walked as rapidly as she could along the boardwalk. When she got to the street where the hotel was, she crossed and went at once to her room. She unlocked the door, stepped inside, and after she shut it, moved across to the window. She watched as Frank came down the street, turned, and entered the hotel. Curiosity came to her even stronger, and she moved to the door and cracked it. She saw Frank reach the landing and turn to his own room. He opened the door and shut it very quietly, as one who didn't want to be heard.

"How very strange!" Lorna murmured. She undressed, washed her face, took a sponge bath carefully, then put on her nightgown. For a time, she sat on the side of her bed wondering what it all could mean. Finally she shrugged. *He probably has a good explanation for it,* she thought, then lay down and went to sleep.

The next morning at breakfast, however, something more disturbing happened. In the middle of the conversation, Middleton said he hadn't slept well. "How about you, Frank?" he asked. Lorna was sitting directly across from

233

Frank, and she saw a break in his features. "I went right to bed and slept like a log," he said and continued eating. *That's a lie!* Lorna thought. *He did no such thing.*

Frank looked up and saw her watching him. "What do you plan to do today, Lorna?" he asked. "Like to take a ride around town? You and Roland and Carmen and I could maybe see a little of the town."

"That would be nice," Lorna agreed.

They went on their ride later that afternoon. Carmen and Middleton were jaded with strange places, but Lorna found Richmond fascinating. Once they passed by a slave market and she said, "Could we see that?"

Frank looked at her strangely. "I suppose so." He drove the wagon to a hitching post, got out, and came to help her down. The four of them made their way into a huge barnlike affair, where the sale was already going on. Lorna found herself disgusted by the entire thing. The auctioneer had just brought a woman in her middle thirties and a small boy to the front. "What am I bid for this fine pair?" he demanded. "Come over, gentlemen. They're worth the money. This buck will make a fine field hand. This woman's capable of bringing lots more like him into the world."

Lorna watched as the prospective buyers went to the front. Some of them prodded the woman's body as if she were an animal. More than one rude remark ran around the room. But the ending was more shocking. One of the bidders made a high bid for the woman, but said, "I can't use the boy."

The auctioneer at once said, "We'll sell them separately."

The woman reached out, grabbed the small boy, and held to him, her eyes defiant and filled with fear. The auctioneer nodded. Two strong-looking men came and held the woman, who screamed while the boy was ripped from her arms.

"Let's get out of here," Frank said grimly. "I've had all of this I want to see." The others were ready, and they hurried to the wagon. The afternoon was spoiled for all of them, and when they got back to the hotel, Frank said, "That's the other part of the South—the ugly part. People get fooled by the magnolias and the nice weather, but any system that'll tear a child from his mother has got to go!"

Lorna agreed at once. "Inhuman slavery was outlawed in Great Britain years ago. I think it's indecent that this country permits it."

"Well, I don't think they'll permit it long," Middleton said. "That's what this war is all about."

★ ★ ★

The play stretched out to a three-week run. And it was in the middle of the third week that Lorna had opportunity to observe Frank Rocklin's strange behavior again. She had noticed that he went out at odd times, and one night while sitting at her window after a play, she saw him exit from the hotel. At once, she knew that he was off on another one of his missions—whatever it was. Instantly she grabbed her coat, left her room, and as she left the hotel, she saw him turn a corner. Without knowing why, she felt she had to know what he was doing. Something in her revolted against the idea that he was not what he seemed. The idea had been growing in her that he was perhaps involved in the Southern Secret Service. She had thought of Maj. Taliferro's questions and had finally decided that perhaps he was Frank's superior. It didn't make much sense to her, but she could not come to any other conclusion.

She had been very clever, she thought, about following Frank. He made his way down the street past the place the last meeting had been, and two blocks later he turned to cross into what appeared to be two vacant lots between two wooden structures. There were no streetlights on this side street, and Lorna felt her way along.

Once she stopped, listening for the sound of voices, but hearing none she kept moving forward. *They've got to be here somewhere,* she thought. Far away the distant tinny sound of a piano came to her from one of the saloons that were still open, but ahead there was no sound at all. Then, abruptly, before she could even move, a pair of strong arms went around her from behind. When she opened her mouth to scream, a hard hand was clapped over her lips, cutting off her cry. She struggled and fear raced through her. Fiercely she kicked with her sharp heel and had the satisfaction of raising a grunt from her assailant, but his hands remained firmly in place. She heard someone else coming, moving from her side, and then she heard Frank's voice demanding, "Who is it, Perkins?"

"I've been watching her. She followed you all the way down the street and turned in here after you did. She's got to be a spy."

Lorna did not recognize the second voice, but she did recognize Frank's. And now she heard him ask, "What'll we do?"

"We can't let her go loose," the first voice said.

Frank said quickly, "Let her talk. I can't believe anyone followed me."

Dave Perkins was a hard man and had done hard things. "We'll have to get her out of here—kidnap her till we find out what she's up to. I think she's one of Taliferro's agents."

Lorna found herself being held tightly, but the hand moved away from her lips. Perkins said, "Who are you? What are you doing following us?"

Lorna said at once, "Frank, it's me, Lorna!"

"Lorna!" Frank was aghast. Then he said abruptly, "It's all right, Perkins. She's one of the actresses in our company."

"It's not all right," Perkins said. "Why is she following you?" A thought came to him and he said, "Is she your woman? Maybe she was just jealous."

Lorna struggled with his grip, and he released her but kept one hand on her arm. "No, I'm not his woman," she said angrily. She looked at Frank and said, "Who is this man, Frank?"

Frank hesitated, then knew he would have to tell the

truth, but not here. "It's all right, Perkins. I'll take care of it."

Perkins said angrily, "You can't take care of it. We'll have to get her out of here. She knows too much."

"You don't know what she knows," Frank snapped. "I said I'd handle it." He reached over and took Lorna's arm. "Come on, Lorna."

Lorna was relieved to feel the man called Perkins release her. She stumbled along as Frank pulled her out of the darkened lot. He said nothing until they were half a block away. Then when she said, "Frank—" he muttered, "Don't talk—not here."

He led her back to her room, and when she unlocked it, he stepped inside, following her, then shut the door. She was trembling and asked at once, "What are you doing, Frank? I have to know."

Frank nodded slowly. "Yes, you do have to know." He hesitated, then said, "Sit down. It's a long story." He waited until she was seated, then began, "I have a brother. The best man that ever lived. . . ."

Lorna sat listening to the story, and when he was through, she stared at him. "So you're a spy for the North. That's it?"

"That's it," Frank said wearily. He drew his hand across his forehead, then lowered it. "I'm sorry you found out about it. It has nothing to do with you. You're not involved in this war."

Somehow, Lorna was feeling a pain she hadn't expected. She could not understand it. Her mind went back to the time when she had stood with Frank and he had held her. She remembered the comfort that had come to her, the strength that had flowed out of him and that she had trusted. That grew bitter now, and anger rose in her. "No, it's not my war, but I hate to be used."

Frank stared at her. "What do you mean *used?*"

"You're using us all," Lorna said, her voice cold. "All of us. None of the rest of them know anything about this, do they? They think you're doing it because it's your profession. But you'll drop the whole company if you want to. Anything to get even for your brother, is that right?"

Frank stared at her. "Don't put it like that, Lorna," he said quietly. "I want this war to be over. This is the way that I've chosen to help." He, too, was remembering how he had held her in his arms and how she'd responded. "Please don't be upset," he said finally. "I couldn't tell you. You wouldn't have come—nobody would've come!"

"That's right," Lorna said flatly. "I wouldn't have come, and I'm not staying."

Frank stared at her. A sense of disloyalty came to him. He had felt the same way when he had been at Lindwood, using his family to get information for their enemies. He felt it now as he stood before Lorna, her eyes angry, her lips drawn tightly together. He felt that he'd like to throw the whole thing over, but he'd gone too far for that, and he hadn't completed his job. "I can't stop you if that's what you want to do," he said at last. "Are you going to tell the others?"

Lorna found herself trembling. "No," she said. "And I'll stay. It wouldn't be fair to them for me to leave. I care about them, even if you don't."

It was a hard moment for Frank Rocklin. He had learned to admire this young woman, and he'd lost her trust. That moment of harmony and gentleness they had shared together was now gone, he saw. He said wearily, "Well, I thank you for that. I'll keep you clear of it. Hopefully, it won't be for too long. Then we can go back." He stood, then moved to the door. When he got there, he turned back to her again and said simply, "Lorna, I'm sorry." Then he turned and left the room.

Lorna closed and locked the door behind him, then she went to the bed, fell across it, and began to weep.

PART FOUR
The Last Act
NOVEMBER–DECEMBER 1863

CHAPTER NINETEEN
Josh Gives a Challenge

"I'm glad to be back in Richmond." Carmen was sitting in the dressing room, applying her makeup. She looked up at Lorna, who was doing the same at the other makeshift dressing table. "I've seen about all of the South that I want to see," she added.

Lorna carefully put the final touches on her face, murmuring, "It was interesting to me. I was surprised at how small most of the so-called big cities are, here in the South." They had gone on a short tour, playing in Montgomery for two weeks. After the first two days, the troupe had found little to draw their attention.

Rose, who had come in with dresses freshly pressed for the two women, listened as the actresses talked. "I thought it was fun. I wish we could travel some more." She helped Carmen put on her dress, and when the actress left the room at her call, she said to Lorna, "You think I'll ever get to be a real actress, Miss Lorna?"

"I'm sure you will." Lorna smiled with encouragement. "Though I'm not sure it's what you really ought to do. It's a hard life—as you've found out on this tour."

"Not as hard as living on a farm," Rose insisted. She fastened up Lorna's dress and stood back in admiration. "Now, you look right pretty," she said. Then she held her skirt out and said, "How do I look? All right?"

241

"You look fine, Rose, just fine."

The two women left the dressing room and went to stand in the wings. The timing on the play had become so perfect that Lorna had learned how to leave the dressing room with only seconds to spare. As she arrived in the wings, she heard her cue and walked out on the stage speaking her opening line: "Why, Davis! What are you doing here?"

Frank turned as she entered, showing his profile to the audience, and spoke his line: "I had to get away. I had to see you, Alice." He crossed the stage to her and took her hand. The two stood there speaking their lines until the culmination of the love scene. Lorna's face was half turned toward the audience, and she kept a loving expression on him. "I love you, Davis," she whispered, reaching up to pull his head down. When his lips came down on hers, she could not help but remember how close they had been for a time. And even now, in view of a full house, she was moved more than she liked to admit by his kiss. He clung to her, pressing her closer, and seemed to savor the kiss more than was necessary. She broke away and continued the scene.

After the two had left the stage and the Hardcastles were heard doing their part of the play, Frank said, "That was well done, Lorna."

Lorna stopped and looked at him. She'd been distant since discovering what his actual purpose was in raising the company, and now she said sharply, "I don't think you have to hold me quite so tightly in that scene, Frank."

Turning to look at her, Frank lifted his eyebrow. He knew that she was distrustful of him. He was disturbed that they had lost the warmth that had existed. "As an actress you ought to know we've got to live our roles, at least out on that stage."

"I think I know the difference between acting and what you've been doing."

Frank stared at her, but could say nothing, for he knew that she was partly right. He ducked his head, bit his lip, then he lifted his eyes to her, saying, "I'm sorry." He tried to think how to explain, and finally shrugged. "If I feel something for you, I guess it comes out when I'm close, especially in a kiss. I don't know how to kiss a woman without some sort of response." The other actors moved about, getting into their places, and although there was no time, he said, "I'd hoped that we'd get back to what we were once, Lorna. I think about you all the time."

Lorna hesitated. There was a faint longing in her that stirred to life as she thought about their past. She had been drawn to Frank Rocklin as she never had been to any man. Yet, the memory of her tragic experience with Michael Dennis was still with her. She had raised a wall since discovering Frank's activities with the Secret Service and could not seem to put it behind her. Wearily she said, "I'm sorry I said anything. Forget it, will you, Frank?" Turning, she walked away and entered the dressing room.

After the play was over, the company went out to eat. But Frank noticed at once that Lorna did not accompany them. As he was sitting down with Carmen to drink his coffee, he mentioned the fact.

"I expect she's just tired from the tour," Carmen answered carelessly. "She's not tough enough for things like that, I suppose." Finally she reached over and put her hand over his. "These English ladies are meant for drawing rooms and tea and things like that."

Frank reached over, picked up her hand, and held it for a moment. He smiled, saying, "You've been great for the company, Carmen."

Disappointment rose in the woman, for she had been hoping for something more intimate. She, too, had noticed the cooling off between Frank and Lorna and had hoped that it meant that Frank would be devoting more time to her. When he released her hand, she felt a vague sense of dissatisfaction. "I wish we could stay here for a long time," she said finally.

"There's not much money in it," Frank replied. "You certainly don't need the experience."

Something about the remark displeased Carmen. She had thought much about herself during the days of the tour and about Frank Rocklin. Carmen was perhaps oversensitive about her age. At thirty-two, she was past her youth, and Frank was so much younger. She had known men to marry older women and was aware that she did not look her age. Nevertheless, his remark about her "experience" somehow hurt her. Finally, when the two rose and left, she said, "It's not too cold to go for a walk, is it?"

"No, of course not. Just a little snappy is all. Nothing like our Northern falls, is it, Carmen?"

The two walked along the streets, the brisk wind snatching at their clothing, making it flutter. "There might be some snow in that," Frank observed, walking along. "The sky looks like it wants to, but I think it's too warm for that. I wouldn't mind seeing a little snow. I always liked it." She stumbled slightly, and he took her arm and held lightly on to it. "I like to make snowmen, have snowball fights, and go sledding."

They took two turns around the block, then entered the hotel. He accompanied her up to her room, and, opening the door, she turned to him. "Thank you for the walk. It was nice," she said. She waited for him to say something, and it was on her mind to invite him in. She sensed that would be a mistake. She had been free, too much, with her favors in the past, and it had to be different with Frank. Still, she knew how to look up and entice a man, and so when she did, he leaned forward and kissed her on the lips. She pulled away at once and whispered huskily, "That was sweet. Good night, Frank."

As the door closed, Frank turned and walked to his own room. He was thinking about so many things. He had been concerned about Perkins, who had been hinting at some great action that would have to take place, although he would not say what. He was also buried in thought about keeping the company going. He had discovered one thing— that acting was the life for him. Entering his room, he shut the door and locked it, then undressed and went to bed. For some time, he lay thinking about problems that existed, especially about his brother. He still felt a bitterness at what the war had done to his family and could not shake it off.

"Got to stop thinking like that," he said. His mother had talked with him, as had others. He remembered how Bob had smiled and said, "You can't let bad things turn you sour. God's too good to let that happen. He's going to do something in you, Frank."

Frank Rocklin thought of these words and finally drifted off to sleep. His last thought, however, was of the softness of the lips of Lorna Grey. "Stage kiss," he murmured, "but I wonder if it will always be like that."

★ ★ ★

"I'm going to do something about it, Rena." Josh Yancy had been walking with Rena along the stream that bordered Gracefield. It was a favorite place for the two of them. They had caught pumpkinseed perch, fat and thumping, in the summer. And they had seen deer drink from its waters, then bound away in that airless fashion of the breeze. It was here that they had come to talk when they had had problems. And now as they walked along, a thought came to Josh. "You know," he said, "I hardly ever stutter anymore. You broke me of that habit."

"I think you did it yourself, Josh," Rena said. She was very pretty that day, wearing a dark-green dress and, on her head, a felt cap that she and Melora had picked out. It had been expensive, but Josh had liked it, and that had been enough. Now they came to a narrow place in the creek. "Let's cross to the other side," she said.

"All right." Josh followed behind her, saying, "Don't fall in. It's too cold for that."

They moved along the north side of the creek. The grasses were brown and dead now, and the trees were orange, red, and a brilliant yellow. "What is it that you're going to do, Josh?" Rena asked.

"I'm going to do something about Rose. She can't go on like she's been doing."

"But what can you do?" Rena asked. "She's grown up. She's eighteen. If she wants to be an actress, you can't stop her."

"Maybe not, but I'm going to try," Josh said. He was filling out now, his lanky frame showing the beginnings of strong muscles, his shoulders broadening. There was a maturity in his face that had not been there a year ago. "I'm going to Richmond tomorrow for Pa, and while I'm there I'm going to have a talk with Rose. Maybe even with Mr. Frank Rocklin. I sort of like him, even if he is a Yankee."

"Well, he's a Rocklin—part of my family," Rena said quickly. "He is nice, and good-looking too."

Josh glanced at her, and a mischievous light came to his eyes. He lost his troubled expression for a moment and reached out and took her arm. She squealed as he held her toward the creek, leaning over. "I think I'll just dunk you in the water," he teased. "That'll stop you from looking at these good-looking actors."

"You let me go, Josh Yancy!" She struggled in his grasp, but was powerless in his strong hands. "Please, Josh!" she said. "Don't let me fall."

At the piteous tone, Josh hesitated, then pulled her back. "I wouldn't do that," he said. "But don't be looking at any of these handsome fellas around here. Mr. Rocklin's your cousin, but I saw you looking at Sam Goodwin the other day in church. He's plumb loony over you." He hesitated and said, "Some would even say he's good-looking, even better looking than me."

"Those with eyes," Rena said pertly. Then at the look on his face, she laughed and hit him, then took his arm. "Come on, let's walk. I'm not interested in Sam Goodwin."

The two finished their walk. He took her back to the house, and before he left he had a word with Susanna. He had great confidence in Rena's grandmother and talked with her for some time about his concerns for his sister. Melora came in while they were talking and listened quietly. Finally, he turned to her and said, "Melora, why don't you go talk to Mr. Rocklin? He'd listen to you."

"It's not Mr. Rocklin that you need to think about. It's Rose. She's headstrong, and there's nothing Mr. Rocklin can do about that. I don't think you ought to go, either."

Josh was usually an agreeable young man, but it had hurt him that his sister had gone on the stage. For some reason, he had strong feelings about people in the theater. He had heard enough stories about the immoral lives of actors and actresses, and he wanted none of that for Rose. He shook his head stubbornly and said, "I'm going to talk to her and Mr. Rocklin, too."

When he had left, Melora turned to Susanna, saying, "It won't do Josh any good. Might even make Rose more stubborn. I wish he wouldn't go."

"Well," Susanna said, "he's going, and that's all there is to it. You Yancys have a pretty stubborn streak." She reached over and patted her daughter-in-law on the shoulder. "But I'm proud of all of you. Clay couldn't have had anything better happen than to get you, Melora."

★ ★ ★

As soon as Josh had finished the business for his father in Richmond, he went to the theater. He found Frank Rocklin without any trouble and said quickly, "Can I talk to you alone, Mr. Rocklin?"

"Why, sure, Josh. Come on to my dressing room. We'll have a little privacy."

Josh sat down, then began nervously, "I'm worried about Rose, Mr. Rocklin." He went on to explain his difficulties, and Frank felt a great sympathy for the young man.

When Josh had finished with a plea for Frank to do something, Frank spread his hands out and said, "Josh, I appreciate your concern for Rose. I wish I could do something, but the only thing I could do is fire her. If I did that, what would happen?"

Josh thought hard and said, "She'd be madder than hops."

"That's right, and disappointed, too. Your father allowed her to travel to Montgomery with us, so he must have some confidence in our ability to take care of Rose. And after working with us for a while, maybe she'll learn that the theater isn't too good a life. Why don't you just let her stay? Mr. Middleton and I are looking out for her, and so are Miss Montaigne and Miss Grey."

At the name of Middleton, Josh seemed to bridle. He said nothing, but a rebellious streak rose in him. He wanted to argue, but saw that it was useless. "Well, thank you, Mr. Rocklin. I appreciate your looking out for my sister."

At the same time that this pair was talking, Rose and Roland were riding in a buggy. She had teased him into taking her for a ride, and the two had driven out of the city. She had shown him around the parts that she knew of the countryside, and now they were on their way back.

"Oh, it's been such fun, Roland!" she said. "Can't we stay a little longer?"

"Not if we're going to make the curtain tonight," Roland said. He glanced at her, admiring the rosy complexion stirred by the wind. She had the clearest eyes he had ever seen; they were the most peculiar shade of green. He had noticed the same shade of green in the eyes of Melora Rocklin and also her brother Josh. "You look very pretty," he said, paying her a rare compliment. "Those Confederate officers that line up to meet you, I'll have to fight them off with a stick tonight."

Rose flushed and shook her head. "You won't have to do that."

"Does it make you feel good to have men flocking around you like bees after honey?"

"I don't care about that," she said sharply. Then she glanced at him quickly. "I didn't mean to be short with you, but I'm happy as I am. I don't need to be thinking about any officers. All I want to do is be an actress."

They had had this conversation many times, and Roland had given up trying to argue against this desire to act that burned in her. They drove along at a leisurely fashion, Rose speaking freely and gesturing with her hands, as was her way. Roland sat listening, enjoying her company. Finally they came into town and returned the buggy to the livery stable.

As they made their way back to the hotel, he began telling her, at her request, of some of the famous people he had met. "I have some pictures somewhere of Mr. Booth—not John, but his father—whom I met when I was a child. And some other famous stars of the theater."

"Oh, could I see them? Do you have them with you?"

"I think so," he said. "I think they're in the bottom of the trunk, if I remember."

When they got to his room, she said, "Please, Roland! Let me see the pictures. It won't take long. We have time."

"Well, all right. Come in." Prudently he left the door ajar and said, "Sit down, and I'll see if I can dig them out."

Five minutes later Roland had found the pictures and then carried in the chair from Rose's room—since his room only had the one chair—and sat down next to her at the small table in his room. Spread out on an oak table were various tintypes and daguerreotypes. Rose was exclaiming with delight as he pointed out the famous actors he had known.

"This is the whole cast of *Macbeth*." He grinned and asked, "Can you guess which one is me?"

"Why, of course!" Rose said indignantly, putting her finger on the photograph. "That's you right there." She looked up at him and smiled. "I don't like you with whiskers."

"Well, I don't either, to tell the truth." He rubbed his smooth cheek with his hand and smiled. "All for art's sake. You sometimes have to suffer to be an actor."

For a few minutes they sat there; finally she gathered the pictures up and put them neatly in a stack. "You need to put these in a scrapbook," she scolded. "They're going to get scarred if you don't."

"Don't have time."

"Well, I do," she said. "Do you have anything I could put them in? We can buy a scrapbook, and we'll start right away. You can help me, but I'll paste them in after you show me the order."

"I don't think it's going to be a very valuable scrapbook. Not like Frank Rocklin's. I think he'll be a great star one of these days."

"You could be a star." She held the pictures carefully and looked down at one of them. "You could do it if you wanted to."

"I guess I've just lost my ambition. A man gets tired of trying to keep up a front."

"Why are you so sad sometimes, Roland?" Rose asked.

He hesitated, then said, "I've never told you this, but I got hurt pretty bad once."

Rose Yancy was an intuitive girl and at once asked, "Was it a woman?"

"Yes, it was. I guess I've forgotten most of it."

"No, you haven't." She looked into his eyes, and her face had grief in it. "There's something in your voice when you talk about it. It's like echoes from your past. I'm sorry," she said simply.

"Things like that happen, but it seems like it's hard to get over."

Rose impulsively took one of his hands in hers. Looking up to his face she whispered, "I wish I could do something to help you. You've done so much for me!"

Knowing that it was not right, Roland reached over and pulled her closer. He gave her plenty of time to reject him—to shove him away—but she did neither of these. Her eyes grew large, but she said nothing. Her hand was trembling in his, but he saw that there was no real fear of him in her eyes. "You're a sweet girl, Rose. I wish I'd met you a long time ago." Then he bent and gave her what he meant to be a quick kiss, but somehow it was not. The touch of her lips stirred him, and he put his arm around her and drew her close. There was a youthful innocence in the girl, and her lips were soft and pliant under his. It was different, he knew, from other women's kisses, and he knew that he would not forget it.

Rose had been kissed a few times, but she had grown very fond of this tall, thin man who had been so kind to her. And now as he held her, she felt drawn to him and put her hand on his neck. He was gentle, and she knew that he was feeling something of the same emotion that had risen in her.

Suddenly a voice broke out, startling both of them. "Rose!"

Rose broke away from Middleton and leaped to her feet to face Josh, who had entered through the half-opened door. Rose flushed, for she knew the situation looked bad. Middleton turned pale, and he said at once, "Now, Josh, this isn't what it seems—"

"I reckon I can see what it is!" Josh stated flatly, his face drained of color, his mouth drawn into a thin, straight line. "I knew you were no good," he said in a shrill voice. "I knew it all the time! I knew what you were like."

"It's not what it looks like," Rose said. "We were just—"

Josh ignored her. "I don't know what you Yankees do when you catch a fellow messing with your sister, but I know what I'm going to do. A friend of mine will call on you. I don't care whether it's guns, knives, or what, but I'll have satisfaction."

"Don't be ridiculous," Roland started. "I'm not going to fight a duel with you."

"That's up to you," Josh said. "Either you'll fight me on those terms, or I'll shoot you out of the saddle when you go out for a ride."

"Josh, don't be foolish." Rose ran to him and shook his arm, but he jerked away from her, his eyes cold.

"Are you going home with me and forget all about this, Rose?"

Rose hesitated. "No, I can't."

"Then it'll have to be a fight." He turned and left the room, slamming the door.

"He'll do it, Roland," Rose said. "You've got to leave town."

Roland said, "I can't do that." Then he knew the despondency that could only come with despair. "You'll have to go now, Rose," he said.

She gave him a strange look, then turned and left the room. Roland Middleton stood there feeling bleak despair. Finally he looked up at the mirror on his wall and said aloud in the bitterest of all tones, "Well, Roland, you've done it again, haven't you? Not content with messing up your own life, now you have to ruin the life of an innocent young girl."

He slammed his fist against the raw pine-board wall and then leaned against it, pressing his face against his arm—and wishing he could go back and be the man he once was.

CHAPTER TWENTY
"Why Hast Thou Forsaken Me?"

"Well, we've got another invitation from my family."

The company had been having breakfast together, and all of them looked up as Frank spoke. "Not to a ball this time." He held up a letter that he had just opened. "It's from my grandmother. She wants us all to come to church. It's a Thanksgiving service."

The response to his announcement was mixed. The Hardcastles eagerly agreed to go. But Albert Deckerman and Carmen shook their heads stubbornly. "I had enough of being made to go to church when I was growing up," Albert boomed. It seemed as if he couldn't speak in a normal voice, and some of the people at other tables looked over at him with distaste.

Carmen said quickly, "I think I'll stay in and rest today."

"I'd like to go," Rose said, casting a quick glance at Middleton.

"I suppose I'd better go, too," Middleton said. "I need it." He had been depressed since Josh had made his threat. He had told Frank about it, and Frank had tried to comfort him. "Too bad it had to happen, Roland. But he's just a hotheaded boy. I'm sure we can calm him down." He had ridden out to Gracefield and spoken to Melora, explaining the matter to her. And Melora had talked with Josh and her father. The matter seemed to have calmed down, but Middleton was still depressed about it. He knew he had been in error, and his low self-esteem had dropped even lower.

"I'll rent a carriage," Frank said. "We'll leave about eleven o'clock. It's a special afternoon service."

Frank finished breakfast and an hour later was in his room reading when a knock came at his door. Thinking it was one of the cast, he said, "Come in."

The door opened, and Frank was shocked to see Dave Perkins slip inside. He came off the bed at once, saying, "Perkins, you shouldn't be here! We don't need to be seen together."

"I was careful." Perkins had a strange catlike walk, and he was very quick despite his short barrel shape. He moved over to the window, looked out, then turned back to Frank. "I was careful, but I had to see you."

"What is it? Something happened?"

"I've got this thing penned down." The quick, black eyes of the agent gleamed as he looked at Frank. "Our people have been having fits trying to interpret the ciphers of the Confederates."

"I thought they had it all figured out," Frank answered.

"They did for a while. Do you know much about ciphers?"

"No, not a lot."

"Well, here's one here." Perkins pulled out a small slip of paper and handed it to Frank. It was a square with letters in random fashion, in different rows. "Here's the way it works. First, you have to have a key. The key to this one is the words *complete victory*. You have to have that to make the cipher work, but once we got that, we were able to interpret all the messages pretty well. Lucky for us, the Confederates don't have their own lines. They have to use the public lines, so we can pick them up."

"What's the trouble then, if you've got the message?"

"They've gotten on to us. They know we can read this code." He took the paper back and stuck it in his pocket.

"What they've done is gone to another method." He reached into his inside pocket, pulled out an object, and handed it to Frank. "Ever see anything like this?"

Frank took the object, which was a large, brass disk. It had letters from *A* to *Z* around it on the outer edge. There was an inner ring that moved also with the letters from *A* to *Z*. In the middle, U.S.A. was printed. "How does it work?" Frank asked. He listened as Perkins explained.

"To encode each letter, you have a *key letter*. Let's say it's the letter *B*. Then you put this letter under the letter *A* on the outer wheel. Then all you have to do is take the letters of the message on the outer wheel, and right beneath each of these letters, you substitute the letters on the inner wheel. We've got to have it, Frank! If we can get it, every time they send a message, it'll be just like sending it to General Grant."

"Where is it?" Frank asked. "They keep it pretty safe, I imagine."

"Yes, that's the trouble." Perkins frowned and shook his head. "We're pretty sure it's in Taliferro's office. He's got a safe there that's pretty well foolproof, right in the middle of the Secret Service department." He bit his lips and shook his head again with despair. "But we've *got* to get it out of there. One of our agents," he explained, "got the information somehow that it's in there."

255

Frank examined the cipher and handed it back to him. "How do we get it? We can't bust in with guns, can we, and hold up the Secret Service?"

"No, we're going to have to turn burglars."

Frank stared at him. "How are we going to get into the building?"

"There's a back way—an alley. There are guards, of course, but nobody's looking for anybody to break into the Secret Service offices." He grinned, saying, "It'd be a first if we pull it off."

"All right, I'm in," Frank said. "I'd like to see a little action instead of all this sneaking around. What do we do—take the disk?"

"No, that wouldn't do any good. We've got to see the cipher, make a copy of it and put it back. They can't know that we've seen it. That's the secret of the whole thing."

Frank stared at Perkins and shook his head. "Well, I can't open a safe. I'm no safecracker," he said. "Can you get into it?"

"No, but we've got a man that made a living along that line for a while. He claims he can open any safe in the world if he has enough time. That's where you and I come in." Perkins took out a cigar, bit off the end and spat it out the window, then lit it with a kitchen match. When he had it drawing, he said, "We'll get him in and get him out. Hopefully we won't be spotted. But if we do get caught, we may have to fight our way out. Do you have a gun?"

Frank nodded. "Yes, but I don't want to use it. If we get caught, we get caught."

"If we get caught, we get hanged, so use it if you have to. I'll give you word when it's on. Be ready! I'll be outside the Secret Service building about a block down, checking the outside."

"All right." Frank watched as the agent disappeared. He sat down on the bed and thought of what was about to take place and tried to feel comfortable about it. "Well," he said finally, "that's what I came here to do, so now I've just got to do it."

He changed clothes, went out, and met the others. They had a pleasant carriage ride to the church in the country. The sun was shining, and the wind was much warmer than it had been. When they arrived at the white frame church with columns in front, he saw Susanna Rocklin standing and waiting. "I hope we're not late," he said. He tied the team and helped the women down, and then the group hurried to the church.

"I'm so glad you could come," Susanna said.

"Are we late?"

"No, just right. Come inside."

As they entered the church, Lorna looked around curiously. She was accustomed to large, ornate Anglican churches in England, though she had not attended in years. This was far more to her liking. The pews were made out of white pine and heavily coated with varnish. The ceiling was high, and the tall windows along each side let in sunlight. Up in the front on a raised platform two men were sitting, talking quietly, and there was a cheerful aspect to the entire congregation, she thought.

"Here we go. We'll have the whole pew," Susanna whispered. Lorna found herself sitting between Susanna and Frank and felt strange about it all. She glanced at Frank and saw that he was tense, and she wondered why that should be. The singing began, and although she did not know most of the songs, she quickly picked up some of the tunes by the second verse. When Susanna whispered, "You have a beautiful voice, my dear," she turned to her and smiled, whispering back, "My two talents: I have a little singing voice, and I can see for a mile. I like your church," she said.

Susanna smiled at her, then the two began singing again.

The service was very simple. Frank had been in many services like it, for his family attended an evangelical church in Washington. He joined in the songs, but he knew the words so well he could sing them without thinking of them.

His mind actually was on the robbery. It was not that he was afraid. He had seen battle and was not troubled about that aspect of it. But somehow he felt disloyal to his relatives. He glanced over to the two women and saw the placid calm on the face of Susanna Rocklin, and guilt washed over him. *I shouldn't be using them like this. Lorna's right—it's wrong to use people, no matter what the excuse.*

Finally the song service was over and the minister got up. He was a tall, well-built man with a pleasant baritone voice. He began by reading a group of Scriptures and spoke for a time about being thankful. "That's what we're here for," he said, "to remember that we owe everything to God. But I'm going to do something a little bit different this afternoon." He looked down over the congregation and said, "Open your Bibles, if you will, to the fifteenth chapter of Mark's Gospel."

The leaves of the Bibles rustled all around him, and Frank was startled when a man behind him handed a Bible over his shoulder. He took it, mumbled his thanks, and found the place.

The minister said, "This, of course, is the chapter that deals with the death of the Lord Jesus Christ. And I would like to read you a portion of it." He began reading at the first, when Jesus was brought before Pilate, and then later, when the soldiers led him away and put a crown of thorns on his head. His voice slowed to solemn cadence when he read, "And they smote him on the head with a reed, and did spit upon him, and bowing their knees worshipped him. And when they had mocked him, they took off the purple from him, and put his own clothes on him, and led him out to crucify him. And they compel one Simon a Cyrenian, who passed by, coming out of the country, the father of Alexander and Rufus, to bear his cross."

He looked out over the congregation and paused briefly. Then he continued, "And when they had crucified him, they parted his garments, casting lots upon them, what every man should take. And it was the third hour, and they crucified him." The minister began to speak about the death of Jesus. Frank, even though he had heard the sermon or one like it many times, found himself putting aside his own problems and listening. The minister made it so graphic that he found himself entering into it. A strange feeling seized him as he heard how Jesus suffered on the cross. And finally the preacher said, "Let me read you what Jesus said: 'My God, my God, why hast thou forsaken me?'"

Frank felt strong emotions stir within him. He had heard and read the words many times, but somehow this was different. He looked down at his hands and found that they were clenched tightly together. Deliberately he unclenched them, but the tension in his spirit did not lessen. He sat listening while the minister said solemnly, "Why did God forsake Jesus? So that he would not have to forsake you. We're here for Thanksgiving, and I'm going to preach you the gospel this morning—for that is the Good News. That is what every man, every woman, and every young person on the planet needs to hear—that Jesus died for their sins. That is Thanksgiving."

For the next forty-five minutes, the preacher roamed through the Bible, pulling Scriptures out from the Old and New Testaments, and tying them together. The longer he preached, the more miserable Frank got. He could not keep his hands from trembling, and there was a thickness in his throat.

He was not unobserved. More than once Lorna glanced at him, and Susanna was very much aware of her young relative's problem. She, unlike Lorna, knew what was happening. *He's under conviction. God's dealing with him,* she thought and, bowing her head, began to pray.

When the minister reached the end of his message, he said, "We're going to pray now, a prayer of thanksgiving for what Jesus has done for all of us. If you have not let him into your life, if he is not your Savior, one simple cry will make all of that different. As the thief on the cross cried out, 'Remember me,' will you not cry that today? For he will remember you. If you will turn from your sins and believe on him and call, you will be a new creature in Christ."

As they stood, Frank was aware that his eyes were filling with tears. He blinked, but could not keep the tears back. Quickly he pulled his handkerchief out wiped his eyes, and when he turned his head, he saw that both Lorna and Susanna were watching him. With some embarrassment, he turned his head from them and endured the prayer. But as the preacher prayed, he began to feel a misery and a hope. He knew that Christianity was true and he prayed simply, "Lord, I've been far away. Don't give up on me! Help me!" He cried out within his spirit, and he *knew* that something remarkable was happening to him.

And then it was over. Frank did not remember much about leaving the church. But when he did, he found Susanna waiting for him. She took his hand and said quietly, so only he could hear, "God is going to do a work in your heart, my dear boy."

Frank did not say a word. He made his way back to the carriage, helped Lorna inside and, when the others were settled, began to drive back to town. The Hardcastles talked freely behind him, and Lorna joined in. But finally they reached the hotel. When he got down and he and Lorna were moving toward the hotel, she asked, "Something happened to you in church, didn't it?"

"Yes," he said briefly. "I'm not sure what it was. But I know one thing—I know that God is real, for he came and rescued me."

Lorna marveled at him. He had seemed so far away and thoughtless. And now there was a brokenness in him that she did not understand.

★ ★ ★

Carmen had been upset, and Frank could not understand why. If he had known women better, he would have read her emotions a little more easily. In fact, she was disturbed that Frank had not insisted on her going to church. She had known that she would *not* go under any conditions. But when they returned from church, she had been watching as Frank and Lorna had paused to speak outside the hotel. She had noticed later that they had had several long conversations, and a rash jealousy arose in her. *Maybe things are not as distant between them as I assumed,* she thought.

Lorna was aware of this, but Frank was not. She did not mention it to him, for she felt that it was not her place. The day after the service, she was greeted during a noon meal by Maj. Taliferro. He appeared suddenly and she invited him to eat with her. He was charming, as usual. But now that Lorna understood the deadly duel going on between him and Frank, she was more apprehensive. However, when he asked, "Would you like to see where I work and what goes on in those mysterious offices in the War Department?" she agreed at once. "Why, yes, Miles. I'd like to see it very much."

He was delighted at her response, and after lunch he engaged a carriage to take them to the department. When they were inside the building, he took great pleasure in showing her the operation. When they went into one room, he said, "Have you seen anything like this?" He handed her a doll, consisting of a rag-stuffed body, but a hard, plaster-of-paris head. "Why, it's just a doll, isn't it?"

"Not quite." Miles grinned at her and, taking the doll, deftly removed the head. "Look at this," he said. "See, the head is hollow. We use it for getting things through the lines. Medicine and other drugs for one thing. You'd be surprised how easy it is to get a doll like this past even watchful guards." He picked up a ring and showed her how it came apart. "Inside, you see, you can put a very tiny message on onionskin." She was holding the ring, and he looked down at her and said, "Here I am giving away secrets. You're not an agent of the Union, are you, Lorna? I'd have to arrest you, you know."

She looked up at him and smiled. "Would you really do that?"

"I'd arrest my own mother," Miles said with a curt smile. "That's what they pay me for. Come along now, and you can go into the inner sanctum." He led her to his office and seated her at the desk across from him. He showed her several papers and spoke, if not a little boastfully, of his triumphs in tracking down Union agents.

The door opened and a sergeant came in. "Sorry to interrupt, sir, but Gen. Williams says he has to have the papers on the . . ." He looked over at Lorna and hesitated. "The papers you're doing for him."

Lorna said at once, "Shall I leave the room?"

"No, that won't be necessary. I'll get them, Sergeant."

Rising from his desk, he walked over to the safe, stooped down, and began to work the combination. Soon, it opened with a click. Reaching inside, he removed an envelope. Closing the safe, he moved across the room. "There you are, Sergeant. Tell the general they're all intact."

"Yes, sir."

After the sergeant had left, Lorna said, "I really must be going now."

"So soon? Well, you must allow me to take you out for a drive tomorrow. I know some of the better places."

"That would be nice," she said. She allowed him to drive her back to the hotel, and when he left, she went to her room to lie down before the performance. She woke up half an hour later refreshed. She dressed and was brushing her hair when a knock came at her door. "Come in," she said. She turned and when she saw who it was, she said, "Why, Frank."

"Can I talk to you for a moment? It's important."

"Of course. Come in. Here, take this chair."

Frank shook his head. "It won't take long. There's something I have to tell you—two things really." He took two or three steps, back and forth; then he paced across the room apparently trying to put his thoughts together. Then he came over and sat down in the chair across from her. "I have to tell you this, Lorna. You were right to be upset with me when you found out what I was doing. I should never have done it."

"Being an agent, you mean?"

"Not that so much as using my family. I could hardly stand to look at Susanna in church. I feel like a—a snake! I just can't do it anymore."

Lorna felt a great pleasure from his speech. "I'm glad you feel that way, Frank. I know there are spies and agents and that they're honorable men—some of them—but I just hated for you to be one of them."

"I was doing it for the wrong reasons. I was angry because of my father being captured and my brother being blinded. I just wanted to strike out. I guess soldiers get angry at the enemy sometimes." He paused and said, "Slavery's wrong. But if I want to stop it, I'll have to do it another way."

"You're giving up the tour?"

He paused and nodded. "I have one more thing to do, then I'll call it off. We haven't made enough money to claim any success. I don't think anyone will be too surprised if we pack up and head back to the North."

She looked at him curiously. "What's the one thing you have to do?"

Frank hesitated. "One job that I have to help Perkins with will be over this week. If we can pull it off, I'll have done enough to pay for the training they gave me."

She hesitated, then said, "What's the other thing you came to tell me?"

Frank Rocklin was not a man who had trouble with words, ordinarily. This time he did. For a while she thought he wouldn't say anything. He looked out of the window silently. She could tell something was troubling him greatly. "What is it, Frank? You can tell me," she said softly.

He looked at her and said, "I think I can. It's—what happened in church. I don't understand it, but I know one thing—I've got to serve God. I've got to call on him and find out what he wants with me. I'm going to do it, too!"

Lorna was accustomed to church being a thing of habit.

She said, "I don't understand this intimacy. People talk of knowing Jesus, and all I know is that he's in the Bible."

"There's more to it than that," Frank insisted. "I've seen it in my parents and in my brother Bob. Jesus Christ is in him, with him, and all around him. And I guess now he's in me. That's how I know Jesus still wants to be with people. That's the only way I know to put it." He rose to his feet and she rose with him. Putting out his hands, he took hers and said, "I'm sorry I got you into all of this, Lorna. I'll do my best for you, though." He hesitated, then said, "I've never known a sweeter, more generous woman."

A flush rose to Lorna's cheeks. She was very conscious of his hands holding hers. Then without meaning to, she whispered, "I feel—I feel very strongly about you, Frank."

He stared at her, incredulous, then reached down and touched her cheek. "It's something we'll have to talk about, isn't it?"

"Yes, it is. I want to."

He said no more, but turned and left the room. Lorna went to the window and looked out, but she did not notice the view. She reached up and touched her cheek where he had put his hand. It seemed to burn under his slight caress, and she felt pleasure when she recalled his words. "Nothing can come of it," she whispered, but she did not believe it in her heart.

CHAPTER TWENTY-ONE
A Time to Embrace

Roland Middleton had known little of contentment. His life had been fragmented by a disastrous love affair, and he had taken a downhill turn ever since. Somehow, though, as he finished shaving and put his razor carefully away, he had a sense of well-being which was unusual for the actor.

"Must be going into my second childhood." He smiled into the mirror at his lean, aristocratic face, then picked up a set of brushes and began to brush his hair. When he finished, he put on his coat and left the room. Still, he was thinking of his future, and although he realized he had wasted his talent, he was still young enough at twenty-seven to turn around. *I just never had the desire to do it before,* he thought as he moved down the street toward the theater. *But a man can't go drifting along like I've been all of my life.* Inevitably his thoughts went to Rose, for he understood himself well enough to know that her coming into his life had made a change. She had the same youthful exuberance that he himself had once had, and being around her had restored this quality to him. As he passed by a store window, he saw a bottle of perfume and on impulse went inside and bought it. "Put it in a nice wrapping, will you?" he instructed the clerk.

"Is it a birthday present, sir?"

"No, just a present." He waited until the clerk wrapped

the package, tucked it into his pocket, then went out of the shop and began whistling. He was a little shocked at himself to feel the excitement that ran through him as he approached the theater. But once again he knew that it was Rose Yancy who had brought this new quality into his life. He entered and was met at once by Albert Deckerman, who had a strange, serious look on his face. Albert usually had a rather foolish grin, but now his lips were drawn down, and he said soberly, "Mr. Rocklin says for you to come to his dressing room right away."

Surprised, Middleton gave the young man a look. "What's the trouble, Albert?"

"You'll have to go ask him."

Middleton's eyebrows went up, for Albert was always willing to talk on any subject. *It must be bad,* he thought, *if Albert's not going to talk about it.* At once he made his way to the rear of the theater and went to Rocklin's dressing room. When he knocked on the door, Frank's voice said, "Come in," and he entered. As soon as he got inside, he saw Josh Yancy standing with his back against the wall, his face set in a determined look. Quickly, he glanced over and saw Rose, who stood across the room from him, and at once knew what had happened.

"Come in and shut the door, Roland," Frank said quietly. He was sitting at his dressing table, but was not putting on makeup. He gave Middleton a direct look and said, "Got some news that you're not going to like." He glanced at Josh and said, "Rose's father sent a letter."

"He wants me to come home, Roland," Rose said. She lifted her face, and he saw that her lips were trembling. She was a highly charged girl emotionally, and he knew her well enough to recognize that she was on the verge of tears.

"I see." He looked at Josh and was silent for a moment. "Is this because of what you saw—Rose and me, together?"

"Yes," Josh said defiantly. "I won't have my sister playing loose with an actor, or anybody else for that matter."

266

Rose cried out angrily, "It's none of your business, Josh! It's my life, and I'll do with it what I please."

Josh shook his head stubbornly. "Pa says for you to come home, and you'll have to do it, Rose." He looked at Middleton, his face set with grim determination. "I don't know you, Mr. Middleton. I do know that Rose wouldn't be happy with a man like you. You're just not steady."

"Been asking questions about me, Josh?" Middleton inquired mildly. All the lightness had left him. At first he wanted to lash out at the boy, but then he thought, *I've got to try to see it from his point of view. To him, I'm just a seedy, run-down actor that's had maybe a lot of women. That's the way it looks to him and his father, too.*

Josh flushed but did not flinch. "Yes, sir, I have been asking about you, and what I've heard hasn't been very good."

"He is good!" Rose cried out. "He's just had a hard time."

Josh cast his gaze on her and then said, "Maybe that's so, but you're my sister, Rose. Pa's worried about you, and he says to come home and talk about it. It'll have to be between the two of you."

Frank said, "No more of this crazy duel business, Josh, is that right?"

Josh dropped his eyes. He had been ashamed at his rash threats to shoot the actor. And now as he raised his head and began to speak, some of his stutter returned, as it did occasionally. "I c-can't—I was wrong about th-that," he said. "But I'm not wrong to ask you to go see Pa. That's the least you can d-do, Rose."

Rose saw that there was nothing else to do. "I'll have to go," she murmured, dropping her head.

"I think that's probably best, Rose," Frank said quickly. "You and your father talk about it, then we'll see." He rose to his feet and came to her, putting out his hand. "You've done a fine job, but you have to listen to your father." Rose took his hand, shook it, and then turned to leave.

"I'll get my things, Josh." Her voice was dead, and all the liveliness had gone out of her face. When she left the room, Josh looked worried. "I didn't want to hurt her, but I just don't think she's going down the right road." He turned to Middleton and said, "I may be all wrong about you. Rose says I am, and she's always b-been an honest girl. But I don't want to take a chance when it comes to one of my sisters. I'm sorry it turned out like this."

Middleton smiled and said, "I'm glad you see it that way, Josh. I only want what's best for Rose. I hope you believe *that.*" He turned and walked out of the room, saying, "I'll say good-bye to her." Once outside, he turned quickly and went to find Rose putting her things together. It wasn't much, and when she turned and saw him, tears came to her eyes. "Oh, Roland, I don't want to go," she whispered.

Roland wanted to put his arms around her but knew that would not be the thing to do. Instead, he took her hands and held them quietly, saying steadily, "I know it hurts, but you've got to pay attention to your family." He bit his lip and shook his head. "I went to the devil and never listened to anything my family said. If I'd listened, maybe I'd have turned out better. I've regretted it ever since."

She looked up, and her green eyes were filled with tears. He could tell her heart was breaking. Holding to his hand tightly, she asked, "Roland, can I ask you something?"

"Of course, anything!"

"Do you—you do care for me, don't you?" Her voice was so low he could barely hear it.

He knew at once that he had to tell this girl the truth. "Yes, I do care for you. You've been like a light in my life, and I've had a dark life. But I'm not fit to take a young wife like you. You deserve better, Rose."

She said quietly, "I love you, Roland."

Middleton flinched as she spoke simply and knew then that he had made a serious mistake. *I shouldn't have let it go this far,* he thought bitterly. Aloud he said, "Sometimes it happens like this. I care for you very much, Rose. But my life is not anything to share."

"You can change," she said. She squeezed his hands hard and said, "You can do anything you want to, Roland. I know you can."

Against his better wishes, Roland said, "I believe I will, but I can't ask you to wait."

Swiftly she reached up, pulled his head down and kissed him. There was an almost fierce look in her vulnerable face as she said, "I will wait. Come to me, Roland. I'll be waiting." Then she grabbed the small bundle and left him standing there.

★ ★ ★

"It was difficult for Rose to go back to the farm." Carmen was talking with the Hardcastles. They were having tea in a restaurant near the Spotswood. It was late afternoon, and they had spent some time rehearsing. Without Rose the play was a little different, and they had had to make adjustments for her absence.

"Yes, it was," Elizabeth Hardcastle answered. She touched her white hair, her thin face kind and troubled. "She's such a sweet girl. I don't see why Roland couldn't have married her."

Carmen looked at her. "Why, Roland's not a man to marry."

"He is if he loves the girl." J. Harold Hardcastle slapped his hand on the table, his blue eyes steady. "And I think he did. I think he's making a mistake. They'd have a hard time perhaps moneywise, but if they love each other, they'd make it."

Carmen stared at the two with envy. "You two have made it." She smiled and said, "I don't think there are many in this world that stick together like you have. I wish I could find a man like you, J. Harold." She rose, went over and patted his shoulder, then said, "I think I'll go rest for a while."

When she left, J. Harold said, "That girl makes me sad."

"She's not exactly a *girl*, J. Harold," Elizabeth said. "She's getting old enough to worry about what's happening in her life. She's had a career, but she wants a man—a husband."

"She could've had men lots of times, a good-looking woman like that!"

"Well, I guess she has *had* a few men, but that gets old. She's thinking about a home now." Elizabeth hesitated, then said, "I may be foolish, but I thought at times she looked at Frank as a woman looks at a man that she wants to come to her."

"Frank? Why, he's too young for her."

"Perhaps so, but women in love don't always think straight." She looked in the direction of the door through which Carmen had disappeared and said, "I hope she doesn't get hurt in all of this."

If Carmen could have heard their remarks, she would have recognized the truth in them. She was thinking of Frank as she climbed the stairs, wondering how he felt. He had been attentive to her, and once or twice she had seen in him that her presence had affected him. But that was not enough. She was indeed tired of the life she now led. When she got to her room, she began listlessly working with her hair before the mirror. Finally, the desire to talk to Frank came to her, and she rose and left her room. Frank's room was down the hall, and when she arrived there she saw that the door was half open. Surprised, she stopped, then heard voices. She hesitated for a moment, then recognized Lorna's voice. She tensed at once. She glanced around and saw nobody in the hall. Stepping closer to the door, she listened carefully to what they were saying.

Inside the room, Frank was standing in front of Lorna. She had accompanied him to his room after a brief walk, and he had asked her to come in just for a moment.

Now he faced her and said, "I've decided to tell you something, Lorna." He reached out and put his hands on her arms and held her quietly. "This thing that's come to me about God—it's all mixed up. But somehow I know I'm going to have to follow him—and I know something else."

Lorna was surprised at his intensity. She was conscious of his hands on her arms and said, "What is it, Frank?"

Quite simply Frank said, "I care for you, Lorna. We haven't known each other long, but we do spend a lot of time together. I've never known another woman like you." Hesitating, he said, "I don't know how you feel about me, but I love you as I've never loved another woman."

His simple statement brought consternation to Lorna. She looked up at him with shock in her eyes and said, "Why, Frank!" She was an honest young woman, and now, quickly, the memory of Dennis's betrayal came to her. Somehow, as she looked into his eyes, the past seemed unimportant. And she said quietly, "I care for you, too, Frank."

"You do? That's good to hear." Frank pulled her into his arms and kissed her gently, then he held her. There was a moment's silence, then he released her, saying, "We'll have to talk about this more."

"Yes," Lorna said, "I'll expect a little more courting than this."

A smile flashed across Frank's face, and he said, "You'll get it. We'll be going back to the North soon. As soon as I do this job for Pinkerton."

"What is it, Frank? Can you tell me?"

Frank spoke quickly, revealing the plan, and Lorna said, "Why, I saw that safe when I visited in Taliferro's office."

"That's the one. We'll be going after it tomorrow night, just after midnight. Once that's over, we'll do another week of the play, and then I want to get out of here."

Out in the hall, Carmen had stood stock-still as she listened to the two speak. An anger had begun to rise in her. She had seen the interest Frank had had in Lorna, and now she felt rage run along her nerves. A sound behind her caught her attention, and whirling, she saw a couple coming up the stairs. Quickly she walked away. She went back to her own room and, looking into her mirror, she saw that her face

271

was pale but her eyes were glittering. She had not realized how much hope she had placed in making Frank Rocklin love her. And now that that had been suddenly blasted apart, her hope was replaced by a bitterness. She felt scorned and rejected.

For a long time she tried to get a grip on herself, but she was a woman of emotional instability. She was given to rash impulses, and finally an idea came to her that stopped her dead still. Quickly, thoughts ran through her mind, and her lips turned up in a cruel smile. "We'll see if you'll go back to Washington, Mr. Frank Rocklin." Sitting down, she snatched a piece of paper; then taking a pen and ink, she began to write: "To Maj. Miles Taliferro: I must inform you of a plot that I have become aware of. . . ."

When she finished the note, she folded it, put it into an envelope, and sealed it with wax. Putting Taliferro's name on the front, she marched downstairs and motioned to one of the young men who helped with the baggage in the hotel. "Timmy, I want you to take this and deliver it for me. It's very important." Then her voice lowered to a whisper, "And very confidential. Can you do this and keep quiet about it?" She handed him the note and a ten-dollar bill.

The young man's eyes opened wide as he took the envelope and the cash. "You bet, Miss Carmen! I'll do it right now."

"Thank you, Timmy." Carmen turned and walked slowly back up the stairs. She went into her room and sat down. Anger still consumed her, and she sat staring blindly at the wall. More than once she had had second thoughts. Once she had almost risen to go after the messenger, but the memory of the love scene between the two rose in her, and she finally let her lips settle into a straight line. She turned and began to fix her hair again, only this time she looked so hard she scarcely recognized herself.

That night at the performance, Frank noticed that Carmen seemed strangely aloof, unlike herself at all. "Don't you feel well, Carmen?" he asked.

"I feel very well, Frank," she said. Her voice was very quiet, but her face was pale. She could not resist saying, "How long do you think we'll stay here in Richmond?"

Frank glanced at her quickly, for her voice sounded odd. "We've got an engagement here for the rest of the week. After that, we'll see. Why? Are you getting homesick for the North?"

Carmen did not answer him, but turned and walked away. She went into the dressing room she shared with Lorna. With one look at the young woman's face, so glowing with health and beauty—and youth—her heart hardened within her. She said nothing, but waited silently for the notice to appear. *They deserve it,* she thought. *He's nothing but a spy!* Somehow that thought did not comfort her, and she grew restless, glad when the call came for her to appear on the stage.

CHAPTER TWENTY-TWO
A Brave Man

Frank started as he heard a sound off to his left. He put his hand in his pocket, seizing the handle of his revolver. It was a dark night with only a sliver of a moon hidden behind a screen of dark clouds. The stars were faint, and he had to peer to see through the darkness. A sentry appeared at the end of the street, stopped, then turned and marched back away alongside the War Department building.

Frank let his breath out and realized that he had clutched the revolver so hard that his fingers ached. *Got to calm down,* he thought. *We ought to make it fine.* He thought quickly of how easy it had been to gain entrance into the building. He had met with Perkins and a smallish man named Simms, the safecracker. Perkins had given orders in a terse voice, and the three of them had moved to the back of the building. There were two guards, but they came along the back of the building once every fifteen minutes. "Plenty of time," Perkins had said. He had jimmied the back door and had whispered, "Frank, you stay here. I'll go in with Simms. There shouldn't be any trouble."

Frank had kept his place rather nervously. Twice a guard had made his measured paces along the back of the building. Each time, Frank had jumped inside the door, holding his breath.

Now as he stood outside watching again, he wondered

what was keeping them. "How long does it take to open a safe?" he muttered. He was still wondering ten minutes later, when suddenly a sound caught his attention, and he whirled to see Perkins step outside the door. "Did you get the thing opened?" Frank whispered.

"Not yet." Perkins' voice was tense, and he stared up and down the street. "It's taking longer than Simms thought. Anything happening here?"

"Just the guard. He goes by every fifteen minutes. He's due anytime now." He hesitated and then asked, "What if he can't open the safe?"

"Then we'll have to come back tomorrow night and try again—with someone else."

"Once is enough," Frank muttered. "What do you think—" He broke off, for a movement had caught his eye. He whirled quickly to his right and hissed, "We're in trouble, Perkins. Look there!"

Perkins had seen the movement at the same time. He whirled the other way and froze. "They're onto us! We've got to get out of here."

"I'll go get Simms."

"We can't get out this alley. There must be twenty soldiers coming this way. Somebody turned us in. Come on." Perkins stepped inside the door, followed by Frank. He locked it firmly, then the two ran along the hall. Coming to Taliferro's office, Perkins called out, "Come on, Simms. We're caught."

"They'll be waiting at all the doors," Frank said, thinking quickly. "What'll we do?"

"Come on! We'll go up on the roof." The building was two-storied, and the three men quickly ran down the hall, then up the stairs. They found an attic door and quickly clamored up. The attic was pitch-dark, and the three stumbled along until they got to the windows in the gables. Perkins looked down and muttered, "Can't see a thing; it's too dark. But we'll have to go this way. They'll be working their way up."

"That's a long jump," Simms whined. "We'll break our necks."

Perkins hesitated. He knew that Simms was probably right. "OK, we'll go fight our way out. Come on."

Frank paused, then said, "We'd better jump, Perkins. There are too many of them, and you know what it means if we're caught."

Perkins shook his head, the faint moonlight outlining his tense face. "If we break our legs, they'll have us anyway. There are several doors down there, and they can't watch all of them. And in the darkness, we'll have a chance."

Frank hesitated, then said, "Not me." He pulled the revolver out of his pocket, then handed it to Perkins. "You take this, Dave; I'm going to jump. It's soft ground down there. I think they're in the building, so we've got a chance. Come on, let's try it!"

But Perkins and Simms both protested. Simms, whispering hoarsely, "I ain't jumping out of this building!" turned and walked back down the ladder quickly, and Perkins stopped long enough to say, "I'm sorry I got you into this, Frank. Good luck."

"You, too, Dave." The two men had not been close, but in the darkness of this attic they felt a kinship. Frank waited until the two had gone downstairs. Then he opened the window and put his feet out over the ledge. He could barely see the ground beneath. He could not afford to wait. A strange thought came to him. *I remember once,* he thought, *the preacher preached on Jesus and his temptations. How the devil told him to throw himself off some high place. What was that Scripture? "The angels will bear you up in their wings."* He smiled grimly and said, "Lord, if I'm going to get out of this, you'll have to send some angels. I'd appreciate it if you'd help me." He gritted his teeth, hesitated for a moment, then shoved himself free from the window. He remembered hearing once that when you fell from a high place you should keep yourself relaxed, and he forced himself to do that. The wind whistled by as he plummeted toward the ground. He seemed to fall for a long time. Everything was very clear, and he was concentrating solely on hitting the ground. If he broke his leg, he knew it was all over. His feet struck the ground, and he allowed his legs to fold. He sprawled headlong, but he had fallen on soft earth and not the hard pavement over to his left. There was a flower bed he recognized, as he wallowed in the dirt for a moment, pain running through his feet and legs. He gasped, "Nothing broken!" then got to his feet shakily. His fall had made a thumping sound, and he looked around wildly.

Suddenly the silence of the night was broken by the sound of gunfire. *They got Dave and Simms!* Grief ran through him, but he knew he could do nothing. He stumbled out of the flower bed and moved quickly down the street. The gunfire continued, rising in intensity, and then broke off abruptly. As Frank disappeared, heaviness came upon him, for he knew that Simms and Dave Perkins were either dead or captured.

He made his way back to the hotel, and when he got to his room, he examined his clothes. He quickly stripped them off, washed his hands and face, and got into bed. He lay there, thinking mostly of Dave Perkins. "In a way I hope they shot him," he said. "Better to be shot than hanged!"

He had not been in bed for more than an hour when he heard measured footsteps coming down the hall. He had expected it. "They must know I was with them. I didn't think Dave would tell, but I can't blame him."

He waited for a moment; then a hard fist hammered on his door. He let the hammering go on until a voice said, "We know you're in there, Rocklin. Open the door!"

Throwing the cover back, Frank moved to the door. He pushed his hair down over his eyes, then made himself look like a man awakened from sleep. Opening the door, he stared at the face of Maj. Miles Taliferro. Behind him were two armed guards holding their muskets carefully. "You're under arrest, Rocklin," Taliferro snapped with satisfaction.

"Arrest?" Frank feigned the speech of a man awakened

out of a sound sleep. He rubbed his eyes and shook his head. "What are you talking about?"

"We know you're a spy, and I arrest you as such. Get your clothes on."

Frank began to protest, but Taliferro stood there coldly saying nothing. When Frank was dressed, he nodded to the guard. "Bring him along. If he tries to get away, shoot him—and shoot to kill." He gave Rocklin a cold look of hatred. "We know how to handle fellows like you. We've got all three of you now."

"I don't know what you're talking about, Major. What are you arresting me for?"

"You'll have a hearing. It'll be short, and the hanging will be even shorter. One of your friends is dead, but we'll hang you and Perkins. Take him away!"

Frank stood there for a moment while one of the guards put irons on his hands, then he was hustled down the corridor. As they passed through the lobby, he saw the clerk's eyes follow him and knew that his company would soon enough hear of what had happened.

★ ★ ★

The interrogation had gone on for hours. Frank and Perkins sat at a table across from Maj. Norris and Miles Taliferro, who shot questions at them endlessly. It was Frank that they were mostly aiming at. They tried in every way they could to get Perkins to implicate him. But steadfastly the stubby man refused to speak. Perkins had looked at Frank when he was first brought in, asking, "Who is this man?"

Taliferro had directed most of the interrogation. Again and again, he had tried to make a connection between the two. But Perkins had merely said, "I tell you, I don't know the man."

Finally it was Maj. Norris, who had said little and allowed Taliferro to do the interrogating, who spoke up and said, "Look, we know you, Perkins. We've been after you a long time. Now, we've got you. You know what that means."

Perkins had an iron nerve. He turned to Norris and nodded slightly. "It means the rope. I've always known that."

Norris looked surprised. He said, "You've got courage, Perkins. It's a shame you're on the wrong side."

"I'm on the right side, all right," Perkins said adamantly. "You just do what you've got to do, Major."

Norris lowered his head and thought hard for a moment. Finally he said, "It doesn't have to be death. If you'll cooperate with us, I'll see that you don't get the death sentence."

"Cooperate? You mean like tell you the names of all my men?"

"Yes," Taliferro snapped. "Including this one," he said, motioning toward Frank Rocklin.

Dave Perkins lifted a gaze that was almost lazy to Rocklin. Their eyes met and for a moment Frank thought, *He's going to do it!* But he was mistaken, as he soon discovered.

"Let's get on with the trial and whatever it is you have to do. I don't know this man."

Frank asked the two men suddenly, "What makes you so sure that I was with these men? You have no evidence at all."

Taliferro said, "We have information that you're a spy."

"Put it before me," Frank challenged.

Taliferro flushed and said, "It's a private communication."

"Anybody can give a 'private communication,'" Frank scoffed sharply. "Either produce it or let me go."

Taliferro flared up. "You're not getting out of this, Rocklin. I'll get the truth out of you."

Maj. Norris said abruptly, "That's enough for now, Major. We'll continue the questioning tomorrow. In the meantime, you see if you can get more information on Rocklin here."

Frank was taken to a cell, separated from the other man. But as they paused in the hallway to put him inside, his eyes met Dave's. Rocklin admired the man more than he would have thought possible. He could say nothing in front of the guards, but Perkins made it easy. He put his eyes on Frank and said, "Good luck, whoever you are. I wish you well."

"Thanks," Frank said. He had to let his eyes do the rest, for he could not say more. When he was inside the cell, he sat down and thought about Perkins. *They're going to hang him,* he thought bitterly. *And nothing could save him. He could save himself, though, but he won't do it. A brave man!*

★ ★ ★

Morning came, and Frank was given a meager breakfast. Immediately afterward, the interrogation began again. Taliferro this time had him all alone. There was a cold anger in the officer that Frank could not understand. He could sense that Taliferro had no evidence, or little at least, and finally after what seemed like hours he looked over and said, "Major, I don't know what's in your head, but you and I both know you've got to have evidence before you can hang a man for being a spy. What evidence do you have?"

Taliferro was coldly furious, and he was disgusted enough to reach into his pocket. "I have this," he said.

Frank took the envelope, opened it, and read it. He recognized the handwriting at once as being Carmen Montaigne's, although it was not signed. He had no idea what was in the woman's heart to accuse him. She had learned somehow of his activities. *She must have been listening outside the door when I was talking to Lorna.* He let nothing show in his face and handed the paper back, saying, "It's not signed. Anyone could've written that note—maybe even you."

"I'll find out who wrote it, don't you worry. And I'll see you swing for this."

Frank was taken back to the cell. Later that afternoon, he had a visitor. He looked up to see Clay Rocklin coming down the hall. He stood up at once, and when Clay was admitted by the jailer, he said carefully, "Hello, Uncle Clay."

"Hello, Frank." Clay stood there silently and then said, "I just heard about the charges. I've been talking to Maj.

Norris." There was a resistance in his voice, and he stood there for a moment saying nothing.

"What did the Major say?" Frank asked finally.

"He says some of his people are sure you're involved in a spy ring. Is it true?"

For one moment, Frank was silent. He wanted nothing more than to deny the charges. But something had come into him that he could not explain. He had betrayed his family and found he could do it no more. "Yes, it's true," he said simply.

Clay stared at him and then said, "Tell me about it."

The two sat down, and Frank told him the whole story, beginning with his service in Vicksburg and his bitterness over the wounding of his brother and the capture of his father. He explained how he was determined to go into the army and fight, but Pinkerton had talked him out of it. Finally he said, "That's the truth, Uncle Clay. I might add one thing, though," he said defiantly. "You can believe this or not, but before this happened I'd already determined to go back. I guess it's all right to be an agent—that's part of war, but it's not for me. I agreed to do this one thing, but I've already told—somebody—that it's all over."

Clay Rocklin leaned back in the chair and stared at his nephew. "You didn't have to tell me that, Frank," he said finally.

"Yes, I did have to tell you, Uncle Clay." Frank got up and walked around the cell, squeezing his hands together. "It's been hard. Especially deceiving you and the family. That was wrong, using you like that."

"Has that young woman got anything to do with your decisions—Lorna Grey?"

Surprised and confused, Frank stared at his uncle. Then he nodded slowly, "Yes, she does."

"And what happened at the Thanksgiving service? My mother told me. Does that have anything to do with it?"

Frank sat down and spread his hands. "You know more about me than I thought. Something did happen there. I know this: I'm going on with God, and I'm going to marry Lorna if she'll have me. And I'm not going to be a spy anymore."

Clay's eyes grew warmer. "You made a mistake, Frank—but not as big a mistake as I made when I was your age." He sat for a while talking to the young man. Once he mentioned Rose. "I think she's in love with the Middleton fellow. I don't know him, but I'd hate to see her make a mistake. Melora's worried about her, and so am I."

"I think that's over, Uncle Clay. Roland told me he'd said good-bye to Rose. He's a better man than you think, though. He could be a good man, if he'd just put his mind to it."

They talked for a few more minutes, and Frank asked about his father. "I tried to see him when we got back from Montgomery, but the guards said he couldn't have any visitors. What happened?"

Clay smiled. "I'm not surprised they haven't told you. It's a pretty embarrassing thing to admit. Your father escaped from Libby while you were away."

"How?" Frank asked, shock evident on his face.

"He had some outside help. Forged orders and fake guards. It was a very convincing charade, the guards say. If you hadn't been in Alabama, Taliferro would try to pin that on you as well."

After a while, Clay rose and called for the guard. He turned to Frank, saying, "I think as long as they don't have any more evidence than they have now, you'll be set free. Taliferro hates you, though. He'll do all he can to get you hanged."

"Dave Perkins won't speak. He'll hang first. I admire that man! Don't know if I could do it. Good-bye, Uncle Clay. Explain the best you can to Melora, would you? And anyone else that needs to hear it, especially your mother."

"I'll tell them." Clay reached out suddenly and gave his nephew a hug. "You'll be all right. You're on the Lord's side now. He's not going to let you fall."

★ ★ ★

Taliferro had used all his authority and one at a time had drilled every member of Frank's company. He had gotten nothing out of them, however. When he talked with Carmen, he thought he saw something in her and said, "Miss Montaigne, I've received information in the form of a note. I haven't been able to trace it, and it's not signed. But it is from a woman. Did you write that note?"

Carmen shook her head. "I did not, Major. I'm just a member of the company."

Taliferro hesitated; then he kept probing the woman, but she did not bend. Neither did other members of the company. He had saved Lorna for last. Finally when she sat down before him in the interrogation room, he felt anger run through him. "Did you know about this, Lorna?"

"I don't know what you mean."

"I mean about Frank Rocklin being a spy."

"That hasn't been proven. A charge has not been final. In my country, we hold a man innocent until proven guilty."

Her swift defense of Rocklin infuriated Taliferro. He began to ask her questions, firing them one after another in a slashing manner. But she answered them quietly, and finally she said, "I can tell you no more."

He stared at her and felt the power of her gaze. However, there was nothing more he could do. He released her, then went to Maj. Norris's office.

"Well, do you have anything else?"

"Not yet, but I haven't given up. I'm going to hold Rocklin over until I look further into this case."

"You can't hold him long," Norris said. "We don't have any evidence."

"I know he's guilty!"

Norris's face turned hard. "Your knowing isn't the same thing as proving it. I'll give you until tomorrow."

When Lorna returned to the hotel, the company seemed to be drawn together. All of them except Carmen met in Lorna's room. They crowded in and talked about the problem. They were disturbed and Hardcastle said, "I suppose this is the end of the play."

"It isn't any such thing!" Elizabeth Hardcastle said. "Mr. Rocklin will be released. There's no evidence on him. Everyone says that."

Middleton said little. He was shocked at the affair and totally unconvinced that Frank was guilty. So was Albert Deckerman, who loudly protested that the government ought to be sued.

Later that evening when Lorna was preparing for bed, she heard a knock on her door. Going quickly, she found Carmen standing there. Her eyes were red from weeping, and she asked, "Can I come in?"

"Why, of course. Come in, Carmen."

When Carmen entered, she stood there wringing her hands for a moment, then said, "I have something to tell you. I—I don't know how to do it."

Lorna said, "The best way is just to say it. What is it?"

"I'm the one who gave Frank's name. I heard you two making love."

"We weren't making love. We merely expressed our feelings for each other."

"But you do love him, don't you? I know you do."

"Yes, I do."

Carmen began to weep. She threw herself into a chair and began to sob, saying, "I don't know what got into me! I lost my mind. I do that—I've been that way since I was a little girl. Oh God, how I hate myself!"

Lorna stared at the woman for a moment, then sat down beside her. Putting her arm around her, she said, "Let's talk about it, Carmen. God is always willing to forgive, and so is everyone else."

CHAPTER TWENTY-THREE
The Company Gets an Ultimatum

Maj. Miles Taliferro looked up from his desk with surprise. His face had fatigue lines around the eyes and mouth, and he snapped irritably at the sergeant, who had opened the door wide enough to stick his head inside. "Well, what is it, Sergeant?"

"It's a young lady to see you, sir."

"A young lady? What's her name?"

"Miss Grey."

Instantly Taliferro straightened up in his chair. "Send her in," he said almost harshly. He waited, leaning back in his chair until Lorna entered the room. As soon as she was inside and the door was shut, he said abruptly, "What is it, Miss Grey? I don't have time to waste this morning."

If Lorna felt any rebuke, she did not show it. Coming over to stand before his desk, she said quietly, "I'm sorry to bother you, Major. I know you're busy, but I had to see you."

"Well, you see me," he snapped crossly. "What is it?"

"Might I sit down for a moment?"

"Yes, yes, sit down." Even as Lorna sat across from his desk, Taliferro could not help but admire her appearance. She was wearing a pearl gray dress with white trim around the wrists and neckline. It was smoothly cut and showed off her figure to the best advantage. A small hat with bright

287

feathers was perched on top of her blonde hair, and it irritated him that she looked so fresh this early in the morning while he was rather disheveled. Leaning forward, he clasped his hands together on the desk and asked, "What is on your mind? It must be about Rocklin!"

"Yes it is, Major," Lorna said with a nod. "I've come to ask you to think about releasing him."

"He'll be released when I have evidence that he's innocent."

Lorna gave him a direct look. "But there's no evidence that he's guilty, is there? As I understand it, the other man has refused to implicate him."

"He's lying. I know he is!"

"That hardly seems likely. If you offered to remove the death penalty for identifying him, why should he insist on refusing?"

It was a question that Taliferro had asked himself. He had gone over and over the evidence and was well aware that he was not on sound ground. He was as certain that Frank Rocklin was one of the burglars as he was of his own name. Still, proving it in court, even a military court, would be quite a different matter. He started to speak angrily, but at that moment, there was a knock on the door, and the sergeant stuck his head inside. "There's another lady to see you, sir."

"I can't see her now."

Sgt. Ames bit his lip and said, "She says she will only take a minute, if you could step outside. The sergeant looked at Lorna and said, "I think it's about . . . the burglary." Instantly, Taliferro got to his feet. He was determined to leave nothing untried, and he had sent word to his agents to send anyone who might have seen anything the night of the burglary. "I'll just be a moment, Miss Grey," he said and left the room. As soon as he stepped outside, he saw an elderly woman with white hair and a thin face standing just past the sergeant's desk. He remembered her and asked impatiently,

"Mrs. Hardcastle—I'm very busy. Do you have something to say to me about the burglary?"

"I've been trying to think about it all," Mrs. Hardcastle said slowly. "I don't remember as well as I used to. Why, when I was a young woman I could name you all the presidents of the United States and the dates that they were in office." Her eyes were bright as a bird's, and she added proudly, "And I knew the lyrics to almost any song you wanted to name and I could—"

"Yes, yes, I'm sure. That's very commendable. But what about the burglary?" He looked around at the sergeant, who was listening, and said, "Step over into this empty room, please, Mrs. Hardcastle."

He turned as she went down the hall and said quietly, "I'll be back. Don't let Miss Grey leave."

"Yes, sir."

As soon as the major was inside the room, he began directing questions at Mrs. Hardcastle. She was a difficult woman to interrogate, for no sooner had he asked a question than she would begin trying to answer it. But her attempts always led her off into some vague memory of years ago. Still, she said enough about the night of the burglary to keep talking for some time. Finally, however, he said with some asperity, "Mrs. Hardcastle, was your employer in the hotel the night the burglary took place?"

"Oh, I'm sure he was. He went to bed early that night, I think."

"But you couldn't know that he stayed in his room, could you now? Did you see him leave the hotel?" This time the answer was a little vague, but he cut through it by saying, "Yes or no? Did you see him leave the hotel the night of the burglary?"

"Why, no, I didn't, Major, but—"

"Well, what in blazes did you come here for then?"

Elizabeth Hardcastle looked hurt. "I thought I might help get Mr. Rocklin out of jail. He's such a nice man—"

"Good day, Mrs. Hardcastle." Stomping to the door,

Taliferro opened it, and when she left—still protesting that Mr. Rocklin was a nice man—he ignored her. Going back past the sergeant, who gave him a covert look, he entered the office and stood behind his desk. "Can you swear to me that Frank Rocklin was in the hotel all night?" A crafty look came into his eyes, and he said, "Perhaps he was with you all night, Lorna," using her first name almost with a sneer. "That would get him off, if you just tell me he spent the night in your room."

"No, he didn't do that, Major," Lorna said evenly.

"But you are in love with him, I take it, or you wouldn't be here."

Lorna hesitated, then said, "Yes, I am. But I just want to see justice done. If you don't have evidence, Miles, you'll have to let him go."

Anger raced through Taliferro, and he shook his head. "You may go now, but I may send for you later."

Lorna rose, and there was a look of regret on her face. "I'm sorry that it's all come to this." She turned and left the room. As soon as the door shut, Taliferro picked up a pen that was on his desk and threw it with all his strength at the wall. The point of it stuck into the pale green wallpaper and quivered there. He stood staring at it with frustration and finally pulled his uniform tunic down and walked out the door. "I'm going down to see Maj. Norris. If anyone else comes, tell them I won't be back for a while."

He moved through the building, coming at last to Norris's office, and found him busy with a stack of papers. Looking up, Norris said, "Well, do you have anything on Rocklin?"

"Not yet, but—"

"Then you'll have to release him."

"He's as guilty as Judas!" Taliferro's face grew red with anger. There was a nervous tic in his right eye. "Just give me a few more days and I'll pin it on him. We'll make Perkins talk!"

"I don't think he will." Norris looked critically at

Taliferro. "Legally we're on shaky ground. We don't have a thing on Rocklin except your suspicions, and those are not enough."

"You mean we're going to have to turn him loose?"

"Yes, right away." He listened as Taliferro argued, then snapped, "You heard the order, Major." He hesitated for one moment and said, "I hate this almost as much as you do. You can do this at least—run him out of town. Use any threat you have to."

"Yes, sir."

Taliferro turned and walked slowly away. As he went back to his office, he called the sergeant in. "Have Rocklin brought to my office, Sergeant."

"Yes, sir."

Taliferro sat down, and ten minutes later the door opened and Frank Rocklin stepped in. He had not shaved, but his eyes were clear and his face was filled with curiosity. Taliferro wanted to smash his fist into the face of the actor, but he got a grip on his temper and said, "We're releasing you, Rocklin."

Frank nodded. "Thank you, Major."

"Wait a minute. That's not all." Taliferro tried to take some triumph out of his defeat. "If you're not out of Richmond in twenty-four hours, you and your whole company, I'll arrest you again and every member of your company. Maybe I can't make the charges stick, but I can make it pretty uncomfortable—especially for your lady friend."

Frank stared at him expressionless and nodded. "Looks like you hold the best cards, Major. We'll be out of Richmond tomorrow."

"If I hear about you in any other Southern town, I'll follow you. Get out of here. I know you're a spy, and nothing would please me more than to see you hang. I can't do that apparently, but if I find you in Confederate territory, I guarantee you I'll make it unpleasant for you—you and all your troupe. Now get out of here!"

Rocklin stared at him but said nothing. He turned and walked out of the office. Taliferro came to the door. "Write out a release order, Sergeant. See that he's out of here right away."

"Yes, sir, I'll take care of it."

When Taliferro slammed the door, the sergeant looked up with a grin. "Well, I don't see the major losing his temper like that very often." He smiled slyly. "You've been kind of an irritation to him. Come along, and I'll see that you get your stuff."

Ten minutes later Frank Rocklin left the jail and paused to take a deep breath. The air was cool and fresh after the inside of the prison. He made his way back to the hotel, where he was greeted by the entire company. They gathered in his room, and he looked around and said with regret, "We'll be leaving tomorrow."

"We're going back to Washington, I take it," Roland said.

"That's right, by orders of Maj. Miles Taliferro. It wouldn't be comfortable for any of us in Southern territory." Frank's face showed regret. "I'm sorry for all of you. You'll be paid up until the time we get back. I wish it hadn't turned out like this."

"Why, it's been a rich experience, my boy!" J. Harold Hardcastle exclaimed. "I'm glad you're out of that jail. Maybe we'll do something together back where decent theater is appreciated."

Frank grinned at him and shook his hand warmly. He had noticed that Carmen was not in the room, and when Lorna came to him, he asked about her.

"She's feeling pretty bad, Frank." Lorna hesitated, then said, "Why don't you go talk to her?"

Giving her a curious look, he said slowly, "I think maybe I know something about why Carmen's feeling like that."

"Maybe you do," Lorna said. She put her hand on his arm and said, "Be kind to her, Frank. She's a lonely woman."

"Sure, I'll talk to her."

Going to her room, he knocked gently on the door, and Carmen's voice sounded muffled. "Come in." He entered and she turned to face him. Closing the door, he walked over to her and said, "Everything's turned out all right, Carmen. I'm out of jail, but we've got to get out of the South."

Instantly Carmen's eyes filled with tears. "Frank, I've got to tell you something." She hesitated, then with torment in her face said, "I was the one who wrote the letter to Taliferro. I don't know why I did it. I was jealous of you and Lorna. Frank, I'm so sorry."

"Carmen, it's all over. I'm sorry if you got hurt."

"But you could have been killed."

"Sure could," Frank said cheerfully. He came over, took her hand, and held it for a moment. Finally, he put one arm around her and squeezed her. "We all take wrong turns from time to time, Carmen. I've taken too many to blame anybody else. I don't want you to worry about this. As for me, I forgive you freely."

Carmen looked up, then fell against him and held on to him for a moment. Awkwardly, Frank held her. Then she stepped back and dabbed at her eyes with a handkerchief. "We're going back to the North?"

"Yes, so get your stuff packed. If we hang around here, we may see the inside of a jail again. I'm not really sorry to go back, though. I'm really glad." He went to the door, opened it, and then smiled. "Maybe we'll do something in the way of acting together."

"I'd like that, Frank," she said, managing a smile.

When he closed the door, he went to Lorna. "She's all right," he said. "She made a mistake, but don't we all. You'd better start getting ready. I'll go get the train tickets." They looked at each other, and then he put his arms around her. He held her gently and said, "This has been a rough tour, hasn't it?"

"Yes, it has, Frank."

He kissed her cheek, then stepped back, holding her hands warmly. "I don't regret it. I found you, Lorna. That's made all the difference to me." He turned and left the room. And as he did, he knew that this was not the end but the beginning.

CHAPTER TWENTY-FOUR
"A Role You Were Born For!"

Buford Yancy looked up from the small anvil where he was pounding on a piece of iron with a ten-pound sledge. He watched as the horseman dismounted somewhat awkwardly, tied the animal to a hitching post, then looked around helplessly.

Tossing the hammer onto the anvil with a clang, Buford moved out of the small shed and said when he approached the man, "Howdy, Mr. Middleton." He had recognized the actor at once. He offered his hand and noted the softness of the actor's flesh. "Surprised to see you way out here, Mr. Middleton."

Middleton gave him an embarrassed grin and shook his head. "I got lost three times, Mr. Yancy. It's not as easy finding your way around here as it is in Washington or New York."

Yancy laughed and shook his head. "I'd get plumb lost in one of them places," he said. "Come on and sit on the porch. I've got some coffee on the stove—or what passes for coffee in these parts lately."

"No, I wouldn't care for any, thank you. I have to talk to you."

"I figured that." Yancy studied the thin face of the actor

and said, "I reckon it's got something to do with Rose. What is it?"

"I've come to ask you for your permission to court Rose," he said. He saw the surprise that flashed through Yancy's green eyes and grew intensely sober. "I know you don't have much of an opinion of actors, maybe with some grounds. I don't know what Rose has told you about me, but I want to be honest with you."

For the next five minutes, Roland gave a stark account of his life, leaving out none of the harsh facts. When he finished, he shrugged saying, "That's what I've been, Mr. Yancy. I didn't hide anything from you. I'll answer any questions that you want to ask. But before you do, I just want to tell you one more thing." Middleton straightened his shoulders, and his gaze was steady as he looked into the eyes of the other man. "I love Rose, and I'm determined to live a different kind of life. I've been a hard drinker. Well, that's all over now. I haven't had a drink in two weeks, and I hope to never take another one. It was something to hide behind, and I wouldn't need that with a wife like Rose. As for my future—" a humorous light came to his eyes—"I'll stay here and work for you on the farm until you see I mean business. I won't be much good at it, but I'll do my best."

Buford Yancy was amazed. He'd expected almost anything out of Middleton—except this. There was an earnestness in the man that he could not deny. He reached up and scratched his head thoughtfully. He thought slowly, turning it over in his mind, and said finally, "Well, Roland, I reckon it'll be up to you and Rose." He looked around the farm and said with a touch of sadness, "This kind of life was all right for the rest of my kids, but it's not for Rose. She wants something more than this. I don't know if she'll be happy with it or not, but I reckon she's going to have to try it." He paused and nodded with his head. "You see that path there? You take that. At the end of it, you'll find some of the finest hogs you've ever seen. Rose is feeding them. You go talk about it with her, then we'll all sit down and see what comes of it."

Roland gave a gusty sigh of relief. He had dreaded facing Buford Yancy, but he saw now that he had a chance. He nodded and a smile touched his lips. "Thank you."

He took the path, and as Yancy said, it was impossible to miss. It was worn smooth by many feet. Before he had gotten very far, he had heard the sounds of hogs grunting and squealing. Slowing his pace, he came out into the opening where Yancy had built pens out of stout saplings. He glanced at the hogs that were gathered around the slender form of Rose, who was putting feed from a wheelbarrow into a trough. The squealing was so loud that she evidently couldn't hear him, and he got within five feet of her before he said, "Hello, Rose."

Instantly Rose whirled and, seeing him, her eyes got large and she dropped the bucket of feed at her feet. "Roland!" she cried. She stood stock-still, unable to speak. She had thought of him constantly since coming back to the farm, and there had been a sadness in her that she could not control. When he came to her, she put her hands out and he took them. "What—what are you doing here?"

Roland allowed a smile to touch his lips. "Came to learn how to feed hogs," he said. "Haven't had much experience, but your dad tells me he may need another hand."

"Why, you can't do that," Rose said indignantly.

"I probably won't do very well at it, but I told him I'd stay as long as he wanted." He hesitated, then his face grew serious as he looked down at her. "I told him I was going to stay long enough to prove that I'd make a good son-in-law." He saw her eyes grow large, her lips parted in amazement. "We can talk about it," he said. He pulled her forward, and she came to him, putting her arms around his neck. As he kissed her, she held him tightly. He was very glad that he had not gone back to Washington with the rest of the company. She was firm, strong, and smooth in his grasp—all that a woman should be. Her lips were soft and gentle, yet at the same time demanding. They stood there for a moment, and when she pulled back, she said, "Roland, you can't be a pig farmer!"

"No, I think not. After I've stayed a while, we'll get married. Then we'll go back. I don't know what's ahead. I haven't been the best actor, but I could be if you'll help me."

"I'll help you, Roland. Oh, it's going to be so much fun!"

He kissed her again, then said, "Well, introduce me to your friends here. I'll have to at least try to show your dad that I'm able to take care of pigs."

She laughed and began naming them. "That's Mammie, and that's Paul, and that's Hamlet, and that's Romeo."

"And that's Juliet, I suppose," he said.

She laughed at him and squeezed him. "No, that's Pete. You do have a lot to learn about hogs."

The two of them laughed, and as he held her he found himself looking for the first time in many years toward the future with hope.

★ ★ ★

The makeshift wood-burning engine pulling the dilapidated cars rattled and clanked over the trestle. Frank looked down at the white water below as it rushed around the support, then turned to say, "I'd like to come back to the South someday, when this is all over—the war, I mean."

"So would I," Lorna said. "There's so much good there. The people are so fine, especially your people."

The two had obtained the seat at the back of the car and spoke quietly as the train wound its way along the serpentine pathway through the hills. There was peace in Lorna's face, and she seemed happy.

Frank spoke for a while about his family and how he hoped to make up his wayward years to them, and she said finally, "You're not much of a prodigal, Frank. They'll be glad to kill a fatted calf for you."

He shifted restlessly and put his arm around her shoulders. She protested, but he grinned and held her tighter.

Finally, after they had remained silent for a while, he said abruptly, "Only one thing bothers me."

"What's that?"

"Well, I went to all this trouble, took all the risks—" he shrugged with a futile gesture, and his face grew sober— "and all for nothing. I mean, I was no help at all to Pinkerton. Maybe that's something I shouldn't grieve over, but I'd like something to show for what I've invested."

Lorna looked at him with an odd expression in her eyes. "I've got a present for you," she said, her lips turning up into a smile. "I suppose an engagement present."

Curiously, he looked at her. "A present? What sort of present?"

"I'll let you decide." Lorna reached into her reticule and came out with a rather flat box about four inches square. It had a string tied around it, and she handed it to him. She watched as he untied the string, and when he took the lid off and gazed down at it, she was pleased to see him blink with shock and astonishment.

"Lorna! Where did you get this?"

She took his arm and held it, saying, "I wanted to do something. You told me the cipher was in the major's safe. When I was there before, he opened the safe. I have very good eyesight." She smiled at him, and there was a delightful charm about her. "I read the numbers as he opened the safe. Then when you were in jail, Mrs. Hardcastle and I made up a plan."

He stared down at the wax impression of the ring and muttered, "It won't be hard to make a brass impression of this. How did you get it out of the safe?"

"It was very simple. I went in to see the major, and after I'd been there a few minutes, she came asking to see him outside. While he was gone, I just went over and opened the safe, took the cipher ring out, and pressed it into some soft wax that I had brought in my bag. Then I put it back and closed the safe."

"Lorna, you shouldn't have done that! Why, if you had been caught—"

"It only took two minutes. Now, are you proud of your fiancée?"

Frank stared down at the wax impression, and a smile came to him. "Mr. Pinkerton will be impressed."

He turned to her suddenly and said, "I'm going to have to give you a reward for this." He leaned over her, but she pulled back.

"Stop!" she said. "I only take rewards in private, not in a public place like a railroad car," she said demurely.

He laughed at her and leaned back. "Well then, I'll give you a double reward later."

The two rode on, and after a while she said, "Frank, I hate to mention this, but I don't have a cent."

"Neither do I. We're a pair, aren't we?"

"What are we going to do? I've got to get work."

"Don't worry about that for now. You're going to stay with my uncle and aunt and brother Bob. I want you to get to know my family. I'll stay at home and introduce you to my parents." He looked out the window at the rolling hills and said nothing for a while. Finally he turned to her and said, "God has been good to us."

"I—I don't know much about God," she said. "You'll have to teach me."

"We'll learn together." He took her hand, and they sat there quietly, listening as the rails made a clickety-clack steel cadence as the train wound around through the hills.

★ ★ ★

Lorna was sitting alone in the parlor, reading one of Amos Steele's lighter books of theology. It had been Bob Rocklin who had gotten it for her. He had smiled at her, saying, "This isn't quite so heavy. Even I can understand part of it. Why don't you read it to me, and we'll see how it goes?"

Lorna had never felt so comfortable as she did with the Steeles and with Bob Rocklin and, of course, with Frank, who was in the house almost constantly. She had fallen in love with all of them. She had gotten to know Melanie and Gideon only slightly, as Melanie spent most of her time taking care of Gideon, who was still recuperating from illness and malnutrition from his time at Libby Prison. The time she spent with them, however, was very pleasant.

She looked up suddenly as Frank entered and came to sit beside her. "What are you reading?" he asked. "Another one of Uncle Amos's books?"

"It's one I've been reading to Bob," she said. "Written a long time ago by a man called Thomas à Kempis."

He looked at the book and read the title. *"Imitation of Christ.* I don't know this one."

"It's amazing," she said. "Here's a man that lived back in the fifteenth century, but he loved God so much. He said that had to be first before anything else."

Her lips were gentle as she spoke, and there was a calm look in her eyes. "Bob's been telling me that that's what theology is. I asked him once what he really believed about sin and doing wrong, and he grinned at me and said, 'Love Jesus and do as you please.'"

Frank laughed out loud. "That sounds like Bob. He's doing fine, isn't he? He's going to make a good preacher."

"Yes, he is," Lorna agreed. "You're so different, and yet you're somehow alike."

Frank gazed deeply into her eyes, saying nothing, and she looked up at him curiously. "What is it, Frank?"

"It's about a new role for you."

"A new role?" Her eyes grew bright and she asked, "What is it?"

"Well, the story's about a happily married couple. They love each other very much, and you play the role of the wife. I play the role of the husband."

Her lips curled upward and she said, "I see. Do you think I can play that role, Frank?"

He put his arms around her and whispered, "Lorna Grey, it's a role you were born for!" He leaned over, and she

301

turned her face up to him. "It'll be a fine drama—Frank and Lorna love each other and live happily ever after." He leaned closer and kissed her. As he held her, peace ran through him. He did not know what the future held, but when he lifted his lips, he said huskily, "With you beside me, Lorna, I can do anything."

"Frank, I love you as much as any woman ever loved any man!"

The tiny yellow canary in the wire cage by the window had been pecking at a piece of apple that Lorna had thrust between the bars. Now he stopped and put one bright eye, as he cocked his head, on the pair. Then his throat swelled and poured forth a high melodious song that carried with it a joy that filled the room.

Gilbert Morris is the author of many best-selling books, including the popular House of Winslow series, the Reno Western Saga, and The Wakefield Dynasty.

He spent ten years as a pastor before becoming professor of English at Ouachita Baptist University in Arkansas and earning a Ph.D. at the University of Arkansas. Morris has had more than twenty-five scholarly articles and two hundred poems published. Currently he is writing full-time.

His family includes three grown children, and he and his wife, Johnnie, live in Orange Beach, Alabama.

If you're looking for more captivating historical fiction, you'll find it in these additional titles by Gilbert Morris . . .

THE APPOMATTOX SAGA

#1 A Covenant of Love   0-8423-5497-2
#2 Gate of His Enemies   0-8423-1069-X
#3 Where Honor Dwells   0-8423-6799-3
#4 Land of the Shadow   0-8423-5742-4
#5 Out of the Whirlwind   0-8423-1658-2
#6 The Shadow of His Wings   0-8423-5987-7
#7 Wall of Fire   0-8423-8126-0

RENO WESTERN SAGA

A Civil War drifter faces the challenges of the frontier, searching for a deeper sense of meaning in his life.

#1 Reno   0-8423-1058-4
#2 Rimrock   0-8423-1059-2
#3 Ride the Wild River   0-8423-5795-5
#4 Boomtown   0-8423-7789-1
#5 Valley Justice   0-8423-7756-5
#6 Lone Wolf   0-8423-1997-2 (Coming Fall 1995!)

THE WAKEFIELD DYNASTY

This sweeping saga follows the lives of two English families from the time of Henry VIII through four centuries of English history.

#1 The Sword of Truth   0-8423-6228-2
#2 The Winds of God   0-8423-7953-3
#3 The Shield of Honor   0-8423-5930-3